THE CREW

CAPTAINS & CANNONS
BOOK II

BY
GALEN SURLAK-RAMSEY

A TINY FOX PRESS BOOK

Tiny Fox Press LLC
North Port, Fl

For all the doggos in the world

Chapter I
The Island

Something sinister tore at Ethan's insides.

Zoey had called it "hunger" at some point during their three days' worth of travel on the open sea, but Ethan was certain it had to be some ravenous, acidic creature trying to burst out of his stomach. If women had to go through even a tenth of what he felt during childbirth, they would forever have his undying sympathy from this day forth. He'd have shot himself in the head an hour ago if Zoey hadn't taken his pistol away.

Bitch.

However, now that he had Maii cornered below deck, things were starting to look up for the newest member of the vampire race, assuming the ahuizotl cooperated, which at this moment was in doubt. The mystical creature, standing nearly as tall as a pony at the withers, bristled his dark fur and snarled, fangs as long as daggers bared. And despite the fearsome maw and razor claws, not only on Maii's four feet but also at the end of his elongated tail, the only thing stopping Ethan from trying to devour the ahuizotl companion was Zoey's iron grip on Ethan's shoulder.

"C'mon," Ethan said, trying to reign in his drool. "Just a nibble. That's all I want."

"No, Ethan," she scolded. "If you're that hungry, drain a fish if you won't take another rat."

"I'm sick of rat and fish taste like piss."

Zoey laughed. "Taste much of that, do you?"

"I should've eaten you when I had the chance," Maii said, growling.

"Except you couldn't," Ethan replied, narrowing his eyes before he waved the ring of command he had on his finger through the air. "You belong to me. So I order you, sacrifice your blood to me. Right now."

"Doesn't work that way," Maii replied. "And if you attack me, I'm free to defend myself."

"Ethan, stop," Zoey said, pulling on him again. "We'll be at the island soon. You can dine all you want then."

Ethan tore free of her grasp, swearing up a storm and marching off a few steps before he started pacing. "I can't believe you turned me into this! A vampire! An undead, bloodsucking fiend!"

"Excuse me for wanting to save your life," Zoey huffed, crossing her arms over her chest.

"Yeah, well, you neglected to tell me just how batshit crazy it would make me, I mean—"

Ethan bolted for Maii, mouth open and fangs ready to sink into tender, sweet, sweet flesh, but Zoey made the intercept with ease. Not only did she manage to do that, but she threw him over her shoulder, and as the air blew out of his lungs, she straddled his chest, pinning him to the floor.

"There was a time when this would turn me on," Ethan said with a frown.

Zoey looked down at him and gave a wry grin. "Was?"

Ethan nodded. Though he had a wonderful view and her silky legs were a hair away from a kiss, the insatiable gnawing at his stomach demanded his immediate attention. He lifted his head and craned it as much as he could so he could look past her hips. "I can literally hear his blood moving inside his body."

"I know. You'll get used to it."

"Used to it? It's driving me insane!" Ethan struggled against her pin, but since she was a vampire, too, a much more experienced and aged one at that, his strength was no match for hers. Ethan huffed and relaxed. "This is so unfair."

Zoey patted him on the top of his head before dropping a kiss on his forehead. "You're doing really well," she said with not nearly as much sincerity as Ethan would've liked. "Way better than I did my first week."

Ethan arched his eyebrow.

"Okay, maybe not *way* better," she said. "But honest, this will all be over soon, and we can look back and laugh."

"I seriously doubt that."

Something caught Zoey's attention, and her head snapped up, and her eyes lit with excitement. "Maii! Get that rat!"

"Ugh! I'm sick of rat!" Ethan said, facing souring.

The ahuizotl appeared at their sides a few seconds later with one live, squirming rodent firmly grasped in his jaws. The thing was the size of a small house cat, with red eyes and teeth that looked like they could chew through an anchor in under a minute. But despite that, it hung limp in Maii's jaws.

"Here," Zoey said, taking the rodent and shoving it in Ethan's face. "Maii charmed it. Poor thing won't even fight back."

"These are disgusting," Ethan said. "At least fish are normal, and I really don't want fish."

"No, fish aren't normal for us," Zoey replied. "The closer something is to a human, the better it'll taste. And since rats are mammals and fish aren't, they'll be better for you in the long run."

Ethan turned his head to the side and continued to argue. "I'll probably get the plague if I haven't already."

"You're a vampire, sweetheart," she said. "You can't get the plague."

"I still think Maii would taste better."

"Maybe, but he gets to defend himself if you try. And I hate to be the one to break it to you, but he'll win that fight."

"You're only saying that because he nearly killed you."

Zoey nodded. "And I can kill you," she purred. "Where do you think that puts you on the food chain?"

Ethan, refusing to admit defeat, tried a different tactic. He'd managed to semi-free one of his hands, and with it, he reached up and pinched her ass.

Zoey's only reaction was to shoot him a deadpan look. "Eat the stupid rat, Ethan," she said, pushing it in front of his face again. "You're sailing back into annoying waters again."

"Maybe I'll have to work my unholy, yet devilishly charming good looks on you."

"Can't, sorry," she said. "They won't work on other vampires. Quit fussing and get this over with."

Ethan pressed his lips together and seethed just because he could. But Zoey didn't budge, and her face stayed hard and unyielding. Moreover, the rat stayed where it was, and as its musky odor filled Ethan's nostrils, his mouth salivated, and he could feel his fangs sharpen.

The rodent's heart beat once again, and Ethan lurched forward, unable to control himself any longer, and sank his teeth into it. The critter's blood immediately poured into his mouth as it let loose a tiny squeak. To Ethan's surprise, what he took in tasted like flat soda. Not terrible by any stretch of the imagination, and while it certainly could've been much better, it quenched his thirst.

Ethan swallowed several more times, draining every bit of life he could from his meal. Tiny bits of blood ran out of the corners of his mouth, and Zoey smiled, wiping it off his cheeks with a finger and sucking it clean.

When he was finished, she tossed the desiccated body to the side. "There," she said. "Was that so bad?"

"No," he reluctantly admitted.

"Now, then, we need to see where we are," she said, taking to her feet and offering him a hand up. Once he was upright, she pointed to his pockets. "Check your character sheet again. Maybe it's updated."

"You said that last time," he replied with a shrug.

"I know," she said. "But I get the feeling we're about to start a new chapter, game-engine wise."

"That matters?"

"Definitely. Now look."

Ethan complied with her request and pulled the sheet out of his pants. To his surprise, the moment he unrolled the parchment, he saw that it indeed had a few new items on it that hadn't been there a few days ago. "I've got three new traits," he said, looking at the new list. "One is *Fast Metabolism*."

Zoey snarled. "Bleh."

"It's bad?"

"I think so," she said. "You get hungrier and crankier much faster than normal—which I was starting to suspect."

"But?"

"But you also don't suffer ill effects from alcohol or drugs, and you do regenerate health quicker, too."

"That seems good."

"Yeah, but again, the need to feed can be problematic," she said, sighing. "What about the other two?"

Ethan shrugged. "Don't know. There are just a couple of other lines with question marks written across. Is that good or bad?"

"The traits could be either," she said. "All that means is we have to discover them as we go on."

"That figures," he said.

With that, they headed for the deck of the *Victory*. When they got there, a salty wind kissed Ethan's face, and blinding rays from a noonday sun beat down upon him.

"Are you sure I'm not going to burst into flames?" he asked, shielding his eyes. "I can barely see a thing."

"I'm sure, and next time eat when I tell you to," she said with a playful scold of the finger.

"What's that have to do with anything?"

"Your senses dulled, and now they're back," she explained. "Of course, everything's going to seem more intense."

Despite her reassurances, Ethan checked his sheet once more. To his relief, the question marks remained. "Well, there's nothing on here like a deadly allergy to sunlight," he said, stuffing it back in his pocket. "I guess you're right."

"You'll find that I am from time to time," she said, grinning. Something caught Zoey's eye, and she trotted to the railing on the port side. There, she leaned over and looked far ahead of the bow. Her eyes lit up almost immediately, and she reached back and waved Ethan over.

"We're here," she beamed, pointing to the horizon.

Ethan cupped a hand over his brow and squinted. It took a second for distant objects to come into focus, but when they did, he saw a large island in the distance. From what he could tell, it was in the shape of a crescent with brilliant, sandy white beaches on the shore and a single mountain forming the bulk of the land. Low-lying clouds obscured the peak, but Ethan could see that a thick rainforest covered the sides and base.

"That's Lenada?"

"It is," Zoey said, hopping back before making her way to the wheel. "You'll never find a more wretched hive of scum and villainy."

"Are you serious, or are you just wanting to throw in a reference joke?"

Zoey flashed him a smile. "Little bit of both. Always wanted to say that coming into a port, but it's not like I'll be in Mos Eisley anytime soon, you know?"

"Right."

"We should drop in on the tavern, though," she said. "They've got some of the best rum for a thousand leagues, too. You'll love it. I promise."

"As long as getting drunk doesn't end with you passing out and us running afoul of another bounty hunter," Ethan said.

"No promises," she said with a wink. "Now run up to the bow, will you? Make sure the way is safe."

Ethan nodded and trotted across the deck, thinking the task simple enough. However, after a few moments of being there, he felt at a loss. "I'm not sure what I'm looking for," Ethan admitted. "It looks clear."

Zoey rose on her toes so she could see a little better. "This isn't a deep water harbor," she said. "That means we'll have to lay anchor about a hundred yards out and row in."

"Okay, but that still doesn't answer what I'm looking for."

"Make sure they aren't readying the shore cannons," she said. "That's our only real worry at this point."

Ethan felt his brow furrow, and he wasn't sure if she was joking or not. "Why would they be shooting at us?"

"Why not?" Zoey replied matter-of-factly. "This port may be small, relatively speaking, but the people here are as unsavory as any others and ready for a fight. So if someone in the watchtowers realizes we're coming in without even a skeleton crew, they might decide this ship of ours should be a ship of theirs."

"Doesn't that figure," Ethan muttered, turning back around. His hopes of finding a willing crew were quickly drowned by worries of having cannon-firing, pistol-toting Lenada berserkers trying to steal his ship every chance they got.

"Cheer up, Ethan," Zoey called out with a bright smile. "I never said this was going to be easy, but we're vampires who just took down a lich. We tell them that, and I bet we get half our crew on that reputation alone—well, if we tell them the lich part, that is. We still need to keep the vampire bit quiet."

"Okay," Ethan said. "I can do that."

Ethan then redirected his attention back to the shore, and over the next several minutes, he scoured the place for any sign of anyone about to fire the coastal batteries. At first, he only saw the limestone embankments that flanked each side of the port where the cannons would be. But it only took him a few more seconds to realize *all* he could see were the embankments, and not a single cannon or carriage was anywhere to be found.

Creases formed on his forehead, and he tapped the railing with his fingers anxiously as he directed his attention to the port. As they drew closer, more and more detail could be seen, and none of it put Ethan at ease. Not a soul walked the streets, nor crossed the docks. Dozens of buildings barely stood, burnt-out hulks of their former selves, while twice as many had collapsed into piles of rubble.

"Zoey?" he called back, only half turning as he kept his eyes ahead. "We've got a problem."

"What?"

"I think the town is destroyed."

"Destroyed? What do you mean, 'destroyed'?"

"Well, not completely razed to the ground, but there's not a tavern, blacksmith, shipwright, or whatever still standing that's going to win any OSHA awards, that's for sure. Hell, I don't think there's a building over there that has three standing walls, let alone an intact roof."

In a flash, Zoey looped the rope she had nearby onto the *Victory*'s wheel, holding it fast, and ran up next to him. Her nails dug into the railing the moment she took it all in, and her mouth hung open.

Eventually, she simply shook her head, like the simple act would wake her from a bad dream. When it did, she ran both hands through her hair and muttered. "What the hell happened?"

"I don't know," Ethan said. "Do you think we should sail on?"

Zoey's brow dropped, and the grief that had been slowly surfacing to her face hardened into determined resolve. "No," she said. "I need to know what happened. There might be survivors, too, that need our help."

Ethan nodded, though an unsettling feeling grew in his stomach that said there probably wouldn't be, and whatever they'd find would prove deadly. Thank a recent encounter with a lich for that one.

Zoey went back to the wheel, and as she kept them on course, Ethan leaned over the side of the ship a little more, hoping the extra few inches would be what he needed to see someone, anyone, mulling about that could give them hope. He didn't see anyone for several minutes, despite the little bit of distance he gained. When they were within about a quarter mile, however, he spied someone laying sprawled out in the entryway to one of the buildings.

"There's one!" he shouted, pointing. "I think—"

Ethan cut himself off when he realized said person looked a hell of a lot more like a corpse than a living body—ashen skin, sunken chest, withered frame, and tattered clothes being the first thing that clued him in.

Then he caught the unmistakable, sickly sweet scent of death floating through the air and cringed. "Oh crap," he grumbled. "He better not get up."

"What are you on about?"

Ethan wiped his nose, some part of him thinking it would clear the smell from his nose, and turned around. "There's a dead body by the docks," he said.

"Damn," she said, shaking her head. "Knew I smelled something. Let's furl that last sail and drop anchor. Then we can row in."

The two went to work; all the while, Ethan kept half of his attention on the port, thinking something awful would happen the moment he looked away for more than a minute. Nothing did, but once they'd finished and were about to lower one of the longboats, Ethan happened to spy something at the end of the docks that seemed new.

"What is that?" he asked, pointing to a bulletin nailed to a post with its own makeshift peaked roof. The parchment didn't have much to it, some writing for sure that Ethan couldn't read, but across the top was a faded, rust-colored X that had been painted with a couple of broad strokes of a brush. "I think it's a warning?"

Zoey came to his side and leaned over the bow to look for herself. As soon as she saw it, her shoulders fell, and she cursed under her breath. "It's a notice."

"For?"

"The plague," she answered, her voice barely a whisper. After a few beats, she shook her head and straightened. "Okay," she said, taking a deep breath. "That doesn't change anything. We still go in. Look for survivors."

Ethan's hands went up, as did his eyebrows. "But...the plague?"

A forced smile flashed across Zoey's face. "We'll be fine. Perk of being a vampire."

Despite her assurance, Ethan still had reservations. "We're actually immune to the plague? You're sure about that."

"I am," she said but then immediately sighed heavily and shook her head. "Usually," she corrected. "Most of the time. There have been a few diseases throughout this world's history that have jumped between humans and vamps. But they're rare. I promise."

"Ugh. I knew you were going to say that."

"Do you want to leave?" she asked in all seriousness.

"I get the feeling you don't. Surely we can find a crew elsewhere, still."

"We might be able to find a trustworthy crew in time," Zoey said with a shrug. "If we had a month to prepare? Sure. That's easy. A day or two to spare at the most? That's something else entirely—especially given our nature."

"Right," Ethan said, frowning and drumming his hands on the railing.

"I know I said that girl was obsessed with not only me, but being turned, but she could still be there, maybe, and need our help. Others, too," Zoey added. "And I know I owe you my life, so if you insist on moving on, then we'll go and figure something out. But it would mean a lot to me for us to at least spend a little bit of time ashore."

Ethan turned his options over in his head for a few moments, trying to weigh the pros and cons of staying versus going. Basically, they boiled down to avoiding the plague (good) and rolling the dice when it came to being infected (bad), and neither option seemed to guarantee him a crew, which he desperately needed. Then he thought of one last point that drove away any indecision: As Zoey had said, people could still be alive on that island that needed his help. And he couldn't leave them, no matter how dangerous said island might be.

"Okay, let's row over and see what we can find," he said.

Zoey smiled and kissed him on the cheek. "Aye, aye, Captain."

CHAPTER II
LENADA

"I always thought rowing was hard," Ethan confessed once they were about halfway between shore and ship. "I mean, other than being a little warm in the shoulders, I feel pretty good."

Zoey, who sat at the bow of their little craft, craned her head over her shoulders and grinned. "Try it for an hour as hard as you can and let me know how you feel."

"Ah, right," Ethan replied.

A few minutes passed, and in that time, Ethan brought them to the dilapidated docks. The waves ended up being a little more aggressive than Ethan had anticipated, so instead of gently brushing up against one of the wood pylons, it became more of a controlled crash that nearly tossed Zoey from the boat and into a face full of barnacles.

"Easier on the gas next time," she said, annoyed.

"Sorry. I'm not specced rowboat. You okay?"

"I'll be fine, but I'd rather not have to deal with a split hull."

Ethan raised an eyebrow. "I don't think I was coming in that fast."

"You—" Zoey cut herself off and sighed heavily. "No, you weren't. Sorry. I'm anxious, is all."

"I figured. No worries, " he replied as Zoey jumped up on the docks and tied a line from their craft to the pylon. When he stepped out of the boat and joined her on the docks, he wrinkled his nose. The stench of decay assaulted his senses, and he had to force rising bile back down to where it came from. "God, this place reeks," he said.

"Focus on something else," she said. "That'll help."

"It will?"

"A lot," she said.

Ethan shut his eyes a concentrated on what scents floated through the air. He nearly lost his stomach contents once more when the first thing that struck his mind was gooeyness from whatever poor dead sap still lingered. But he quickly turned his attention to other parts, and the easiest to pick out was the salt coming off the ocean. Though he did pick up floral notes coming from the nearby rainforest—as well as the scents of mint, copper, and chocolate of all things—he worried they were too faint to last, and he'd be right back to taking deep whiffs of a corpse. As such, he kept his mind on the salt.

Which wasn't that bad at all, and having general fond memories of being at the beach as a kid, he simply stuck with that.

"Okay," he said, slowly drawing a deep breath to make sure he got it. "I think I can manage. Let's go."

"Lead the way, Captain," she said with a bow and sweep of her hand.

"I get the feeling this deferment isn't out of respect for the position."

Zoey shot him a playful look. "Creepy, desolate town ravaged by the plague? Not sure why you wouldn't want to lead the way."

"Exactly."

With that, Ethan started walking. When he was about halfway down the docks, he noticed a small sunken ship two dozen yards away and about ten feet underwater. Even with Ethan's limited view and even more limited knowledge, he could tell it was a small cutter, probably forty or fifty feet long.

"What do you make of that?" Ethan asked, nodding his head toward the vessel.

Zoey pressed her lips into a thin line before frowning and shaking her head. "I don't know, but I know I don't like it."

"Enforcing quarantine, maybe?" Ethan proposed. "You know, keeping anyone from leaving and whatnot?"

"That's as good a guess as any," Zoey said. "If that's true, if we find anyone still alive, they might not be too keen on letting us leave, either."

"Should've brought Maii," Ethan replied, looking back to their ship.

"Still think you had the right idea leaving him, actually."

"You do?"

"I do. As you said, we want to make sure we have a ship to come back to," Zoey said. "And a territorial ahuizotl on guard duty is a great way to make that happen."

"I think he just wanted a chance to eat someone," Ethan said.

"That, and he didn't want you to take a bite out of him as well," she replied. "Still, good call on your part keeping him there."

Ethan nodded, feeling a little bit smarter than he normally did, and continued down the docks. Aside from the *clomp-clomp-clomp* of his hard leather boots on the weathered boards and the occasional call of one unseen tropical bird to another, the area held an unsettling quiet.

"Man, he looks like hell," Ethan said once they reached the body they'd seen from the *Victory*.

Though Ethan had pegged him for dead long ago, he hadn't appreciated up until now exactly how dead this guy was. Withered skin clung to a skeletal frame, and tight leathery lips were pulled back, revealing a blackened mouth devoid of tongue and most teeth. His eyes had long disappeared, be it from scavenger or rot, Ethan didn't know.

"He looks like more than that," Zoey said, kneeling and picking at his clothes with the tip of her cutlass. "He looks like he can tell us quite a bit."

"Such as?"

"Plague didn't kill him," she replied matter-of-factly.

"How can you be sure?"

Zoey dropped the tip of her weapon and looked up at him. "You tell me," she said. When he balked, not understand where she was going, she quickly tacked on. "Go on. It'll be good for you. Stretch that new plus three intellect of yours."

"Do I get a reward if I'm right?"

"Why would you get a reward?"

"You know, classic Pavlov conditioning," he said. "It's a psych thing."

"I know who Pavlov was," she replied, rolling her eyes. "Does this mean you want me to get a bell, too, and make you drool?"

"I was thinking something a little more girlfriendy in terms of a reward," he said. "The bell doesn't quite do it for me."

Zoey toyed with her necklace as she looked at him out of the corner of her eyes. "Oh, girlfriendy," she said. "I could probably come up with something should you come through on a couple of things first."

"Such as?"

"Knock my socks off with this investigation, for starters," she said. "Because smart is sexy."

"And the second?"

"Kick Maii out of our cabin for the night. Bells might not do it for you, but he really doesn't do it for me."

Ethan interlocked his fingers and turned his palms out, so they all cracked together. "Consider it done."

"Good," she said before motioning to the body. "Now go on. Tell me what you see."

Ethan shot her an air kiss before redirecting himself back to the corpse. He had no idea what the hell he was looking for. He was a pirate, damn it, not a doctor. The guy was dead. How the hell was he supposed to know what he died from?

Ethan drummed his hands on his thighs, working out his initial frustration. It only took a few seconds for him to realize that if Zoey was pushing him this hard, and if she had picked up on what was going on that fast, he wasn't going to need to do a full autopsy to figure this out, let alone any kind of specialized bloodwork.

His eyes studied the body, going over every inch from top to bottom. The first thing he decided was that the elements had taken their toll on everything from skin to fiber. Then he realized the man was missing his cutlass as the scabbard was empty, and there was a sizeable gash on the inside of his right forearm.

But that wasn't lethal, was it?

Surely not.

But why wasn't it bandaged?

Lacking an immediate answer, Ethan moved his investigation on. The man's clothes didn't seem like anything of note, unless worn-out, caked-with-dirt shirts and trousers were somehow special, but he was missing his boots. Gnarled feet covered in callouses rested on the ground, splayed outward.

Ethan frowned. The feet didn't tell him anything either. He huffed, frustrated, but then his eyes went back to the man's torso. It was at that point he realized that it wasn't just dirt clinging to the fibers. There was a sizeable stain in the man's left chest—a stain that surrounded a small hole, about as large as his thumb was wide.

"He was shot?" Ethan said, more speaking his thoughts than anything else.

"He was," Zoey said with a pleasant tone of approval. "What does that mean?"

Ethan looked at the ground. It looked ordinary. Lots of dirt. Some bits of grass. When that led him nowhere, he turned his attention to the building, or rather, what was left of the building. It, like all those around it, was a charred mess.

"He wasn't killed because of the plague," Ethan said.

"Are you sure?"

"Yeah," Ethan said, more confident this time.

Zoey's eyes brightened. "Which means?"

"He got in a fight with someone, going by the wound to his arm," Ethan said. "Whoever that was, they killed him and left his body out here while the town burned. But why?"

Zoey sucked in a breath through clenched teeth. "Close," she said. "Want to try again and really impress me? Or do you just want to take the consolation prize?"

Ethan shook his head. "No. I want the whole thing," he said. Ethan rubbed his hands together and knelt at the corpse's side. His eyes studied every crack in the skin, every wrinkle of cloth, every hair on his head.

Ethan straightened.

"You see it?" Zoey asked, sounding hopeful.

Ethan didn't reply right away, though he felt like he was right there. His eyes went from the body, to the burnt-out building, and back to the body several times. The distance between them couldn't have been more than a foot from one blackened wall to the top of his head. "He was killed after the fires," Ethan said. "Something put them out first. Rain, maybe? He's too close to have not burst into flames, or at the very least, not to have had his hairs and clothes singed."

"Exactly."

"So what does *that* mean?"

"That, my dear, sweet, clever boy, is what we need to figure out."

Chapter III
The Black Sea Devil

The Black Sea Devil.

That's what the name of the tavern was. Ethan knew this because of the two-foot-by-two-foot sign hanging above, gently swinging on rusted iron chains as the wind swept through.

"Question for you," Ethan said, looking up at said sign. "Is that a devil from the Black Sea or a sea devil that's black?"

"Good question," Zoey said. "I'm guessing it's the angler fish, but who knows. They could've at least provided a picture."

"Remind me to complain when we get inside," Ethan said. "Maybe we'll score some free rum."

"I imagine the barkeep has bigger worries. Let me know how that goes for you."

Ethan ignored her playful pessimism and pushed through the rickety, mostly intact door. It opened with a screech of metal on metal thanks to the hinges, but only after he coaxed it with a stiff shoulder.

Two things greeted them when they stepped through: rubble and a charred interior. Most of the furniture had been reduced to coals, though portions of tables and chairs still remained, most notably those off in one corner. Even the bar was standing, likely due to its mostly brick design. The stairs leading to the second floor appeared suspect, and the ceiling looked blacker than the abyss—but it was there, as were six of the eight load-bearing columns, each a foot thick.

A gaping hole did exist in the ceiling where two of the columns had failed. Light from the late-morning sky poured in, illuminating not only the rubble that remained, but also a fair amount of water that pooled around it.

"I guess that answers that," Ethan said, pointing to the damage. "The rains came before everything was wiped out. Must have been a big storm, though, to put out this big of a bonfire."

Zoey nodded. "Big storms happen a lot around here. Something to keep in mind later as we're sailing."

"Which do you think came first, the plague or the fire?" he asked. "Or maybe someone set the fires to battle the plague?"

"That would be my guess," Zoey said with a heavy sigh. "And if I had to guess more, I'm thinking whoever set them probably was infected and died not long after. Maybe our friend back at the docks was trying to leave, and they stopped him, trying to protect the rest of the world."

Lines of worry formed across Ethan's brow, even though he tried his best to remain optimistic. "We've still got time to look around," he said. "Maybe we'll find some of your friends further inland."

"Maybe," Zoey replied, but she didn't sound hopeful.

Ethan went for the bar, and Zoey started for the second floor. She only took a few steps before she drew her sword and pulled the pistol from her belt. "Care to join me?" she asked.

Ethan pulled his sword, too, feeling her unease, and came to her side. "Sense something?"

"No, but if there is something deadly up there, I don't want to die from a classic horror movie mistake," she admitted.

Ethan chuckled. "Yeah, I mean, this place is screaming the 'get out now' vibe, isn't it?"

"Exactly."

The two climbed the stairs, wood creaking with every step. At the top, they found themselves in a long hall with a peaked ceiling. Doors lined both sides, spaced at regular intervals. Not surprisingly, each one led to a guest room, and like the rest of the town they'd seen so far, they found not a soul.

"Unrelated question," Ethan said as they stood in the hall. "About this girl that lives around here."

"The obsessed one?" Zoey asked.

"Yeah," Ethan said. "Why didn't you turn her? I mean, I'm assuming you two were friends and all, and she obviously knew what you are."

"It's not that simple, for starters," Zoey said. "The vampire lords, the absolute top of our lineage, take it very seriously. If they found out other vampires were giving away immortality to every commoner they came across, they'd hunt down and kill everyone involved."

Ethan, not expecting such a thing, stiffened. "Seriously?"

"Seriously," she said. "This is a very exclusive club, which is why we need to be lowkey about it all. Yeah, there are humans who like to think of themselves as vampire hunters. And the overzealous clergy or crusader can be a pain in the ass to deal with, too, especially if you don't *want* to have to kill them. But when it comes to a vampire lord hunting you down—let alone several—all bets are off."

Ethan slumped against the wall, exhaling. "Damn." He stayed quiet for a few seconds before asking his next question. "But...but we're okay, right? You and me?"

Zoey's face went grim, and she shrugged. "I don't know. I hope so," she said. "The truth is, I rolled the dice for both of us in a big way making you. I definitely can't make any more for another fifty years or so. And you? You better not for at least a century."

"Believe me, I have no intentions of turning anyone," Ethan said, holding his hands up in the air.

"Good, because if you do, we'll all be killed. You. Whoever you sired. And me, for turning you. And when they do put an end to us, it won't be pretty, either. It'll be long and drawn out, taking full advantage of our natural regeneration. I'd tell you specifics, but—"

"You don't have to," Ethan said, holding up a hand and feeling his stomach go queasy.

"Good," she said. "So, promise me, no matter what, you won't ever, *EVER* turn anyone."

"I promise."

"I mean it," she said. "I don't care what they say. What they bribe you with. Or threaten. Or whatever—"

"I get it," Ethan said, holding up his hands. "I promise. Sheesh, you make it sound like this is going to be an ongoing problem."

Zoey sighed. "It shouldn't ever be, but if Katryna's still around, she might try with you. And I really want to impress upon you just how bad of an idea that would be. Okay?"

Ethan took her hands and pulled her close. "I won't. I swear."

The anxious look on Zoey's face stayed for a few seconds before fading. "Okay, good," she said. "Now then, what say we get back to this search of ours?"

"I say that's a good idea."

The two dropped the conversation and continued on. After searching a few more rooms with nothing of note to be found, a thought struck Ethan as he stood a couple of feet inside the threshold of a guestroom, looking at a messy bed with its sheets tossed to the side. He nudged Zoey with an elbow to share his thoughts. "That's not right, is it?"

"What do you mean?"

"I mean, every bed we've come across looks as if someone flew out of it," he said. "That's not exactly the behavior you'd expect from a plague victim, right?"

Zoey furrowed her brow and tilted her head as she walked forward. When she was a couple of feet away from the bed, her hands found her hips, and she started drumming her fingers on her side. "The sheets aren't soiled, either."

"I'll wager ten crowns none of the others are as well," Ethan said. "In fact, I'm going to wager another ten crowns on top of that that says there's no plague at all."

Zoey cocked her head, and she looked at him with equal parts skepticism and amazement. "I'm really, really tempted to call. Why do you say that?"

"Because we should've found a makeshift ward by now," he said. "And I don't know what the rest of the town looks like, but if you're overflowing with sick people, wouldn't you convert at least the tavern to some sort of hospital?"

"Yeah...yeah, you would..."

Chest filling with pride, Ethan crossed his arms over his chest and beamed. "I suppose that's ten points to me, then."

Zoey bit down on her lower lip as her gaze wandered around the room. "That doesn't make a lot of sense, though. Why would anyone fake a quarantine?"

Ethan didn't have an answer for that; at least, not right away. "Because you don't want people to come," he finally said. "Because you found something you don't want anyone else to have or even know about."

Zoey nodded, her eyes staring off to infinity. "True," she said slowly. She then shook her head, snapping herself back into the moment. "Still, that's a lot of speculating. How do we test this theory of yours?"

"That's going to be hard unless someone was kind enough to leave us a diary," Ethan said. "But…"

A grin spread across his face, one that spanned from one ear to another.

Ethan's infectious smile spread to Zoey. "I trust that look means you have something brewing beyond flipping a coin and relying on luck to decide," she said.

"No, I won't do that," Ethan said, laughing. "I've got something else in mind."

"Awesome. Do tell."

"I was thinking, there's got to be a graveyard around here," he said. "Let's see when the most recent were buried. Even if they ended up burning bodies by the boatload, the first few people to die probably would've gotten their own graves dug and marked, right?"

"That, Ethan, is an outstanding idea," she said, eyes lighting up with hope as she headed for the door. "Come on. I know right where it is."

Ethan took a few quick steps to fall in line next to her. "You do? How?"

"Yup. It's on the north side," she replied before flashing an evil grin. "Put a few people in it myself."

Moving at a fast pace, the two left the tavern and snaked through the empty streets of Lenada. Along the way, they found a few more bodies. Like the first they'd stumbled across, they'd all died by means other than the plague. Three shot in the chest, one in the head, and two more stabbed through the gut. Other than their tattered clothes, a few of which included tricorne hats clinging to weathered scalps full of stringy hair, not a one had any possessions.

The graveyard ended up being at the top of a grassy hill overlooking the bay. A wrought-iron fence encircled it all with stone columns offering support at the corners as well as every ten paces or so. The road they took from the city ended at a set of large gates, latched closed but apparently not locked. Beyond the gates, Ethan saw hundreds of plots, all slowly succumbing to encroaching vegetation to one degree or another.

"If we don't find anyone, we could always raise a crew here," Ethan said as Zoey swung open the gates. "I mean, there has to be plenty of material, right? And we do have Lord Belmont's spell book."

"I said it before, and I'll say it again: I'm not about to mess with it," she said. "But if you want to risk the backfire from that kind of dark art, by all means, don't let me stop you."

"Yeah, I know, but I can still dream."

"You like dreaming of the dead?" she replied. "Never really pegged you for the type."

"Technically, you're dead."

"True, but I'm the hot kind of dead," Zoey replied, not missing a beat. "What you bring up here, I promise, won't be pretty."

Ethan laughed and then started looking at headstones. Most were upright, nearly three feet tall and curved at the top, though some were simple rectangular slabs that were planted in the ground. He was surprised at the skill and delicacy in the letters that had been carved into each face, as well as the scrollwork etched above and below the names and dates. But more importantly, each also had a small shrine carefully put together at the base, one that reminded Ethan of the ancient temples of Rome and Greece.

"These graves took a lot of time and care to make," Ethan said, pointing to the one he was at. "Why?"

"The people of Lenada honor their dead like no other," Zoey explained, her voice soft with respect. "A wild group, but a respectful one to the deceased in their own ways."

Ethan nodded before kneeling down and pulling some of the weeds away from the headstone he was at. If he was treading on such sacred ground, the least he could do, he figured, was to make it a little nicer. He could spare the moment. As he did, he looked at the date. "Eleven sixteen to eleven fifty-five. How far back is that? I guess I never bothered to look at a calendar."

"A little over a century," she said. "We're in the year 1277."

"From what?"

Zoey laughed with a shrug. "Honestly, I have no idea what the calendar is based on. I've always gone with it."

"Well, this guy didn't die of plague then. That's for sure."

"Or this one," Zoey remarked, motioning to the grave she was at. "This girl died a decade ago."

It took them less than ten minutes to check out each marker, and by the end of it, they had only one answer and a thousand more questions.

"No plague," Ethan said as the two met at the final spot. It sat next to a sprawling oak tree that had a wreath made of rope and copper, and of the entire site, the marker seemed cared for the most, which wasn't surprising, as this spot seemed to hold the most honor, being at the top of the hill. "Most recent one I found was from last year."

"Same."

Ethan made a slow circle, not really sure what he was looking for, but hoping something would stand out. As he did, some lingering questions on the world's lore popped into mind. "Hey, question," he said. "You said everyone in this world is real, right? I mean, like, they aren't mindless NPCs. They're alive."

"As far as I can tell, yeah. Why?"

"Do they hear Narrator, too? Or pick levels? Or any of the game stuff we get to do?" he asked. "Or do they not know about any of that, and they'll think we're crazy if they heard us talking about such thing?"

Zoey laughed. "Yeah, they'll definitely think you're either crazy or trying to pull a worn-out, thoroughly unfunny joke on them. Sometimes you'll get labeled as a cultist. Depends on who hears you."

"A cultist?"

"Mhmm," Zoey said. "Fanatical cultist of the double seas."

"How's that?"

Zoey smiled, and she laughed again, shaking her head. "Whoever started that tale a few hundred years ago misunderstood whoever they got it from," she said. "Instead of the double seas, undoubtedly, it was C&C, e.g., *Captains & Cannons*."

"Ah, gotcha," Ethan replied. "Still, you'd think someone by now would've managed to explain it all."

"Why?"

Ethan shrugged. "Why not? It's a simple concept."

"In theory, sure," Zoey replied. "But imagine being back in our world, and some guy ran up to you claiming you were in a giant game and whatnot. You'd never believe him. In fact, you'd probably—"

Zoey cut herself off, tilting her head to the side as if something grabbed her ear.

Ethan held his breath, sensing danger, and listened intently to everything around him. The world seemed to come alive in more vibrant detail than before. He could smell the nervousness drifting off Zoey's skin, could see the hairs on her arms rise, taste the way her sweat left a tinge of salt in the air. And then he heard it. The crunch of grass, a couple of blades at the most, coming from behind.

Ethan whipped around with Zoey spinning at the same time, both with swords drawn. A tall, lanky man halted in place, ten feet away, dressed in worn breeches and a black open vest. A couple of gold earrings hung from his ears. One hand rested on the hilt of a cutlass, while the other stayed on the butt of a pistol tucked into his waistband.

"Easy, mates," he said, taking a half step back. "Only looking to talk."

The look in the man's eyes, however, said otherwise.

Chapter IV
Standoff

Ethan adjusted his grip on his cutlass, and his gut tightened. Though he'd come a long way in a short period of time, skill and combat-wise, he knew he was hardly a master swashbuckler, and the guy who squared off with them had probably won more fights in a week than Ethan had birthdays under his belt.

"You want to talk?" Zoey asked, voice filled with skepticism.

The man nodded. "Aye. Name's Bill. Nothing fancy with it. Just Bill."

"Well, nothing fancy Bill," Zoey said with a snort. "If all you want to do is talk, why not have your friends come join us?"

"Friends?"

"Don't take me for a lass who can't see a hole in a ladder," she said, face hardening. "Tell them to come out, or this gets ugly."

When the man hesitated, Ethan joined in, realizing he needed to back her. "I'd listen if I were you," he said. "She's not the first mate because she plays nice."

The man grunted and threw a glance over his shoulder. "Alright, lads," he said. "Two of you best be coming out so our guests don't get jumpy."

Ethan watched as from behind a couple of large, weed-infested headstones, maybe eight yards away, two men popped up and approached. They wore similar garb and tanned skin that told of life on the open seas like Bill's, and both had swords hanging from their hips, though neither had a pistol.

"And the other," Zoey said, narrowing her eyes.

"Afraid, miss, this is it," the leader said, throwing up his hands with a shrug. "Your nerves are getting the best of you."

Ethan cocked his head. His vampiric ears picked up Zoey's heart, beating strong and true in her chest, and he quickly realized how in synch his own was with hers. He also could hear the hearts of the men before him pumping away. They sounded quicker than he would've expected, but he didn't dwell on that for long. A fourth heart beat somewhere nearby.

"He's over there," Ethan said, hitching his thumb toward another large headstone.

The leader grunted again, this time with irritation. "They're on you, too, Giddon," he called out. "Might as well join the fun."

The fourth member pushed himself up and warily made his way over. Giddon turned out to be the shortest of them all, with a pot belly and a bald head but arms that would give any blacksmith's a run for his crowns. "Told the lot of you that was a bad spot," he said in a rough voice.

Bill ignored the remark and instead flashed Ethan and Zoey a weaselly smile. "Can't blame me for being too careful, yes? Not like there's many a sane man who'd risk the plague."

"Maybe," Ethan said. Though he did his best to keep his affect flat, tension built in his muscles—a tension he knew the source of: Zoey. The vampire was expecting a fight. No, not expecting, looking for the opportunity to start one. How he knew that, he wasn't sure, only that it was a deep-seated gut feeling. "You said you wanted to talk," Ethan said, refocusing. "Talk."

Bill nodded. "We saw your ship, wanted to tell you and your crew to get away before the black fever took you all."

"Black fever?" Ethan repeated. "Is that what swept through here?"

"Aye, it is," he said. "Came two months ago on the morrow. Stole half the town in a week."

"I assume you burned the town, then?" Ethan asked.

"Aye, we did," he said. "Dying at the time, or thought as much. Seems we've recovered a bit, but even I'm not such a scoundrel to say being 'round us is safe, if you know my meaning."

Ethan didn't believe a word he said, or at least, he didn't believe they were being given the whole truth. Inside his heart of hearts, he knew Zoey felt the same. It was like her soul whispered to him on a deep, intrinsic level. A glance to the vampire only confirmed the thought. "What do you think?" he asked.

"I think we should leave the same way Han did."

Ethan cocked his head. "Han?"

"When he was at Mos Eisley."

The words had barely registered in Ethan's head when Zoey whipped out her pistol and fired. The shot hit the lead man square in the chest, and he fell to the ground, lifeless.

"Cleave her to the brisket, lads!" Giddon shouted, drawing his sword.

Instinctively, Ethan yanked his pistol free and fired as the three men attacked. The magical weapon kicked hard in his hand, and with a deafening rapport, it shot a lead ball straight at the closest attacker. Unfortunately, his aim wasn't nearly as lethal as hers had been. The bullet ripped through the man's left shoulder, much to Ethan's dismay.

Corsair hit!
Corsair lightly wounded!

Ethan, having not heard Narrator's voice in his head for a few days now (that he could remember, at least, as the blood hunger had made things extremely fuzzy), had his attention focused on what he was saying so much that he barely had time to react when the melee was upon him.

The first pirate to reach them issued a straight thrust for Ethan's heart, which he barely parried, catching the sword with the strong part of his own blade and deflecting it to the side with the handguard. However, he overcompensated on his move, swinging his hand far too wide so that when the man dripped his blade under Ethan's guard and slashed it back across, Ethan couldn't defend against it.

A searing pain erupted across his collarbone as sword cut through fiber and flesh.

A corsair hits you!
You are lightly wounded!

A second attack came, this one from the next pirate to join the fray. He issued a backhanded chop, intent on taking Ethan's head from his shoulders. As the blade flashed through the air, Zoey yanked him to the side and used her own blade to defend Ethan.

Ethan, somehow having anticipated the yank, moved with the momentum and let his body spin completely around. His blade clashed against the last pirate's weapon when the man took a stab at Zoey and knocked it aside.

The pirates pressed their attack, only this time, they fanned out and spent a half second to coordinate their attacks. Steel cut through the air, steel from vampire and pirate alike, and Ethan found himself moving out of pure instinct. But he wasn't merely reacting to parry attacks against himself or even those that went for Zoey as well. He was moving alongside her in tandem as if they'd been given a dance to master together.

Their hands found each other's in concert, offering support or a well-timed pull to safety, while their weapons kept their attackers at bay. At first, the ballet they entered seemed to only keep them safe, but when one of the corsairs came in too close, Ethan trapped the man's blade as Zoey thrust hers straight through the pirate's heart.

Corsair hit!
Corsair killed!

Narrator hadn't finished his last announcement when the vampiric pair spun around and issued another combination attack of beat-and-thrust, this time Zoey knocking away the next pirate's weapon as Ethan, operating in complete unison, stabbed the man through the gut, dropping him immediately.

Bonus attack!
Corsair hit!

Corsair killed!

Zoey, with a hold on Ethan's forearm, spun the two of them around so that they now faced off with the last remaining pirate. The man, the one who'd come out from hiding last, backed away, sword and free hand raised defensively and a panicked look in his eyes.

Ethan opened his mouth to speak, but before he could, the sounds of two distinct gunshots filled the air.

Corsair hit!
Corsair hit!
Corsair killed!

Ethan straightened but kept his guard up. The pirate staggered forward with a pair of gaping holes in the middle of his chest. The man fell to his knees, then to all fours, then collapsed in a bloody heap.

"What the hell just happened?" Ethan asked.

Before Zoey could answer, a woman stepped out from behind the oak tree, wearing a pearl-white bodice with a black corset and form-fitting pants tucked into leather boots. She carried a smoking pistol in each hand and an impressed look upon her face. As she continued forward, eyeing the dead corsairs with a glint in her dark eyes, a long scimitar swayed off her hip.

"Never thought I'd see you again, Zoey," she said, her refined voice sounding like it came from Eastern Europe or whatever the equivalent was in this world. "Dare I hope you came for me? Or is this just a chance meeting?"

Zoey nodded. "No, we came for you."

"Thank God," she said as she came close. The corner of the woman's mouth drew back, ever so slight, as if the act of smiling came unnaturally—or maybe it was that she couldn't quite bring herself to believe Zoey. "Do I get a hug?" she asked stiffly. "Given how we parted, I'd rather not assume."

Zoey nodded again. "You can have a hug. I'm glad you're still alive."

"I've missed you," she replied once she had Zoey wrapped in her arms. Zoey returned the embrace, albeit with obvious reluctance, and that reluctance didn't go unnoticed. "And let me also say, thank God you shot first. I saw them heading your way, and I was worried I might not reach you in time."

Zoey laughed. "Ha! As if I'd believe any of them were locals. Of course, I was going to shoot first."

"How did you know that?" Ethan asked.

Zoey pulled away from the woman and pointed to Bill's body. "See that tattoo with the flag and irons? It's a slaver tat. His friends have them, too. That alone makes them shoot-on-sight worthy. I assume the only reason they didn't shoot us first—or try and take us—is they were worried we actually had a few hundred troops nearby."

"Ah, gotcha," Ethan said. "Wonder if they have anything good."

"Only one way to find out," Zoey said. "But if they have any rings, don't go putting them on right away like last time, yes?"

"You're just saying that because I ended up with Maii," Ethan said as he searched the fallen corsairs. He didn't come up with anything exciting, but even splitting the coin, he was happy with his share. Narrator, as always, gave the rundown.

You have taken six shillings!
You have taken the pistol!
You have taken powder and shot!

"Your pistol is much better than his," Zoey said.

"I know," Ethan said as he adjusted the new weapon's place in his waistband. "But I figure we might need to sell it at New Port Royal. I'd take the swords, too, for the same reason, but I have a feeling walking around with all of those attached to my body would be awkward."

"Fair enough," Zoey replied with a nod.

The woman cleared her throat. "Care to introduce me to your new pet?"

"Right, sorry," Zoey replied. "Katryna, Ethan. Ethan, Katryna."

"And I'm not a pet," Ethan tacked on.

Katryna raised an eyebrow, and Zoey confirmed. "He's not."

"Then who is—" Katryna cut herself off as she sized the two up for a moment. "Oh. I see. Well, I'm happy for you, Zoey. I imagine he's quite skilled, then, if he's the pick of your crew."

"He's the captain, actually," she said.

"And you're looking at the crew," Ethan finished.

"The crew, as in, she's part of it?"

"The crew, as in, all of it," Ethan replied.

Katryna's jaw dropped. "Tell me you're joking. Tell me you've got a full battalion of marines on board."

Ethan shook his head, though he wished he didn't have to. "Afraid not."

"That's insane," she said. "How did you even get the ship sailing?"

"Very carefully," Ethan replied. "We were hoping to find a crew here."

The woman pressed her lips together and frowned. "This world, I swear, always trying to plant a pig on me."

Ethan furrowed his brow. "What?"

"Plant a pig," she repeated. "It means to cause trouble and play dirty tricks. You come here with a ship and get my hopes up—but have no crew." The woman sighed and shook her head. "Doesn't matter. We will work with what we have, yes? But we best be moving fast in the meantime."

"Why?" he asked. "What's going on?"

Katryna started walking and motioned for them to follow. "I'll catch you up on the way to the others," she said. "Hopefully, we'll be long gone before the corsairs realize they're missing their friends."

Chapter V
Marcus

"The corsairs raided the town a couple of months ago," Katryna said as she blazed a trail through the jungle with Ethan and Zoey following close behind. "In under an hour, they had all of the survivors in chains."

"Damn. That was fast, but they've got to be more than simple slavers," Ethan said. "Why are they still here?"

Katryna glanced over her shoulder and nodded. "They are. They sank our ships, took Lenada's shore guns, and erected a fort on the other side of the island. It doubles as a labor camp."

"A labor camp? For what?"

"They're digging for something," she said. "What, I'm not sure. A few others and I escaped the carnage by pure luck. I didn't exactly run up and ask what they were doing."

"That dig must be why they faked the quarantine," Zoey said. "Whatever they're after must be insanely valuable."

"How many of them are there?" Ethan asked.

Katryna shrugged. "Couple hundred, give or take a few dozen."

"Did Marcus escape?"

"He did. We're going to his place, in fact."

"His place?"

"He built a spot hidden away, far from town," she explained. "To work on his 'art' without having to listen to people complain about the noise. Or smell."

Ethan barely caught that last part, for his stomach rumbled, signaling the impending return of that invisible, ravenous monster who'd made a home in his gut. It wasn't the first time it had made such a noise during their trek, but it was the loudest. It rumbled so loudly, in fact, that Katryna stopped and turned around.

"Skip breakfast?" she asked.

"No," Ethan said, setting his jaw and trying to push his pangs away. It wasn't easy, and he wondered how much longer he'd be able to do it before he lost his mind. "I guess I didn't get enough, is all."

Zoey grimaced, her hand clutching her midsection, and leaned against a tall, thin rubber tree. "You and me both," she said.

Katryna joined the vampire. With one hand, she took Zoey by the shoulder, and with the other, she offered her wrist. "Here. This will help."

Zoey pushed her arm away and shook her head. "We'll catch something later," she said. "I get the feeling you'll need your strength."

Katryna offered her wrist again. "And you need yours. You look like a squeezed lemon."

The exchange went on, and as it did, Ethan felt his teeth sharpen and his mouth water. His feet carried him forward with a will of their own, and his eyes never left the gentle curve of Katryna's soft neck.

Katryna turned and shot him an incredulous look. "Down, tiger."

Her words were short and sharp enough that Ethan regained his self-control. "Say again?"

"I said, 'down tiger,'" she replied, crossing her arms over her chest. "Look, I don't know what fantasies you're entertaining when it comes to the three of us, but we're stopping that right now. We are not peas in a pod, so stop gawking at me and drooling like we are."

Ethan blew out a puff of air and laughed. The tone in his voice grew dark, and as he sized Katryna up, memories of his first night with Zoey ran through his mind. "Katryna, can I be honest for a moment?"

The woman rested her hand on the pommel of her scimitar. "If you like, but I can't promise you'll keep your tongue."

"You look absolutely delicious."

Katryna opened her mouth to reply, but before she could, Ethan lunged.

"No! Don't!" Zoey yelled, dashing forward. She managed to underhook one of her arms in Ethan's shoulder and used it to hip-toss him to the ground.

The move caught Ethan by surprise, but it didn't stop him. He slipped from her grasp and tried to drive forward again, but Zoey pounced on his back. Ethan flattened out on the ground. He reached out with his hands and used them to claw forward, dying to sink his fangs into human flesh.

"I just need a little," he growled, pulling himself and Zoey along. "A liter at the most."

"No, Ethan. Now's not the time," Zoey shot back. As he continued to argue and struggle, Zoey slipped one arm around his neck from behind and soon got him into a rear-naked choke.

Ethan kept going with all he had. The gnawing in his gut demanded nothing less. His throat felt scratchy and dry, and Katryna's heart tempted him to such a degree that any siren would be jealous.

A few seconds later, his fingers tingled, and goosebumps formed across his skin. His vision dimmed, and then oblivion took him.

The next thing Ethan knew, he was lying on his back, staring up at a jungle canopy as two women stood over him. His hunger pangs were gone, and it took him a few seconds to realize who they were, but he had it figured out by the time Katryna spoke.

"Wow," Katryna said, eyes wide. "Wasn't expecting that. I guess that explains why he was drooling over me. Is he part of your coven, or did you two meet somewhere else?"

Ethan perked at her question, realizing he didn't know a lot about how vamps worked in this world. "You're part of a coven? That's actually a thing here?"

"We met back in Bartigua," she said.

At first, Katryna didn't react, but after she studied him for a few seconds, a little resentment showed on her face. "Ethan, how old of a vampire are you?"

"A few days," he answered, taking to his feet.

Katryna arched her eyebrows. "A few days? Who turned you?"

"I'm afraid that's on a need-to-know basis," Ethan said, figuring it best for all involved not to name names.

His ruse, a poor one admittedly, didn't last half a moment. Katryna slowly turned her head to Zoey with a deadpan look upon her face. "I can't believe you did that."

Zoey groaned and rolled her eyes. "Look, it's nothing personal—"

"Of course, it's personal," Katryna interrupted, throwing her hands up in the air. "How could it not be? We were like drops of water together. At the very least, tell me you two have a long history together. Known since diapers, yes?"

Zoey balked.

"He's a noob you don't even know?" she said with a huff of disdain.

Ethan crossed his arms. "I am *not* a noob."

"Oh yeah? When did you get here, then?"

"A while back."

"So, a week ago," she said with a smirk. "Two, tops."

Zoey sighed and rubbed her temples. "Please stop. You're going to make me regret ever coming here," she said. "I didn't have a choice."

"You don't expect me to believe that, do you?"

"I wish you would, because it's the truth."

"Fine. Whatever," Katryna said. "But you know what? I'm not jealous at all. Why would I be? I mean, I've only been in the game three times as long as you, made sure you didn't die when hunters came looking for you, and now you're telling me you wasted the best gift you could give anyone on a complete noob."

"Ahem," Ethan said, puffing his chest. "As I said before, I'm not a noob."

"Sure, you aren't," she said. "Let me see your character sheet."

Ethan stepped back, feeling put on the defensive. "Let me see yours."

Katryna reached into her bodice and whipped out a neatly folded piece of paper. Keeping it clamped between two fingers, she flipped it out toward him. "Be my guest."

Ethan warily took the paper, unfolded it, and read aloud. "Name, Katryna. Race, human. Class, swashbuckler. Strength, fourteen. Endurance, fifteen. Intelligence, ten. Charisma, eleven. Reflex, fourteen. Luck, nine. That doesn't seem all that special."

"Keep going."

So, he did, but not for much longer. He stopped when he saw her level and skills and whistled. "Thirty-four? Holy crap, and a *master* at *Swordplay*?"

"Among other things," she said. A smirk formed across her face. "Going by your look of astonishment, I'm going to stand by my original point: you're a noob. You don't have to show me yours."

"Yeah, well, could a noob kill a lich?" he countered.

Katryna shook her head and grinned. "No, but a noob would lie about it."

"He's not lying," Zoey interjected.

"He's not?"

"No."

"Not only did I kill a lich, but I saved Zoey's life in the process," Ethan said, feeling smug as he puffed his chest. "Impressed?"

Katryna's mouth hung open for a few seconds before she seemed to realize she needed to say something. "Maybe."

"Maybe?"

"Maybe," she repeated. "Question for you, though, while I'm thinking about it."

"Shoot."

"Why are you here?"

"Playing against Azrael," Ethan replied as he handed back her character sheet. "I'm assuming you know about him."

"I do," she answered. "That's why most come. Who are you playing for?"

"Anne," he replied.

"Wife? Girlfriend? Kid?"

Ethan shook his head. "She's my dog."

Katryna stiffened as if she'd been belted across the face with a leather strap. "Your dog?"

"Yeah."

"You're risking your life for a dog."

"Yeah," Ethan said again, this time feeling annoyed. "I love my dog."

"Your life, I guess," she said with a shrug before turning to Zoey. "Did you know this?"

"I did," Zoey replied. "I think it's sweet."

"I think it's dumb," Katryna said. "Don't get me wrong, pets are nice, but hardly something I'd risk my soul for. Not sure I like the idea of following someone like that."

Ethan, feeling himself start to seethe, shot the swashbuckler a glare. "Who are you playing for, then?"

"No one."

"No one," Ethan tutted with disbelief. "Then why are you here?"

"I won a game at the fair—back when I could go," she said. "This is my prize. To live in this world as long as I like, which as far as I'm concerned, will be forever."

"Forever? Like, forever, forever? Like never see your friends and family again, forever?" he asked.

Katryna's face hardened as she popped her knuckles and her eyebrows knitted together. "Exactly like that."

"Well, okay," Ethan said, not sure what to make of her reaction. At that point, his stomach growled, and he hunched as his gut tightened. "I'm really going to need a bite soon," he said.

"We've got snares set not far from here," Katryna replied. "Hope you like rabbit."

Ethan didn't know if he did or not, but since Katryna wasn't on the menu and she hadn't offered him a rat, he decided he'd give it a go. Thankfully, they didn't have to go far. Ten minutes later, they reached the first snare, which had a seven-pound rabbit alive and kicking. Two minutes after that, Ethan decided rabbit was a step up from rat, but Katryna probably would've tasted better.

Ethan shuddered at that last thought, no doubt the result of what humanity he still had left in him.

Post-snack, Katryna led them through the jungle at a brisk pace. When two hours had nearly passed, they reached a secluded thirty-foot waterfall with a small, crystal-clear basin. Giant red cedars lined the perimeter. Strangler figs wrapped about half of the trees, and between them all, oil palms grew by the dozen.

The air held a refreshing, almost magical feel to it, and tiny golden fish darted around the water, while a few emerald-green parrots sat perched above, divvying their attention between the fish below and the newcomers to their side. All the place needed, as far as Ethan was concerned, was a large hammock to climb in.

"Damn, this is incredible," Ethan said as he took it all in.

"It's definitely one of the island's hidden gems," Katryna said, carrying on.

Ethan could only nod in agreement as she led them around the left-hand side of the pool. He took care not to lose his footing on the few slippery spots of rock Katryna pointed out along the way. When she reached the side of the waterfall, she took a couple of handholds on the rock face, and once her feet found what little purchase was available, she started to shimmy across.

"It's right on the other side," she said as water crashed down from above, only inches from her head. "See you there."

With that, the woman slipped through the cascading water and disappeared.

Zoey started to follow, but Ethan caught her by the elbow, rooting her in place. "Hang on a sec," he said. "I had a thought."

"About?"

"Our need for a crew," he said. "I was thinking, maybe it's not such a good idea that we *only* have skeletons."

Zoey cocked her head. "What do you mean?"

"I mean, I don't know how trustworthy this Marcus guy is, and I don't like the idea of him being in command of the entire crew," Ethan explained. "He'd essentially be captain, and, well, I doubt he's invested in the race as much as we are."

Zoey folded her arms over her chest and drummed her fingers as her mouth twisted. "I have a feeling the more we're together, the more I'm going to hate you for doing that," she said with a laugh.

"Doing what?"

"Making poignant observations."

Ethan grinned sheepishly. "What can I say? I have a mighty eleven INT now."

Zoey blew out a puff of air and stuck her hands on her hips. "Right, so, we're going to need more crew," she said. "But before you go in there and try and get us one, there are a couple of things you absolutely need to know first."

"Why do I get the feeling this is serious."

"Because it is."

"Okay," he said, steeling himself for whatever it was she was going to throw at him. "Go ahead and break it to me. We've been through worse, I'm sure, unless you're hiding some other godawful curse from me that's going to get me killed."

Zoey laughed. "It's nothing like that, relax," she said. She stopped, dropped her brow, and briefly touched her lips with a finger. "Well, in a way, I suppose it is."

"Ha. Ha."

"I'm not joking," she went on. "We're vampires. People react—how do I say this without scaring the crap out of you—in a variety of interesting ways when learning such things."

"Like how? Stake through the heart?"

"Yeah, or the polar opposite, completely fanatical, which comes with its own problems," she said.

"Like Katryna."

"She was one of the more mild cases, but along those lines," she said. "Most people, though, generally don't trust us, and for good reason. Almost as many simply despise us. For those two reasons alone, we've got to keep things quiet."

Ethan nodded. "Can do. What's the other thing I need to know?"

"You're the captain."

"Yeah, I know."

"No, I mean, whoever is in that cave is potentially going to be our crew. They need to see you like that from the start," she said. "You're going to have ten, twenty seconds at the most to convince them you're a savvy, salty dog who has his own ahuizotl-guarded ship, who knows exactly what he's doing. If you don't, we're sunk."

"Well, I've got the first half at least," Ethan said with a sheepish shrug. "But honestly, I'm making most of this up as I go."

"So am I."

Ethan jerked back reflexively. "You are?"

"More than you realize," she said. "It's not like I'm an expert in all things around here, but I fake it well enough, don't you think?"

"Uh, yeah," Ethan stammered.

Zoey scooted forward and rose on her tip toes to kiss him lightly. "That's all you have to do," she said. "Play the part. You're the captain. They're the crew."

"Got it. Play the part," Ethan said. He repeated that last bit again for his own benefit. "Right, play the part. I can do that. I can totally do that."

"Good."

"Should I talk more piratey?" Ethan asked as he tried to solidify the role in his mind. "Toss in some more 'Arrs' and what not?"

"Talk however you want, but it's more about attitude than anything, which is why I said remember you're the captain," she said. "If it helps, pretend to be your favorite leader from whatever book or movie you can think of."

"I always liked Aragorn," Ethan said.

"Perfect."

"Maybe mixed with a little William Wallace?"

"Who?"

"The main character from *Braveheart*," Ethan replied. When she looked at him with a blank stare, he added, "You know, 'Freeeedom!'"

"Oh, right. The guy with the painted face."

"Yeah, him," Ethan said. "And topped off with Jack Aubrey, of course. *Master and Commander*." Again, the blank stare, to which Ethan shook his head. "Never mind. The whole picture works for me, I promise. I'll play the part as if our lives depend on it."

"Good," Zoey said as she grinned. "Because they do."

A split second later, Zoey slid across the rock face and disappeared through the waterfall.

For a few seconds, Ethan stood there, his thoughts churning over her last words. He wanted to believe she was joking, at least somewhat, but no matter how he tried to perform his mental gymnastics to say otherwise, he knew she wasn't.

He also realized he couldn't stand there for the rest of time, either. The tips of his fingers dug into wet rock, slipping once as they tried to dig into ledges that weren't quite what they needed to be. Likewise, his feet couldn't grip the portions of rock he tried to set them on nearly as well as the girls had. Though he managed to quickly find his starting position, he didn't get but a foot or two before he nearly fell off, thanks to a combination of water pouring down on his head and his inability to see, let alone find anything.

"Come on, Ethan," he said to himself after freezing in place. "It can't be that hard."

It wasn't that hard. It was harder. No matter where he stretched his hand through the waterfall, he couldn't find anything to grab hold of that wasn't exceptionally smooth, hard, and wet. Frustrated, he pulled back and tried a foot next, which ended even worse. His other foot slipped off the rock, and it was only a miraculous scramble that kept him from taking an unplanned dip.

Frustrated, Ethan collected himself once more. This time, he found the tiniest of holds for his fingertips about four feet in. Something for his feet? Not so much. He wasn't sure what to do, but after standing under the waterfall for several moments, getting thoroughly drenched, he came up with a well-thought-out plan that could be summarized in two words.

"Screw it." Ethan launched himself sideways, using the finger hold to add extra reach to his sideways jump.

Once he flew through the water, he shook his head midair to clear the hair from his eyes and did so just in time to see himself hurtling at a rockface. A dry rockface with plenty of places to grab, at that.

Ethan quickly attached himself to said rockface, smacking into it with a slight grunt, before then climbing the four feet that remained from him to the edge above. Once he cleared the top, he found Zoey and Katryna waiting for him, each smiling with amusement as their wet hair clung to even wetter bodies.

What stood behind them was not the damp, moldy cave with a dirty bedroll that Ethan had envisioned, but rather, an interior so lavish, it would be the envy of any. A fire burning in a nearby hearth provided a warm glow to the place, and four more high-back satin chairs had been placed nearby with three small end tables set between them. A half dozen brass oil lamps hung from iron hooks mounted in the walls, providing additional illumination as well as giving off a cinnamon-like aroma that Ethan enjoyed. If there was one breakfast food he could've survived on for his entire life, it was cinnamon toast.

Off to the side of the cavern, built up against one of the walls, was a full bar with overhead hooks holding a slew of steins, as well as a couple of racks that contained both fine glassware and dozens of bottles of what had to be wine and rum. While no one currently tended to or sat at said bar, there were four salty men of varying ages—but equal grit—who'd gathered around a massive round oak table. Though they were clearly in the middle of a card game and partaking in plenty of drink, their focus wasn't on the game.

The moment their eyes found his, the entire group jumped from their seats, pistols flying out of waists and a few curses sailing through the air as well.

"All of you, stop!" Katryna shouted, hands up. "He's with me, too."

"Bah," was the only response Ethan caught, though there was a low grumbling that accompanied it as well before the men settled.

Once they had, Ethan spent a moment taking the place in. "Damn," he finally said with a long, slow whistle. "This is quite the hideaway."

"Tell me about it," Zoey said. "How the hell did Marcus get it all in here?"

"Lots of pulleys, rope, and patience," Katryna replied, pointing to a block and tackle stored in one of the corners.

"What in the blackest abyss are you three doing?" bellowed a thunderous voice. Ethan jumped, and from a side passage in the back, a monstrous thing marched out that bulged more muscles than a championship strongman competition. It towered over everyone by at least a couple of feet, and the curved horns jutting from his bullish head looked like they'd drop an elephant with a single gore.

Short ebony hair clung to the minotaur's hide, and from his chin were three long braids to form a beard, each wrapped in copper wire. The creature wore chestnut-colored breeches tucked into black leather boots, while an equally dark vest topped a bone-white long shirt. A pair of skulls hung from a chain belt around his hips, and a barnacle-encrusted tricorne hat sat atop his head. "Drip over there!" he shouted, pointing to the fireplace. "See the flames? Feel the heat? I swear to Great Lord Charethes—may he always infuse my soul with his undying power—every last one of you is as useless as a barrel of soaked powder!"

"Ugh," Zoey said, rolling her eyes and head in tandem. She grabbed Ethan by the wrist and pulled him along to their designated spot by the hearth. "Come on, Ethan. Best keep Marcus happy."

Unable to look away from the minotaur, Ethan felt his eyes bulge as she pulled him along. "He's Marcus?" he stammered.

"*He* is going to go on a rampage if people don't stop leaving puddles everywhere!" he roared as he stomped his way over. When he got to Ethan and Zoey, he bent low so his forehead was but an inch away from Ethan's. "Did I not make myself clear last time?"

"Easy, Marcus," Katryna said, putting a hand on his side. "They both just got here. They didn't know."

Marcus straightened. "They did? Bah. How was I supposed to know? You humans all look alike." At that point, Marcus dropped his brow and grunted, huge puffs of air steaming out of his nostrils as he did. "Wait. When you say they just got here—"

"She means we literally just got here," Ethan finished. "As in, I have a ship that could use some extra crew for a few weeks. You help me. I help you."

"A ship could be useful," the minotaur said, sounding like he was talking more to himself than to Ethan. His head dropped, and he tapped his giant hands together several times as he thought things through. "Hate to leave my home unattended, but there might be less of a chance it'll be found if we left for a spell."

Though Marcus seemed to still be on the fence, the group of men—all save one at the table—jumped to their feet, hope shining in their eyes. The lone dissenter kicked his boots up on the table and eyed them skeptically. "And what, pray tell, are we helping you with?"

"Reaching New Port Royal to start," Ethan said. "After that, we'll be sailing in the regatta."

The excitement in everyone's eyes sank faster than a galleon with a split keel.

"The Grand Regatta?" Marcus asked with a disturbing chuckle. "I think I speak for everyone here and say we'll take our chances with the corsairs. Now, if you'll excuse me, I have work to do. Feel free to see yourself out."

Chapter VI
Plans

"Scared of a little race, are you?" Ethan said, crossing his arms and trying to give off the best look of disgust he could manage. He realized this tack was a gamble, both in terms of success and reaction, but deep down, he felt questioning the room's toughness would yield the fast results he needed. "I expected more from the lot of you, but then again, I suppose that explains why you lost your town."

The men at the table growled and looked ready for a fight. Marcus, on the other hand, with his eyes narrowing and nostrils flaring, looked ready for war. "If you're looking to test your mettle, this old seadog will be glad to send you to the bottom of the abyss, but only a fool would agree to challenge Azrael not knowing the captain he'll be under. And from the looks of you, I'd say there's not much you can boast about."

"Is that a fact?"

Marcus nodded with a smug grin. "Aye, it is, but since I'm feeling charitable, I'll give you ten to be explaining who you are, else I'll take your words for what they are, insulting and begging to be answered."

"Minutes?" Ethan asked.

"Seconds."

That wasn't the word he was hoping for, but Ethan did his best to play the part to win them over. He did, after all, have fifteen points in Charisma now, and he wasn't sure how his vampiric charms worked, but they had to help, too. "Well, Marcus," Ethan said, taking his time smoothing out his clothes. "I'm the one who went to Gibbon Isle with only my first mate and jackal at my side and not only acquired a hefty bit of treasure but killed the lich who lived there and took his ship."

The room grew silent, save for the nearby crackle of fire. Marcus eyed Ethan with a tremendous amount of skepticism, but at the same time, respect, too. "You want us to believe you slew Lord Belmont?"

"*We* slew Lord Belmont," Ethan corrected, motioning to Zoey. "I'll not have anyone sail with me thinking otherwise, especially as she's first mate."

"What proof do you have?"

"I have his ship, the *Victory*," Ethan said. "And..." Ethan let the pause hang for a couple of seconds to emphasize what he hoped would seal the deal. "We have his staff and spell book. I'm willing to let you use them to raise even more members for our crew if you want a taste of that power because, I'll be honest, right now, our numbers are thin. We could use a full complement of skeletal minions. Means I have to hire fewer marines when we get to New Port Royal."

Marcus let out a deep, wet snort. "You don't expect me to believe you're simply going to hand over an artifact as powerful as Lord Belmont's staff, do you?"

"What you expect and what I'm willing to do can be very different things, my good bull," Ethan replied, smiling and feeling good about where this was heading. "I'm not worried about letting you use it."

"And why is that?"

"Because I took it from a lich, and I'll take it from you just the same if you get any ideas," Ethan explained. "Furthermore, as an extra incentive to keep things moving smoothly, I'll say this: when we win the race—and win we shall—you can keep that staff as payment for your services."

A deep, rolling laughter erupted from his belly. "Ah, Master Ethan, now you've overplayed your hand. No one in their right mind would give up such a thing."

"I don't care about the staff one bit," Ethan said, unfazed. "All I care about is winning that race."

Zoey stepped forward, joining Ethan at his side. "It's true," she said. "The treasure isn't important to either of us. Only beating Azrael."

Marcus balked, seemingly caught between wanting to believe and wanting to call bullshit on it all. "I'm sure I can find another necromancer to take me up on my offer," Ethan said, hoping that all that was needed was a nudge. "If this bargain doesn't suit your fancy, speak now, and we'll be on our way. But I doubt you'll ever have an opportunity like this again."

Marcus stroked his chin and toyed with one of the braids in his beard as he thought it over. "You drive a tempting offer, Captain. Tempting indeed."

Ethan cocked his head and smiled. "Captain? Is that what you'd like to call me, then?"

Marcus shot out his meaty hand, which nearly crushed every bone in Ethan's hand when he took it. "Aye, it is."

Once the minotaur released his grip, Ethan casually placed his hands behind his back so he could work out the impending soreness without being seen and turned to the others. "Will the rest of you be joining us?"

The man farthest to the right crossed his arms over his chest. Soft, angular eyes narrowed into a wary gaze, and he lifted his large hooked nose into the air as if he could somehow sniff Ethan's character out. A dark, short, and curly beard covered his jaw, while a set of unruly clothes, breeches, and a long shirt hung off his wiry frame.

"And what are you offering us in exchange for risking our lives?" the man asked with a French accent—well, it would've been a French accent if France existed in this world, Ethan reminded himself.

Before he could answer the man, Zoey hopped in. "You get six shillings a day, which is more than twice the pay you'll see anywhere else."

"Oui, but it's a far cry from what he's getting," the man said, motioning to Marcus.

"He's also a necromancer that's going raise the dead, Mister..." Ethan said, letting his voice trail.

"Jean Bayard," the man replied with a sweeping bow. "The one and only."

"Well, the one and only Jean Bayard," Ethan said. "I'll give you each an extra ten crowns once we win on top of what I'm already willing to pay."

"Make it thirty, and then you'll be talking our language," Jean replied.

Zoey gave a mocking laugh. "We're hiring a crew. Not desperate for one. We can pick up who we need elsewhere."

"Paying us each ten crowns says otherwise," the man said.

Zoey went to argue some more, but Ethan held up his hand, not so much because he felt like she couldn't handle the matter, but because he knew if he were to be seen and respected as captain, his word had to be the final say in all such matters. "You'll get twenty crowns each," he said, "as well as making a name for yourself. I reckon being able to brag you helped beat Azrael ought to be treasure enough for a man in charge of his own destiny. In exchange, from this point until we reach the finish line, my word is law, and anyone not working, sailing, and fighting as hard as he can gets tossed overboard without a shilling to his name."

Ethan tacked on that last part on the fly, hoping the men before him respected a cutthroat leader more than an easy pushover. The dark chuckles and gleams in the men's eyes prompted him to finish the offer. "Well, what do you say?" he asked. "I have a regatta to enter, and I'm not in the mood to waste any time getting there."

The group looked at each other, and after a quick semi-huddle where hushed whispers were exchanged, Jean pivoted on his heels to face Ethan once more. "Alright, Captain," he said. "We'll join, but before that happens, I have two requests—simple ones really for a man of your power."

Ethan raised his eyebrow, faking as much as he could borderline indignation at being told what he had to do. In truth, he didn't mind the negotiation, and he was thrilled he'd have more under his command shortly, but as Zoey had said, he had a part to play. "What, exactly, would you ask of me?"

"First, there's a ship out there, the *Red Fish,* that's sailed the regatta the last couple of years," he said. "If we cross her, I want her sunk and her captain keelhauled."

Ethan dropped his brow, unsure what to make of the bloodthirsty request. "Because...?"

"Because she and her crew captured my brother's ship, the *Blind Mako,* three years ago off the coast of Piram. They took his cargo, and after he refused to give up our family ring—a simple copper band worth nothing to anyone else—they killed him and the rest of the crew and sank the ship."

"You were there?" Ethan asked.

Jean nodded and pulled his shirt aside to reveal a large scar on his upper chest. "Shot through the chest and fell overboard," he said. "Managed to pull myself onto a rowboat that broke free once they'd left me for dead. Now, I want my revenge."

Ethan turned to Zoey, looking for more input on the matter, but it was Katryna who spoke first. "The *Red Fish* is captained by a man named Sir Gideon North—part of the Golden Templars."

"Who are they? Pirates?"

"No. They're men who've taken the idea of a zealous crusade to an entirely new level," she said. "At times, they've been known to take 'donations' to help purge the land of darkness."

Ethan shook his head and cursed. "Figures."

"I told you morality was ambiguous at best around here," Zoey said. "And to tack on to the end of that, if there's a Golden Templar in the race, we don't have to pick a fight with him. He'll be looking to sink us on his own. Undead crew and all."

Ethan cursed again, but despite the grim warning, he wasn't about to let it get to him. "Alright, Jean," he said, turning his attention back to the man. "We run into this *Red Fish,* and we'll sink her, but not at the expense of the race. Fair enough?"

The man nodded. "Oui. Fair enough," he said.

"Good. What's the other thing?"

"The other thing is I want you to free our lads from those corsairs," he replied. "I figure a task like that should be easy for the killer of a lich."

"Are you mad?" one of the others exclaimed. "Let's set sail this very instant."

"We're not leaving anyone behind," Jean said evenly.

"They outnumber us thirty to one," the man protested further. "That's not tucking tail. That's being savvy."

"I said we're not leaving anyone behind," Jean said, a deep crease forming in his brow. "I'll have a word outside with any man who says otherwise."

"Easy, Jean Bayard," Ethan said, holding up a hand. "We'll get your friends back. I promise you that, and everyone here is going to help."

Jean Bayard curled his lips into a devilish grin. "Good, because I tire only dreaming of revenge."

Half an hour later, once Marcus was thoroughly convinced Ethan, Zoey, and Katryna were all dry and thus allowed to move away from the hearth, the group of eight stood around the table as Katryna unrolled a large parchment. On it was a rough sketch of the corsair's fort, done in charcoal. Loose, smudged lines formed the bulk of the map, though she had made finer, more intentional strokes for her labels.

"The fort is built up on a small hill overlooking the entrance to the cove," she said, pointing it out. "The mine they've got everyone digging at is about two miles south, and their galleon is anchored nearby with probably thirty or forty onboard at all times. Prisoners are kept in a building here, chained together, and the three buildings here are barracks where the corsairs will be. Last, the fort has six watchtowers spaced around a wood palisade, with embankments for cannons here, here, here, and here."

"Are those the cannons from town?" Ethan asked. "We noticed they were missing when we came in."

Katryna nodded. "They are. They brought them over, two at a time, with oxen, along with other tools and materials looted from town."

Ethan studied the map for a few moments and then a few more to verify his gut reaction. He hadn't a clue what to do given their numbers. "Does anyone have any initial suggestions?"

"What are these?" Zoey asked, tapping a spot on the map near the southern wall.

"Kitchen, armory, and general stores, I think," Katryna replied. "They never gave me the full tour, so it's all guesswork."

Ethan perked. "Armory? How stocked of an armory?"

Katryna shrugged. "Not sure, exactly, but enough to handle the needs of two hundred men."

"Any chance that means other than the guards, they'll be unarmed?"

The woman shook her head. "No. They keep their swords and pistols on them at all times, even when sleeping. The armory probably only has extra powder and shot, though it might have whatever weapons they took from their captives."

Ethan frowned and let slip a curse as his masterful plan was dashed before it had a chance to take off, even if he knew, ultimately, it was nothing more than wishful thinking. But it didn't take long for Ethan to realize it didn't matter if corsairs slept with their weapons if he could take care of all of them in one fell swoop.

"You've got that look," Zoey said, cutting into his thoughts.

"Well, I've got a rough plan," he said as he took a drink from his own stein. "We take out the guards on a couple of the towers and sneak through the gap. Once inside, we use surprise to our advantage and win the day."

"Straightforward. Bold. I like it," Zoey said, raising her mug. "Course, now all we have to do is figure out that bit about using surprise to our advantage."

Ethan drummed his fingers on the table and hummed. Had he specced military genius, he felt as if he could've come up with something truly amazing. As it were, all he could do was voice the top of his wish list. "This would be so much easier if we could just nuke it from orbit."

"I doubt the prisoners would like that plan," Zoey replied.

"Guided missile, then. I heard a tomahawk cruise missile can hit the driver of a jeep going fifty from a thousand miles away. A few of those would take care of those barracks in no time." Ethan paused and glanced at the others, who all looked at him like he was stark raving mad. "Never mind," he said. "I'm rambling."

Confusion continued to plague the other pirates; Marcus as well, but Katryna's eyes gleamed, and the corners of her mouth drew back. "We might not have those, but what you said gives me a grand idea."

Ethan tilted his head. "It does?"

"It does," she repeated. "We've got skeletal minions, right? Or will, at least. We strap some makeshift bombs to their chests, give them each a match cord to hold, and then send them into the barracks. They should be coordinated enough to self-detonate."

"Oh, I like that," Ethan said, feeling the hairs across his arms raise in excitement. "I like that a lot. I mean, not only is it effective, but can we get any cooler than kamikaze skeletons?"

"Blow them up? Bah!" Marcus said, thumping a heavy fist on the table. "All that time and material wasted! Won't even get to see how effective they could be."

"Think of it as an investment," Ethan said. "They're going to create a lot more material for you to use. Now then, what's the downside to this plan?"

"We have to get the skeletons into the barracks before the alarm is raised," Katryna said. "That might be hard enough with the watchtowers and guards posted at each building alone, but there will also be at least three roaming patrols. The moment anyone stumbles on a body or sees a skeleton running around, they'll raise the alarm."

"Or worse, put a shot through one of the powder kegs," Jean Bayard finished.

"Then I guess we better make sure they don't see us," Ethan said.

"And how do you plan on doing that?" Jean asked.

"A little bit of stealth and backstabs, courtesy of Zoey," Ethan said, "and a whole lot of trickery, courtesy of Maii. I'm sure he can stall anyone we need long enough to set those bombs off. Once that's done, we can certainly handle whoever's left."

"Maii? Who's that?" Katryna asked.

"My ahuizotl."

Katryna's eyes went wide, and her jaw dropped. The rest of the room had a similar reaction. "You have an ahuizotl?" she asked.

"Didn't I mention that before?" Ethan said, knowing full well he hadn't and enjoying the surprise on the faces of all.

"How is that even possible?"

"Because I've had him since he was a pup, and he knows who's the alpha in our group," he replied. "Now then, how long will it take to get there? We need to strike tonight, and we've still got to get back to the graveyard, raise an army, and pick up Maii."

"We can't strike tonight," Marcus said. "There's no possible way we can flesh out all the details in such a short period of time. Just coming up with a list of contingencies will take a week, and that's not counting making sure we have an ironclad understanding of our foe's habits now that the fall storms are upon us."

Ethan shook his head. "We don't have to know everything, everything. We'll be fine. You'll see."

"Yes, we do need to know," Marcus said, thumping a heavy fist on the table. "If we're going to be that sloppy, we might as well only rehearse our parts four score and seven times!"

"We strike tonight," Ethan said, deciding he needed to end this objection immediately. "This isn't up for debate. Aside from the fact that I have to be at the race in a few days, those corsairs are going to realize a few of their men are missing soon, if they haven't already, and once they find the bodies, we're going to lose our element of surprise. Trust me. We have to go tonight."

"I'd like to, Captain," Marcus said. "But even with your ahuizotl helping, I need time to familiarize myself with Lord Belmont's staff and ritual book."

"Ethan is right," Katryna chimed in. "There's no point waiting for the grass to grow."

"Exactly," Ethan said, nodding his head. "And surely you've had some success in raising the dead already, Marcus. The staff ought to make that tenfold easier."

"I've had some, yes..." the minotaur replied.

Jean Bayard laughed. "Some. Is that what we're calling it now?"

"I'd call it tremendous if the lot of you would respect my rules!" Marcus bellowed. "How am I supposed to work when I'm dealing with wet floors all day?"

"That has nothing to do with it."

"It has everything to do with it, you ungrateful sack of—"

A single pistol shot ended the argument before it devolved any further. "Sorry, Captain, if I took too much liberty," Zoey said, sliding the smoking weapon back into her waist band. "But I know how much you hate infighting. Figured the proper thing was to at least give them a warning before you start taking limbs."

Ethan hesitated, but only for a moment. His thoughts fell in sync with hers a moment later—a feeling that seemed almost supernatural—and he blew out a long puff of air as he readopted his part of the man in charge. "Let's stay on task, gentlemen," Ethan said. "Exactly how much success have you had?"

Marcus grunted before sticking his pinkies in each side of his mouth and whistling sharply. From the back room, a skeletal dog bounded out. He stood a little over knee-high at the shoulders and kept a knotted sock firmly locked in its jaws. When he reached Marcus, he sat on his haunches while his tail wagged excitedly.

Ethan took one look at the undead canine and sighed, already knowing the answer to the question he was about to ask. "Tell me you have a full kennel with thousands of these guys."

"Not quite," Marcus replied.

"Hundreds?"

"Almost."

"Almost?" Jean repeated, chuckling.

"One is closer to a hundred than a thousand," Marcus growled.

Ethan wanted to slump but forced himself to stay upright. Out of the corner of his eye, he caught Zoey with an amused look upon her face. "What?" he asked.

Zoey jerked back and laughed, clearly having been caught in her own little world. "I was just thinking, at least it's not a skeletal hamster."

The comment hit Ethan just right, and his face lit up as he smiled. "No. No it's not," he said before forcing himself to stay positive. "Alright, Marcus. If you can raise one not-skeletal hamster with that staff, you can raise us an army. I'm sure of it. Now make me a believer."

Chapter VII
Minions

A couple of hours after the sun had set, underneath a cloudless night sky, the group managed to return to the graveyard at Lenada after Ethan had picked up Maii from the *Victory* and grabbed the staff and ritual book as well.

Marcus stood near one of the older graves, gripping the staff tightly with one hand as the other held the leather-bound book aloft. At his side, Katryna kept an oil lamp raised so he could read. The minotaur murmured to himself the entire time as he did, asking himself questions about how things worked, only to chuckle a few moments later when his eyes apparently found the answer within the text.

Ethan and Zoey waited patiently nearby, hands clasped with one another's, while Maii used the clawed hand at the end of his tail to scratch himself behind the ears. Jean Bayard and the rest of the men stood spaced out around the area, hands nervously twitching on the hilts of sabers or butts of pistols.

"I'm telling you, he's watching me," one of them said, his gaze fixated on the ahuizotl.

Jean Bayard shook his head. "No, he's not."

"Don't tell me what my eyes can see," he shot back. "That thing wants to eat me."

"It's your imagination. Nothing more."

"Oh, I definitely want to eat you," Maii replied, licking his chops and flashing his razor-sharp teeth. "But at least I'm willing to admit it."

The man's pistol flew out of his waistband and pointed at the ahuizotl. "What's that supposed to mean?"

"It doesn't mean anything," Ethan said, shooting Maii a displeased look. "He's not eating anyone here."

Maii went into a deep, downward dog stretch. "As you say, master."

"I do say," Ethan replied, hoping to not only nip this potential problem in the bud but also quell any and all fears growing in the others.

Marcus turned, his brow knitted, and huffed. "I'm going to start now. Further interruptions may cause...interesting results."

"What about nibbles?" Maii asked, throwing a wicked look at the snack he wanted.

"That would be an interruption," Marcus said with a growl.

"What if they are quiet nibbles?"

"Maii!" Ethan barked. "I already told you once. You're not eating anyone here."

"Who said I was asking about me? I'm not the one with the rumbling stomach."

A pang of hunger stabbed through Ethan's gut, even more intense than the others had been. The rabbit from before, an adequate snack at best, had become a distant memory, meal-wise. Now, Ethan could feel the approach of invisible claws, claws that would soon tear at his sanity if he didn't eat relatively soon. That said, he managed to keep a stoic face. "I'm sure people can wait. Now stop causing trouble so Marcus can work."

The minotaur grumbled to himself before turning back around. He drew a deep breath and rolled his massive shoulders a couple of times like a prizefighter about to enter the ring.

Marcus cleared his throat and raised the staff high. Words, dark and sourced from some strange language Ethan had no hope of understanding, flowed from his mouth. The tip of the staff started to sway, slave to his wrist. At first, the movements felt stiff and jerky but quickly fell into rapid, flowing motions, as if the necromancer swayed to the sounds of a tribal beat that only he could hear.

The air all around took on an electric feel, raising the hairs on Ethan's arms and the back of his neck. The temperature dropped suddenly as well, at least forty degrees, and breath from everyone hung in front of their mouths.

"Yes, yes," Marcus said as he focused on the ground at his feet. "Feel that? I call, and the grave answers."

Earth cracked into tiny fissures around the grave into a weblike pattern some five feet across. The air chilled ever more, yet at the same time, heat poured from Marcus's staff, drawing everyone close to keep skin from freezing.

A bit of bone pushed its way loose from the soil, drawing audible gasps from everyone—everyone but the necromancer. The minotaur's eyes gleamed with maddening delight, further accentuated by the disturbing laugh that came from deep within his belly.

A small digit pierced its way out of the ground, followed by three more until a fully formed hand—or was it a paw—came forth. It clawed at the topsoil, pulling itself further out so that its arm and torso followed. The skull came next, sliding out sideways, but it wasn't the skull of a person. It was oblong, with large eye sockets and a nasal structure that looked like it belonged more on a dinosaur than a person.

It was at that point Ethan realized the thing was the size of a housecat at best. "What the hell is that?"

Katryna squatted, resting her elbows on her knees as she leaned in closer. "I think...no, is it?"

Zoey laughed. "It is," she said with a quiet laugh. "It's a giant skeletal hamster."

The minion sprang to life a moment later, shaking its back end like a dog ready to play before hopping a couple of times and ultimately dropping its hind end next to Marcus.

The necromancer knelt briefly, scratching the top of its pale skull. "It's not just a skeletal hamster," he said. "It's proof the staff bends to my will, that I can weave energy through it like thread on a loom."

Ethan sighed, not sharing the minotaur's optimism. Even if under other circumstances he would've found the homemade hamster to be quite the accomplishment, it was a tad on the macabre side. "Our plan needs more than an army of undead rodents."

"A practice run, nothing more," Marcus said, gently picking up his creation and placing it on his shoulder. He stood and shook his arms loose. "Trust me. All those buried here will walk once more."

Marcus resumed his work. The intensity of his words jumped tenfold as he whipped the staff overhead in a rapid circle. The skull atop the magical instrument glowed with a sickly green light, and from its mouth, dark tendrils of smoke stretched across the graveyard, writhing as they cut through the air before eventually diving beneath the soil. Spots of brown and black formed on the weeds, and the plant life curled in on itself.

The sweet scent of decay filled the air, and in dozens upon dozens of spots, the ground rumbled and heaved. A bony hand broke through the soil, and three more followed suit. One of the men next to Jean Bayard broke ranks, fleeing into the darkness. No one chased after or said a word. Marcus, however, laughed, his eyes bulging out of their sockets, and the muscles in his forearms bulging as he gripped the staff harder yet.

"Yes! Yes!" he bellowed. "Answer your master's call! Answer and let us take back all that is rightfully ours! Our lands! Our lives! Our pride!"

Zoey slipped an arm around Ethan's and squeezed. "I'm not sure I like how this is making him," she whispered.

"I don't think I like it all," he whispered back.

The skeleton of a man draped in rotted leathers stumbled to its feet. It stood awkwardly at first, slumped forward with one shoulder dropped, and moved in a jerky fashion like it was slave to a drunk puppeteer. But within seconds, it snapped upright with a clattering of bones and marched forward. Its lifeless eye sockets stared out to infinity as it came, and its jaw clacked together with every step.

When it reached Marcus, the minion stepped to the side and waited. Four more joined it seconds later, and within a few minutes, Ethan found himself looking at a total of forty-two skeletons that seemed deadly enough and were definitely not of the hamster variety.

"That's impressive," Ethan said, thinking he needed to say something.

"That's a start," Marcus replied with a nod. "I need rest, and the staff needs to recharge. But in an hour, we shall have thrice what you see here."

A hundred and twelve. Oh, and a half. Ethan corrected himself on that last bit when he made the final count of their skeletal mini army. The last one raised by Marcus ended up being nothing more than feet, legs, and a pelvis. Ethan failed to suppress a grin at its creation, which then turned into a laugh when Marcus shot him a glare, but thoughts of the comedic creation lasted only a moment. Ethan's gnawing stomach ensured that.

The group went about equipping their undead cohorts with an array of weapons looted from the town, or rather, impromptu weapons. Clubs fashioned from table legs or broken handles formed the bulk of what they had, but a quick raid of the town's blacksmith yielded a number of hammers as well as a half dozen swords in various completed states. They even managed to find a few sickles. Despite the paltry arms in use, fashioning the bombs ended up being both easy and, as far as Ethan could tell, effective.

"See?" he said, wincing as another hunger pang shot through his side. "Another reason to love rum. Solves all sorts of problems."

Zoey grinned as she cinched tight the rope that held the last remaining powder-packed cask to a skeleton's chest. "Creates them, too. I'd hate to be in the same room when this guy goes off."

"You and me both," he said. Another pang. Though Ethan managed to stop the grimace, he could feel his eyes water.

"Something the matter, Captain?" Jean Bayard asked, slapping him hard on the shoulder from behind. "Or did you get a good whiff of our dead friend here?"

"Just a little hungry," Ethan said without thinking.

Jean Bayard laughed in disbelief. "Hungry? By the eleven seas, you must be quite the butcher if you can think about having a meal alongside these walking cadavers."

"You have no idea," Ethan replied, shutting his eyes for the moment and drawing a deep breath. Yes, the stench of death felt unbearable, but it didn't have a snowball's chance in hell of overpowering the growing pit in his stomach. Ethan knew he'd have to find a way to eat soon, because if he didn't, there was no telling what would happen or who'd suffer because of it.

Zoey snapped her fingers in front of his face several times to grab his attention. Ethan jerked his head up, and in the moment, everything faded away until there was nothing left except the two of them. It didn't feel like the effects of being charmed, not like before, at least. No, this was something else. Like they had their own little world they could dip into. Before he could give it any more thought, she spoke, her voice both concerned and commanding. "Ethan," she said. "Tell me you can wait."

"I can wait," he said. He took in a deep breath and exhaled forcefully, pushing through the pangs and tension they created to repeat his words. "I can wait."

Zoey smiled and then smiled even more when he took her hand in his and squeezed. "Glad to hear," she went on. "Now, let's go take a fort."

"Not yet."

"Not yet?"

Ethan nodded. "We're missing something."

Zoey tilted her head. "What's that?"

"This." He stepped forward and slid his hands across the small of her back before his lips found hers. As he pressed into her, as her fingertips traveled up his spine and toyed with his hair, he could feel his heartbeat in total sync with hers, and then a moment later, the two seemed to merge into one distinct sensation.

"Would've been bad luck," he explained after they parted a minute later.

"Oh, we wouldn't want to risk any of that," she whispered. "Luck's been a staple for us, after all."

"Exactly."

They shared another moment or twenty in silence, eyes locked on one another until the world reappeared around them. They still stood hand in hand, though now they had acquired a few onlookers surrounding them. In the back of his mind, Ethan realized the encounter was a little strange, both in terms of timing and the sudden urge, but he didn't care. Hell, the fact that this was one oddity he'd experienced in this world that wasn't deadly was cause for celebration, and on that note, he almost initiated round two.

But Jean Bayard cleared his throat and ruined the mood.

"If the lovebirds are done, we can go," he said, raising his hands with a shrug. "Oui?"

Zoey gave a longing sigh and peeled away, much to Ethan's disappointment. "Oui. We can go."

And with that, they did.

Chapter VIII
The Fort

Mist Zoey, the affectionate pet name Ethan gave her right before she dissolved into a fine spray of white, broke free of the tree line and drifted up the hill where the fort sat overlooking the small bay to its east and the wide Gold Monkey Sea to the north. To her right, the ground dropped sharply for a few yards before disappearing over a rocky cliff. Though she couldn't see where it ended, she could hear the crash of waves against the rocky shore.

A ship could never lay anchor there, hence the reason this side of the fort wasn't watched as much as the others, but the edge of the cliff was almost completely obscured from those in the fort. Only those in the northeast tower—a simple rectangular three-story structure that reminded her of the fire lookout towers back home—had a view of the cliff. True, the southeast tower also looked out over the area, but it couldn't see the dip in the topography, and it was certainly too far away to make anyone out at night. Thus, Zoey had only to deal with a few of the night watch at the most.

As her form glided silently along, she caught glimpses of light from inside the fort peeking through the gaps in the palisade. She couldn't tell where it was coming from but guessed the source had to be the oil lamps carried by the roaming patrols. One had to be near, which was both wanted and dangerous. Wanted because it meant once they left, she'd have the maximum amount of time to work, and dangerous because she could feel the strain on her will, the draw of her body trying to reform. She wouldn't be able to stay a mist for much longer, which meant she didn't have much time to find a place to enter and hide.

Zoey waited, hoping the patrol would move on, but when they didn't, and the light persisted, she knew she had to move, regardless. She pushed through a dark section of the perimeter, only a few yards away from the watchtower. She'd barely made it inside when Mist Zoey reformed into just plain Zoey despite every attempt to stay in the form a little longer. That said, she did manage to cloak herself in the inky black shadows smothering the area before anyone noticed.

Sadly, she hardly felt safe. Looking around, it became painfully clear that the light she'd seen wasn't coming from the night patrol's oil lamps but rather oil lamps that had been hung and lit all across the grounds. Worse, she could count at least a half dozen groups of men walking the grounds in sets of three and four, all armed and visibly on edge. They hadn't found the bodies of the men who'd attacked her and Ethan. Zoey had checked on that a few minutes prior to Marcus raising the dead. But they had to have realized they were missing said men, and since there weren't a lot of places for deserters to go on such a small island...

Zoey's thoughts froze as one of the patrols stopped several yards away. One man in the group happened to look her way, but only for a moment. Her *Sneak* skill, she knew, was more than enough to keep her hidden. Once they moved on, she considered aborting the attack, returning to the others, and encouraging them to leave while they could. In the end, she didn't. She knew it was a panicked reaction to the unexpected, no doubt some lingering anxieties about how disastrous her last party had gone when the unexpected—Lord Belmont—claimed them all.

Zoey sucked in a breath and studied the patrols, and after a minute or so, she relaxed. Yes, there were more. Yes, they were on edge, but there were still wide gaps in their routes they could exploit. All they needed to do was sneak a few bombs into the barracks, which she felt had to be exponentially easier than taking down a lich.

With that in mind, Zoey slipped out of her hiding spot, and using her *Sneak*, she darted up the winding stairs of the watch tower quieter than a gentle breeze. The stairs took her to the very top without incident. There she found three guards, with two looking out to the east and into the dark where Ethan and the others lay hidden, and one staring straight at her.

Zoey's eyes darkened, and pressure followed by a deep heat built behind them and spread through her skull. The guard straightened, his hand dropping to draw his sword as fast as his mouth opened to sound the alarm. He did neither. Narrator filled in what she already knew.

Corsair Charmed!

Zoey curled her lips and placed a finger delicately on them. "Shh," she whispered, her voice barely audible even to her own thoughts.

The corsair nodded and did nothing but stand there, staring blankly through her. Knowing her effect would only last a minute at best, she slipped to the side so he wouldn't see her, as any hostile action she'd take would have a good chance of breaking the effect. When she was clear of his line of sight, she drew her dagger and promptly slit the throat of the nearest guard. Again, Narrator chimed in.

Back stab successful!
Critical hit!
Corsair killed!

The body hit the ground, and for a brief second, Zoey wished Ethan had been there to see the kill, to see what she was capable of. The sound the corpse made, however, as it thudded to the floor, snapped her out of those thoughts. She spun to square off with the other man right as he turned. Zoey reacted first, but only by a fleeting instant. She lunged forward and attacked, dumping every bit of *Luck* she had into the attack. She didn't have nearly as much as Ethan, but the ten points she committed to the exchange would hopefully win the fight before the man could raise the alarm.

Thankfully, it did.

The tip of her blade caught the man square in the heart. It sank fully to the hilt. The corsair wheezed and clutched feebly at the weapon before his legs gave out. Zoey quickly scooped him under the arms as best she could to ease the man down. After that, she dispatched the third guard with ease and gave Ethan the signal that she was in by stripping one of the guards of his coat and hanging it outside the tower.

"Six minutes," she whispered to herself.

That's the timer everyone agreed on once she'd set the impromptu flag. Six minutes to sneak into the prison and free everyone there. For a normal thief, it would prove to be a difficult, if not an impossible task, but Zoey was anything but normal. Being a queen of the undead certainly had its perks, as she'd just demonstrated, even if she did have to feed on a blood doll or hapless stranger from time to time.

Speaking of, her stomach rumbled, and she winced as a cramp shot up her side. Zoey furrowed her brow, trying to understand why. It hadn't been *that* long since she and Ethan had dined on rabbit, and on the way to the fort, Katryna had even let her have a brief snack from her wrist when the pair casually lagged behind the group for a few minutes. She shouldn't be hungry. Peckish, maybe, but not hungry. Ethan sported the *Fast Metabolism* trait, not her. Unless...

Zoey shook her head, snapping herself out of all the speculation. She'd have to deal with whatever this was later. She stole the pistols from her victims, thinking they might come in handy, and slipped down the stairs.

Once back on the ground, she darted into the shadows and made her way as fast as she could to a large square building near the center of the fort made from heavy, rough-cut logs. Lanterns hung on iron poles staked at the corners, providing ample illumination, while a pair of guards stood at a single door barred with a heavy piece of timber. Not a single window could be seen, and she doubted there'd be any on the other sides either. After all, it's not as if prisons were known for the luxurious views afforded to their guests.

But she didn't need a window. Or an open door, for that matter. The gaps between the logs would be enough, and she could still turn to mist two more times this day. Once to get in and free everyone. Once to get out and unlock the door, provided they didn't run into surprises.

The vampire shut her eyes and relaxed, letting her body dissolve back into a thin, white mist. She floated onward, grazing the light when she reached the jail, but not a soul took notice. Within seconds, she reformed in the building, where she spent a half moment shaking her right leg free of tingles. A common, mildly annoying side effect when she repeatedly tapped into her shapeshifting ability over a short period of time. When her leg felt tolerable, she surveyed the room.

The prisoners, fifty-two in total, slept in a line on a wood floor. Heavy irons bound their wrists and ankles together, which were then locked and anchored around two of the thick wood columns that ran up to a pitched roof.

Zoey quietly padded across the room and knelt by the first prisoner. She didn't recognize the dark, wiry man before her, but that didn't mean much. Zoey only knew a handful of the people at Lenada.

Zoey gently placed her hand on the man's shoulder to stir him awake. The moment she made contact, the man's eyes shot open, and he jumped against the chains. The links rattled loudly, and the vampire quickly pressed her finger against her lips.

"Shh," the vampire said. "I'm here to free you."

The man nodded with a toothy grin, his movement barely perceptible as if he risked summoning the entire corsair camp by doing anything more. Despite his near statuesque state, when he replied, his tone was both cutting and vengeful. "We better not be running," he whispered in a gravelly voice. "I have a score to settle."

"We're not," Zoey reassured. "We're going to attack from here once the raid comes."

"When's that?"

"Soon as the barracks blow, which will be any minute now."

The man's eyes shined bright with anticipation, and Zoey drew back the corners of her mouth, loving the fiery spirit that still burned bright in his soul. The vampire then directed her attention back to his leg irons. The lock was far from useless, but it was hardly the craft of a master artisan, either. Ten seconds after she started, she popped it open with a soft click.

The man eased out of the cuff around his ankle and, once freed, quietly gathered the chain, wrapping one end around his fist. As he did that, Zoey moved on to the next man in chains who had woken up already. When Zoey's eyes met his, she made a quick check of the slave pen and realized that all of the prisoners lay awake and watched her every move.

"Shouldn't take long," Zoey said to him, and it didn't. The second lock popped open even faster than the first.

Feeling good about how smoothly this was going, Zoey moved through the pen, her fingers delicately working her picks. When she'd freed almost half of the prisoners, the hairs on the back of her neck stood on end as sounds of approaching corsairs filled her ears. There was a group of them, talking loudly amongst themselves. Drunk, no doubt, but definitely headed their way.

Zoey slinked further into the shadows that draped the pen, thinking it best to pause in her work and stay hidden until they passed by. That all changed, however, when the group—five by her count, judging from the different voices—stopped outside the door.

One said something about going in first, and then there was an argument that quickly followed—the precise words Zoey couldn't follow as most of their speech was slurred. But their intent was clear, especially when the heavy wooden beam on the outside fell to the ground with a solid thud.

"Damn," Zoey muttered. She thrust the spare pistols she'd taken off the others into the hands of the nearest two men and drew her sword. "Everyone stays inside till I say," she said as loudly as she dared.

The door to the jail swung open. Five corsairs with swords dangling off their hips and bottles of port and rum hanging in their hands staggered inside. The second one raised an oil lamp, presumably to hang it on a nearby hook. As he lifted it up and the light swept the room, the prisoners attacked.

Chapter IX
The Battle

The rats had returned. Well, maybe not all of them, but there was at least one of the hungry little devils gnawing on Ethan's gut once again. Nothing was going to get rid of it, he knew. Nothing short of feeding.

He should've taken a bite out of Katryna when he had had the chance, back when she and Zoey had lagged, and no one else noticed. Or maybe he should pounce on her now while they waited for Zoey to give the signal. Seeing how she'd been a blood doll already, she probably wouldn't even fight him off all that much. She'd be an easy snack, one way or the other, he told himself.

Ethan shook his head, set his jaw, and growled.

God, what was he becoming? What had he become? A vampire, sure, but until recently, he never knew what that entailed. Worse, he had a feeling he still had a long way to go before he fully understood, and he shuddered to think of what monster he might ultimately turn into.

But Zoey had managed, somehow, to keep her humanity. Or had she? He had seen her ravenous once before, and it shook him to the core. Furthermore, she'd admitted to killing others while feeding, though she never provided the details.

Was she a cold, undead killer in the end? Ethan didn't think so, but God, the gnawing growing worse and worse made it hard to think. All he wanted was a snack. From anyone. Anywhere. And he'd do anything for it. Maybe, in the end, that's how Zoey was, too—controlling her hunger only when it was polite and beneficial to do so.

Maii plopped next to Ethan, derailing his thoughts. "We'd make the most fantastic of teams, you know," he said.

The tone in the ahuizotl's voice gave Ethan pause, and he cocked his head. "Aren't we already?"

"Yes and no," the creature replied. "Yes, in that we travel together, but not when it comes to dining. Between you, me, and Zoey, we could feast on whoever we liked—gorge ourselves till the end of days. Wouldn't that be nice?"

Ethan winced at the bloody picture forming in his mind. As ravenous as he was, as much as he wrestled with his own wants and needs, the dark picture Maii painted struck a sharp chord against his soul. "I don't want to eat anyone," he said.

"Your grumbling stomach says otherwise."

"I don't care."

"You know, there are plenty of powerful and corrupt people out there who could use a good eating," he went on, giving his forepaw a tongue bath. "You'd be doing the world a favor, really, if you drained them and left their bodies for whatever happened by."

"You mean, I'd be doing you a favor."

"Master Ethan," Maii purred. "You sound like I'm trying to trick you, as if my motives aren't plain to see. I did say upfront, I want you to keep me well-fed, and now that you've changed—for the better, I might add—you can really make that happen. Why should innocent men and women suffer under brigands and tyrants when we could put a stop to it all and fill our bellies in the process?"

"And let you grow in power, too."

"Again, my desires are hardly secret," Maii countered. "Or you can continue with this foolish idea you'll beat The Hunger, and when it finally consumes you, you really will drain anyone nearby. Men. Women...children. Do you want those meals on your conscience? Or would you rather still feel good about yourself after a meal?"

"No, I don't," Ethan admitted. He gritted his teeth as another stab took him, and he had to admit that whether he liked it or not, how and what he thought of as food was going to radically change his life from here on out.

That said, maybe the ahuizotl had a viable point. Maybe he could save his humanity, feeding off the wicked and evil of this land. He could be a vampiric Dexter of sorts, and it would certainly go along with one of Zoey's quips she'd made when they'd first met.

"Life here *is* morally ambiguous at best," she'd said.

Another knot came and went. Though it hadn't been as sharp as the previous, Ethan wondered how much self-control he had left.

Katryna appeared from nowhere and dropped a hand on his shoulder. "A few more minutes at the most," she whispered. "Can you wait?"

"I don't know," he admitted. "I need—" He paused a half second to throw a glance at the others and ensure they still weren't paying attention to him. "—something. Anything. Maii here isn't helping."

To his surprise, she nodded. "I know. I'd offer, but I want you hungry."

Ethan narrowed his eyes and let slip a tiny growl. "Why?"

"Hungry vamps are even deadlier vamps, provided they aren't starving," she said. "Trust me on this mechanic. You'll get your fill shortly."

Ethan shook his head. "I don't think I'll be able to control it, though. They're going to see."

"The fight will be chaos," she said. "You should be able to eat where no one will see. But all that hinges on you staying in control long enough for us to blow the barracks."

Ethan opened his mouth to continue the conversation as the mere act helped keep his sanity, but then it came: the scent of blood.

Coppery. Fresh. Absolutely delicious.

Better yet, he could tell its source wasn't that far off.

Ethan tilted his head up and let his nose sniff the air. A couple of seconds later, he was certain the scent was coming from the watchtower Zoey had been heading to. An insatiable thirst welled within, and if Katryna hadn't clamped her hand around Ethan's upper arm and held fast, he'd have been over the wall in ten seconds flat.

"Look, there's the signal," she said, pointing to the coat that now hung outside the watchtower. "Six minutes."

"Might as well be six centuries," Ethan said, shuddering.

"Count with me," she replied. When Ethan balked, she dug her nails into his skin. "Count! One. Two. Three. Four. Five..."

Ethan followed along to her steady pace, using all of his resolve to stay calm. By the time they reached the count of sixty, the tension in his arms and legs lessened, and by one hundred, it had practically disappeared. When they were halfway to three-sixty, Narrator spoke, putting a smile on Ethan's face.

Willpower check successful!
You remain in control!

"Thank God," Ethan said, relaxing further. His stomach continued to gnaw and tear, but at least he didn't feel as if he were teetering on disaster.

Ethan rejoined the count, and when they hit three-sixty, he immediately jumped to his feet and darted out from the tree line. Katryna followed closely behind with Marcus and his horde of skeletons in tow. Several of the undead carried three wooden ladders, while a few more held thick ropes with iron grappling hooks.

They all reached the walls without trouble, and the ladders docked with a soft thump. Ethan scrambled over, hands shaking due to hunger and anticipation of a meal but still finding the rungs in the blink of an eye. When he reached the top, he used one hand to vault over the palisade and the other to draw his sword so that when he hit the ground, he was ready for a fight.

"Damn," he said, instantly taking note of the extra oil lamps hanging and patrols walking. "That can't be good."

"It's not, but that won't be enough to stop us," Katryna said.

Marcus joined them and snorted, his giant nostrils flaring. "I can't wait to see the look on their faces when they realize they're all going to serve me."

"Marcus, take the main bulk to the left," Ethan said, spending a few extra seconds to study it all. "Seems like that's where most of the corsairs are milling around. I'll take our bombs up the right near the cannon embankments and hook into the barracks from there. It doesn't look like they have many lamps in that area."

Marcus nodded. "Agreed. But be fast. They'll see us soon."

Ethan tapped Katryna on the shoulder. "Let's do it."

"Ethan, one more thing," Marcus said. When Ethan turned back around, the minotaur thumped his chest. "May the Great Lord Charethes infuse your soul with his undying power."

"And may he, um, do the same for you," Ethan said, stumbling as he wasn't sure how to respond. Hopefully, that was good enough, and he didn't just anger the gods with accidental blasphemy because he failed some unknown *Lore* check, but when Marcus nodded with approval, Ethan sighed with relief.

At that point, the pair darted to the right, hugging along the northern side of the palisade, and made a run to the embankment that held the shore batteries aloft. The corsairs had nine in total, each one spaced by about ten yards, each one ready to pulverize any ship that wandered into the little cove with a hail of thirty-pound cannon balls. Oil lamps burned steadily near each one, casting a warm glow twenty paces in each direction—no doubt to ward off any saboteurs on top of the general security they provided.

Ethan, staying well out of the light surrounding the embankment, hooked left and led his team across a flat expanse of grass toward the three buildings serving as barracks.

Gunshots pierced the night, two in total, their echoing booms snapping Ethan's attention to the side. Cries born from savagery and desperation immediately followed, and from the prison, Ethan saw two corsairs stumble backward. One clutched his stomach, attempting to staunch the flow of blood, while the other ran screaming with both hands pressed against his face. On their heels came dozens of prisoners who spilled out into the night, making a run for the armory.

Two separate nearby patrols of five men each quickly formed a skirmish line as voices shouted the alarm. Pistols fired from the groups, while muskets shot from the watchtowers.

"Take these two and send them in there," Ethan ordered, directing Katryna to the closest two skeletal bombs he had. "I'll hit others."

"Aye."

Ethan dashed forward, heading for the barracks in the middle as fast as he could, hoping to the gods of this world that the men inside wouldn't pour out in the next three seconds.

They didn't. But not by much.

With less than ten yards to go, the rear door swung open. A corsair appeared in the entryway, half-dressed but clutching both pistol and cutlass in hand. Reflexively, Ethan whipped up his pistol and fired. The weapon spat out a torrent of flame so bright the ground beneath him turned to daylight.

Corsair missed!

Ethan didn't need Narrator's wonderful remark on that one to know what had happened. His shot tore a chunk out of the door frame. Wood splinters showered the man, and he ducked back inside. Ethan started to run again, but that changed six strides later when Narrator spoke again.

Weapon reloaded!

"Reloaded?" Ethan repeated, cocking his head and coming to a halt. A brief glance down shed light on it all. His pistol, magically enchanted and once wielded by the late Lord Belmont, was indeed ready to fire. And so Ethan did.

Corsair missed!

And then a third time.

Corsair missed!

Ethan didn't care. His shots were doing exactly what he'd hoped they'd do: they kept the man (and his friends) from coming out of the door for a few more moments, no doubt not wanting to run into what they thought was a firing line outside.

"Get in there!" he shouted at his nearest kamikaze skeleton.

The minion chattered its six teeth together excitedly and dashed forward, one hand clutching the bomb on its chest while the other held a bit of burning slow match. It disappeared into the barracks, and time seemed to come to a standstill as nothing happened. Not a cry. Not a shot. Definitely not an explosion.

Ethan blinked, dumbfounded, but then it happened. A massive blast sent a shockwave through Ethan's chest, blowing debris in all directions out the door and window, carrying with it the scent of scorched flesh.

Two more explosions followed, this time with the bombs detonating in the barracks to Ethan's left, the ones Katryna had attacked.

Cheers erupted from the chaos of the night, but Ethan knew the battle was far from won. He sent the next skeleton in to finish off anyone still left in the middle barracks. The undead creature easily pushed through the smokey doorway, and by the time it, too, had detonated, Ethan was running across the grounds to the third barracks, some thirty yards away.

Gunfire cracked as bursts of flame and smoke came from the building's windows. A bullet whizzed past his ear, and another drove into the ground several feet to his side.

"Ethan!" Katryna yelled from somewhere behind. "Don't let them escape!"

It only took a split second for Ethan to see what she was talking about. Though several of the corsairs were taking turns shooting from the barracks, more and more were taking their chances running out of the barracks to join the fighting out in the grounds—fighting that even from Ethan's distant view he could see was bloody and relentless.

Ethan's stomach knotted, and he doubled over in pain, clenching his teeth, cursing up a storm. It subsided a moment later, but the pain had been so intense that part of him was shocked he hadn't just been shot through the gut.

Blood filled the air. Blood that called to him. Blood that he had to have.

"No," he growled at himself, holding a tight fist as he pushed himself up. "Not yet."

His hands trembled. Sweat dripped from his brow, blurring his vision, and he could feel the fangs in his mouth lengthen in anticipation. "You two," he said to his last two minions, voice straining. "Go. Now. Through the windows."

The undead soldiers obeyed without question and rushed forward. In an almost immediate response, those inside the barracks answered the charge with a volley of musket fire. The shots tore into the closest of the two skeletons, shattering one of the arms, taking its jaw, and finally sending it sprawling to the ground when its left hip disintegrated.

Before the corsairs could reload, however, the second skeleton reached the building. Ethan watched as it threw itself headlong through the window. Before its feet made it inside, the bomb blew.

Shouts. Screams. Gunshots. The clang of steel on steel continued long after the blast stopped ringing in Ethan's ears. He spent a moment trying to sort out the chaos in the night. On both sides, far off in the dark, bands of corsairs and skeletons hacked away at each other. He wasn't sure where anyone else was. He was about to head for the prison to look for Zoey when the far door to the barracks he was near shot open and out poured dozens of men.

They ran with panicked looks on cut and bruised faces, ran without purpose or organization. Most tried to regroup with those already fighting, but a few others ran for the gates. One, in particular, caught Ethan's attention. He hobbled along, hand clutching his thigh as blood flowed from the leg.

Ethan narrowed his eyes, like a lion eyeing a wounded gazelle. The battle around him faded into nothing as a solitary thought consumed all. He needed to feed.

The ground flew beneath his feet as he drove forward toward his prey, and he covered the forty yards that separated the two in seconds. The wounded corsair didn't even turn around before Ethan struck him from behind, sending both of them tumbling to the ground. They rolled once, with Ethan coming out on top. He grabbed his meal by the head and yanked it sideways, exposing the man's neck, and promptly sank his teeth into flesh.

Fangs scissored for a half second and half inch, opening veins and letting the rich lifeforce fill Ethan's mouth. Ethan shut his eyes, drinking it in. Gooseflesh formed across his arms and ran across his body as hair stood on the back of his neck. His eyes rolled upward as he closed his eyelids, smiling the entire time. This was his first true meal, not some disgusting pittance that involved rat or fish. No, the taste was richer than anything he'd ever experienced, and with each passing second, his body felt more and more energized than it had ever before.

The corsair feebly swatted at Ethan's head and sides, the blows barely a minor distraction. After several more seconds, they ceased altogether. The corsair shuddered once, and then the blood stopped coming.

Ethan reared back, sitting on his haunches while still straddling the man's waist, and took in a sharp intake of air as he wiped his mouth on the back of his sleeve. Ahead of him, some twenty yards away, Katryna drove forward into a dozen men with not even three skeletons at her side. She'd scarcely engaged the first corsair when six more came at her from her left flank.

"Katryna!" Ethan shouted, leaping to his feet and driving forward.

His mad dash slowed after the second pace. His mind reeled with what his eyes took in, and his jaw dropped. The swashbuckler slipped under and around cut after cut, thrust after thrust, dancing through their ranks with a deadly ballet. She opened wounds in the corsairs time and again while not suffering a single one in return. Some maimed. Some killed.

After the tenth corsair fell to her scimitar, being sliced deeply across his belly, the surviving men broke ranks and ran for a small wooden building nearby where others had rallied. The sight of them fleeing snapped Ethan out of his awe from watching Katryna go to work, and he ran after them along with Katryna and a swarm of skeletons.

The corsairs quickly formed a crescent shape with their backs to the building, no doubt trying to make a valiant last stand, and with about sixty of them in total, they had a chance. Pistols fired from their lines, blasting skeletons apart, dropping a few of the prisoners Zoey had freed, too, in the process.

A moment later, the two sides clashed. Ethan shot to the left and then charged when he reached the corsairs' flank. When he slammed into the line, his first strike took the head off a corsair's shoulders with ease. His next skewed one through the heart as his blade drove straight through the man's back and shot out of its chest.

A blur of movement caught the corner of his eye. Ethan instinctively ducked under a wild hack made by another corsair, and he then hopped back to avoid the follow-up blow. His chest burned, and a glance down showed that the corsair's blade had a cut a deep gash across his chest.

The pain that ran through his body, coupled with the sight of his own dark blood now flowing, reignited a burning hunger inside his soul.

"Good, but not good enough," he growled before flashing his fangs. "Now it's my turn."

The man's eyes went wide, and he barely got out a "What?" before Ethan was upon him. He batted the corsair's blade to the side and lunged forward with a tremendous war cry.

The corsair nearly fell over as he tried to scurry backward. He tried to defend himself with his cutlass, but Ethan proved to be faster. A single hack of Ethan's blade took the man's right arm at the elbow, and before the corsair could scream, Ethan bit into his throat.

Blood, sweet and euphoric, pumped into the vampire's mouth. The man struggled vainly against Ethan's grip, but soon his strength gave out, and they both fell to the ground.

The back of Ethan's shoulder exploded in pain, but the sensation was greatly drowned out by another.

Feeding...

The blood ceased, as did the man's struggles. Ethan ripped himself free, driving forward on powerful legs, not bothering to see whether or not the corsair was dead yet. Only one thing mattered: it wasn't giving him what he needed.

Feeding.

Corsairs and skeletons were everywhere, fighting, hacking, killing, dying. Ethan slashed through the throat of another with his razor-like nails and drove shoulder-first into a third. He clawed and bit, drinking as much blood as he could that a couple of seconds would allow before he had to drink from something fresher. The taste of the wounded and dying couldn't compare to that of the unscathed.

After ripping free of another victim, Ethan's next target happened to be a corsair who'd just knocked one of the prisoners off his feet and was about to run him through. Ethan charged, closing the three yards that stood between them in a single bound.

The corsair spun an instant before Ethan could connect and brought his sword in line with the attacking vampire.

The blade sank deep into Ethan's upper hip. The pain would've been more than enough to cripple any man, not counting the horrific injuries it inflicted, but Ethan's mind was still focused on one thing and one thing only.

Feeding...

Feeding...

His fingers dug into the man's face, and he pushed his head to the side before clamping his jaw down on its throat as he had with all the others. His fangs sank deep into flesh and opened up a jugular.

The corsair fought harder than the others had, striking Ethan repeatedly in the side of the face and gut with heavy fists. But eventually, he, too, succumbed to his wounds, and his strength gave out.

Corsair drained!
Corsair killed!
You heal some wounds!

Ethan's vision suddenly exploded into a bright array of starburst lights. The back of his head went numb, and he fell. The chaos of battle loomed around him, but the sounds felt as if everything transpiring were miles away. Despite the stun, Ethan's focus remained.

Feeding...Feeding...

He rolled onto his back right as the most enormous brute he'd seen yet pointed a pistol that could've doubled as a deck gun right at his head.

Chapter X
Buttons

Marcus loved battles, even if they were, on the surface, anathema to proper studies. After all, one could hardly focus on the faded pages of ancient text with the constant clash of steel on steel ringing through the air. And one might as well forget trying to learn the intricacies of proper pronunciation when it came to mastering long-forgotten languages or invoking the spirits when the screams of the dying drowned out any and all thought.

Well, Marcus could forget trying such things. He wasn't as dark or disturbed to be able to relax in such places. Maii, on the other hand, probably could.

That said, the one thing that battles did do was give Marcus an unparalleled opportunity to be at the point where the lines of life and death converged. That, he knew, was the crux of all his studies—for what else was necromancy when boiled down to its most basic, fundamental concept? And one day, when he'd become an expert in his craft, he could finally retire to his labyrinth, where his hordes of skeletal minions would keep the living away, so he could further his studies in peace instead of having to deal with all the damn heroes that undoubtedly would show up, trying to make a name for themselves with nothing but a sword and a ball of string.

Daydreaming, however, would have to wait, especially since the corsair he'd squared off with had proven to be a troublesome man, neither scared of the minotaur's undead minions nor inept at dual-wielding the pair of cutlasses he had in hand.

The man came at Marcus with a series of feints and chops, and with each second that passed, he seemed to get closer and closer to penetrating Marcus's defenses. After a few strikes, Marcus knew he had to regain control of the duel and thus went on the offensive with a well-timed strike of his own.

The man darted backward, narrowly avoiding a cut across the belly. He then trapped the minotaur's weapon with one of his own before lunging forward in an attempt to skewer Marcus through the chest. But the corsair wasn't the only one with two weapons in hand. Marcus whipped his staff around in a high overhead arc, striking the man inside the wrist.

The corsair howled in pain as Marcus put his weight behind the blow, which no doubt shattered the bones in the man's wrist. The cutlass went flying, and less than a second later, Marcus cracked open the man's head with the tip of his staff.

Before the corsair had fully hit the ground, Marcus roared, basking in his victory before charging headlong into the rest of the fray. His skeletal minions had done well catching the corsairs by surprise, cutting their numbers with ruthless efficiency. But most of their success was due to catching the pirates and slavers unaware. Now that skirmish lines had been made, the undead army was suffering as many losses as they inflicted.

That was something Marcus intended to fix right then and there, especially since he could feel his staff warming and sending tingles of energy racing up his massive arms. Energy had returned to the artifact, energy that could be used with devastating results.

He stabbed a corsair through the side after the man had just taken down two of Marcus's skeletons before stepping back from the fray and pointing his staff at the corsair's ranks.

"*Vas Corp Hur,*" he said, his voice slow and deep as he intoned the spell.

The skull's eye sockets on the tip of the staff burned like hot coals while dark tendrils shot out of its open mouth. They curled through the air, hissing and crackling as they went, a dozen in total, each one wrapping themselves around the throats of the slavers.

The men shrieked in unholy unison, dropping their weapons and clutching their necks as they fell to their knees. Their bodies doubled over, and their skin withered. When they each finally fell completely to the ground, they'd become little more than grey husks of their former selves.

"You shall all serve the Great Lord Charethes!" Marcus bellowed, practically cackling as he did.

More skeletons surged from behind, taking advantage of the chaos that poured through the corsair ranks. But that surge broke like a storm-tossed ship on a rocky shore a moment later.

A blur of movement grabbed Marcus's attention out of the corner of his eye. He spun to the right just in time to see something massive plowing its way through his skeletal army, sending shattered and pulverized bones flying in all directions. And before his eyes could even focus on the monstrosity, let alone truly take in what it was, he was met with a massive fist that sent him dazed and spinning to the ground.

Consciousness slipped away shortly thereafter.

Maii sailed through the air, a nightmarish beast of fang and claw, but as far as Ethan was concerned, the ahuizotl was the most beautiful thing he'd ever seen at that moment. The monstrous feline's jaws clenched on either side of the corsair's face, crushing bone as five sets of claws from legs and tail tore flesh into ribbons.

"Thank God," Ethan said, exhaling and thoroughly elated he was still alive.

Maii didn't reply. Instead, he shot further into the fray, and then Zoey suddenly appeared at Ethan's side, smiling and drenched in sweat.

"Come on, lazy," she said, hoisting him up. "We've got a battle to finish."

Ethan's heart soared as a wave of energy rippled through him. Something about seeing Zoey redoubled his resolve, gave him purpose, and invigorated his soul.

Once on his feet, they surged forward, a vampiric pair fighting side by side that could not be matched. Blades flashed, and like the skirmish back at the graveyard, Ethan and Zoey moved in concert with one another, fending off attacks meant for the other while providing their partner with the perfect opening to cut a corsair down at the knees or drive a point through the heart.

As the combat went on, Marcus's skeletal minions picked up weapons from the fallen, as did the prisoners Zoey had released, and numbers the corsairs fielded dwindled from fifty to thirty to twenty at best.

Zoey snapped her wrist high, angling her blade downward to catch a wild overhead chop. She passed the trapped weapon over to Ethan, who'd just come out of a backspin that left another corsair without his right hand. He caught it on his own cutlass effortlessly, as if they'd practiced the trick a hundred times, and slapped it sideways so that Zoey, free of the attack, could neatly lop off her opponent's head.

The decapitated body dropped to its knees and fell forward. But before its chest hit the ground, a skeletal minion crashed into it with such force, its bones shattered in all directions.

Ethan twisted, looking over his shoulder at where the skeleton had come from just in time to see a monstrous thing come at him. Ashen skin covered a muscular frame wrapped in what looked like countless dirty linen bandages. Standing nearly nine feet tall, it towered over all the combatants, snatching, swatting, and throwing skeleton and prisoner alike with oversized, clawed hands. Countless rings, piercings, and chains hung from a disfigured face, all showing off a myriad of voodoo charms and trinkets ranging from shrunken heads to shriveled paws.

Four skeletal warriors shot by Ethan a split second later, intent on bringing the monster down. Three were pulverized with a single backhanded blow, while the fourth managed to stay intact long enough to issue a feeble attack of its own before meeting a similar fate.

A great rallying cry sounded from the corsairs, and their line tightened around the monster. Just behind it all, Ethan caught sight of a witch doctor, wearing nothing but a loose loincloth, a wide-horned wooden mask, and intricate body paint, dancing and laughing with a long, wicked knife in hand.

"Ha! Ol' Sejour have a few tricks for you yet," he called out before reaching behind him and producing a small clay pot seemingly out of thin air. He sent the pot sailing through the air, and when it hit the ground, it erupted into a massive green-and-yellow fireball that spared nothing for ten yards in all directions.

Though the blast had staggered Ethan, he quickly found his footing and charged, Zoey following his lead and the rest of his forces surging back into the corsair line. Ethan lunged at the monster with the point of his cutlass leading the way.

He was fast, but not fast enough. The monster batted him sideways with a well-placed strike to the shoulder. Its claws cut through Ethan's skin while at the same time sending a massive shockwave through his right arm, which sent his cutlass flying and him spinning to the ground.

Buttons hits you!
Buttons disarms you!
You are seriously wounded!

The world became a jumbled mess of shouts and motion. Thankfully, Ethan had the presence of mind to roll away from the monster. A heavy foot smashed into the ground where his head had been only a moment ago.

In the blink of an eye, Zoey jumped between Ethan and the monster, sword raised, body slightly crouched. As Ethan came to his feet, the two squared off with one another. Then the attacks came from each. Zoey lunged forward, which ended up being a feint as she shot to her right and ducked under a heavy blow. Once clear of the attack, she went on the offensive. Her blade sliced cleanly into the monster's upper thigh, spilling bright red blood in all directions.

The monster wailed, sounding more like a toddler having a temper tantrum than something in pain, and before she could issue a follow-up attack, it threw itself at her, managing to get a hold of her forearm in the process. With one giant heave, he threw her through the air like a rag doll. She hit the ground, plowing through a number of skeletons in the process. And though she didn't get up immediately, she stirred, which told Ethan all he needed to know in the moment: she lived.

"I'm going to tear you a new one for that," Ethan said with a growl, narrowing his eyes at the monster.

"Not unless I tear him one first," Katryna replied, suddenly appearing at his side and handing him his recently lost blade. She flashed a smile and threw him a wink before adding, "Half crown says I bring him down before you."

Ethan kept his focus on the monster. "Done."

The two drove forward together, and the giant creature responded in kind. It swung at the two in a wide arc with one of its lumbering arms. Despite already knowing what it could do, the attack still seemed to come impossibly fast for Ethan. While Katryna slipped under the blow with ease, Ethan had to dive sideways to keep his head attached to his shoulders.

Ethan hit the ground, though this time he at least had more finesse in the maneuver. He rolled with the momentum and easily came up into a low crouch, ready to spring away or attack once more as the situation would warrant. Neither, to his surprise, was needed.

Katryna thrust the point of her sword through the monster's chest, just below its left armpit. The monster roared, spit shooting everywhere as it did. It spun around, trying to swat the woman with a backhand, but failed to connect. Katryna's next cut went across its right forearm, and the following took a chunk of flesh from a calf.

The creature continued to wail, punching, swiping, and launching blow after blow in a feeble attempt to put down its tormentor. With every strike it missed, Katryna made it pay heavily with its own blood. She darted inside its reach one last time, cutting it deeply across the back of a knee.

The monster fell forward, hunched over as it tried to keep from toppling completely. Katryna launched herself onto the thing's back, knocking it down to all fours, at which point she drove her blade directly through its shoulder blades.

With his jaw set and his face chiseled with anger and determination, Ethan calmly walked up to the thing, pulled out his pistol, and put a shot through its head.

Buttons killed!
You feel a lot more experienced.
You feel like some skills could improve after some rest.

Ethan smiled, grateful that they'd dropped the thing relatively quickly, and cheers erupted all around. As Katryna used her foot to help push and yank her sword free of the newly made corpse, Ethan took a moment to survey the rest of the battle.

There wasn't much of one.

What corsairs still lived ran, most getting cut down before they could break the lines of skeleton and prisoner, but a few managed to push through. Jean, along with some others, followed close behind, yelling taunts and jeers. Marcus, on the other hand, was found slowly staggering to his feet, but he still retained enough strength to hurl plenty of promises of eternal enslavement.

All that said, the witch doctor was nowhere to be seen.

Ethan, however, didn't give the man's fate more than a fleeting thought before he rushed to Zoey, who was still lying on the ground. Right as he reached her, she pushed herself up into a seated position and groaned as she rubbed her head. "Holy crap," she said, wincing. "That thing hits like a Mack truck. Tell me it's dead."

"It's dead," Ethan said, exhaling with relief as he helped her to her feet. "Are you okay?"

"I'm alive," she replied, wincing again. "Been better. Wouldn't mind a bite to eat to heal up."

"You and me both," Ethan replied, now acutely aware of the pain radiating from his shoulder.

"I could help with that shortly," Katryna said, joining the two of them and sheathing her scimitar in the process. "Looks as if the day is won. Or night, as the case may be."

"Where's Maii?" Zoey asked.

Ethan shrugged, never once looking away from her, inspecting every inch of her body with both eye and delicate touch. "Around somewhere, I'm sure," he said. "Are you sure you're okay?"

"I'm sure," she said, nodding.

Ethan said nothing as he found himself lost in her dark eyes, his heart a jumbled mix of worry and relief. Slowly, he drew her toward him, sliding his hands around the small of her back and resting his forehead on hers. "Good," he whispered. "You scared me for a moment."

"I'm fine. I promise," she whispered back with a smile.

Katryna cleared her throat. "Ahem."

Neither vampire moved, at least, not until she cleared her throat again, to which Ethan sighed heavily and turned partially toward her. "What?"

"If you two lovebirds—or is it bats—are done, there's a couple of things I feel like I ought to say," she said, holding up a pair of fingers.

"Which are?"

"First, you owe me a half crown, and don't you dare argue it." She tilted her head with a slight glare when Ethan did, in fact, start to argue. After he wisely remained quiet, she grinned and went on. "And second, I think you two need to check your character sheets."

To that, Ethan furrowed his brow, and Zoey had an equally confused look upon her face. "Why?" he asked.

"Because this—" she said, using her index finger to make a swirling motion at them both, "—is not normal."

Ethan shrugged. "I don't care."

He then planted a kiss on Zoey and relished every second as she pressed back into him. Euphoria ran through him as butterflies made a home in his stomach and his heart beat feverishly against his chest.

"Just do it," Katryna huffed. "When you two can finally come up for air, that is. In the meantime, I'm going to go find Maii."

Chapter XI
Breaking Maii

Maii ran through the chaos with a deadly, singular focus. The man who'd brought the giant golem—the witch doctor—had broken away from the melee, no doubt realizing it was only a matter of time before Ethan, Zoey, and Katryna brought down his bodyguard.

The ahuizotl didn't care all that much if one man escaped, or even a dozen for that matter. But he'd be damned to a century of servitude if he was going to willingly pass up such a delicious meal where not only flesh would be consumed, but powerful magics as well—and a witch doctor such as the one he pursued had so much magic infused in his body, it practically seeped from his pores. If Maii could consume him fresh, who knew what sort of growth he'd see or new powers he'd develop. By the trickster god, if the ahuizotl dared to dream, he might even grow strong enough to finally break the hold Ethan's ring had over him.

Maii shook his head, narrowed his eyes, and refocused. He was getting ahead of himself, he knew. Freedom would come soon enough. For now, he had to ensure the witch doctor didn't slip away in the forest or make it to a rowboat and get back to the ship that lay anchored not far away.

A flash of steel sent the ahuizotl sideways. One of the few surviving corsairs, locked in a battle with two skeletons, had taken a wild swing at Maii as he passed by—likely purely out of reflex. For a moment in time, as Maii's legs went from one stride to the next, he considered taking a chunk out of the man purely on principle, perhaps out of his neck or groin if he were feeling particularly vicious. In the end, however, Maii drove himself forward even more, leaping three dozen yards to clear the corsair.

The skeletons could finish him off. Besides, the longer the fight in the fort took to ultimately wrap up, the longer Maii could do what he wanted without anyone noticing.

The witch doctor reached a small side gate, some fifty yards away next to one of the watchtowers, and quickly tossed the bar to the ground before running through. Had it been anyone else, Maii would've closed the distance in seconds, but the man worked and ran unnaturally fast, practically a blur of movement in the shadows even to Maii's keen predatory eyes.

"You'll not catch me, stupid beast," he called out with a mocking laugh. "Ol' Sejour has dealt with far craftier than the likes of you."

Maii growled and redoubled his efforts. He could feel the claws on all four feet lengthen in both anticipation and determination. The man threw the gate closed behind him, and Maii plowed through without hesitation, using his shoulder as a battering ram. The heavy door half swung, half disintegrated from the hit, and the ahuizotl found himself several dozen yards away from an open beach. The witch doctor ran on, his bare feet leaving a perfect trail in the powder-white sand as he went.

The chase sent Maii across the beach for a hundred yards, passing by two longboats beached and tied to a thick palm tree. The witch doctor may have been fast, but apparently, he didn't fancy himself as being able to launch, let alone row, the small craft quick enough to get away from the ahuizotl.

The hundred yards between them closed to fifty, and not long after, disappeared to twenty-five. Twenty. Saliva dripped from Maii's lower jaw, and his nostrils flared, desperate to take in more and more of the sweet aroma of power he was about to dine on.

Fifteen yards from his quarry, still racing along the beach, Maii pounced. He careened through the air, silent and deadly. His mouth clamped down on the back of the man's neck, but instead of sinking into flesh, his teeth cut through nothing but air, and Maii passed through the witch doctor as if he were nothing but mist. He slammed into the ground but found his footing quickly enough. Maii spun a couple of times, his head low, eyes darting left and right. His prey, crafty indeed, had not thrown him completely. Fifty yards away, Maii caught sight of the witch doctor fleeing into the jungle.

The ahuizotl bolted after his prey once more. He was annoyed he had fallen for what was a relatively simple illusion, and he even chided himself for thinking such a man would be caught so easily. But when he heard the witch doctor's laughter, taunting and mocking him, those feelings vanished as Maii vowed once he had the man pinned, he'd eat him over the course of several hours. Maybe then the fool would learn a little respect.

Powerful legs carried him through the jungle, padded feet barely making a sound as they struck dirt, rock, or brush. As he ran, he'd occasionally slow to tip his nose upward, ensure that he was following the scent and not another illusion.

Ahead, he saw the man dart behind a large boulder near the top of a small rise. Maii almost cut right, intent on shaving some distance off between them, but then he realized the ground dropped sharply to the left by the giant rock—a drop sharp enough to hide the movements of someone crouching.

Maii cut left, and within seconds, he cleared the top of the drop and smiled wickedly as he saw the witch doctor not even five feet away. Maii pounced with such power and speed that when he connected with the man, he not only drove him into the ground before he could even cry out in fright, but every last rib in his body shattered on impact.

The two skidded across the jungle floor for several yards, and when they finally came to a stop, Maii lazy straddled the broken man, dropping his haunches on the man's hips and digging his foreclaws into the witch doctor's biceps.

"Do you have a preference where I dine first?" the ahuizotl said as he kneaded his claws against the man's skin. "I've always been fond of starting at the fingers thanks to their crunch, but mother always said the best place to start was the calves."

To Maii's surprise, the man grinned, flashing an array of dirty—and bloody—broken teeth that contrasted sharply against his pale face paint. "How about I be making you a better offer, great trickster?"

"Great trickster?" Maii echoed with amusement. "Such flattery will get you nowhere, my delicious fellow, but make your offer if you like. It's always fun to see what people think their lives are worth."

The witch doctor cackled, which turned into a coughing fit, sending flecks of blood into the air. When he finally recomposed himself, he kept his lively attitude, despite his injuries and Maii's threats. "My life? No, no, great trickster. I offer your life."

Maii cocked his head and used the claws on the end of his tail to scratch the top of his head, all of which was nothing more than theatrics. "My life? I think I've got that under control, and I think when you've filled my belly, it'll be even better than before."

"Ah, but it's not yours, is it? Your master owns you, enslaves you," he went on.

Maii clenched his jaw at the thought. Though Ethan had proved to be a surprisingly fun owner to be bound to, and now that he was a budding vampire, even more opportunities crested the horizon in terms of fun, power, and meals, none of those could compare to being free. "Go on," Maii said.

"I be thinking you let Ol' Sejour go, and Ol' Sejour be freeing you in kind," the witch doctor said, pointing a bony, crooked thumb at his chest.

Maii smirked. "And give up such a delectable meal?"

The witch doctor laughed, much to Maii's surprise. "What good is a meal without your freedom, eh? Surely there are things you be wantin' to do."

The smirk on the ahuizotl's faded away, and Maii reluctantly conceded the point. There were a great many things Maii wanted, all of which, however, required him to be free of the ring, which is why he'd been so focused on eating and growing. But if he didn't have to worry about that anymore, he could get on with life: Find a forest to terrorize or even an entire country. Or perhaps take over a ship and be the first pirate ahuizotl to sail the eleven seas. But before he could indulge in such wishful thinking, the monster had a more pressing question that needed tending to. "Tell me, friend," he said. "Why should I believe you can do such a thing?"

The witch doctor shot him a look of indignation. "Why should you be believing I can't? You see my Buttons."

"Buttons?"

"My Buttons! He be fighting your friends. Why you insulting me, thinking I can't break a simple binding spell if I can make Buttons?"

Maii eased his claws off the man's arms. The golem had been impressive, even if it had been constructed of cloth and thread and not metal or stone. "That's an intriguing offer, I must say."

"Then we be doing business together?"

"I think we might be able to come to some sort of arrangement," Maii said. "But indulge me in one other curiosity: where do you plan on going? You'll find no quarter with anyone else."

"Don't you be worrying about Ol' Sejour," he said. "I call the sea turtles and ride them away."

"If you say," Maii replied, unconvinced but ultimately not caring.

"I do say!"

Maii shrugged. "Fine. You say. Now release me."

The witch doctor chuckled and waggled a finger in front of Maii's face. "Not till I have your word that Ol' Sejour be free to go."

Maii sat back on his haunches, thinking such oaths were pointless and stupid. But in the end, if such promises were needed to be free of the ring that held him, so be it. "You have my deepest, unbreakable word, my good man, that if you free me from this ring, I shall let you go."

"And not be attacking me later," the witch doctor quickly tacked on. "I want your promises to include no tomfoolery."

"I'll not attack you later, on my word and my honor," Maii said with a huff of annoyance as he eased off the man. "Now, free me."

The witch doctor stiffly pushed himself to his feet after giving a short nod. With his right index finger, he lifted paint from his body and smeared it across Maii's forehead. After making a few figures the ahuizotl couldn't see, Ol' Sejour began chanting. The words came low and quiet at first, but as warmth built in Maii's skull and radiated through his body, those words grew louder and faster. After several more moments of this, Ol' Sejour popped Maii's forehead with the heel of his hand, and a loud bang, almost like a gunshot, reverberated in Maii's ears.

"Ah, see?" the witch doctor said, grinning wide and backing away like an artist might looking upon his finished work for the first time. "Feeling better now, yes? Just like Ol' Sejour said."

Despite the glow Maii felt in his soul, he still felt a little skeptical. Did the gods actually grant him his freedom so easily, he wondered? Perhaps. He stretched each limb, one at a time, shook it loose, concentrated on how every fiber of his being seemed freer and quicker, and most important of all, seemed as if each was completely his. Gone was the sensation someone or something shared his body with his soul. Gone were the invisible walls that kept him from doing all that he wanted, and gone was the invisible hand that forced him to do things he didn't.

"It seems, witch doctor, you've granted me my freedom," the ahuizotl said, the tone in his voice darkening as a world of limitless opportunities opened up before him. "And for that, I'm compelled to give you my thanks."

"My pleasure, great trickster," Ol' Sejour said with a sweeping bow. "Now, if you'll be excusing me, I've got some sea turtles to call."

Maii smiled. The man before him smiled back and nodded, no doubt first thinking the ahuizotl's reaction was permissive, possibly even friendly or sweet. But when Maii's true nature surfaced, and his eyes glowed red, panic struck the witch doctor's face right.

"But you gave Ol' Sejour your word!" he protested, hobbling back.

A devilish grin spread across Maii's face. "And what makes you think that binds me to anything, pray tell?"

Before the witch doctor could reply, Maii pounced and tore out the man's neck.

Chapter XII
Loot

Ethan and Zoey stumbled, arms tightening around one another, hands exploring bodies, all the while both ignoring the macabre battlefield. Together, they sidestepped a fallen corsair, lips locked, and when her hands plummeted down Ethan's stomach toward his pants, Ethan's desire to ravish jumped tenfold.

He pressed forward even harder, and Zoey giggled as she went for the ride, right up until her back hit the wall. Her breath shot out with an explosive burst, and her jaw clenched tight as she grimaced. In turn, Ethan cringed, feeling as if his own sore ribs had taken the blow.

"Sorry," he said. "Hope that didn't kill the mood."

Zoey shook her head, eyes smiling with amusement. "Given everything else we're ignoring around here, a little roughness isn't going to stop anything."

Ethan relaxed and toyed with her hair by her ears. "Good."

"Now shut up and kiss me."

Ethan leaned into the vampire, ready to oblige, but never made it all the way. A searing pain erupted from his ring finger, and he doubled over, clutching his hand. "Damn it to hell," he said through clenched teeth. "That hurts."

Zoey grabbed him by the shoulders and pulled him upright, eyes wide with fear. "What hurts?"

"My freaking finger," he said. Ethan raised his hand to show it off, half expecting to see the digit in question burnt to a crisp—or at least, split open to the bone—but it looked normal. Minor addenda. While he found his finger as it had always been, the ring upon it looked tarnished along the edges.

"Oh, I don't like the look of that," Zoey said. She reached up and toyed with the ring. It spun freely on his finger, and her face soured. "And I really don't like the look of that as well."

Ethan played with it as well. The piece of jewelry easily slipped over his second knuckle, something it hadn't ever done before. He paused before sliding it completely off his hand and decided to put it back in place. "What do you suppose that means?"

Zoey shrugged, lines of worry appearing on her face. "My guess is Maii is either free or dead. Check your sheet. Maybe that'll say."

Ethan reached into his pocket and pulled out his character sheet. His face lit up the moment he scanned the first few lines. "Sweet! I'm level seven now," he said, but as fast as that excitement came, it faded when he realized, experience-wise, it wasn't that much of a jump.

Zoey wrinkled her brow. "What?"

"I'm only level seven."

"That's more than you were before."

"I know, but I just thought I'd be even higher, what with all the dead corsairs and whatnot."

Zoey laughed. "This place isn't *that* retro."

"Say again?"

"What I'm saying is you don't get to hog all the experience, sorry," she said, smooching him. "It got split between everyone."

"Damn," Ethan said. He then flashed a smile with a heavy sigh. "That would've been pretty awesome, though. I'd have become the fastest formed vampire lord, hands down."

"Well, prince, at least," she said, kissing him again. "Where are you going to spend your skill points?"

"I was going to start working on getting to the next level of swordplay, but then I remembered you said I'd have severe penalties for any untrained skill."

Zoey raised her eyebrow. "I did," she said, sounding impressed. "Glad to see you're still not behaving like someone with eight INT."

"I have eleven now, thank you very much."

Zoey laughed. "I know."

"Anyway, it says I can take *Leadership* now. I think I should bump that to at least *novice,* so I'm not *untrained.*"

"Good idea," Zoey said with a look of approval in her eyes. She then smirked. "Can't believe I didn't insist you do that already," she said. "You crit fail on that, and you're looking at a total mutiny if things go to hell on the open seas."

Ethan felt his gut tighten. "Could that be a problem?"

"Out here? Are you kidding?" Zoey said, laughing with disbelief. "Not only is it a possibility, but if you're lucky, when it happens, all that they'll do to you is maroon you on a tiny island with a pistol and a single shot."

Ethan's gut went from tightening to souring completely. "Ugh," he said. "I get the feeling I'm going to want to level that up even more."

"Absolutely," Zoey said. "Any other thoughts on skill points?"

"What about *Naval Tactics*?" he asked. "You know, the race and all. I figure that could be useful in not getting sunk. I could get that to at least *novice,* as well, and then have a little leftover to start working on the next level for *Swordplay.* I'm still a couple of points shy to get it bumped to *competent* in that."

"*Naval Tactics* could come in handy," Zoey said. "Still, this is a race, not a fleet engagement. Might want to go with something else. That said, I say think about it a bit, especially when since you'll get a new ability next level. It would be a good idea to have that synergize with your skillset."

"Good point."

"What else does your sheet say?" she asked. "Anything about the ring?"

Ethan directed his focus to where all the traits he'd gained were on the page. At the very top of that section, it still listed *Ring Bearer,* but right under that, there was a new one. "Oh, that's weird."

"What is?"

"This," he said, turning the page so she could see and pointing to the line. "*Undying Love: Connected.*"

In a hurry, Zoey fished out her own sheet and confirmed what they both already knew with a nod. "I've got it too."

"What does that mean for us?"

The corner of Zoey's mouth drew back, and she shook her head. "It means having shared both a supernatural bond and intense, life-threatening events, we're stupid for each other in a way mortals will never know."

"Of course, I'm stupid for you," Ethan said, chuckling. "Still, nice to know you feel the same."

"I should also add, it's only going to get worse."

"Worse?"

Zoey shook her head and stuffed away her character sheet. "Stronger is a better word for it," she said. "It has four levels: *Connected, Bonded, Enamored,* and *Devoted.* Each one comes with stronger benefits and well...quirks."

"I like the benefits part, especially since you still owe me a girlfriendy reward."

"Not those kinds of benefits."

"Figures. What are they, then?"

"Small boost to combat skills when fighting together, along with the occasional chain attack and a massive boost to parrying," she said, clearly trying to think back to what she'd learned about the trait at some previous point in time. "Oh yeah, seduction resistance, and increases to crits and damage when the other is critically wounded. Few other things, too, I can't remember. Shared feelings and then thoughts, maybe? We'll need to check the manual when we get back to the ship. Anyway, the stronger our bond, the bigger the bonuses to all of that."

"That sounds handy. What about the quirks?"

Zoey made a face like she'd taken a swig from a carton of curdled milk. "We don't do as well when we're apart. Penalties to everything get more severe the more devoted we are. I'm sure you've noticed that already. I have."

Ethan pressed his lips together, thinking back to recent events and how things simply felt off when she wasn't around. "Yeah. Yeah, I have."

"We also start annoying people when we're together."

"Like with Katryna."

"Yep," she replied. "There are also some other things that are slipping my mind, but we can look those up later when we get the chance. That said, the one that always stuck with me was *Faithful till the End.*"

"Why's that?" Ethan asked, both intrigued and wary as to what it would entail.

"It's an automatic pickup trait when we're *devoted* and can be tragically romantic."

"Explain, because I'm really trying to avoid the whole tragedy here."

"It's simple, really. We'll never leave the other in a fight, regardless of circumstances. It's usually a good thing because of the insane bonus we'll have together at that point, but it's been the undoing of more than one set of lovestruck vamps—ancient ones at that, hence the romantic tragedies."

"I see," Ethan said, trying to decide on how he felt about where this was headed. "I don't mind the romance part or the fighting bonus part, but if it's all the same to you, I'd like to win this thing still and go home, alive, and in one piece."

A new voice joined in the conversation. "Found your pet."

Ethan turned to find Katryna and Maii a few paces away. "I don't think he likes being called my pet," the ahuizotl said, before yawning and entering into a deep, downward dog stretch. "Pride and all."

"I'm *not* your pet," Ethan said.

Maii smacked his bloodstained lips together and looked up at Katryna with a knowing grin. "What did I tell you?"

The smugness on the creature's face put a knot in Ethan's stomach, and he reflexively toyed with the ring he had. When he finally noticed what his subconscious was doing, Ethan spent a few seconds looking back and forth between the metal band and the ahuizotl.

Katryna picked up on his angst first or at least was the first to speak on it. "Something wrong?"

"Raise your front leg," Ethan said, keeping his focus on Maii.

Maii complied with a shrug, hoisting his left paw up into the air like a dog giving a shake for a treat.

"Scratch your head with your tail."

Again, Maii shrugged and complied. At first, he seemed annoyed, but when the claws found the sweet spot behind the right ear, the look of bliss washed across the monster's face. "Ooh, yeah. I like that."

"Hey!" Katryna said, snapping her fingers to grab Ethan's attention. "What's going on?"

When Ethan didn't answer immediately but instead kept his focus on Maii, Zoey filled the swashbuckler in. "His ring's tarnished," Zoey said, pointing to Ethan's hand. "And it burned him not that long ago."

Katryna looked down at Maii with indifference. "Are you free now?" she asked, with about as much concern as she probably had when taking a swig of rum.

"No," he replied.

"Would you tell us if you were?" Ethan asked.

"I see no reason why I wouldn't," Maii answered. "It's not as if I haven't already told you I'd be free of it one day already."

Ethan relaxed a little at that last point. The ahuizotl had indeed made that crystal clear, but even with that in mind, Ethan had questions—questions and worries. "Okay, but why is this ring loose and tarnished if it still controls you?"

Maii leaned forward, examining the piece of jewelry like a minor curiosity found in the bottom of a strong box. "I'm hardly the enchanter, so I can't say I'd be able to offer you a good explanation," he said. "But I'd wager it has something to do with the last spell that witch doctor tried to get off before I ate him. I guess it hit me a little more than I thought."

"You killed the witch doctor?"

"That was implied when I said I ate him," Maii said, flashing the largest predatory grin Ethan had ever seen.

"How much stronger did that make you?"

"Oh, quite a bit more than I'd dared to hope," Maii said. The creature rolled his shoulders a couple of times to show off bulging muscles. As he did, his dark coat took on a bright sheen that rippled with colors. "Do you think we could find another to eat? I'd like that."

"I'm sure you would."

Zoey tugged Ethan by the arm. "Can I talk to you for a second in private?"

"Yeah. What is it?" Ethan replied.

Zoey tightened her grip around his elbow and dragged him away several yards. When they stopped, she dropped her voice to such a quiet whisper, even she probably had trouble hearing it. "I'm not sure we should take him along anymore."

"You think he's lying about not being free?"

"I wouldn't put it past him."

Ethan frowned. He'd had that nagging feeling as well, but he didn't want to be down a pet monster, either. "You know," he said. "You were the one who said I should have a pocket ahuizotl. We even went with that when I started picking abilities."

"Yeah, I know, but that was back when I thought you'd be closer to being a vampire lord than you are now."

"I'm pretty close."

"You're pretty not," she replied. "A lot of things around here would still tear you apart in seconds, him included."

Ethan flattened his lips into a tight line, not liking what she'd said. "We'll have to agree to disagree," he said as he massaged his bruised ego. He didn't want to think about still being weak or incapable of standing up for himself. That was the old Ethan. The new Ethan, Captain Ethan—vampire lord (to be) Ethan—was anything but helpless. And he loved every bit of it. That said, a perfectly valid point popped into mind, one that he was quick to share. "We might need him against Azrael," he said. "And winning that race is the most important thing of all."

"It is, but we can't win if he kills us," she said. "And even if he doesn't, he could still muck things up enough so that we don't win."

"Well, we don't know either way yet, right?" Ethan said after mulling over her words. "We'll keep an eye on him and keep him happy. After all, we're only talking two weeks. We can manage that, right?"

"I hope so."

Ethan nodded definitively, as if such an action had the power to make it so. "We will. You'll see." With that, the two returned. Katryna was lazily reloading her pistol, while Maii simply sat on his haunches, quietly watching him.

"Alright, Maii," Ethan said, "I want you to give me your word you're not tricking us."

"On my honor," Maii said, with a deep, sweeping bow of his head.

"And you're not going to eat us, either," Ethan added.

"Provided you don't attack me, yes, Master Ethan, I have no plans on doing such a thing," Maii said.

Ethan wasn't sure how much he believed such oaths bound a creature like Maii, but he'd wanted Maii to make them simply so he could see how the ahuizotl reacted. Sadly, he felt as if he hadn't gleaned a thing. He still had no idea whether or not Maii was telling the truth, but he was willing to delude himself enough to give Maii the benefit of the doubt. "Alright, good," Ethan said, "because I'm quite certain as long as we're friends, you're going to get your fill."

"I'm quite sure even if we weren't, I'd still get it," Maii tacked on.

Ethan narrowed his eyes. "I believe I said for you not to mess with me."

"Merely stating a truth," he grinned. "But if such things are unsettling, I shall keep them to myself."

"Let's just stay focused on what matters: the race," Ethan said. "And with that in mind, we have a crew to organize and preparations to make."

Three hours after sunrise, from inside the longboat, Ethan hoisted himself up the rope ladder and climbed aboard the corsair's frigate. Jean Bayard, along with a dozen and a half others, had sailed the ship around the island and had dropped anchor about fifty yards away from the docks of Lenada. There it now sat, rocking slowly, surrounded by crystal-clear water, waiting for Ethan and the others to divvy up whatever spoils they found aboard.

"Oh wow, look at that guy," Ethan said, pausing near the top of the rope and pointing. Off to the side, across the tops of vibrant coral, a colorful octopus made his way along, tentacles stretching in all directions. "Wonder if he's friendly. He looks cool."

Katryna grabbed him by the wrist and helped him up the last couple of feet and onto the deck. "Cool, yes. Friendly, no."

"No?"

"No," she said. "Augustus is one of the grumpiest things on this island. Best to leave him be."

"Maybe he's misunderstood," Ethan said, shrugging and thinking he'd still like to meet the creature. "I bet a little shrimp would go a long way to making him friendly. Who'd turn down free shrimp?"

"Trust me, the four separate people he killed last month all thought similar things," Katryna said, drawing back the corner of her mouth. "He goes from passive to aggressive in the blink of an eye, and he's so venomous, I doubt even your special blood would save you."

"I'll take your word for it," Ethan said.

At that point, he redirected his attention to the corsair ship. She held a total of three masts, all sporting a square rig with currently furled sails. Sixteen cannons lined the main deck, eight to a side, each one looking a lot shorter than the ones Ethan's ship held. Those, however, were not the end to the ship's armament. As they'd rowed over, Ethan had counted another eight gun ports on the deck below, putting the total number of cannons she sported to thirty-two, not counting the four small swivel guns mounted near the bow.

"Nice ship," Zoey said as she climbed onto the deck. "Too bad we can't take her."

"Why not?" Ethan asked. "We get first dibs, right? Or rather, next dibs."

"No, you don't," said one Thomas Drake, cutting into the conversation. Thomas was a giant of a man Ethan had met not even an hour ago and was also the appointed leader of the thirty-three men who opted to remain on Lenada and rebuild the town. He stood near the stairs leading to the quarterdeck, built like an ox, dressed in light breeches and an open shirt. A cutlass hung off his hip, while a trio of pistols stuffed into his belt were all within easy reach, and he stared at Ethan with eyes that had thousands of nightmares behind them. "You'll get your share of what's here. No more. No less."

"I'll be deciding what we take, seeing how you'd still be in chains if we hadn't come by," Ethan said, squaring off with the man. Deep down, he didn't want a confrontation, but he also knew from the moment they'd met, Thomas wasn't the sort of person who took kindly to weakness. "Just be glad we're not taking the whole ship."

"As if I'd let you," Thomas said.

"As if you could stop me," Ethan said.

Thomas started for him, and Ethan reflexively went for his pistol. Before the confrontation could escalate, Zoey appeared between them both. "Gentlemen," she said, arms outstretched, voice firm. "You two only have to be cordial for a few more minutes with each other, and fighting helps no one."

"I have a town to rebuild and men to look after," Thomas said, narrowing his eyes. "I suggest you keep that in mind when you tell me what you think you're going to take."

"You do," Ethan said, his words firm but genuine, and to that, Thomas relaxed. "And we don't need much," he went on. "In truth, anything in excess will only slow us down."

"What are you thinking then, extra lines and fabric, or just part of the coffers?" Katryna asked.

Ethan nodded, but as he scanned the ship's deck, he once again took note of the armament it had. "What's with the stubby guns?" he asked, nodding toward the closest one. "They seem a little...weird."

Thomas snorted with a mocking laugh. "Never seen a carronade? What sort of captain are you?"

"One from very far away," Ethan said, not missing a beat. "Mind telling me what's so special about them?"

"They're devastating for their weight at close range, that's what, since they don't have long barrels and can fire much bigger and heavier shot," he said. "The tradeoff is they're terrible at a distance. If you're not up close and personal, a long gun is what you want."

Ethan nodded. "Zoey, are these lighter than what we have? It looks like they might be."

The vampire eyed the guns for a few seconds before replying. "They should be, by at least a few hundred pounds."

Ethan ran a quick mental calculation, hoping his mighty eleven INT points were up to the task. "That means we'd be about five thousand pounds lighter if we swapped our guns for these?"

"Sounds right," Zoey said with a nod. "We'd also be firing thirty-two-pound shot instead of nine."

"So, we'd essentially be fielding nearly four times the firepower for a lot less weight."

"More or less."

"Then how is that not good for a race since we'll also go faster?"

"We'll get chewed to pieces if we go up against anyone who realizes what we have and stays far away," she said.

"Which won't matter if we're out running them."

"True," she said. Her hands found her hips, and she drummed her fingers on them for a moment.

In the meantime, Ethan turned to Katryna. "What do you think?"

"Not sure," she admitted reluctantly. "I could see the decision go either way. You're the captain. It's your call."

"That I am," he said. He still liked his idea a lot, actually, but at the same time, Zoey's point that they'd be weak stuck painfully in his mind. Still, being faster had to be the right choice, he thought, and being unexpected had to have its benefits, too.

"Alright, Thomas," Ethan said, turning to him. "This is what we're going to do. We'll take the carronades, the shot that goes with them, and a hundred pounds to go directly to our crew. We've already found triple the coin back at the fort. You and the others can have everything else, including this ship and whatever cargo it has. That should be more than enough to let you rebuild."

"Absolutely not," he said, crossing his arms over his chest. "I don't mind giving the men their share of coin, but each one of those guns is worth a small fortune. There's no way in hell you're setting sail with all of that."

"They may be worth a small fortune, but you're getting the cannons we have already on the *Victory* in trade," Ethan said. "And from what I can gather, you'll want those on the shore anyway."

Thomas grumbled to himself for a few seconds. "Fine," he eventually said, sticking out his hand. "It's a deal."

Ethan smiled and shook. "Done. Now let's get these moved so we can be on our way."

Chapter XIII
Engagement

One hundred and two.

That was the final count when it came to how many crewed the *Victory* as she set sail for New Port Royal. A little over two dozen of them were the living, breathing kind—the kind who guzzled rum and stank to the high heavens due to want of a bath. They were also the sort whose blood constantly tempted Ethan to take a little sample. Thankfully, he'd managed to keep his *Hunger* under control by coming up with a ruse where twice a day, he'd collect a few ounces of blood using a needle and chalice and tell the donors Zoey needed it to ward off unholy spirits who might look to feast on them all.

It was hardly ideal, and it still left Ethan wanting more, but it worked. And in a way, he wasn't lying, which made making it convincing all the easier.

The rest of the crew, seventy-one in all, were of the long-deceased variety. As it happened to be, they ended up being far more skilled than Ethan had expected. They worked hard, never speaking, tending the rigging, and keeping the night watch as well as any other. A few of them even turned out to love games of dice, which they played on the quarterdeck from time to time—lingering traits of their former personalities, as Marcus had explained.

They also performed decently enough when Ethan ran the ship through basic combat drills (something both Zoey and Katryna insisted on so Ethan would at least have an inkling on what to do before they ended up catching their first broadside). To top it off, the skeletons also seemed more than capable of repelling boarders should the need arise.

On the second day, right as Ethan polished off a delectable sample of AB+ from his chalice, a frantic knock on his door grabbed his attention.

"Captain!" Katryna shouted from outside. "Hunters on the horizon!"

Ethan raised an eyebrow and looked to Zoey, who sat across from him. "Hunters?"

"Ships in pursuit," she explained.

"Crap," Ethan scrambled out of his chair, wiping his lips one last time on a rag to ensure no blood could be found on them, and tossed the chalice into an open foot chest as he ran out the door.

The moment he broke into the sunlight, he had to shield his eyes and spend a moment letting them adjust since he kept his cabin dark. After all, he couldn't have crew seeing what went on in there.

"Both portside, with about five hundred yards between them," Katryna said. "They'll probably close on us within the hour."

Ethan ran up the stairs to the quarterdeck and leaned over the railing to get a better look. Sure enough, a pair of ships, each about three-quarters the size of the *Victory*, sailed the waters, lagging slightly aft and a half league away.

"Any idea who our new friends are?" Ethan asked.

"No," she said. "They're not flying any colors, but I doubt they're friendly."

Wrinkles formed across Ethan's brow as he looked across the water, hoping his vampiric senses might pick up on something useful. They didn't. "Are you're sure they're coming for us?" he finally asked.

"They were both headed west when we spotted them on the horizon. They turned completely around about ten minutes ago," she said. "Given they're on course for a slow intercept, I can't imagine they're anything but pirates."

Ethan snorted. "Pirates. Doesn't that just figure out here. I bet they grow like weeds in this world."

Katryna chuckled. "Worse."

"Still, are you absolutely certain?" Ethan asked. "What if they're merchants who forgot to load their dye this morning? I'd hate to blow them out of the water for a simple misunderstanding."

"Begging your pardon on the interruption, Captain," Jean Bayard said, stepping up to the pair and handing Ethan a spyglass. "But I must agree with the lady's assessment. I've been on many a ship, privateer and naval alike, and those aren't merchant ships. They're looking for a fight."

"Lady?" Katryna said with a snort of amusement. "I think you've known me long enough to know that's not the case."

"I've also seen you work that sword enough to not dare say anything else," he quickly tacked on.

Ethan chuckled at the remark and held the spyglass to his eye. Though the edges of what he saw looked distorted and blurry, the image of the ships was clear, and he instantly realized what he was looking at: two ships built for speed and agility, with a dozen cannons on each, not ones that were fat and slow thanks to tons of cargo being shipped inside swollen bellies.

"I'm inclined to agree with the both of you," he said, handing the spyglass back to Jean. "What would they be fielding?"

"Long guns for certain," he replied. "No more than nine pounds each. Might only be six-pounders if we're lucky."

"That sounds rather pathetic," Ethan smirked.

"We can weather a few nine-pound volleys without much trouble," he said. "But those guns are enough to rip apart our rigging and tear our sails given enough time," he said. "Once we're dead in the water, they can take their time picking us apart or simply grapple and board since they'll have numbers on their side. That said, one or two solid volleys from our carronades will be more than enough to take each one out of the fight."

"Good to know," Ethan said with a short nod. He then turned his head over his shoulder and called out to the helmsman, a wiry man with bronze skin covered in tattoos. "Mister Potts, half a point portside if you would. I'd like to test the waters."

"Aye, sir," came the reply.

"And Jean, ready the carronades," Ethan added. "Solid shot on them all."

"Aye, captain. They'll be ready," he said before hurrying back to the main deck, barking orders as he did. "Man the guns! Cast loose and provide!"

The deck became awash with a flurry of movement, living and undead crew working in what Ethan considered to be remarkable harmony as cartridges were loaded and rammed. Throughout it all, the *Victory* brought herself to her new bearing and sped along on a new course that would see her cross the bow of the leading ship. She ran with a broad reach, the wind mostly blowing from her rear, and though she'd lost a little of her speed with her new course, her guns had a much better angle to deliver a crippling blow when the time arose.

While the minutes ticked by, Ethan watched for any indication as to what their potential opponent might do in response.

He had his response inside a quarter hour.

A puff of white smoke came from the lead ship's side, followed by a distant thud of the gun's report. The cannonball whistled through the air, eventually splashing down at least two hundred yards short of the *Victory*.

"Son of a bitch," Ethan said. Though he'd ducked reflexively, he stood up, laughing. "I can't believe I flinched. Their gunners are terrible. That had to be the worst shot in the world."

"They're ranging us," Zoey said. "Next time, they might add a few more cannons to the mix."

As if on cue, two more puffs came from the ship, and this time, the shots landed much closer, each splashing down about a hundred yards away. After that, three more came with similar results, though Narrator finally decided to chime in—or rather, Ethan took note of his voice.

Pirate ship attacks!
Pirate ship misses!

Ethan snorted at the obvious commentary, and he refocused on what was happening as opposed to what was being told had happened. He turned to Katryna, who stood at his side, gripping the railing with a bloodthirsty zeal in her eyes. "How far away are we?"

"I'd say a little shy of a thousand yards," she replied.

"And we want to be within a hundred for our carronades?" he asked, making sure he hadn't forgotten.

"It would be better to be half that," she said.

"I guess we'd better close the distance before they can reload," Ethan replied before addressing his helmsman once more. "Mister Potts," he called back. "Full point to port if you'd be so kind. Let's run these scallywags down and show them we've got teeth."

The *Victory* turned further with the wind, her sails at full, her hull carving a white-capped path through the deep ocean-blue waters. Eagerness swelled in Ethan's chest, and his lips curled as he couldn't wait to prove himself once more to the woman at his side.

"Does my dear first mate have anything to say before this all unfolds?" he asked.

Zoey shook her head with a bright smile of her own and snuck her arm inside his elbow. "No, but if you wanted to dedicate your first naval victory to me, I'll not complain."

"First? No, you shall have them all."

Katryna let out a long groan and rolled her eyes. "I swear, if this is the tip of the iceberg when it comes to this new trait of yours, I'm going to shoot you both myself."

"Don't be jealous," Ethan teased.

"I'm not jealous," she retorted. "We're in the middle of a battle, and you two are worse than hormone-crazed teens."

"First, we're in the middle of a pause in battle," Ethan said, holding up a finger. "They're still reloading. And second, you'll be someone's Morticia one day. Don't worry."

"I don't know who this Morticia of yours is, nor do I care," Katryna said, shaking her head in disgust. "I'm going to make sure we're ready to repel boarders. Do remember we're trying not to die and save the make-out session for later if you would—*Captain*."

Katryna left the quarterdeck, and with her words still ringing in his ears, Ethan forced himself to detangle from Zoey. "Are we really that bad?" he asked.

"Could be worse," she said with a shrug. "Correction, we will be worse. But she'll live."

The rest of the conversation was interrupted when the trailing pirate ship fired its chasers from her bow. The shots flew wide and short, but then the lead ship made a small turn with the wind to better present her side and unleashed another broadside. Most of the shots from this barrage failed to connect with the *Victory*, but one found its mark.

The cannonball ripped through the *Victory*'s jib, punching a neat hole through the leading sail before dropping into the water. Ethan winced a little at that one, but when a third volley came, this time when they were about four hundred yards away, Ethan cussed up a storm. Iron bars and chain links cut through the *Victory*'s rigging, blowing apart ratlines leading to the crow's nest and tearing gashes in her main and topsails.

Pirate ship attacks!
Victory lightly damaged!
Maximum speed slightly reduced!

"I really didn't need to hear that," Ethan said.

"I'll manage the repairs. You focus on sinking that ship ASAP," Zoey said, giving his hand a squeeze before taking off.

Ethan nodded, and though he took heart she'd get their lines replaced quickly, as much as he tried to stay focused on the developing battle, he couldn't help but long for her to be at his side, watching him sink his first ship. He could picture how her eyes would sparkle, how her lips would turn up, how her cheeks would dimple.

Ethan shook his head, desperate to rid himself of his daydreaming. Orders. That's what he needed to give. Orders that would keep him on task as much as they would the crew. "Steady as she goes," Ethan said to his helmsman before addressing Jean on the main deck. "Those carronades better be ready."

"Waiting to fire on your order," he called back.

Hairs stood up across Ethan's arm and neck. He knew he needed to get as close as he could to ensure a devastating broadside, but at the same time, he also realized he'd have to weather at least one more volley, if not two, from the pirates. Unless, of course, he fired sooner rather than later and got a little lucky in the process.

And luck, Ethan reminded himself, was his specialty.

With the enemy ship a little over two hundred yards away, Ethan committed to his new strategy. After all, he didn't need every cannonball to hit. Just one thirty-two-pound shot had to blow one-foot holes—if not two or three—in everything it smashed through. Sure, he'd made that number up on the spot, but he'd seen how enormous they were, and each one looked like it could ruin any ship's day.

"Two points starboard and bring us to bear, Mister Potts," he said. The helmsman acknowledged the order, and the *Victory* rolled with the turn. The moment she settled into her new course, Ethan gave the order to attack. "Fire at will!"

Jean hesitated. Ethan guessed it was due to the range they were at, but to the man's credit as a member of the crew, he obeyed without a word and spun around, relaying the order to the gun crews. As the first slow matches went to the touch holes, Ethan dumped half his *Luck* into what he hoped would be a spectacular show of marksmanship. Or whatever the artillery version was. He still didn't have a complete grasp on how most things worked in the game, but he did know that sinking ten points into a roll gave him a plus fifty percent—and he really, *really* needed to land this volley.

Thunderous explosions shot from the *Victory*'s side, eight in all, the blasts stealing Ethan's breath and leaving a deafening ringing in his ears. A little over a second later, he counted six splashes in the water.

The Victory attacks!
Pirate ship lightly damaged!

"Come on, lightly damaged?" Ethan protested. "Those cannons can level castles!"

"Not with two hits they can't," Maii said, sauntering across the deck without a care in the world. "Next time, maybe wait until you're closer. That said, I'd like to point out that if these pirates prove to be your undoing, I might get to snack on you after all."

"Hush."

"And Zoey can finally have your boots," he added. "Won't that be nice?"

"I said hush. That wasn't a suggestion. I know what I'm doing." Maii cocked his head, and Ethan felt his skin flush in response. "As if you could do better."

Maii's lips drew back, showing off his razor teeth. "Oh, Master Ethan, I'm quite certain I could command this ship much better than you."

"As if they'd even listen to you."

Maii's grin only broadened. "Not only would they listen to me, but they'd love me," he said. He threw a sideways glance and cleared his throat. "Mister Potts," he shouted in a very Ethan-like voice. "Two points hard to port. I want us on top of that ship yesterday!"

"Aye, two hard to port," called back the helmsman.

"Belay that order," Ethan yelled. He leveled a stare at Maii and growled. "What the hell do you think you're doing?"

"Testing my abilities," Maii said, shrugging.

"You don't ever pretend to be me ever again," Ethan said. "Ever."

Maii chuckled. "Relax, Master Ethan. You have my word I'd not dream of taking this ship. Besides, my order was the right one, I promise."

"How's that?"

"You'll want to be scraping your hull across her rudder when your starboard guns come to bear. I mean, that is what you had in mind all along, right?"

Ethan frowned and gave a reluctant nod even though that was precisely not what he'd had in mind whatsoever. He'd certainly planned on drawing nearer, but could he even get that close? Apparently, not only could he, but he had to.

"Apologies, Mister Potts, I jumped the gun before," he called out, keeping his eyes on Maii the entire time. "Two points hard to port right now, if you would."

"Two hard to port, aye, Captain."

The *Victory* swung around with the order, sailing nearly perpendicular to her foe. She cut fast through the waves thanks to the broad reach of the wind filling her sails, and it was clear that given her course, she'd indeed cut right behind the pirate ship's rear. That is, provided it didn't turn into them so that they'd simply circle each other, trading broadsides the entire time. Why they weren't, Ethan wasn't sure.

"They can't," Maii said as if reading Ethan's mind. "If they swing toward us and into the wind, they risk getting caught in irons."

A pair of shots from the other ship's bow chasers cut off any reply Ethan might have had. Thankfully, both missed, but not by much. Plumes of water leaped into the air, not even twenty yards away.

A split second later, a hundred and fifty yards now separating the *Victory* and her closest foe, the enemy fired another broadside. Four of the five shots tore through the *Victory*, ripping sails even further, cutting lines, and obliterating several skeletons in the process.

Pirate ship attacks!
Victory lightly damaged!
Maximum speed reduced!

"Damn it," Ethan cursed. He fought the urge to order a broadside of his own in reply, and a moment later, the pirate ship began turning away. Yes, she'd present her aft to the *Victory*, but only for a moment, and then, Ethan knew, they'd be weathering another broadside.

Shouts came from his gun deck. Panicked ones. Questions. Demands. The battle took on a surreal nature as Ethan felt himself detach from everything around him. Among the chaos, the only thing he became crucially aware of was how lacking he was when it came to both commanding his ship and winning a naval engagement.

A sharp pain exploded across his calf, snapping him back in the moment. He looked down to see Maii taking a nip out of his lower leg.

"I suggest more doing than...well, whatever it was you were doing," he said, easing back on his haunches. "Unless you'd like me to take over?"

Ethan's brow knitted, angry and embarrassed he'd lost his composure. He glanced over the waters just in time to see the pirate about to present him with yet another broadside.

"Mister Potts! As hard as you can to starboard!" he yelled.

"Aye, Captain!"

The *Victory* rolled heavily as she turned, and as she did, Ethan activated his *Luck of the Devil* talent, hoping it would carry over to the evasive maneuvers he'd just launched his ship into. Hopefully, he wouldn't need the skill for a week since that's how long the cooldown was.

A swell in the ocean lifted his enemy right as it opened fire once again. Despite the close range—less than fifty yards at this point—the abrupt change in pitch was enough that the entire broadside missed wildly, which Narrator spoke about.

Pirate ship attacks!
Evasive maneuvers! (automatic success)
Pirate ship misses!

"Bring us back around!" Ethan yelled, clenching a fist in triumph. "I want us scraping his hull before we unleash hell! And Jean Baynard, tell me those carronades are ready."

"Aye, Captain, they're ready," he shouted back.

"Perhaps make them double-shot," Maii suggested.

Ethan hesitated, not sure what that was but realizing he didn't have the luxury of time for any sort of explanation or question. "Double-shot, Mister Baynard!"

"Aye, double-shot it is," he called back. "It'll take a moment to load, however."

"A moment is all you have!"

The other ship tried to turn away, but the *Victory* had both the speed and angle that any maneuvers it made would only be done in vain. Less than a minute later, the *Victory* drew within five yards of her prey.

Katryna shouted orders from the main deck, and both her living and undead marines began firing pistols and muskets into the enemy ranks. In the fighting tops, Zoey and several others began raining down fire of their own, picking off the pirates with deadly accuracy.

Grapples flew from the pirate ship, five altogether. Before the first one tangled itself on the *Victory*'s rails, Ethan gave what he hoped would be the order to end it all.

"Fire!" Ethan boomed.

Eight carronades erupted in flame and smoke, and the double loads—grapeshot packed on top of solid balls—cut through the enemy's ship with devastating results. Men lay strewn about, bloodied, clinging to wounds and each other. Not a single one stood upright.

"Cut those hooks free!" Ethan shouted, not wanting to be tied down to what was now essentially a ghost ship.

His crew reacted immediately, hand axes from Katryna's marines swiftly dealing with the grapples attached to their ship.

"Mister Potts, keep that ship between us and the other until we have time to reload," he said, realizing they still had another foe to deal with.

The helmsman complied as Jean and the gun crews feverishly worked to reload the carronades. Three minutes later, the guns were ready to fire right as the *Victory* swept past her first target and caught sight of the other. To Ethan's surprise, the remaining ship had given them her aft and was sailing fast away with a broad reach of the wind filling her sails.

Cheers from his crew erupted across the deck. Jean looked up at Ethan from his position near the bow and gave an enthusiastic salute, while Marcus, who happened to be next to him, simply gave an approving nod. Despite the celebrations and praise, Ethan felt sick to his stomach. He could feel the sweat dripping down the back of his neck, and no matter what he did, he couldn't rid himself of the tremor in his fingers. The battle, though ultimately a victory, was not one that had been won due to anything he'd done.

"Mister Potts, put us back on our original course for New Port Royal," Ethan said after sucking in a deep breath and letting it out slowly. "We've got a race to get to."

"Aye, Captain."

"Hang on," Katryna said, cutting in. "We're not boarding?"

"No," Ethan replied.

"I'm sure they'll wave the white flag moment we grapple," she said. "Think of all the coin we could have."

"I don't think it's worth risking their friend coming back while we're tied up," Ethan said.

Katryna groaned as she set her jaw. She clearly wanted to argue but didn't in the end.

"Is money that important to you?" Ethan asked.

"No, but living is," she replied.

Ethan cocked his head and folded his arms over his chest. "I'd think us not taking risks, then, would be more to your liking."

"I get why you'd rather not take a chance now with needing to be at the regatta," she said, "but running away isn't living."

Chapter XIV
The Call

Maii casually knocked over a chair inside the captain's quarters. Its heavy thud did nothing to slow down either Ethan or Zoey from ravishing each other. Their kisses found every exposed inch of skin on the other while fingers ran through hair or gripped shoulders. When Ethan started to slide Zoey's shirt over her head, and she got stuck, she giggled, and Maii tried to put a stop to the two vamps once and for all.

"There are others in this cabin who can see you," he huffed before knocking over the other chair for added effect.

All he got for his efforts was Zoey's top hurled with uncanny accuracy. It struck him square in the face, wrapping around his eyes, so he had to spend a moment shaking it free. After it hit the ground, he'd wished it had stayed there. Ethan had Zoey pressed against the wall now, the two half-naked and rapidly approaching completely naked, which meant they were going to give him a show whether he liked it or not.

And Maii did not like it at all.

It wasn't that he had any sort of hang-up about naked humans (or vamps, even). In fact, he quite preferred them without clothes. It made eating them much, much easier. Nothing ruined a good meal faster than accidentally biting down on a metal buckle or getting a leather strap stuck between some teeth.

Sadly, *these* naked humans weren't ones he could bite (or naked vampires, as the case were). At least, not and get away with it. To his dismay, he still had to pretend to be under the ring's command for a while at least, and he knew, ultimately, he still couldn't pick and win a fight against the pair. Ethan, most likely— though as the fledgling vampire grew, he'd have a harder and harder time, even if Maii was growing himself.

But Zoey? Possibly. Maybe. As much as he hated to admit it, he'd only done as well as he had against her back in Lord Belmont's throne room because the lich had cast a number of temporary spells on him right before the fight, which had greatly enhanced his strength and reflexes. Now that those had long expired, she'd be a much deadlier opponent.

Then, of course, he'd have to deal with Katryna. Even before he saw her fight, he knew the world would be hard-pressed to find her equal when it came to the blade. Hell, it was one of the things that attracted him to her so, but that fact also meant he had to be careful in all that he did. To cross paths with her would certainly be fatal.

Sure, Maii did genuinely find Ethan entertaining still, so he didn't want to bite an ankle to get him to stop the romp he was enjoying with his girl, but at the same time, all the ahuizotl wanted to do was enjoy a quiet, peaceful rest inside the cabin and bask in the magical glow it provided. He could feel the subtle energies humming from every plank from bow to stern on the *Victory*, but the cabin was where they felt the strongest. Whenever he curled up there, it was like curling up near a lit hearth on a cold day.

Ethan picked Zoey up as she straddled his waist. Together, they flopped to the bed, and Maii let out a groan while rolling his head. Then, with a huff for good measure, Maii saw himself out of the room, using his clawed tail to work the door.

Warm, humid night air greeted his face while the clacking of bones danced in his ears, the only sounds made by the skeletal crew who tended to the ship at night. They tirelessly kept the *Victory* on course without comment or complaint so that those who still belonged to the living could enjoy a night's rest.

Ahead, about halfway to the bow, Maii spied Katryna. The swashbuckler leaned over the railing, resting herself on her elbows, her gaze focused far beyond the horizon, where dreams played, and stars were born. He regarded her for a few moments, wondering what captivated her so, and his curiosity grew even more when she let out a long, content sigh and smiled pleasantly to herself.

He thought about asking, thinking that knowing more about the depths of her wants and the makeup of her mind could only serve him well in the end. After all, one didn't need to be strong to move the powerful. One only needed to know where to put the right pressure—like how the smallest of rudders could move the mightiest of ships.

And Katryna was mighty, indeed.

A split second before he opened his mouth, a new thought occurred to him. Perhaps he was overestimating her, or along the same lines, perhaps he was underestimating himself. A simple test, he thought, would do.

With that in mind, the ahuizotl crouched lower than a panther stalking its next meal and slinked across the deck so that he'd ultimately come up directly behind her. A whisper of a whisper escaped his lips, and his coat darkened, so he was nothing more than a shadow that moved more quietly than those that moved across the deck.

Ten feet to his goal, Maii froze as Katryna spoke. "And to what do I owe the pleasure of your company tonight?"

The woman didn't turn whatsoever as she addressed him. In fact, she seemed to relax even more, if such a thing were possible, and fully let herself be swept into a sea of wanderlust.

"I know you're there, Maii," she said, laughing quietly.

The ahuizotl grunted and sat on his haunches. "I'm always here," he said, trying not to sound annoyed that he'd been caught so easily. "It is a small ship, after all."

"And what does that have to do with you trying to creep up on me?"

Maii let slip a tiny growl out of frustration. "Nothing. It was practice. Nothing more."

Katryna turned about and casually leaned back on the rail. "Looking to see when you can test your mettle?"

"No," he lied.

The corners of Katryna's lips drew back. "Neither one of us believes that. But you know what? I don't care. It's in your nature, I know. Just behave whilst you're on board, and I promise I won't make a coat out of you."

"I wouldn't dream of behaving any other way," he said.

Again, the lie was hardly a secret, but Katryna said nothing more on the matter. She turned back around with a short nod right as the most peculiar of aromas tantalized the ahuizotl's nose. It smelled like the nerves of an anxious explorer descending into a newly found, gloomy cave. He lifted his head and sniffed the air, focusing all of his thoughts on the matter. Angst wasn't the only thing he picked up. There were notes of wonderment and awe, along with hints of potential dread.

Maii went to follow the scent, but Katryna stopped him in his tracks. "Before you go," she said. "Why are you here?"

For a brief second, Maii considered his answer. At the very least, Katryna suspected he was free of Ethan's ring, but at the same time, she didn't seem to care, either. Perhaps that attitude was a ruse to get to the truth. After all, that's what he'd do. But then again, perhaps she really didn't care. Either way, he didn't want to flat out give away such a valuable secret if it weren't already known, but at the same time, her ability to pick apart his lies and see through his deceit seemed to grow with every second he spent with her. And that, along with the fact that she was clearly one of the deadliest swashbucklers on the sea, intrigued Maii more and more.

"I'm here for the same reason you are," the ahuizotl said.

"Which would be?"

"To see the world. Much harder to do without a ship and crew, wouldn't you agree?"

Katryna glanced over her shoulder, studied him for a moment, and nodded once again.

She turned back around without a further word, and at that point, Maii moved on. The scent he'd noticed earlier still lingered, and as he slowly worked his way toward the bow, he realized that not only was it stronger, but it was coming from below deck. Quickly, he took to the stairs that led into the crew quarters. Sailors slept soundly in their hammocks, rocking gently with the sea as the *Victory* sailed on. Most did so quietly, though a couple let loose a snort here and there as they shifted in their beds. Not a one woke to Maii's presence, but every last one stank of hard work, powder, and smoke.

Maii was hardly the type to complain about humans needing a wash, but he had a hunch that it wouldn't be long before he'd make an exception to that rule. Perhaps it would rain in the near future, and they might all do with a wash.

He pushed such wishful thinking aside and continued following his nose. This took him through the gunroom, which Katryna had taken over as her own, but offered nothing of particular interest to the ahuizotl. She kept her bed neat and the one table clear of anything. He suspected her footlocker was empty, as he hadn't seen her bring anything aboard when they'd first set sail. Whether that was because she traveled light or she'd simply lost it all when Lenada burned, he didn't know. He didn't care, either.

The hairs across his back bristled. The flow of magical energy around him suddenly became stronger. He could feel it moving through the floorboards, hear its quiet vibration in the walls. Something was happening, not just on the ship, but to it.

Instinctively, Maii dropped into a crouch and darted out of the gunroom and down one more flight of stairs so that he was in the very belly of the ship. Stores were packed all around, barely visible in the gloomy dark. Casks of fresh water and rum. Sacks of flour and bags of tack. Barrels of meat so salted that if they weren't soaked in constantly refreshed water for hours on end before consuming, a single bite could lead to an aneurysm.

He slipped by piles of linen, whole cloth by the dozens of yards. Spare blocks in crates. Lines coiled together. Then he passed through heavy, wet curtains to where the gunpowder was stored in the magazine. There it sat below the waterline, in relative safety, until needed.

While this area should've been the darkest of all, as lanterns were not allowed anywhere near, let alone beyond, the wet curtains that separated this room from the others, at the far side, a sickly green light slipped beneath one last set of curtains that led to the aft stores.

Maii cocked his head at the sound of deep, gravelly words. They were words he didn't know but certainly understood. Words of power. Words of calling to the dead. Words that, he realized in a heartbeat, belonged to Marcus.

The ahuizotl crept forward, not so much because he feared being caught, but because he wanted to see what the minotaur was up to. Something dark and fun, perhaps? Maii didn't know, but he could dare to dream.

Something heavy crashed, sending a shockwave rippling through the hull, and the green light that had been only an instant before was no more.

"Bah!" Marcus cried. Another heartbeat passed, and some grumbling, and then the minotaur spoke again. "*In Lor.*"

Light, bright and white, cut through the darkness. Sensing that whatever was going on had also met an abrupt end, Maii pushed through the curtains. On the other side, Marcus sat hunched over a small, square table. In the middle sat a hefty, leather-bound tome splayed open to somewhere in the middle, its worn pages covered in crimson text and intricate symbols, while off to the side, several barrels lay knocked on their side.

"What?" Marcus growled, dropping his brow and leveling his gaze. "Can't you see I'm working? I swear, to the Great Lord Charethes—may he always infuse my soul with his undying power—I'm going to lose my mind one of these days."

For a fleeting moment, Maii thought about making a jab, as pissed-off minotaurs always made for good times, but he quickly decided against it. He did, after all, have a mystery to solve, and he knew Marcus was the key to unraveling it all. Work first. Play later.

"It's your work that brings me down here," Maii replied, casually taking a seat across from him.

"And how might that be?"

"There's something odd 'bout this ship," the ahuizotl went on. "Have you noticed?"

Marcus glanced at his tome before folding his hands in front of him and leaning forward. "Noticed what, exactly?"

"From the first day we set sail on the *Victory*, I could feel *something* stir inside of her," Maii explained, his eyes growing a little vacant as he dove into the memories. "Subtle, but constant. Like the call of a lone cicada, miles away, whose song is lost to all but the most intently listening ears. But it's not a sound—it's an energy. Magic. A life...almost."

Marcus tilted his head slightly but didn't say a word, and so Maii finished his thought. "And tonight, that presence grew in the most unexpected of ways. It was stronger, rose and fell to a tempo I didn't follow, as if it were talking to someone, or perhaps, some *thing*."

"Ha!" The minotaur yelled, jumping to his feet only to strike his horns against the low ceiling above. He snarled and shook his head, muttering a few curses, before settling back in his chair. "I knew it! I knew the very second I stepped aboard I heard the song of the netherworld carried on the softest of wind!" He paused and rubbed his chin as his gaze drifted to the side. "Then why did the séance fail, I wonder? Too much nightshade in the incense? Or should I have forgone the shade wards so I could hear the *Victory's* call?"

"You did a séance?" Maii asked, straightening and unsure he heard right.

"Some time ago, yes," Marcus said. "But no answer. Unless..." His voice trailed. "Did it take this long for her call to reach me, I wonder? Perhaps her voice is what broke my concentration tonight."

A devilish grin spread across Maii's face, and his tail swished back and forth with eager anticipation. He'd been speaking poetically, never once thinking any of it might be remotely true, merely trying to describe the sensation the ship gave him. At best, he'd figured it had been enchanted in some fashion or housed some long-lost artifact of some sort. Both would certainly not be unheard of, as the ship had once belonged to a lich. But a ship with a spirit? A life of its own? That opened up all sorts of possibilities for the ahuizotl. Still, he had to be sure he was hearing the necromancer correctly and wasn't simply letting his imagination get the better of him. "You're saying, then—"

"The *Victory* most certainly has a spirit, yes," Marcus enthusiastically cut in. "Faint. Dormant, even, or perhaps so far gone into the netherworld, she doesn't even remember the cord that attaches her to this plane. But there's a spirit here nevertheless."

"Inside the ship," Maii went on. "The entire ship."

Marcus nodded and sat back, crossing his arms over his chest as a fire lit in his eyes. "Exciting, is it not?"

"Quite," Maii replied. He chewed the revelation over a few times in his head, wondering what to do with it all. After a few minutes, during most of which Marcus dove back into his tome and furiously began scanning the text, Maii realized he was going to need a lot more time to mull this over. A lot more time. "When do you think you'll know more?" he finally asked.

Marcus shrugged. "A few days at the very least," he said, shrugging. "I should proceed with caution from here on out. Make plans. Revise plans. Make contingencies, and contingencies for the contingencies."

"All of that?" Maii asked, dropping his brow.

"All of that and then some!" Marcus replied, thumping the table with excitement. "Calling such a powerful spirit back to a world it left is not without danger. I'll need time to do it right, lest we all risk her wrath when she returns."

Maii pressed his lips together into a tight line, understanding the necromancer's concern. Only a fool disregarded the haunted, regardless of whether or not it was a home, an object, or in this case, a vessel. The heaps of misfortune they could bring upon the hapless or arrogant were often second to none.

"I suppose then, that I should inform the captain of this new development," Maii said, lazily turning around. He paused at the curtain. "Would you like me to relay anything?"

"Only that I'm not to be disturbed until I'm done," Marcus grunted, face still stuck in his tome. "The skeletons can take orders without me."

"Very good," Maii said as he let a devilish smile grow.

With that, the ahuizotl left, wondering how best to take full advantage of this unexpected discovery.

Chapter XV
New Port Royal

By the next morning, all of the repairs to the sails and lines of the *Victory* were complete, and she cut through the blue waters with all the grace and speed of a mako. The start of the day went by without incident, but when midmorning rolled around with clear skies and the occasional seagull floating effortlessly overhead, a welcomed and much-anticipated cry cut through the air.

"Captain! New Port Royal on the horizon!"

Ethan's eyes shot up to the crow's nest, where one of the men leaned out and pointed to the line where the sky met the sea. Ethan beamed and made a quick adjustment of his tricorne hat before straightening his jacket. It was important to look the part as best he could, he knew, and with what he felt was an important moment in their adventure, he wanted to get this just right.

"If you'd be so kind as to bring us in, Mister Potts," he said. "And Katryna, see to the details once the longboats come to tow us to the docks."

"Aye, Captain," she said.

"If you need me, I'll be talking to my XO in my quarters," he added.

"Aye, Captain," she replied yet again.

With that, Ethan led Zoey away while Katryna took over, barking orders. When they entered his quarters, Ethan shut the door behind them. As far as a captain's area went, what he had was quite nice, and a thousand steps above the cramped rope hammocks the crew had to sleep in down below. A single bed lay tucked against the wall with ample room for one, or in Ethan and Zoey's case, decent room for two. Red satin sheets covered the mattress, and several glass-covered candlesticks were mounted on the wall nearby. The aft wall held five large, arched windows, which allowed plenty of sunlight to illuminate the room.

To the left sat a couple of chests, mostly empty at this point, as Ethan hadn't much when it came to personal effects to store. The one on the right, however, did hold a hefty amount of coin that they'd taken from Lord Belmont's estate. In the middle of the room was a round table, anchored in place, with four chairs spaced around it.

Zoey headed for the closest one and dropped herself in it. "What's on your mind?"

"The race," Ethan said, grabbing the seat across from her. Nervous energy filled his body, and he tried to drum it out on the table with his hands, but it didn't seem to help much.

"You're worried?"

"A little, maybe."

Zoey laughed with relief. "Good," she said, leaning forward with a smile. "It's about damn time."

"Good? How is that good?" he replied. "I've been faking this whole thing the entire time. I have no idea what the hell I'm doing, and well, the battle we just had that I practically got us all killed in made everything really, really, *really* real."

Zoey reached over and grabbed his still-drumming hands. "Yes, good," she said once she held his gaze. "You should be nervous, Ethan. You're challenging Death to a race, and there's no coming in second. You've got to win."

"Is that supposed to make me feel better? Because it doesn't."

"I'm saying that it's good you're freaking out because that means you're taking both this race and this world seriously," she replied. "We'd be in a hell of a lot more trouble if you thought this was going to be a walk in the park, you know?"

"I guess. Felt like we were already in a hell of a lot of trouble, and those were just a couple of pirates."

"Ethan, you did well," she said.

"Only because I listened to Maii and blew my once-a-week skill," he said. "I didn't really do any of that on my own. Not really."

"Hey, I wouldn't lie to you," she said. "You did well for your first engagement—a two on one, at that, and no matter how you feel about what you did or didn't do in the heat of the battle, remember, it was your idea to trade for the carronades. They absolutely proved their worth ten times over."

"Yeah...yeah, I guess they were my idea," he said.

"Exactly."

Her words helped calm him, some, but Ethan hardly felt inspired. Furthermore, despite his recent last few days of accomplishing things he never would've dreamed of being able to do back home, deep down in his soul, he was still just Ethan—a guy with a mediocre-at-best job who was terrified of even talking to the girl across the hall.

Zoey squeezed his hands. "What?"

"I'm still faking it, regardless of what you say."

"What's wrong with faking it?"

"Everything?"

Zoey shook her head but kept her smile. "When I first started as a nurse, we had this guy in ICU, multiple system failure. Actually, check that. Total system failure. He was my second case I had when I was let loose on my own. Guy was fifty-something, long history of substance abuse, and it was probably a miracle he lasted that long before his body just gave up. Anyway, I walk in there one morning, and his sister is there like she usually was. Most days, she didn't say much, but for whatever reason, that day, she gave me both barrels completely out of the blue, yelling, screaming, calling me names, all because she said I didn't know what I was doing, and her brother should be better."

Zoey paused for a moment as her eyes drifted to the side as if she were watching her story play all over again in her head. "And you know what?" she said, returning to Ethan after a smirk. "I didn't know what I was doing. I mean, I was trained, obviously, and I aced every class I ever took. But no amount of nursing school could've prepared me for that absolute disaster of a patient, both in terms of his physical condition and all the goddamn family drama he was involved in—let's just say, if you knew even a tenth of the abuse he suffered, you wouldn't have been surprised if he'd blown his brains out at twenty instead of poisoning himself to fifty.

"Anyway," she went on after another pause. "Long story short—"

"Too late."

"Yeah, yeah," she said, grinning. "I held it together until I got to my floor supervisor and just bawled my eyes out for the next hour. I was in over my head. The family wanted way more than I could provide, and all I wanted was out. Laura, my boss, told me something that absolutely saved my career. She said, and I quote, 'I might be the only person to ever tell you this, professionally, but sometimes you just have to fake it until you make it. So, get back in that room, and at least pretend you know exactly what you're doing.'"

Ethan leaned back in the chair, letting her words soak into his mind. "She actually said that to you?"

"Yeah."

"But like, what if you killed the guy? I mean, no offense. I'm not calling you stupid, but you even said you were in way over your head."

"The guy was going to die, regardless of what I did," she said. "The family needed reassurance we knew how to care for them, and if I was going to get better as a nurse, I needed to face a situation I wasn't ready for. You don't get better, Ethan, if you're doing the same easy thing over and over and over."

"I guess," he said. "I don't think that quite works here. Katryna, Maii, the crew—"

"Need to feel like you know what you're doing," she said. "They're watching you. You know that. I know you know that."

"Yeah, but at least you knew the basics of nursing. What the hell do I know about racing Death?"

Zoey laughed and rolled her eyes. "You want the basics?" she asked. "Here they are. Pay attention. There are three things to make all of this work. First, you need a ship. Second, you need a crew. And third, the most important, you've got to cross the freaking finish line first. You've got two of the three down. Tap into anyone and everyone else with better expertise to make number three happen."

"Yeah, but—"

"Ethan," Zoey said, cutting him off. "Being captain doesn't mean you do everything. It just means you're responsible for everything. Empower the crew. Respect their abilities. *Listen* to their suggestions and advice, but ultimately, you've got to at least pretend that when you speak, that's the law, and that's the course we're going to take. If you do all that, they'll follow you. And if they follow you, we can win this stupid race."

Ethan put his elbows on the table, clasped his fingers together, and rested his chin upon them. "Do you honestly think we can do this?"

"Since we're having a heart-to-heart, I'm not going to lie," she said. "Azrael will probably win. So, if he ever offers you some sort of deal that lets you out of this, I won't blame you for taking it."

Ethan snorted. "As if he'd offer."

"He might," she said with a shrug. "I've heard tattle where he's shown a little favor to opponents he likes."

"Maybe, but I doubt that deal would help you."

"Probably not. He's already given me one break, remember?"

"Then I won't take it."

"Ethan—"

"No," he said. "I'm not leaving you behind. I promised."

Zoey sighed. "Fine. That's sweet, but I'm used to living here. I'll manage and find another way. I always do, right?"

"I don't care," Ethan said. "I'm getting you out of there and helping you save your kids. Anyway, you said he'd probably win. That means there's a chance he might not."

"There's always a chance, but no one's been that lucky."

"I'm the pirate king of luck, remember?"

Zoey snorted. "Sorry, that's one stat will need at least another zero attached to it before we can effectively rely on it."

"Then what can we rely on?"

"Honestly, I'm not sure," she said. "But we do have one thing definitely going for us: we're the underdog. And no matter what anyone says, the underdogs have a propensity for being underestimated. Azrael will have a few other challengers this year he'll be paying more attention to."

Ethan nodded, as that simple point made a lot of sense to him. "How long is the race in total?"

"A thousand leagues, give or take," Zoey replied. "Which, if you don't stop at all, takes two or three weeks, depending on how well the wind favors us. We'll get a chance to see the waypoints tonight after registration is closed, and we can make plans then on what routes we want to take."

"There are routes?"

"Some minor choices in a few spots, but yes, ultimately, we won't all sail the exact same path," she explained. "They each have their own advantages based on which ship is sailing them."

"Gotcha," he said. Then, after some thought, he added. "That means we have time then to figure things out."

"We do. Got anything on your mind yet you want to try?"

"No, but you said Azrael would be watching other competitors more than us."

"I would be if I were him."

"Then my first thought is we don't sail as fast or as hard as we can at the start," Ethan said. "If they think we're slower than we are, we can make them pay for that assumption later on—maybe by taking a route they aren't and coming out ahead."

"I like," Zoey replied, face brightening as a genuine look of hope washed over her. "I mean, it's simple, but it has a lot of merit to it."

"Right. I guess we should get back on deck, then."

"Probably," Zoey said, standing. "It'll give you more practice at faking things."

The splash of the anchor falling preluded the *Victory* easing to a halt by the docks. Immediately, the skeletal crew threw lines to a couple of the men who jumped over the rails and onto the docks. Said men then quickly tied the ship down to the heavy iron cleats.

"I think that's the best docking I've done yet," Ethan said, admiring how quickly and smoothly the process had gone.

"Helps to have a crew who knows what they're doing as opposed to one guy that just learned how to tie a sheet bend four days ago," Zoey said. "Not to mention, a longboat with a veteran harbor pilot to tow us in."

"That's why I'm such a good delegator," Ethan replied, bumping her with his shoulder as they made their way across the main deck. "I know my limitations and direct accordingly."

"You mean Katryna directs accordingly," Zoey replied. "She's the one giving all the orders."

"True, but I'm telling her where I want to go, so it all works out."

As if on cue, Katryna's voice cut through the air as she barked orders from the poop deck, accentuating Zoey's point. "Finish furling those sails, damn you all!" she yelled. "I'll feed every last one of you to the next leviathan we see if I have to say it again!"

Ethan cocked his head, focusing more on her threat than Zoey's warning. "Does a leviathan eat skeletons?"

"They eat anything," she said. Zoey pulled him toward the plank that had just been set between the *Victory* and the docks. "Let's go register so we can at least relax the rest of the day before the race starts. Maybe pick up some extra stores afterward."

Ethan, agreeable to the suggestion, took the lead and hurried off the ship and onto the docks. The entire harbor, a massive area stretching nearly a mile, was crammed with ships, three score of which were participants in the regatta. Regarding the immediate area of the docks they were in, a few other ships shared that space: a couple of sloops along with a single rowboat lashed to one of the pylons.

At first, Ethan didn't pay much attention to who happened to be nearby, but it only took a few moments for him to realize that a small crowd had formed—and continued to grow—at the far end. The cause for said crowd was easily determined by their gapes and points toward his ship, something even his previous eight INT likely would've figured out.

A skeletal crew was *not* the norm.

"Are they going to be a problem?" Ethan asked, hitching a thumb back toward their crew.

"Shouldn't," Zoey replied, though the angst in her face belied her words. "Unless..."

"Unless what?"

"Unless there's an inquisitor around on some sort of holy quest," she finished. "But they usually stick to the mainland and wouldn't come here, and as long as our guys stay on the ship, we should be fine either way."

"Well, that's good, at least," Ethan said with a shrug, not sure what else to do, and kept walking.

"There will be extra eyes on us, however," she went on. "Keep that in mind when you get hungry."

"Ah, I take it that's frowned upon here."

"It's frowned upon everywhere," she said with a laugh. "You should know that."

"Know? No. Suspected, yes," Ethan said.

"Yeah, well, if you get caught, not only will you have angry townsfolk to deal with, but the lords I told you about will hear about it, too," she said, voice hushed. "And then—"

"We're in serious trouble," Ethan finished.

"Exactly."

The conversation ended, and the two continued down the docks, Ethan keeping a wary eye on the crowd as they did. The mass of sailor and citizen parted a few seconds later, and from it strode a large man with bronze skin, lustrous black hair that fell in curls, and a tricorne hat.

He approached with speed and purpose, like he could command the world with a single word. He walked upon polished leather boots with black trousers tucked and bloused over the tops. A ruffled, ivory-white shirt covered his torso, and over that, he wore a giant blood-red jacket with gold trim and embroidery that hung an inch above his knees. Across his chest, held fast by leather straps, were three flintlock pistols, their wooden butts polished to perfection.

But the armory the man sported didn't stop there. He also wore an ornate rapier off one side and carried an elegant main-gauche off the other. Ethan had no idea how much either of those cost, but he had a feeling they'd each fetch enough to feed a small army, especially if the intricate runes inscribed across their blades were any indication of the craftsmanship involved.

As Ethan gawked, Zoey took him by the arm and whispered into his ear. "That's him."

"Who?"

"Azrael."

Ethan blinked, and in that infinitesimal amount of time, Death went from being several dozen yards away, leisurely walking toward them, to standing but a pace away.

"Master Ethan!" Azrael said, his voice full of energy and his face lit with excitement. "How splendid of you to make such a grand entrance at the last hour. I see the tattle regarding you is nothing but poppycock, not even fit for the breath of a whore. Told every last one of those vagrants and vagabonds you'd show in time to register, and not one of them believed me."

Death shifted his attention to Zoey. After a theatric gasp and an even more theatric bow—one that saw his tricorne hat sweeping through the air—he addressed her. "And my dear Lady Zoey, you look as lovely as the day we first met. It warms my heart to know the life you live here is a full one, and I look forward to renewing our duel. Unless, of course, you're ready to go home?"

Zoey scowled as she squared off with him. "Never. You're not taking my kids."

"One day, my good woman," Azrael replied as he flipped his hat back atop his head. "One day."

Ethan extended his elbow to Zoey, and she promptly wrapped her arm around it once more. "A pleasure," Ethan said as he started forward. "Now then, if you'll excuse us, we have business to attend to."

Azrael stepped to the side and gestured with his arms for them to walk by. "By all means, Master Ethan. I was only coming to admire the new ship that's graced us with her presence and to pay my compliments to whoever captained such a fine vessel. In fact—"

Death cut himself off so abruptly that Ethan stopped as well, unsure what to make of it. Azrael then shook his head, laughed, and then quickly recomposed himself. "Pray tell, Master Ethan, is that actually Lord Belmont's ship? Up until a moment ago, I'd have sworn it was one of her sisters, but I'll be damned to the bottom of the abyss if that's not her."

"She *was* Lord Belmont's ship," Ethan corrected. "Once he lay down to rest, she became mine."

"Ah, I should have guessed," Azrael said with a chuckle. "He never would have willingly parted with her. I must say, I'm eager to see her sail in the regatta."

"Um, thanks," Ethan replied, not sure what to make of his continued politeness.

"Then, of course—" Death paused, cocked his head, and after a perplexed look crossed his face, he raised his right hand and slowly moved it to and fro, as if he were painting the *Victory* from afar, all the while keeping his eyes closed. "Interesting," he said, opening his eyes and lowering his arm. "I believe you have something special there—or horrifying, as the case may be."

Ethan retreated a few steps, eyes widening. "What are you talking about?"

Azrael chuckled, and his face filled with pity as if he were a curator trying to explain art to a patron who could never appreciate the work he currently stood in front of. "I hear her call," he said. "It's one I haven't heard in a long, long time, but it's definitely hers."

Ethan waited a moment, and when Azrael went no further, he prodded. "And she would be...?"

"She'd mean nothing to you, but everything to your lovely first mate, though she'd not believe me if I gave it," he said.

Zoey crossed her arms over her chest. "Try me. Or are you simply playing games?"

"No, no, my dear," he said, chuckling. "I'm quite serious. I suspect if you look hard enough in the captain's cabin, you'll find your answer."

"What am I looking for, a stowaway?" Ethan asked.

"No, she's definitely not a stowaway," he replied, chuckling once more.

Ethan twisted his mouth to the side, drumming his fingers on his side. The tone and certainty in Azrael's voice for all of this told him that Death wasn't lying. Not in the least. It also told him, much to his own frustration, that Azrael wouldn't be providing any further details.

"Should we go back and look?" he asked Zoey, throwing a glance to the *Victory*.

The vampire hesitated. "Not yet," she finally said. "Let's get registered first. We need to get to the office before it closes."

"A wise decision, if there ever was one," Azrael said, clapping her shoulder. "Oh, and before I'm accused of lacking when it comes to manners, tonight, Captain Ethan, if you would take a seat at the Sword and Spear promptly at nine, I'd be much obliged."

"What for?"
"Tradition, my good man," Azrael said. "For tradition."

Chapter XVI
Invitations

Sword and Spear.

A cozy tavern and inn at the edge of New Port Royal, if there ever was one as far as Ethan was concerned. Sure, the rock and brick walls that formed the three-story structure groaned against the slightest breeze, and yes, he did find it a little strange that more than one window was missing glass, and more than a dozen vines took advantage of those missing panes by snaking their way inside. And then there was the whole unsettling air outside the place that made it seem as if one were to walk in and just happen to stumble upon a few corpses slumped over, that would be business as usual. But all of that, Ethan told himself, simply added to the charm of the establishment.

"I still think we should go back to the *Victory* and make plans there," Zoey said, her face wrinkling in disgust as a foul odor wafted through the air. "I mean, I know you're curious to see why Azrael invited us, and you probably want to explore the world, but this place is practically a hole in the ground—literally. I swear, three weeks from now, the foundation is going to sink another ten feet into the earth."

"All great historical places are like that," Ethan said, trying to put a spin on things he could get behind. "Think of it like the Leaning Tower of Pisa."

"No, it's more like a dilapidated Kehoe House."

"A what, what?"

"The Kehoe House?"

Ethan paused long enough to throw her an inquisitive look before plopping down on a stool at a small table, shrugging as he did. "I have no idea what that is."

"You don't?" she asked with genuine surprise. "It's only one of the most famous haunted houses in the United States, or the world for that matter."

Ethan continued to look at her with a blank face.

"In Georgia?"

Ethan shrugged again. "Still not ringing a bell. How do you know about it, anyway?"

"It's in Georgia!" she said with a bit of a laugh as she sat down across from him. "I told you when we first met, I love Georgia."

"No, you said you loved peaches. I'm the one who said they came from Georgia."

Zoey rolled her eyes and shook her head. "I clearly had a lot on my mind at the time," she said. "Now stop arguing with me on this and just admit this place is a dump."

"Dump or not, I like it," Katryna said, pulling up a third stool to join them. "Rum flows. Drinking tunes are awful. And I'll bet you each two shillings at least two fights break out before the top of the hour."

Ethan snickered. "I honestly don't know which of the three you're going to enjoy the most."

Katryna flashed a grin back at him. "Me either."

"Well, before any of you get sloshed, shatter ears, or start swinging, what say we take a look at the race and plot our course?" Zoey said, pulling out the map they were given after they'd registered and paid their entry fee.

"Probably a good idea, but I think we can at least get a start on the sloshing," Katryna said, drumming her hands on the table. The woman then stood and stuck a finger in each side of her mouth and blasted a whistle to rival a locomotive, silencing the tavern. "Barmaid! There's no rum here!"

"And there goes not attracting attention," Ethan sighed, rubbing his temples.

"When did I promise not to do that?" she countered. When Ethan didn't react, let alone answer, she jabbed him in the shoulder. "Relax some, Captain. Live a little. It's not good to be so tense."

"Last time I relaxed at a tavern, things did not go well."

"Should've had me around then. Or Zoey, for that matter. I promise it would've been much different."

Zoey cleared her throat, clearly wanting to avoid delving into the topic. "Right. So, I took a peek at the map as we were walking, and I think our course is fairly straightforward if we want to take advantage of our shallow draft."

"I didn't realize we had one."

"Compared to Azrael's ship, the *Griffin,* we absolutely do," she said. "Since he's the reigning champion, any strategy that doesn't focus on defeating him is moot."

"Makes sense. What's he sailing? Nothing too dreadful, I hope."

"It's not too dreadful if you don't mind going up against a sixty-something gun frigate," Zoey said.

"Crap."

"Exactly," she said. "But at least it's not his flagship. That thing's a monster's monster."

Ethan cringed. "Do I even want to know?"

"Beyond knowing it can pulverize a first-rate ship of the line, probably not," Zoey replied. "But back to the race. I think we need to decide upfront whether or not we want to sail to Little Bargadine. That's going to matter on the route we take."

"Little Bargadine?" Katryna repeated. "What in the name of the eleven seas does that place have to do with the race?"

Zoey spun the map so she and Ethan could see it better and dropped her finger on its location. "Little Bargadine is where this year's bonus treasure is," she said. "It's a small island a few hours off course. There's an old abandoned fort there, and inside its chapel is wind in a bottle."

"Like, actual wind?" Ethan said.

"More like a storm, but yes," Zoey went on. "Usually, it's enough to make up for lost time, but sometimes they stuff a little more tempest than usual. No one really knows until they use it."

"So going there might not convey much of an advantage," Ethan said, shrugging. "What's the point? Because I'm assuming there's only one, so if we get there after someone else does, we're screwed."

"You assume correctly," she said. "But as I said, it's considered the bonus treasure, which means, if you cross the finish line with it, or in this case, even just the bottle sans wind, your prize is doubled."

Katryna's eyes lit up. "Oh, I like the sound of that."

"So do I, but it also means we'd have to be winning to have a chance at it," Ethan pointed out. "I can't imagine being far behind and being able to take the time to lay anchor, row ashore, find the damn thing, and whatnot."

"Most likely," Zoey said. "Still, something to keep in mind."

"Right. What about this bit with our shallow draft you mentioned?"

"That's something we can definitely take advantage of," Zoey said as she pointed everything out on the map. "Here, here, and here are all places with miles of reefs we could sail through that he can't. It won't be much, all things considered, but we could gain a couple of hours if we dart through these coastal islands instead of going around them."

Ethan nodded, easily following along. "Sounds easy enough."

"It will be," she said. "That said, our best place to make a sizeable gain will be near the final leg," she went on, tapping the map. "It's the Isadora Strait and amounts to nearly a full day's shortcut on average. Not everyone will be able to use it, but we can."

Ethan whistled and leaned over to get a better view of what she was directing his attention to. Near the finish line, a winding channel separated the mainland from a large island that extended far to the west. While it looked narrow, it didn't look impossible, assuming the map was even remotely drawn to scale. "What's the catch?"

"Catches," she corrected. "First, there are plenty of rocks and sunken ships hiding right below the water. It's a risky run on that alone."

"And second?"

"And second, there's hardly any room to maneuver. That means if anyone follows us in—like someone else who also wants to beat Azrael—we're potentially looking at a brutal knife fight that'll do us both in."

"Sounds exciting," Katryna said, taking both bottles of rum from the barmaid who'd just arrived at their table.

"Sounds desperate," Ethan said. "Are you sure this course would even be legal? It doesn't seem right that we can just make up our own route when it comes to a race."

Zoey poured herself a drink in one of the crude glasses provided and downed half of it in a single shot. "I'm sure," she said. "As long as we take no hostile actions at the start and finish line."

"Where are they?"

"Lighthouses mark the safety zone at the start of the race," she replied. "And there are buoys that mark the safe harbor zones at the finish. Pretty simple and not a lot to remember."

"Other than we still need to cross the finish line first," Katryna added, tipping her own glass at them both before enjoying a drink of her own.

"Yeah, with the ship, I might add," Zoey added. "That means the captain has to personally be touching her with colors raised. Otherwise, it doesn't count."

"I thought that was implied," Katryna said, rolling her eyes.

"Thought I'd mention it before Ethan gets too creative with his planning and suggests we just turn into bats or ravens or something and fly there," she explained. She threw him a gin. "You know how you get sometimes."

Ethan shrugged unapologetically in return. "Never said I don't, but on that note, I think maybe later tonight, you should be my tutor and give me a private lesson. You know, make sure I really know the rules and whatnot."

The tip of Zoey's tongue flicked across her lips, and she toyed with her pendant. "Oh, that has possibilities," she said. "Who knows where that will take us?"

"For the love of all," Katryna said with a groan, lolling her head to the side. "Want me to get you two a room?"

"Here? No," Ethan said, shaking his head. "But I'm ready to ditch this whole tradition thing if you are."

"Would be more fun to start our own tradition," Zoey replied.

With a stir in his groin, Ethan popped off his stool. "No time like the present."

Zoey giggled, and he took her hand and tried to lead her away. He didn't get far. One blind step away from the table had him slamming into something large and unyielding. His face bounced off a short-haired, leathery hide rippling with muscle, and as he stumbled back, a rough hand twice the size of his head grabbed him by the collar. The next thing he knew, he was hoisted into the air and was staring at something with dark, narrowed eyes and a wide set of black horns jutting from its head.

"Jumpy little runt, aren't you?" the minotaur said with an explosive snort. "Do you sail your ship so recklessly?"

In a flash, Katryna leaped to her feet and drew her sword, but before she could swing, Zoey clamped down on her forearm. "Relax, it's fine," the vampire said. She then turned to the minotaur. "Hello, Sedra. Mind letting go of our captain, or are we about to get ugly?"

"I doubt either of you can get anymore wretched than you already are," Sedra replied, grinning and snorting again before swinging Ethan over to his stool and dropping him back in it.

Ethan hit the seat with a thump, and once he did, he got a better look at the creature before him. The minotaur stood nearly eight feet tall with shoulders as wide as a broadside. Long, unruly hair fell from the top of his head, and other than rags cinched around his waist and thick iron bracers around his wrist, he wore nothing. A pistol hung from one hip, and off the other, he sported a heavy war hammer that looked as if it could crack a cannonball with ease.

Not that the minotaur would need it. Ethan was fairly certain that between the ten tons of muscle he had and the rock-solid fists he could make, Sedra could easily shatter bodies with his bare hands alone.

"You two know each other?" Ethan asked, realizing he probably needed to say something.

"She knows the aft of my ship," Sedra said with a chuckle.

Zoey flashed the minotaur a glare. "*Second mate* Sedra Blackhorn," she said, putting extra emphasis on the creature's rank, "likes to think he had something to do with *The Popinjay* knocking my ship out the last time I raced."

"If memory serves, it was our broadside that tore down your mast—a well-timed broadside I ordered," he said with another deep chuckle. "And as long as we're correcting the record, *The Popinjay* is under new command. *My* command."

Zoey huffed with a half snarl. "Your captain and first mate have a little accident? There's no way you bought that ship on your own."

"No," the minotaur said. "What happened to them was very much intentional."

"At least mutiny made you honest."

"Wrong on both," he said before coming up behind Ethan and dropping both of his heavy hands onto his shoulders. "So, Captain Ethan, are you excited about the regatta?"

Ethan craned his head up so he could look at who he was talking to. In kind, Sedra looked down with a smile and a grunt that left Ethan wishing he could give the guy a breath mint or fifty. "I am," he said. "But mind taking your hands off my shoulders?"

Sedra whacked Ethan strongly but playfully on the back. "Relax, captain," he said. "I've been sent by Azrael himself to escort you to an exclusive gathering, and I'm of the opinion that any man who earns that invitation must carry a bit of clout."

Ethan spun on his stool and eyed Sedra warily. "What sort of gathering?"

"A traditional one," Sedra said, tipping his head. "But if you'd like a more specific answer, I'll be glad to oblige. A group of us get together on the eve of the race every year and play Thirty-One and Bone. Azrael would like you to join us. You do know how to play, don't you?"

Ethan looked to Zoey and Katryna for input on what to make of it all, and when both seemed agreeable, he stood with a nod. "I do," he said. "I suppose we'll take you up on the offer. Lead the way."

"Ah, yes. About the whole 'we' business," Sedra said with a heavy air of smugness about him. "But this is a captains-only game. No crew allowed."

"Then forget it," Ethan said, crossing his arms over his chest. "Where I go. She goes. No exceptions."

Sedra grunted and went to speak, but Katryna beat him to the response. She took Zoey by the arm and pulled her to the side. "No, Ethan. Go," she said. "We'll see you back at the ship."

"But—"

"No," she said, cutting him off with force. "You two need practice being apart. It'll do you good."

Ethan still balked, but Zoey sighed heavily with resignation. "Go," she said. "I might not like it, but I think it would be a good idea to meet our opponents."

Ethan's heart sank, but the lonely ache in his chest flew from his mind when Sedra whacked him on the shoulder hard enough that he nearly toppled off the stool.

"Marvelous," he boomed. "Let's go while they're still sharing drinks and laughs instead of daggers and threats. Oh, and before I forget, I hope your purse is full. Our blood is richer than mere pennies."

Chapter XVII
Traditions

When a pair of well-dressed attendants with white cotton wigs opened the heavy double doors, Ethan got his first glimpse of the parlor. He didn't have any words, but he did have a whistle—long and slow.

Oil paintings the size of his first apartment covered fifteen-foot walls made from teak, while several full-length windows offered a majestic view of the bay. Exquisite silk rugs with red and golden fibers accented a hard cherry wood floor, and he had no doubt that the cleaning bill for a single one would likely eat up a month's worth of wages. Three chandeliers made from gold hung from the ceiling, their candles offering warm light to all those below. In one corner sat a grand piano, and at its bench, a young blonde in a sky-blue satin gown let her fingers dance across the ivory keys, providing a soft but upbeat melody.

Wood burned steadily in a fireplace to Ethan's right, while directly ahead, eight men sat around an elongated table filled with bottles, steins, bread, cheeses, a spattering of cards, and a small pile of silver coin loosely gathered in the center. Out of the eight men of varying ages and demeanors, Ethan recognized only one: Azrael.

Death still wore his ensemble of blood-red jacket, black trousers, and ivory-white shirt, but whereas last time they'd been together, he'd been empty-handed, this time, Death held a long, fat, lit cigar in one hand and a fan of five cards in his other. When he saw Ethan standing in the doorway, he set his cards facedown and beckoned him over.

"Ah, there's our newest contender," he said, face beaming. "Come, Master Ethan, and introduce yourself to everyone."

Ethan balked in the middle of the doorway until a nudge from Sedra sent him forward. "Hello?" he said. "I'm Ethan, from North Carolina."

All those at the table gave him an apathetic grunt, mixed with a couple of half-hearted salutes with steins, save one. One man, a thirty-something fellow by Ethan's best guess, dressed in a sleeveless tunic that was all white and trimmed with gold, arched an eyebrow. "North Carolina?" he repeated, his voice sounding like he'd gargled a few pints of acid in his youth for fun. "What place is that?"

"In the US?" Ethan offered. When the entire table, the man included, stared at him blankly, Ethan sighed, realizing not one of them happened to be from back home as Zoey was. "It's out west," he finally said. "Far, far west."

"Past the Dry Tantorgas?"

"Yep."

"And the Western Andies?"

"Yep."

The man snorted and pressed his lips together, seemingly impressed. "That's a long way to sail for one race," he said.

"You don't know the half of it," Ethan said.

"Tell me, Captain Ethan," the man went on, his face hardening and his tone adopting a more confrontational tone. "Are all of these North Carolinians as depraved as you?"

Ethan stiffened. "What?"

"Sailing around with an unholy abomination of a crew?" he went on, his beady eyes narrowing. "A slave to the twelve depths of the Abyss?"

"Sir Gideon, if you'd be so kind as to rein in your crusade," Azrael said, pointing his cigar at the man and chuckling as he did.

"I assure you, Master Ethan is a captain of the highest caliber, a man worthy of not only our respect, but also a seat at this table."

"And I assure you, Captain Azrael, the Golden Templars will not rest until we've purged every blight upon this land with holy fire."

"Tell me, does your little crusade include participating in piracy?" Ethan asked. "I hear you've become quite the robber as of late."

The man leaned back in his chair, amusement dancing in his eyes. "Sounds as if you've heard a tale or two from the sea. Be careful, lad, believing them. Many are lies spun from desperation."

"Maybe," Ethan said. "From what I hear, you sank the *Blind Mako* off Piram three years ago and killed the captain and crew, all because he wouldn't hand over a copper ring. That sounds like piracy to me."

The man leaned forward and playfully pointed a finger at Ethan. "Ah, that story," he said. "Did it come with the sad tale of how that captain was merely trying to deliver grain to a hundred starving children at an orphanage a hundred leagues away? Or is this the one where he was sailing home to reach his beloved wife of twenty years, who was now on her deathbed, and he was desperately trying to see her one last time before the banshee came calling?"

Ethan raised an eyebrow. "Are you saying it never happened?"

"Oh, it happened, alright, but not as you say," Sir Gideon said, settling back in his chair. "I chased that ship for weeks, but they were the pirates, not me, every last one of them. Nothing more than lawless vagabonds, the very dregs of society. Each one of them would've had their necks stretched soon enough had we not found them."

"That's quite a different version," Ethan said.

"Aye, it is because I was there. You'll not find a closer source than me."

Ethan smirked. "Funny. My source was there, too."

"Your source."

"Yes, my source," Ethan repeated. "He was one of the crew you tried to kill—the captain's brother, to be exact."

Sir Gideon clenched his jaw and let loose a growl. "And what sort of person are you, I wonder, to side with such a despicable soul?"

"Shall we discuss this matter outside, then, Sir Gideon?" Azrael asked, cocking his head to the side. "Or would you rather continue with the game and maybe learn a thing or two about the good Master Ethan?"

Ethan didn't know what to make of Azrael's unexpected defense and praise. Was Death setting him up for something? Probably? Almost certainly? But at the same time, Ethan couldn't shake the feeling that what he'd said had been genuine praise and honest defense of Ethan's character. Maybe Death happened to be a good sport after all? Going by Sedra's previous remarks, that certainly could be the case. Ethan's general wary nature, however, kept him on edge.

That said, however, he wasn't about to come across as rude or ungrateful. Something about the room told him that if he committed such a faux pas, he'd pay for it dearly later on. "My thanks, Azrael, for clearing the air about me," he said, putting on the best smile he could while tipping his head and offering a two-fingered, informal salute.

"Think nothing of it, Master Ethan," Azrael replied before motioning to the empty seat at his side. "Have a seat here, if you'd be so kind. I'd like the pleasure of your company."

With Sedra making for the only other empty seat at the table, Ethan obliged the request. The moment he dropped onto the chair's satin cushion, one of six attendants, dressed in a tan coat and breeches, left his station at the wall and came to Ethan's side.

"And what would the gentleman care for?" he asked in the most butler-like voice Ethan could've ever imagined.

"Port?" he said, not sure what was being offered but figuring that was a safe bet.

"Very good, sir."

Right as the servant turned, Ethan caught him by the elbow. "And I'll have one of those, too, if you have one," he said, pointing to Azrael's cigar.

"Very good, sir."

Azrael grinned. "Master Ethan, I was unaware you took pleasure in such things."

"First time for everything," he replied with a shrug. Though Ethan had always been of the mindset that inhaling smoke wasn't the brightest thing in the world, he wanted to fit the part there at the table, or at least, seem a little more seasoned.

"Well, Azrael, are you going to take another card or not?" asked a man with a frazzled grey beard and a scar that ran through his left eye. "I'm sick of listening to yer jibber jabbers."

"I'll lay anchor and see what the fair winds have dealt you, Captain Horal," Azrael said, folding his hands and resting them atop his cards.

For the next couple beats, Ethan did his best to study each man as best he could, looking for anything he might later use as a tell. Azrael looked calmer than a lake of glass, while Captain Horal had a nervous twitch going on with the side of his mouth.

"Twenty-nine," the man said, flipping his hand of four over for all to see.

Azrael's eyes didn't even as much glance at the cards thrown. He calmly took a puff from his cigar and slid his cards across the table, face down. "Then I believe the pot is yours," he said. "Well played."

Captain Horal laughed heartily and scooped up his winnings. "Knew you were bluffing."

Ethan raised an eyebrow when Azrael didn't react in the least to the charge. On the surface, it certainly would've seemed as if Azrael had had a bad hand, but his proficient skill in *gambling* led him to believe that perhaps Azrael had conceded a hand he'd actually won, perhaps setting Captain Horal up for a later sweep.

"I believe that makes it my deal," Sedra said, grabbing the cards in his meaty hands. He shuffled them faster and with more skill than Ethan would've ever thought possible given his fat, sausage-like fingers. Once done, he paused, thumb resting on the top of the deck. "Ante up, gentlemen," he growled. "I'll not deal a single card till I see the pot full."

Coins flew into the center of the table from all the players, hitting the table with a distinct clank. Ethan watched one bounce off the wood and roll, wobble, and then spin a few times before finally settling down. When it did, that's when Ethan realized Sedra wasn't kidding. They didn't play for pennies. Every last one of them had tossed in a full shilling at the start. And if Ethan had done his math right (or rather, Zoey had done hers right when he asked and she'd explained it all), a shilling was worth about sixty bucks, and given the stacks of coin he saw everyone hoarding, he had no doubt they'd be betting crowns—each one worth the equivalent of nearly a thousand dollars—in no time.

A hard pit formed in the center of Ethan's gut. Despite still having some bounty left from the ettin, as well as spoils from Lord Belmont, he wondered how fast the betting would get out of hand for him.

"Is something the matter, Master Ethan?" Azrael said.

"I—" Ethan cut himself short when he realized how much he was sliding back into his old ways. He hadn't gotten this far in the world by being meek. And it wasn't as if he didn't have decent skill and perks when it came to playing cards, not to mention, he did also have one hell of a luck stat.

He could win and win big here. All he needed was a little boost to his initial purse, and the rest would sort itself out. And to get that boost, all he'd need to do was aggressively spend some *Luck* on the first few hands to win the pots.

Ethan faked a cough, put a fist into the center of his chest a couple of times, and shook his head. "I'm fine," he said, coughing once more. "A tickle in my throat is all."

"Then I believe that's a crown you owe for ante," Sedra said evenly.

"That it is," Ethan replied. He coolly reached into his purse and pulled one out, trying not to let on to the fact that he only had a few more. A desperate gambler, he knew, was one easy to take advantage of.

Ethan sent the coin flipping through the air. Once it came to a halt in the middle of the pile, Sedra dealt. As players took cards as they saw fit, Ethan kept his eyes on each one as much as possible. He already knew what he had: a nine, a two, and a five, meaning he'd take two cards at the very least.

On the first round, Sedra sent him a seven, bringing his total to twenty-three. He'd have to take another card the following if he had a prayer to win. That was without question. He didn't want to seem eager, however, or balk too much, for that matter.

Ethan counted to two before tapping the table, indicating he wanted another. As he did, he made a mental note to use a few points of luck to try and land on thirty-one.

Three points of Luck used.
Luck countered!
You feel a little off!

Surprised at Narrator's sudden intrusion, not to mention off-putting news, Ethan straightened and soured his face, purely by accident. Immediately, he tried to cover it by staring at his stein of port.

"Are you ready for your next card, Master Ethan? Or are you ready to hold?"

Ethan turned his attention back to the table to find Sedra staring at him with impatience.

"Yeah, sorry. I'll take another," he said. As Sedra started to deal, Ethan tried his luck again, even more this time.

Three points of Luck used.
Luck countered!
You feel a little off!

The hairs on the back of Ethan's neck rose, and his chest and face felt warm. What in the nine hells was going on? he wondered. He made a mental note to ask Zoey later, as well as comb over the manual once more to see if it might provide some answers. But both of those would have to wait, obviously, and he knew he couldn't spend any more time on it.

Another seven. Ethan sat marvelously at thirty.

"I'll stay," he said, putting a little fidget into his hands to hopefully throw off his opponents.

Sedra nodded and continued around the table. When he was done, only two of the men went over, cursing up a storm as they did. Then came the final bets. Three rounds went in total, each one raising the pot by three shillings. Of the eight players that remained initially, only four were left, including Ethan, by the time the betting was over.

At that point, cards were revealed.

Captain Ord, a withered old man with fiery red hair and a handful of teeth, led the way with twenty-nine. Sir Gideon flipped his over, showing the same, at which point, Ethan showed his hand of thirty. Azrael, the only other player still in, merely nodded and slid his cards, face down to Sedra.

"A masterful run for your first time," Azrael said, puffing on his cigar.

"Thanks," Ethan said, trying not to let his relief show.

The second round, Ethan lost, as he did the third and fourth. Not due to misplaying or misreading, but simply because his cards were awful. By the time the fifth rolled around, he'd at least bet smartly and folded promptly, and thus was still up overall. He won the fifth pot, which ended up being a hefty purse of seven crowns.

Rounds six through eleven, however, all ended in disaster, at which point he realized his purse was far lighter than it had been when he'd first come in. Worse, he'd used several more points of luck, trying to offset his losses, only to be told yet again that his luck had been countered. Now, Ethan sat quietly in his chair, his stomach in knots, mouth dry, and mind reeling at the unshakable feeling that he wasn't able to read anyone in the room.

That changed, however, when a solid deal set him at exactly thirty. Better yet, the pot held a fair amount of coin in it. Not enough to make him think anyone would steal the game, but enough to make him think at least two at the table probably sat at twenty-nine. The only bad thing about all of it was, to match Sir Gideon's raise, Ethan would have to throw in everything he had, aside from three pennies and two farthings.

Ethan toyed with one of his four last crowns. He knew he was going to toss it in. He had to, but he wanted to play the room as best he could. "Okay, I'm in," he finally said, flicking it into the pot.

The clink of metal on metal still rang in Ethan's ears when Captain Horal threw in his coin, too. "Aye. I'll be seeing what everyone has, too."

Sir Gideon drummed his fingers on the table as his eyes studied each one of his opponents. After several uncomfortable moments of silence, he pitched his one crown in and then slid in another five. The moment he did, Ethan's heart sank. Per the rules, if he couldn't call, he'd fold automatically. There were no all-in options.

Sir Gideon flashed Ethan a knowing grin but spoke to the next player in line. "That's an extra five to you, Azrael."

Death took a long puff from his cigar before letting out a billowing cloud of smoke into the air. He watched it for a few seconds as he rolled his cigar between his thumb and forefinger with a look of disappointment in his eyes. "Master Ethan here does not have five crowns extra," he said, nodding at Ethan's small stack of coin without judgment. "He won't be able to call."

"I'm aware of that," Sir Gideon said. "Perhaps he should've brought more to the table or played better if he wanted to stay in."

"Perhaps," Azrael said. "But a poor show, nevertheless."

Nothing more was said between the two, and Death put an extra five crowns in the pot, which then made it Ethan's turn once more. His muscles tensed under stress and anger, and he wanted to launch into a tirade of expletives, maybe even toss his drink, for being cheated out of the pot. Sir Gideon was the only one he was worried might have thirty-one, but now Ethan was convinced he had at most twenty-eight and was trying to buy his way to victory.

Before he did, however, he had a thought. No, a winning strategy, he corrected, pulling his pistol and thumping it on the table. "This, I believe, will be enough to cover five crowns, as well as raising an additional ten."

Captain Horal whistled. Sir Gideon's eyes bulged, and Azrael picked it up for a moment like a curator might with a new find. "This, Master Ethan," Azrael said as he gently returned it to the pot, "is a first-rate pistol crafted by none other than master gunsmith, Victor Caslon. And together with its enchantments for rearming and accuracy against the living, it's worth at least ten times what you say."

Azrael's appraisal sent a sharp stab through Ethan's gut, and he did his best not to show any surprise. "So it is," Ethan said, staring down Sir Gideon. "That's an additional hundred, then, as long as we're keeping things on the up and up."

Sir Gideon returned the stare, never blinking. "Betting limit is fifty crowns. You sure you want to risk that over fifty crowns?"

"I'm sure I want to take your fifty," Ethan countered.

Captain Horal leaned back in his seat, tossing his cards down. "Those waters are too bloody for me," he said. "I fold."

Sir Gideon, still watching Ethan like a hawk, simply pushed a stack of crowns forward. He looked as if he were going to raise again for a brief moment, but after his eyes flicked to Azrael, he held fast.

Death matched the pot without word. Then the cards came out.

Ethan had thirty.

Azrael had thirty.

Sir Gideon sat on thirty-one.

"I hope you race better than you play, Ethan," Sir Gideon said, scooping his winnings. "For your crew's sake, at least. Otherwise, you're liable to get them all killed on the first day."

A kraken-sized headache landed squarely on Ethan's head and crushed his skull. Thanks to it, he didn't pay much attention to what more was said by the man or what was exchanged between others around the table. At some point, after spending several moments rubbing his temples and trying not to be swept into a death spiral of pity and self-doubt, Ethan looked up when Azrael cleared this throat loud enough to grab his attention.

"I believe you still need to ante, Master Ethan," Azrael said, pointing his cigar at the pot.

Ethan slowly nodded his head, though it was simply reflex at this point. He knew he'd been beaten soundly, and at this point, it was only a question of how little did he want to leave the room with. The answer to that was simple. He needed to call it a night.

"I think," he said, gently nudging the port away from its position in front of him. "I'd best retire for the evening."

"Presenting the stern already?" Sir Gideon asked with a smirk.

"You'll have plenty of opportunities to look at my stern when I cross the finish line before you," Ethan replied. "You can bet on that."

Sir Gideon grinned and set his drink to the side. "A side wager, then? Thirty pounds, held by the magistrates."

"One crown," Ethan countered. "I don't care about the money. I just want to see your face when your coin becomes mine."

Sir Gideon's eyes narrowed as he studied Ethan for a few seconds. "A crown it is."

"If that's done, I'd like to deal," Sedra said with a gruff tone. When no one else said a word, cards flew from his hand as each player took his turn.

As they went about, Ethan leaned back in his chair and tried to exhale all the tension he'd been holding in his neck and shoulders. It didn't work. So he tried again, and when that failed as well, he gave up and decided once this hand was done, he'd return to the *Victory*.

With that in mind, Ethan quietly watched as Sir Gideon finished his turn.

Sedra flicked the card off the top of the deck toward the man. It spun across the table and came to a rest a few inches from his drink. The Golden Templar, still looking at his cards, reached for it, almost out of pure reflex. Two of his fingers dropped onto the card back and pulled it toward him, but only a half inch.

"No, I don't want it," he said, looking up from his hand.

"Too late, it's yours," Sedra said, scowling.

The rest of the table looked equally as irked, and even more so when the Golden Templar pressed the issue. "I never looked at it," he said. "And I never put in my two crowns to buy another card."

"You asked for it."

"And I changed my mind," he said. "Stop trying to cheat."

The minotaur jumped from his seat, hand now clenching his hammer. Though Sir Gideon was technically out of reach of the monster, Ethan didn't doubt one bit that Sedra could close the distance and cave the Golden Templar's skull long before the man could pull his weapon. "You're accusing me of cheating?" Sedra roared. His nostrils flared, and he leaned across the table, the muscles in his forearm bulging even more as he tightened his grip on the hammer's shaft. "Say it again, and the next thing that flies is your head from your shoulders."

"Rules are rules," Sir Gideon said evenly. "I never put in. I still have the opportunity to change my mind."

After a few tense seconds, all eyes around the table went to Azrael, who sat there, cigar in mouth, apparently waiting for precisely this moment when he was asked to weigh in. "Rules are rules, Sir Gideon," Azrael replied. "And the rules clearly state the moment you touch the card, it's yours."

"That only applies if I'm challenging the deal," he countered. "Not for a case such as this."

"That is neither the intention nor the spirit of the rule, Sir Gideon. Now take the card and be a sport. Perhaps you'll still win."

"And why should I take to heart your words on the matter?" the Golden Templar asked with a snort. "You're still in the pot. That hardly makes you a neutral arbiter. More like a cheat."

A few of the men gasped. One choked on his port and ended up in a coughing fit. Azrael, however, merely smiled, much like a shark might upon spotting a wounded seal. "I believe you're right, Sir Gideon," he said unexpectantly. "I propose then that our esteemed opponent, Master Ethan, settle the matter at hand. He no longer has a stake in this pot and thus far has shown quite the mastery of the rules tonight."

Ethan jumped, nearly knocking over his own drink in the process. "I'm not—"

"Now, Master Ethan," Azrael said, setting his cards face down. "No need to be modest. You're fully capable of deciding this matter. It's not as if a man's life hangs in the balance."

"Not yet, at least," Sir Gideon tacked on.

A few snickers circled the group, though Azrael, as well as Sedra, didn't share the humor. Ethan drummed his fingers on the table for a few moments trying to weigh what little of the rules he knew in his mind. He obviously had a full grasp on the basics, but when it came to the intricacies of what was essentially tournament play, he felt lost at sea.

Not only lost at sea, but he finally understood what the Greeks meant by being caught between Scylla and Charybdis. Azrael, no doubt, was a dangerous man—being literally Death and all—but Sir Gideon seemed to be no one to trifle with, either. And he had a deep feeling that whoever he ruled against would take it personally. His only hope, he figured, was that if he ruled fairly, the other captains around him might rise to his defense.

So, where did that leave him? The Golden Templar, true to his defense, hadn't technically bought the card, nor had he seen what it was. As such, he certainly made a strong case. However, he did both ask for said card and did touch it. The fact that Sedra might have jumped the gun when dealing a split second before the coin officially hit the pot seemed a technicality of the worst sort.

"I believe," Ethan said, trying to find the most diplomatic way to deliver bad news, "That Sir Gideon did indeed decide on taking an extra card, which is further reinforced by his reaching for it. And while he may not have benefited from seeing the card, he certainly benefited from seeing the rest of the table's reaction. And can one put a price on that knowledge? I'd say that's worth at least the ante."

Sir Gideon soured his face and leveled a glare. "You've come to your decision, then?"

"I have," Ethan said with a short nod. "The card is yours, and you owe the pot."

A pistol appeared in Sir Gideon's hand, one that had been tucked into his belt only a heartbeat ago. Though he had it pointed square at Ethan's face, he didn't fire or even look as if he were about to. That little bit was probably only due to the fact that Azrael now had two pointed right back at him.

"I think this is one storm you'll find unable to weather, my good captain," Azrael said with a smirk. "Lest you want to test what sort of tempest all of us may bring upon ye."

"You'd best pray the wind favors you tomorrow, Master Ethan," the Golden Templar said, tucking his pistol back in his belt. He then pulled a crown from his purse, flicked it in, and scooped up the card on the table that had caused so much trouble. The man sneered with disgust before flopping the rest of his hand on the table for all to see.

Thirty-two.

"Seems the pot is mine," Azrael said, raking it in. Once he had it secured in his purse made of red leather, he patted the bag and stood. "I believe, gentlemen, that'll be the evening for me as well."

The group dispersed at that point, Azrael looking quite content at his haul for the night, and Sir Gideon looking at Ethan like he was going to shank him in an alley on the way back to the docks.

Chapter XVIII
The Deed

"How much did you lose? I didn't quite catch that."

Ethan paused, hands resting on the lid of the small chest near his bed, and glanced at Katryna. The woman was relaxing in one of the two chairs in the room, feet kicked up on the table. She'd taken the spot and a break from searching the cabin as Zoey pressed for details on the card game. She'd only been paying half attention to it all, right up until he'd confessed his losses. At which point, she'd perked and asked the question.

"Twenty-two crowns, four shillings," he repeated.

"And your pistol," Maii tacked on. "Let's not forget that."

"Yes, and my pistol."

"Your magical pistol," Maii said. "Enchanted with who knows how much magic. Able to reload on its own and blast apart dragons with a single shot."

"It can't blast apart a dragon," Ethan said with a heavy sigh.

"How do you know?" Maii asked. "We never tried."

Ethan shot the ahuizotl a glare. "Why do you always insist on antagonizing me?"

"Why does the fox slip into the hen house?" Maii asked, rolling onto his back and letting his feet stick up in the air. "Because it can."

Zoey, who sat on the edge of their bed, frowned. "Jean's not going to be happy about that," she said.

"You should've shanked him in the alley," Katryna said.

Ethan shook his head. "I'm not shanking anyone."

"He's not only anyone," Katryna went on. "He's a self-righteous prick that's caused ungodly amounts of suffering in the wake of a misguided crusade."

"Yes, I've heard," Ethan said. "I'm sure we'll cross paths in the race. We can deal with him there."

Katryna shrugged. "Still would've been easier to deal with him in the alley."

"And what would I have done with the body?"

Katryna shrugged again. "Stuff it in a barrel. Light it on fire. What do I care? Or bring it back here if you like."

Ethan stiffened, certain he'd heard wrong. "Why would I ever bring a body back?"

"Marcus could've had some fun with it, I'm sure," Katryna explained. "And Jean, no doubt, would've loved to see his mortal enemy turned into a mindless zombie."

Before Ethan could answer, Maii rolled onto all fours and sat up with a huff. "As if he'd do that. He never brings back bodies."

"First," Ethan said, holding up a finger. "I'm not a serial killer who brings back trophies. And second, Maii, I feed you plenty."

"But you could feed me more."

"You were like...that big when I first met you," Ethan said, holding his hands about two feet apart. "And now you're like...like...well, look at you. A lot bigger. So hush."

"Look, what's done is done," Zoey cut in as she took to her feet. "Ethan lost, and Sir Gideon is still very much alive. None of that's going to change."

The argument quieted, and Ethan held up a finger to ask something that had been weighing heavily on his mind. "There's one other thing," he said. "I tried to use some luck at the table, and every time, someone or something countered it."

Zoey frowned, and Katryna shared a similar look. "Someone has a new trait," the vampire explained with a sigh. "Or enchantment. There are a few out there. They keep anyone from tapping into luck points, essentially."

"*Even the odds* is the most common," Katryna tacked on. "Midlevel. Could've been any of them."

"Great," Ethan replied with a heavy sigh. "So at least one of our opponents nullifies my primary stat. Lovely."

"Only when they're in range," Katryna went on. "Even fully developed, you're only talking using it within ten yards, five times a day."

Ethan's face soured even more than it already had, and Zoey squeezed his shoulder. "The upside for you is that when active, they can't use luck points either. Regardless, it's nothing we can do anything about right now," she said. "As such, I suggest we continue looking for whatever it is Azrael referenced before the sun rises. That *is* something we can do."

Ethan nodded, and deep down, despite not having any answers as to who was blocking his *Luck* points, he was more than happy to let the matter of the disastrous card game drop. He hated that he'd lost so many crowns, but he really hated losing his weapon. Not only was it a fine pistol, and one he felt could be instrumental in surviving whatever foes the future had in store for him, but he also worried how it might be used against him— perhaps fatally this time. After all, he had been on the receiving end of the pistol when he'd squared off against Lord Belmont, and that was an encounter he'd barely survived.

Ethan pushed those thoughts away and concentrated on searching the room. He popped open the chest he knelt at while others continued inspecting the floorboards, walls, and what modest furniture adorned the room. This was the third time he'd opened the chest, and like all the other times he'd peeked in, there wasn't much to it. Iron hinges squeaked as it opened. The smooth bottom was only an inch thick at the most, as were the walls and lid. As such, there didn't appear to be any sort of hidden compartment, and there didn't appear to be any markings that might offer any sort of clue as to the true nature of the *Victory*.

"Oh, I think I've got something," Zoey said, her voice suddenly energized.

"What?" Ethan said as he shut the lid and looked up. The vampire was kneeling near the head of their bed and ran a finger alongside the bottom panel of the frame.

"There's a puzzle lock here," she explained as she pressed the wood with her forefinger. As she did, a two-inch section of the wood sank into the frame and stopped. For the next several seconds, Zoey kept her focus on the bedframe, occasionally prodding it here and there, but nothing happened.

"What are you looking for?" Ethan asked. "Maybe we can help."

"Anything that moves," she said, gently rubbing her chin. "The craftsmanship on this lock is exquisite. I barely saw the seam for that first part, and that was after missing it a dozen times. Whatever is next isn't going to be obvious."

"Unless that's it over there," Maii tossed in. The ahuizotl ambled to the other end of the bed and used the claws on his tail to pull on the trim. A section slid out a few inches, and Maii shot a smug grin. "Looks like it was obvious after all."

Zoey drew back the corners of her mouth and threw up her hands. "I stand corrected. Let's find the next step, then. We're definitely onto something."

The group quickly came together around the bed and kept working it from every angle they could. The third step finally presented itself a half hour later—a spot underneath the feather-filled mattress. The fourth, fifth, and sixth also took about a half hour to find. The seventh, the final, only required half that time. Ethan found a tiny latch hidden at the midpoint of the headboard. And once he flicked it, a small panel fell open above that, revealing a slender compartment with a single sheet of parchment, bound with a thin satin ribbon.

"Do you think it's a treasure map?" Ethan said, taking the item and hoping it was. Nothing said pirate more than a hidden map to even more hidden treasure.

"No idea," Zoey said. "Open it up, and let's see."

"But don't read out loud," Katryna said. When Ethan shot her a confused look, she quickly explained. "If it's a magic scroll, you might activate it, and I'd rather you not drop a fireball at our feet."

"Ah, good point," he said. Ethan slipped off the ribbon and unrolled the parchment before setting it on the table for everyone to see. It held a rough texture and felt cold to the touch. Across the top of the page sat a graceful ink drawing of a twin-mast ship sailing across the water. Beneath that were six words written in elegant calligraphy, which Ethan read. "Know all men by thefe prefents."

"Those are *s*'s, not *f*'s," Zoey said, sounding amused.

"They are?"

"They are."

"Why the hell didn't they just write them as *s*'s, then?" he asked. "Because they sure as hell look like *f*'s to me."

"That's just how they come sometimes," she explained.

"Well, that's just stupid. What moron came up with that?"

"Asks the captain who said 'thefe prefents,'" Maii teased with a snicker.

Ethan let a little groan slip, and he rolled his eyes before deciding to move on and read the rest:

That the undersigned have settled all debts, fees, and obligations, and shall forthwith have and hold the title of Captain for The Duchess *for the entirety of service to her.*

In witness whereof, the undersigned have hereunto set his Hand and Seal on this day and year.

Beneath that was a list of names, or at least, Ethan assumed they were all names. About a dozen existed, all made in varying inks and handwriting. All had a single line scratched through their middle, including the most recent, which read *Lord William Belmont*. That name was simple enough to read. But as Ethan looked at the ones that came before, the letters became more and more strange, and by the fifth one from the bottom, he couldn't read them at all.

Ethan looked to the others, hoping they'd chime in on who these other mystery captains were. To his shock, all three of them stared at the page with mouths agape.

"What's the deal with *The Duchess*?" he asked. "I take it she has some notoriety?"

"You might say that," Zoey said, shaking her head in disbelief.

"Because...?"

"Because on the darkest of nights, when the waters are still, and the fog is heavy, she sends any ship she comes across to the bottom of the sea," Zoey said. "The men who survive, what few there are, lose their minds. They ramble, incoherently for the most part, but all sing the same mournful song."

"The tattle says just hearing the song will give you nightmares for a week," Katryna tacked on. "Singing it...well, singing it is gambling with your life."

Ethan felt his gut tense, and then again when he asked the natural follow-up question. "How's that?"

"Because they say if you sing even a single note, you invite *The Duchess* to come find you within a fortnight," she explained.

"You're serious?" Ethan asked. He didn't need a reply. He could see the look in everyone's eyes that not only she was, but that Katryna hadn't been more serious about anything else in her life. "Why the hell would you sing it, then?"

Katryna shrugged. "I wouldn't. But it's also supposedly the only way you can get a survivor to talk to you—to find out what happened. It returns their sanity for a minute or two—supposedly."

"Others say if you sing the whole song, you'll be granted a vision of your future," Zoey added. "Not saying I'd be belting out those lyrics any time, but I can see how, if you were desperate, you might."

Ethan drummed his fingers on the table and nervously looked around, half expecting the cabin they were in to twist into some horrific monster. But when it didn't, doubt—or rather, denial—kicked in. "This ship can't be her," he said. "She's the *Victory*. Says so on the little plate on the back. And she's hardly see-through, and we're hardly insane."

"Unless we are," Maii grinned. "Maybe all of this is in our head."

"You'd just love that, wouldn't you?"

"I respect that," he said as if the clarification somehow made all of it better.

Zoey leaned across the table so she could give it a closer read one last time. When she was done, she read it a couple more times out loud and sat back down. "I have no idea whether or not the *Victory* is also *The Duchess*," Zoey said, "but I'm a thousand percent sure that this deed is the real thing. As long as no one signs it, I think we'll be fine."

Ethan wanted to believe that. He really did. And as much as he tried to argue and swim in denial, one inescapable fact loomed.

Ethan frowned, and his shoulders fell. "Except Azrael said what we'd find would be horrifying. Not sure how an unsigned piece of paper will give us nightmares."

"Right," she said with a sigh of resignation. "Forgot about that."

"So, what do you want to do?" Katryna asked. "Abandon ship? Tell the crew? Sail on and hope for the best?"

"We can't abandon ship, and I'd rather not spook the crew—at least, not until we have definitive answers," Ethan said. "The race is tomorrow. I have to win it."

"What do you think happened with Lord Belmont?" Zoey asked.

"What do you mean?"

"I mean, do you think he signed the deed before or after he became a lich?" she asked.

Ethan shrugged. "No idea. Does it matter?"

"It might," Zoey replied. "What if he was normal before he found her? What if *The Duchess* twisted his humanity, so he wanted to be a lich and conquer the world?"

Zoey's questions, poignant as ever, ran rampant in Ethan's mind. Pain suddenly erupted across both sides of his head as a crushing headache took hold of him. "Cripes, that hurts," he said, spending a few seconds rubbing his temples.

"You okay?"

"Yeah, just stress, I'm sure," he said, only half believing his words. "At any rate, I think at the very least we need to consult with Marcus. He is, after all, our resident necromancer and expert in all things dead. Maybe he'll know what to do."

"Worth a try, but this isn't a zombie ship," Zoey said.

"I know. But you guys said *The Duchess* was a ghost ship, so we can only hope," Ethan said. "Maybe we'll get lucky, and he'll do something or other, and this will turn out to be all one big misunderstanding. Should I toss some points into the whatever-lore roll we're about to make?"

Maii took to his feet and stretched. "I'll fetch him, but there's no misunderstanding."

Ethan cocked his head, finding Maii's tone and statement both curious and troubling. "What do you mean?"

"Marcus told me the other night he'd sensed a spirit aboard," he explained. "He's been trying to speak to it for some time now, but to no avail."

"Are you freaking kidding me?" Ethan exclaimed, slamming both palms onto the table and digging his fingers in. "Why didn't you tell me?"

"You were busy," Maii said.

"I was not!"

"The moaning between the two of you and Zoey's top hitting me in the face said otherwise," Maii replied. "Besides, what would I have told you? That your precious new ship might be haunted? I honestly had no idea what we were dealing with, as Marcus had no idea what he was dealing with."

Ethan's lips pressed together into a tight line as he clenched his jaw. "Fine. Whatever," he said. "Go get Marcus."

Ethan, Zoey, and Katryna stayed quiet as the ahuizotl left the room with about as much speed and care as a housecat lazily wandering into the next room to find a sunbeam to lay in. Zoey broke the silence first, but only by a microsecond.

"We're not actually keeping him, are we?" she asked.

Ethan dropped his brow. "Who? Marcus?"

"No, not Marcus. Maii," she said. "He's plotting something, I'm certain, and there's no way in hell that ring still has control of him."

"What do you think?" Ethan asked, turning to Katryna.

"I think your ring is worthless now," she said. "It's even more tarnished and corroded than before."

Ethan held up his hand and inspected the band of metal. The edges had turned green and black, with some spidery veins working their way into the center. "Yeah. Yeah, it is," he said reluctantly. "But even if it lost all its power, we can't just get rid of Maii, can we?"

"I don't see why not," Zoey replied.

"Aren't you the one who said we should keep him to begin with? That having an ahuizotl would be a good thing?"

Zoey nodded. "Yes, but I also figured he'd grow a lot slower so we could be a lot more powerful by the time you lost control," she explained. "If he's scheming against us now, it might not be long before we're just another snack to him."

"All the more reason we can't get rid of him here," Ethan said. When Zoey clearly didn't follow, he explained. "We can't just let him loose in the city. He'll really cause trouble then. Hell, he'd probably eat a couple dozen of the townsmen before just wandering off, bored of how easy it is to kill them all."

Zoey frowned, conceding the point. Before she could say anything, however, Katryna jumped in. "Don't worry about Maii," she said. "I'll keep him in line."

"You sure you can?"

Katryna let out a snicker and playfully rolled her eyes. "I'm quite sure," she said. "And you know what's even more important than that?"

Ethan turned his hands up. "What?"

"Maii knows that, too," she said. "He tried to sneak up on me the other night and failed—badly. He'll behave as long as I'm around, and honestly, I still think it's a good idea to keep him. He could come in handy during the race."

Ethan blew out a tense puff of air and leaned back, folding his arms over his chest. "God, I hope so."

"You hope so, what?"

Ethan spun around at the sound of the ahuizotl's voice to find Maii and Marcus standing just inside the doorway. Ethan hesitated a moment, caught off guard at how both of them had gotten in without him noticing. Maii? Sure. Ethan had no doubt the monster could slip underneath the nose of a starving dragon, slathered in BBQ sauce if he wanted. But Marcus? The minotaur? The way he clomped around, owners of china shops halfway across the globe probably had coronaries every time he moved. So what did that mean? Had Maii done something so they could both slip in without being noticed? And if so, how long had they been standing there, anyway?

Those last couple of thoughts did not sit well with Ethan. But instead of being quiet on the matter, he tackled it head-on. "Does this still work on you?" he asked the ahuizotl as he showed off his ring.

Maii nodded. "Yes."

Ethan narrowed his eyes. "Are you lying to me?"

"No."

"Are you lying to me?"

"*No.*"

Ethan narrowed his eyes even more. "Would you tell me if you were?"

With a slow, deliberate drawing back of his mouth, Maii showed off his razor teeth. "What do you think?" he asked.

"I think you're playing with fire," Ethan said as he leaned forward.

"Ah, you're so much more respectable when you're like this," Maii said. He dropped onto his haunches and used his right forepaw to clean behind his ear as he went on. "Look, Master Ethan, if it makes you feel better, I should probably remind you that you were never going to own me forever. With that in mind, what difference does it make if it's now or later? The important thing is that we all get along in the meantime, yes?"

Katryna's hand fell to the hilt of her sword. "How much effort are you going to make to see that happen?"

Maii eyed the swashbuckler for a few seconds, his ears flattening in the process. "You don't trust me?"

"I have no reason to," Katryna replied. "Furthermore, I know what you are—what your nature is."

Maii nodded. "Indeed." At that point, He turned his attention back to Ethan. "I suppose in the end, you don't have to trust me," he said. "You only have to realize, even if you think I'm quote-unquote, 'evil,' you also have to know I'm not stupid. I'm not about to take on the likes of her, and I'm certainly not about to do that while she's paired with a couple of—"

"Of what?" Zoey interrupted.

Maii cocked his head and threw a quick glance at Marcus before grinning with understanding. "Ah, yes. We're not all friends, are we? Can't let the bat out of the belfry."

Marcus snorted as he stomped his way to the table. "What's he talking about?"

"Lovers," Ethan said, jumping on the first thing that came to mind. "She's not just the first mate."

The minotaur grunted. "And?"

"And that's it," Ethan finished. "Crew from time to time don't like it when the first mate gets...favors."

Marcus waved a meaty hand at them both. "Bah. You humans have such ridiculous hang-ups."

"Good; since that's out of the way, there's something you should know," Ethan said, clapping his hands and leaning forward with his elbows resting on the table. "The ship we're on apparently isn't the *Victory*. It's *The Duchess*."

Marcus tilted his head before his eyes went wide, but instead of abject terror being reflected in them, what shone brightly was something more akin to total mania. "*The Duchess*! Of course! Any other spirit would have yielded to my call, but not her...oh, no. Not this one," he said, chuckling. "*The Duchess* is a tempest no one can tame."

"Perhaps, but what do you make of this?" Ethan said, showing him the deed.

Marcus took the parchment, and once he was finished studying it, he slid it back across the table to Ethan. "I think one of us will be visited by her shortly," Marcus said. "She doesn't reveal this deed until she's fancied herself a new captain."

"Reveal? No, you don't understand. We found it," Ethan said. "The three of us, after Azrael made a few comments back on the docks."

Marcus chuckled darkly. "If that's what you want to believe. So be it."

"How and why we found it doesn't matter," Zoey said. "We really need to know if we're in danger. All of us."

"We're always in danger," Marcus replied. "But from *The Duchess*? I don't think we are, at least, not until someone's accepted her call. What happens after that? I have no idea."

"Right," Ethan said, clapping his hands together. "Then as the first order of business, or last, or whatever, as captain of the *Victory*—and *only* the *Victory*—I am hereby ordering everyone not to accept said call under any circumstances. Okay?"

Everyone agreed without the faintest hints of objection, after which they all left, save for Zoey. Once they were gone, the vampire closed the door and waited for a few beats to ensure no one was returning before asking Ethan one last question on the matter. "What are you going to do with that?"

Ethan looked down at the deed, unsure of the answer himself. "I think it might be best if I keep it on me," he said.

"You don't want to lock it up? Or maybe burn it?"

"Someone could still find it, and I've got a feeling burning it might be the worst of all our options."

Zoey bit on her lower lip, her face awash with anxiety. "Well, I hope you know what you're doing."

"You know I don't," Ethan replied, forcing a smile. "But hey, we've been through worse, right? We'll figure it out."

Chapter XIX
The Duchess

"Ethan...it's time...we...spoke," spoke a slow, raspy voice. The words barely reached his ears, as if hissed by someone using their last breath. And though there was no force behind the words, the ancient power they exuded ripped Ethan from his dreams and sent him rocketing out of bed.

His feet hit an icy floor, and he felt like he hadn't slept for a week. For the next several seconds, he watched his breath hang in the air as his brain tried to wrap itself around what had become of his cabin. Pale-yellow light filled the center of the room, muting all the colors to give it a surreal appearance. Shadows blotted out the corners, while dark tendrils seemed to grow from their depths and retreat a few seconds later in a tidal fashion. Seated on the other side of his table was a ghostly woman, translucent and white. Soulless eyes stared at him, while long, brushed hair fell well past her shoulders, and a teardrop pendant hung from a chain around her neck. A flowing dress with long sleeves and a delicate cape covered her frame with an intricate bodice cinched about her top.

From her lap, she drew a long dagger and motioned with it to the chair opposite her. "Sit."

Ethan didn't. Not even when his brain restarted. He jumped back and fumbled for weapons at his side that weren't there, all the while trying to raise the alarm. "Zoey!" he shouted. "Zoey, wake up."

"Sit," she said once more with an eerie calm.

Ethan still didn't. "Zoey, wake up!" he yelled once more. When she didn't, he dared a look over his shoulder to find that only darkness filled his bed and not a sign of her could be seen anywhere. He raced over, clawed at covers that disintegrated in his hands.

"Ethan, sit," she tried once more.

Ethan spun, backpedaling as he did. His heel struck the corner of the bed, and he nearly toppled but found the wall in time to keep from going over. All the while, the ghost kept her unnerving gaze upon him, sending icy shivers up his spine.

"What did you do with Zoey?" he demanded.

She didn't answer.

Ethan glanced to the door. "Katryna?" he yelled. "Maii? Marcus!"

No one answered, and so Ethan did the only thing he could think of. He ran out as fast as he could. He yanked open the door with such force, it was a small miracle that he didn't rip the handle off the door in the process, and before it was fully open, he'd already barreled through.

Ethan froze two steps into his stride. He stood, dumbfounded, two steps inside his cabin, with his back to the door and the ghost sitting, as it had been, watching him patiently.

"What the actual hell," he stammered.

"Sit, Ethan," she hissed. "Or run...if you like...in the end...you will...sit."

"The hell I will," he said, shaking his head. Again he pivoted. Again ran out the door. Again, he found himself right back where he'd started. His legs weakened, and he dug his fingers into his scalp, trying to ward off whatever insanity had taken hold of his psyche. One last time he went to the door, trying to tell himself this was some sort of nightmare he could break free of if he ran fast enough. But this time, when he flung open the door, he didn't rush headlong through. He simply stood there to see what was on the other side.

She was. Unmoving. Uncaring. Seated at his table inside his shadowy cabin, exactly as she was if he turned back around.

The corner of her mouth drew back, ever so slight. "Sit. Ethan...We have...much...to discuss."

This time, Ethan obeyed. He cautiously drew near, his eyes darting left and right, hoping to find something he could arm himself with. With each step he took, however, the more and more he realized how bare his cabin had become, and none of his belongings could be seen anywhere.

"Who are you?" he finally asked, easing himself into a chair.

"You know...who...I am."

"The Duchess?" he asked, feeling like it was a wild stab in the dark.

She nodded.

"You're...you're the ship?"

She shook her head.

"Then what, a ghost?"

She shook her head once more.

"Poltergeist?" he tried. When that was met with the same response, he rattled off a list of everything he could think of, not really knowing what the differences were between them all, especially in this world, but thinking he'd feel at least somewhat better if he had something specific to work with. "Apparition? Manifestation? Spirit? Specter? Class Five full-roaming vapor?"

The Duchess tilted her head and let a smile slowly form across her face but said nothing.

"Will you at least tell me what you want?"

The ghost nodded. She set her dagger to the side and used one hand to push a parchment across the table he hadn't noticed was there before. "I want...you...to sign."

Ethan took a better look at what she'd sent toward him and quickly realized it was the deed they'd found earlier. Only this time, the letters didn't appear to have been written in ink, but rather they were made from red-hot coals, still burning with deep yellows and oranges.

He didn't know what the consequences of such a thing would be, but he had no doubt whatsoever he wanted nothing to do with it. "I'm *not* signing that."

"I...disagree," she hissed.

"You're going to have to do better than that if you're going to threaten me," he said, tapping into a strength he'd forgotten he had.

"I've tackled baby krakens, ornery ettins, hordes of skeletal minions, as well as the lich who commanded them."

"I...am not...threatening you," she said. "But...I think...out of...everyone...you...I...would like...the...most."

"Out of who? The crew?"

"You...Zoey...Katryna," she listed slowly, "...and...the pet..."

Ethan wrinkled his brow. "The pet? You mean Maii?"

She nodded. "Yes... I've considered...you all...Now...sign..." she added, pointing at the deed.

Ethan glanced at the paper but kept his hands far away, fearing she'd trap him in some sort of Faustian bargain simply for touching it. "No. Find someone else."

"No," she replied. "I want...you."

"Why? What's so special about me?" he asked.

The Duchess leaned forward and gave a most unexpected reply. "Nothing."

Ethan straightened and blinked. "Nothing?"

"Nothing," she repeated.

"Then why do you want me?" he asked, wondering if his INT had dropped back to eight without his knowledge.

"You are...new...and...shapable," she explained. "Those are qualities...I desire."

Ethan cocked his head. "Desire for what?"

Her smile grew, and her eyes darkened three shades blacker than the abyss. "Vengeance."

Ethan's heart skipped a beat at her answer, and he reflexively pulled away from the table.

"You...will be...compensated...well..." she said, nodding slowly. "And...you will...have...a ship...at...your...command...like...no other."

"I don't care," Ethan said, backing away further and shaking his head. "I just want to win this race and go home. I wouldn't be good for you, anyway."

"I've not had...a...vampire...before," she said, tipping her head. "I suspect...you are exactly...what...I need...and want. The solution...to...my eternal...problem."

Ethan scooted his chair back one last time and crossed his arms over his chest. "I'm not signing that, so you might as well leave me alone."

"You are free...to pretend...otherwise," she said. "But you will...sign...Eventually."

"She left after that? Or...?" Zoey asked.

Ethan, who sat slouched in his chair at the table inside his cabin with bloodshot eyes and his arms dangling to his side, rolled his head to his shoulder to look at her. She'd woken up not long ago to find him seated where he was, and since that time, he'd told her everything that had happened with the Duchess. Apparently, she hadn't been paying attention to the details because he'd already answered that question. As frustrating as that was, at least he wasn't trapped in whatever nightmare area he'd been in before. Color had returned, and the choking shadows were gone. Best of all, he discovered he could actually leave the cabin if he so chose and go out on deck.

With that said, however, it would've still been nice if Zoey had been paying attention.

"No," he replied with an irritated groan. "That's what I've been telling you. She hasn't left at all. Ever."

"Ever?" Zoey echoed. She twisted in her chair and looked around. When she turned back to face him, she didn't look afraid or startled or anything else he'd have expected. Only concerned.

"She's right there!" he shouted, throwing both hands toward the far-side corner. "Right there! Standing! Watching! Not saying a damn thing!"

Zoey turned again and looked right at where Ethan pointed. But instead of seeing the Duchess as he did, it was clear Zoey still saw nothing. "Ethan, I don't know what to say."

"Just say you believe me," he said, collapsing forward onto the table. "Why won't you? Why is it so hard to believe she came to me?"

"Because *The Duchess* is a ship. Not a ghost, or banshee, or whatever."

"Well, you're wrong," he said. "And if we had some sort of monster manual I could look her up in, you'd see I'm right."

Zoey gently took his hands in hers and squeezed. "I believe you definitely saw something," she said. He went to correct her, but she tightened her grip and went on. "But maybe you need to consider the fact that the ship is driving you mad. If that's the case, it's not safe for any of us. We should go. Maybe you can renegotiate your contest with Azrael."

"I'm not doing that," he said. "And I'm not crazy. The Duchess came to me. She wants me to sign the deed, and she's apparently not leaving until I do."

"And you can't ignore her."

"Right," Ethan said. "She's everywhere. Wherever I turn. Wherever I go. I can't even close my eyes to get rid of her. She's right there in my mind's eye. Standing. Waiting."

Zoey sighed heavily and looked to Katryna, who stood near the door. "Thoughts?"

"I think he's telling the truth," she said. Her face then soured, and when she spoke again, Ethan wished she hadn't. "That said, he might still go crazy if she keeps hounding him like that. Who knows what will happen at that point?"

Ethan fished in his pocket and pulled out his character sheet. "I'm not crazy, and I can prove it," he said. He unfolded the paper and dropped his finger to where his traits were listed. "See? Doesn't say anything about being crazy."

"No, but it does say something else," Zoey said, tapping the sheet with her index finger. "*Haunted.*"

Ethan snorted. "I've been trying to tell you that for a while now."

"Regardless of whatever your sheet says, I think you should let me hold the deed," Katryna said. When the two of them shot her an inquisitive look, she explained. "Someone has to, other than him, I mean. Might as well be me."

Ethan's hand dropped to the hilt of his blade. "Why?"

"Because you're the one in danger, not us," Katryna said. "And I'm a stronger fighter than Zoey. I'll have a better chance at keeping it safe if someone tries to rob."

"You mean, you'll have a better chance at getting *The Duchess*," Ethan said, staring at the woman. He knew on the surface, she was trying to help, but by the same token, he also knew deep down, she was plotting against him—even if she didn't know it yet. He could see the jealousy in her eyes, hear her covetous nature in her voice.

"Ethan, relax," Zoey said.

"Relax?" he repeated, voice growing sharp. "How can I relax when I've got some ghost girl trying to steal my soul, and she's trying to steal my ship?"

Zoey exchanged a nervous glance with Katryna, and an unspoken conversation was shared between the two in under a second. The vampire then pulled her hands away, and the anxiousness in her face disappeared as her features sharpened and her eyes grew dark and stern. "Ethan, give me the deed," she said.

"No," he said, shaking his head. "I found it. I mean, it's my responsibility."

"I don't care," she said. "Give it to me. Now."

"I told you already. It's mine," he snapped.

Zoey shot out of her chair and slammed both her hands on the table. "Do not mistake my patience for weakness," she yelled. Though the fierceness in her eyes continued to burn brightly, when she went on, she softened the tone in her voice. "Let me help you, Ethan, so neither of us has to hurt you."

With his senses returned, Ethan nodded weakly, and before he could think himself out of the decision, he took the deed out of his pocket and slid it across the table toward her.

"Careful with that," Katryna said, tipping her head at the deed.

"Way ahead of you," Zoey replied. Using a black cloth that she pulled from her pocket, Zoey took the deed and stuffed it in a leather pouch, all the while taking extra care not to directly touch the parchment. "There," she said, exhaling sharply and passing the bag to Katryna. "That's that."

Only, that wasn't that. The Duchess still remained in the corner, and Ethan felt as exhausted as ever. "What now?"

"Now, try and get some rest," Katryna said. "We've still got an hour till sunrise."

Katryna excused herself and left right after. Once she was gone, Zoey led him back to bed and tried to help him relax by stroking the top of his head.

"Better?" she asked after a few minutes.

Ethan nodded. "A little. I'm sorry I snapped at you."

"It's okay," she said. "Is she still there?"

Ethan didn't even have to glance to know the answer to that. "Yeah. She's sitting in my chair now."

"Watching us?"

"Yeah."

Zoey kissed him lightly on the forehead. "Don't worry," she said. "I won't let her get you."

Ethan smiled and sank into her embrace. The impossible happened a moment later. He fell asleep.

Chapter XX
The Race

With a half hour till noon and the start of the race, Ethan stood near the bowsprit of the *Victory*, watching some dolphins play in the distance as a bright-yellow sun warmed his skin. He'd managed to sleep for nearly five hours, which was hardly enough to leave him refreshed, but it was enough to make him functional.

Joining him there was the Duchess, who floated quietly nearby, still invisible to all but him, while the *Victory* lay at anchor in the bay, rocking gently with the water in her position at the starting line, as her colors—a simple gold cross on a white field—flew proudly in the wind. A dozen and a half other ships floated off to either side, some hundred or so yards apart. Most were brigs or sloops of similar size to Ethan's ship, though he did notice a couple of cutters at the far ends. The captains of those small vessels had clearly opted for an as-light-and-fast-as-possible approach, as each one had less crew than Ethan had fingers, and not a one carried a single cannon of any kind.

That, of course, contrasted sharply against Azrael's *Griffin*, which was the reigning champion and had the honor of being a full three hundred yards ahead of all the others at the start. The frigate dwarfed every other ship in the race, and it bristled with nearly thirty cannons on each side. And though Ethan had assumed and even commented that such a ship had to be bogged down by its own weight and therefore incapable of racing, Zoey had assured him, repeatedly, it was not.

"Beautiful, isn't it?"

Ethan turned to see Katryna a few feet away, leaning against the foremast, one foot kicked up and pressed against it. She held a dark bottle in one hand, and a long, thin lit cigar dangled out of her mouth.

"The *Griffin*?" he asked, once he realized he ought to reply.

Katryna laughed and shook her head. "No, I meant the ocean," she said before sighing longingly. "I love looking across it, its horizons promising endless adventure, and the sunrises here are gorgeous. Ones back home have nothing on the ones here. I don't care what the brochures say for the Bahamas or Fiji."

"Never really noticed, to be honest," Ethan admitted.

"You should. It's a great way to start an adventure. Trust me on that," she said, tipping her bottle toward him. She then took a swig and whistled. "Whew. That's good stuff. Like Papa used to make. Want some?"

Ethan eyed the bottle. "Better not," he said reluctantly. "The race is about to start and all."

"I'm not saying get drunk as a skunk, but it might help take the edge off," she said, offering it again. "Especially given your...royalty problem, which I'm assuming you still have."

Ethan sighed heavily, and when he glanced at the Duchess, she flashed him a smile. "I do," he answered. "Why? Dare I hope you've found a solution?"

"I think so, but let me ask you something first," she said, kicking herself off the mast and making a slow approach. "What are your plans after the race, assuming you win? Are you leaving this little world of ours for good? Or are you going to come back and play for more souls?"

"I still have to save Zoey and her kids in ICU," Ethan said. "Which means I'll be here for a little bit longer at the very least."

Katryna nodded and tipped her bottle toward him again. "Exactly, and Azrael will undoubtedly fight ten times harder than he's going to now if he knows you can beat him. Which means you're going to need all the help you can get when that happens."

"I don't doubt that one bit," he said.

"Good, because here's my solution," she said. "After we win the race, you make me like you and sign the deed. Everybody's happy."

Ethan laughed and backed away. "Yeah, no. That's not happening."

Katryna's face hardened. "Why?"

"You know why," Ethan replied. "We can't just bring people into the club whenever we like. There are consequences, consequences I'd like to avoid, and I'm sure you would too."

Katryna's eyes darted to each side as she checked to see who was close enough to be within earshot. The nearest group were several skeletons standing idly about ten feet away, and the closest living crewman was twice that. More than enough to continue on with the conversation, but she still dropped her voice and kept things quiet as she went on. "I know the risks," she said. "Trust me, Zoey has made them quite clear. But I'm thinking once the race is over, instead of waiting around for vampire lords to hunt us down, we go after them with *The Duchess*. Any experience, skills, and loot we pick up on the way can only help with your next challenge with Azrael."

"Whoa, let's back up a few steps," Ethan said, raising his hands. "I might be tired, and I might be haunted, but I'm not stupid. There's no way the three of us are tackling vampire lords. If they're even a tenth as strong as Zoey has alluded to, there's no possible way this will succeed, and there's no way Zoey is going to agree to any of this."

"We can convince her," she said. "I'm certain. You two are a pair of shoes. She listens."

"She's already dead set on not making more of us," he replied. Then a new thought dawned on him. "Why do you want this so badly, anyway?"

"I want to live, Ethan. Here and forever," she said. "Being eternally young will help make that a reality."

"I've got a feeling there are lots of people who want to be turned who are seeking eternal youth," Ethan said. "So, I don't see how that's going to convince her, and it's certainly not going to convince her when you throw eternal servitude into the mix."

"That, my dear Ethan," Katryna said, pointing a figure at him as her eyes lit up, "is where you're wrong—where we're all wrong."

Ethan cocked his head. "How's that? The deed was clear."

"It is," she admitted. "But it says, and I quote, *'That undersigned have settled all debts, fees, and obligations, and shall forthwith have and hold the title of Captain of* The Duchess *for the entirety of service to her.'* And that implies that the service will eventually come to an end."

Ethan turned her point over and over in his head. It was an interesting angle he hadn't thought of before, but it seemed too hopeful, too naïve, to be true. "Let's pretend that you're right on that, that I won't be a slave to her for the rest of time," he said. "There's nothing in that contract that says I won't lose my mind, or not be compelled to commit acts of atrocity, or even be able to protect the three of us from—let alone hunt down—the vampire lords."

"I know," Katryna admitted, much to his surprise. "But I think we can strike a bargain with her."

"I seriously doubt that," Ethan tutted.

"You've never seen me deal. I can be quite persuasive," Katryna said.

"Trust me on this. She wasn't in the bargaining mood," Ethan said. "There were exactly zero negotiations involved. It was just 'sign,' 'sign,' and 'sign' some more."

Katryna took a swig from her bottle and kept her upbeat attitude on the subject. "I know, but that doesn't mean we still can't work something out. Besides, I don't think she's as evil as we've assumed."

Ethan snorted. "Easy for you to say. You're not the one she's driving mad."

"It is easy for me to say, and let me tell you why," she replied. "I could take the *Victory* from you if I wanted."

"No—"

"Yes."

"No."

"*Yes,* Ethan," she said, laughing. "It wouldn't be hard. I'd kill you faster than I'd out you, and with the crew seeing me as their savior, they'd sail under my command in an instant and without complaint."

Ethan grumbled to himself, wanting to argue. But he didn't. He knew she was right. He'd seen how effortlessly she cut through the corsairs, how lackadaisical she was around Maii, and how much of a wide berth the ahuizotl gave her. Even back in his eight INT days, he'd have known how completely outmatched he'd be squaring off against her.

"Or maybe she's a tortured soul," Katryna said. She held up a quick finger, bidding Ethan to let her continue when he opened his mouth to cut in. "Think about it. If I could take this ship from you anytime I want, but don't, doesn't that tell you I'm not a cutthroat? That I'm *not* looking to rob you? That I *want* to help you?"

Ethan nodded. "Okay, that's probably a reasonable conclusion."

"So, if she's as dangerous as all the tattle—and I have every reason to think she is—and she's *not* forcing you into service, I think we can conclude she's not evil."

Katryna had a point. Ethan hated to admit it because if she happened to be wrong, the consequences of going down this path were terrifying—and those were only the ones he could come up with. He thought about it for several moments, but then he noticed that the Duchess had come closer to the two of them. Furthermore, she stood taller and more expectant.

"Captain…" she whispered. "If…it is…vampires you wish…to hunt…I…will be…more than…happy…to assist…in that…regard."

Ethan felt his jaw drop, and for a brief second, he stood there, dumbfounded, as Katryna looked at him with confusion. Before he could offer an explanation or she could inquire about one, the heavy toll of the giant shoreline bells carried across the water, signaling the arrival of noon in fifteen minutes.

"I'll fill you in shortly," Ethan said, jumping into gear. He spun around to set his crew into motion, but the deck had already become awash with a flurry of activity. Men and skeletons alike scrambled up ladders and took positions at their cannons or readied to weigh anchor.

Zoey ran up to his side and rubbed her hands together. "We're ready as we'll ever be. If you want to make a speech, now would be the time."

"I wouldn't even know what to say," Ethan admitted, forcing himself to shift gears, and then again when he realized the spirit had disappeared.

"Be the captain," she said, giving him a nudge. "And be yourself. But be the captain, first and foremost."

"I don't think the adorkably sweet, slightly naïve hero is going to go over well with them."

"It won't," she said. "Save the adorkably sweet for me. Let them have the hero part. Definitely lose the naivety." When he balked, she gave him a quick squeeze of the shoulder. "Go on. They're watching. They might not look like it, but they are."

Ethan balked, and Katryna took a few steps, so she came to his other side. When she got there, she stuck a pair of fingers into her mouth and whistled sharp enough to grab everyone's attention. "Stand fast," she bellowed. "Captain's got something he'd like to say, and if anyone makes him repeat himself, I'll flay the skin off your back myself."

With that, Katryna moved aside with a sweeping bow. Ethan immediately dropped into character as best he could, stepping forward and catching a wink from the swashbuckler.

"Though we've only sailed together for a short while, already I'm convinced there's not a fiercer, more capable crew to be found anywhere," he said. "You've stormed a fortress in a single night. Avenged those at Lenada, and now, wait for the start of the Grand Regatta."

Ethan paused for a second and scanned the men before him. The skeletons were expressionless, but the men, despite their attempts to show otherwise, were not. Anxiousness and fear hid behind the surface of their stoic faces. He could see the twitches of nervous hands, the widened pupils. He could hear their hearts beating faster than they should. He didn't know what to do with that other than acknowledge it. It seemed to work in the movies, at least. So he started with the only speech he could think of and recall at the same time, tweaking as needed and hoping for the best.

"And looking out at all of you, I see in your eyes the same fear that would take the heart of me! A day may come when the courage of this crew fails, when we forsake our love of the sea and break our oaths. But it is not this day. This day we sail! This day we race! By all that you hold dear, I promise you we shall win, and years from now, the entire world will know that you were the ones to steal the crown of victory from none other than Azrael himself! Your names shall be sung in taverns till the stars burn out, and your story here will be told for a thousand generations. So man your stations, and let's show them all how a true crew sails the ocean blue!"

A mighty cheer erupted, and as they went back to work, Zoey nudged Ethan with her elbow. "Nice job," she said. "Hope Aragorn doesn't mind that you ripped him off, though."

"I think he'd understand," Ethan said, shrugging. "Besides, I did put my own spin on it."

"That you did."

The heavy toll of bells started again, interrupting what was left of the conversation. They rang twelve times in all. On the last toll, a dozen massive shore batteries fired in unison, and the race began.

Chapter XXI
Initial Exchanges

"Weigh anchor!" Ethan yelled. "The game is afoot!"

"The game is afoot?"

Ethan twisted in place to see Maii sitting on his haunches, using a front paw to wash behind his ears, all the while looking rather amused. "Yes, afoot," Ethan said. "It means to begin."

"I know what it means," he said. "I'm impressed you do, is all."

"I have eleven INT, you know," Ethan said.

"I've noticed," the ahuizotl replied.

Ethan disengaged from the monster and turned his attention back to his crew. "Jean, unfurl the sails and keep a single reef."

The man nodded and started to repeat the order but caught himself looking back at him as if he'd misheard. "Single reef, Captain? There's hardly any wind. We won't make even eight knots at full."

"I'm aware," Ethan replied. "But there's a bloodbath coming. I'd rather pick through the wreckage than supply it."

The man glanced at all the other ships Ethan gestured to and nodded in understanding, after which he relayed the orders.

With a snap, the sails took the wind and became as taut as drums. The *Victory* drove forward, sleek and powerful, her bow cutting effortlessly through the water. Even with the single reef on the sails, the ship barely lagged behind the rest. In fact, Ethan noted he was keeping pace with a few others on either side as well.

"She's fast, even when not running her fastest," Ethan said, admiring the way she glided over the water. "I guess I hadn't really appreciated it before."

Zoey took a grip on the railing and looked down the length of the ship. "Trading the cannons for carronades helped a lot."

"See? I knew they were the right choice."

Minutes passed—five, then ten. Ethan tensed as they drew near two small islands, each with a red-and-white lighthouse, as once they passed those, a ship's armament could be used per the regatta's rules. Would be used, he corrected.

Ethan took a spyglass and scanned what lay ahead. Spectators filled the shoreline of both islands, and even more could be seen on the lighthouses as well, each one no doubt eager to see the carnage that was about to take place.

They didn't have to wait long.

Azrael's ship, the *Griffin*, made her northerly run to open waters close to the western island, practically scraping her sides against the coral reefs. The moment she passed by the line that stretched between lighthouses, the *Griffin* turned two points starboard from her course, listing sharply to the side as she came around.

Barely a heartbeat passed when she settled her roll and a single gun near the bow cracked. The shot struck the water ahead of the *Golden Mako*, a large schooner Ethan had taken note of when he'd learned that was Captain Ord's ship. Water leaped into the air some thirty yards from the *Golden Mako's* bow, and before it had a chance to fall back to the sea, the rest of the starboard guns on the *Griffin* roared to life.

"Holy crap," Ethan said, his eyes taking in the devastation. The *Golden Mako's* foremast split halfway up its rise, the severed piece smashing into the deck. The schooner cut a single point to the starboard as well, desperate to bring her own guns to bear and get clear of the *Griffin's*.

Whether or not she would've stood a chance if she'd succeeded, Ethan never found out. Sedra Blackhorn's *The Popinjay*, a sloop-of-war that rumors had was heavily enchanted, entered the fray. Like the *Griffin* had earlier, she swung starboard as well but only needed one point in the wind to bring her portside guns to bear. But whereas the *Griffin* had been a hundred yards away when she attacked, *The Popinjay* had barely two dozen yards separating her from her prey.

Nine guns fired in even sequence, their roars seeming to be three times as loud and more ferocious than any of those on the *Griffin*. Wood disintegrated along the *Golden Mako's* side, and then a quarter of its aft disappeared when an explosion rocked the ship. Immediately, she listed sharply on her side. Flames leaped into the air, along with a huge column of smoke and the cries of panicked men.

"Damn," Ethan said as his jaw dropped. "I mean...damn. That was fast."

"That's the race," Zoey said, her face grim.

"It wasn't even a fair fight," Ethan said.

"Again, that's the race," she said, nodding. She then pointed to the side. "Watch."

Ethan turned right as a similar exchange happened when four more contestants crossed the line, and three pounced on the unlucky ship in the middle, obliterating it with a trio of broadsides. Though the remaining three disengaged with each other shortly thereafter, they didn't do so nearly as cleanly or quickly as Azrael and Sedra had parted ways. Each one took a few shots at the other, damaging sails and cutting a few lines, but not a one caught fire or remotely came close to sinking.

"Captain! We've got sharks looking to make us a meal!" Katryna yelled.

"Sharks?"

The swashbuckler leaned over the edge of the nest, her hand directing his attention to either side of the *Victory* where two ships sailed, each one angling its bow slightly inward, so they slowly closed the distance between themselves and the *Victory*.

"*Fortune* and *Sea Storm* two hundred yards," she called out. "They'll be at half that, I'd wager, once we're out to sea, and they're definitely looking for a fight."

Ethan's face soured, agreeing with her assessment. "Thoughts?" he asked, turning to Zoey.

"If we do nothing, we haven't a prayer, and from the looks of things, we won't outrun them—not without giving them several shots unanswered at our aft. We could drop anchor, let them get by, but we'd be close enough once they cross the line, they might still send volleys our way."

"Looks like we're taking hits one way or another, then," Ethan said. "If that's the case, I think we take our chances slipping by one. Mister Potts! One half point starboard, if you'd be so kind."

The helmsman nodded and turned the wheel. "One half point starboard. Aye, Captain."

"Be ready to make that a full two points in the other direction if need be," Ethan added before issuing his next two orders. "Sails at full! Let her run as fast as she'll go! Carronades! Chain and bars on both sides. If we fire, I want their sails in tatters and their masts fallen!"

"Aye, sails at full, and chains and bars on starboard!" Jean called back.

As his crew worked and prepared the broadside, Ethan turned his attention to the *Fortune,* the pursuing ship they'd turned away from. He'd hoped that she wouldn't give chase, that her captain would rather get distance on the seas than risk damage in a fight. To Ethan's dismay, however, the *Fortune* swung around with the *Victory*, keeping parallel with her line to keep her choked off from an easy escape.

"Hope you have a better plan than simply 'turn,'" Maii said with a large smirk. "But if you don't, let me know. I'll start swimming for shore now."

Ethan ignored the jab as he let his novice-rated mind in tactics go to work. It didn't come up with much other than quickly realizing he was outgunned and outmanned, and he'd never survive a sustained engagement. He likely couldn't even take one of them with him, either, thereby escaping with some sort of threat of mutually assured destruction.

"Any chance you can make us disappear?" Ethan asked.

"Completely? None," Maii said with disappointment. "Still need a few more meals in my belly before I could pull that off."

Ethan's gut tightened. He knew it was a long shot, but still, it was a long shot he really needed to have made. With a grunt, he forced himself to quit dwelling on what couldn't be and instead focus on what he had: a ship, a skeleton crew, and maybe a volley or two of carronade fire at the most before it was all set ablaze.

"Perhaps you should sign that deed," Maii offered. "I imagine the Duchess will send them running in terror in no time."

"No," Ethan said.

"Could be fun."

"For who?"

Maii shrugged. "Me. But you, as well, if you'd stop being so noble and simply play the cards dealt to you."

Ethan groaned, but when an idea jumped to mind, he straightened and changed subjects. "Zoey, any chance they'd fight each other if we were out of the mix?"

The vampire shrugged. "Maybe? Probably? Tensions are high, so who knows? Do you have a giant potion of invisibility on hand I don't know about?"

"No, but we have barrels of tar."

Confusion marred Zoey's face. "For?"

"Burning."

"Are you crazy?" she asked, eyes widening. "You want to set fire to the ship?"

"No, just a barrel."

"Which will quickly become the ship," she said.

"Captain, we're almost to open water, and they're still in pursuit!" Katryna yelled.

Ethan took Zoey's hands in his and squeeze. "Trust me, please," he said. "We're about to get blown to pieces. We've got to be a little unorthodox."

"This is beyond unorthodox," she said, shaking her head and laughing with disbelief. "But I've got nothing better, so make me a believer."

"It will. You'll see," he said, feeling better and better about it all the more he thought about it.

"You four," he then called out as he pointed to a group of skeletons. "I need a barrel of tar brought up from the stores along with one of our oil lamps."

Without a word, the undead crew scurried across the deck, their boney heels clacking loudly against the wood, and disappeared down below. Less than a minute later, which as far as Ethan was concerned was all they could spare, the group reappeared with a hefty wooden barrel.

"Portside and keep it out of view of those chasing us," Ethan said, gesturing off to the side. "And make ready with the oil lamp."

He tried to sound calm and play the part, but as the skeletons obeyed, he realized how dry his mouth felt and how fast his fingers toyed with one another. His eyes darted to the rest of the crew. The dead went on about their duties as they always had, but the living were noticeably distracted as their eyes were all but glued to the unfolding spectacle.

"I really hope you know what you're doing," Zoey said, crouching slightly and letting tension creep into her voice.

"Me too," Ethan quietly admitted. He then raised his hand, keeping only his index finger pointed to the sky. "On my command, Mister Potts, I still want a full two points to the port side."

"On your command," he repeated.

The next half minute crawled to an unbearably slow pace. Ethan's eyes darted from crew to lighthouses a hundred times over, and with each pass, he watched his pursuers as well and second-guessed himself a dozen times.

Then they crossed the line marking the open sea, and time sped practically faster than Ethan could keep up.

"Starboard carronades! Fire at will!" he bellowed.

Gouts of flame along with thunderous billows of smoke erupted from the *Victory*'s side as a half dozen carronades fired. The shockwave from their combined fire put a tremor through the entire ship and thumped heavily against Ethan's chest. Chain and bar from a half dozen blasts ripped the jib and mainsail. They even snapped a few lines, ruined blocks, and tore a chunk from a boom, but it wasn't enough to see the *Sea Storm* crippled.

The smoke had yet to clear when the *Sea Storm* replied in kind. Her cannons, seven in all on that side, shot one at a time to a slow, steady beat, her gun crews no doubt taking the extra second or two to line up their shots. Only two missed their mark completely, one sending plumes of water far aft of where the *Victory* sailed and the other landing short by not even six yards. The rest tore into the *Victory*'s side, sending fragments of wood in all directions and shattering the legs of a skeleton, as well as punching a hole through the ship's hull only a few feet above the waterline.

To the crew's utmost credit and Ethan's utmost relief, no one faltered or panicked. Worms and sponges were rammed down each gun to clear them of leftover wadding and extinguish any remaining embers. As they worked, Ethan prayed his gambit would work. At this point, it had to.

"Light the barrel and sound the alarm, but all hands off the flames!" Ethan yelled.

Immediately, the skeleton holding the oil lamp used it to set the tar inside the barrel alight. Thick, putrid smoke started billowing forth and obscured half the deck in a matter of seconds. His eyes watered and burned, and he reflexively covered his nose and mouth with one hand. A split second later, the ship's bell rang with such a furious tempo that even the denizens of the darkest deep no doubt roused from their slumber.

That said, despite what Ethan felt was a fantastic ruse, his heart sank when he realized the *Fortune* was still in pursuit. The ship kept on the same heading it had always been, and for a moment, Ethan worried her captain wasn't convinced the *Victory* would sink on her own.

"Zoey," Ethan called out, coughing. "They're not buying it. I'm up for suggestions."

"Dump the barrel," she said. "We'll have to—" The vampire cut herself off as her eyes lit with excitement. In a flash, she disappeared into the thick of the smoke, and two breaths later, a skeleton came staggering out, completely ablaze. It ran aftward, leaving a fiery streak for all to see. The moment the *Victory* crossed the bow of the *Sea Storm*, it hit the railing, flipped over, and left a fiery trail as it plunged into the waters below.

Ethan jumped, throwing a clenched fist high in the air as he realized what she was doing. "Three more!" he yelled.

He'd barely gotten the words out when a trio of skeletons dressed in fiery rags bolted across the deck. Like the one before them, they went over the railing.

Ethan staggered under the onslaught of smoke but kept his gaze shifting between the *Sea Storm* and the *Fortune,* the latter of which now had her choice of targets.

"C'mon," Ethan said. "Work. Work. Work. Work."

And it did.

The *Fortune* suddenly opened up with a broadside that ripped through the *Sea Storm* with devastating results. Ethan brought up his spyglass to inspect the damage. Chaos ruled the *Sea Storm's* deck. Men lay strewn about, or portions thereof, and more than one of her cannons had broken free of its carriage or anchors. While a few sailors took to small arms, including two in the masts, and returned fire with muskets, the peppering had little to no effect on the *Fortune* or her crew.

"Tar overboard!" Ethan shouted as he dropped the spyglass.

Within seconds, three more skeletons grabbed the flaming barrel and hoisted it over the railing. The air quickly cleared on the *Victory's* deck, but before it did, Ethan was already grinning from ear to ear.

"Clever, Ethan," Maii said, sounding genuinely impressed. "Mind telling me how you came up with the idea?"

"Card trick 101," he said, chest swelling with pride. "Little misdirection and cultivating a lot of faulty assumption. It just happened to be a card trick with a ship, is all."

"And what do you plan on doing with the two of them now? Leave them be?" Maii asked.

Ethan raised his spyglass, unsure of the answer himself. The *Sea Storm* was still in dire straits, and it didn't look like the *Fortune* had much to worry about. The sensible thing would be to turn two points and get back to the race.

"They did fire on us first," Maii pointed out, cutting into his thoughts. "I suspect, given the opportunity, they'll fire on us again."

"Then we'd best not give them that opportunity," Ethan said before issuing his next set of orders. "Mister Potts. Four points, portside. See us completely turned around."

"Four points, aye, Captain."

"Jean, are the carronades ready on that side?" he asked.

"Ready on your command," he replied.

Ethan glanced at the deck where the gun crews waited eagerly at each carronade, the look of vengeance in their eyes and slow matches burning and ready.

"Aim slow and true," Ethan said. "I want the *Fortune* dead in the water with a single volley."

He gave the order to fire right after, with not even fifty yards separating the two ships. The series fired in slow succession, each gun crew taking a moment extra to ensure their aim was on target. For the most part, they were. Shot after shot tore up the sails and split lines. The last two, however, bar shots from each, took down the *Fortune's* main mast, first about halfway up, and the second knocking out another four-foot section.

The giant piece of timber groaned as it came down, falling heavily toward the bow, nearly toppling the foremast, but managing to rip through the jib sail in the process. The crew of the *Victory* erupted in cheers, leaving Ethan thrilled, especially when Narrator chimed in.

The Victory attacks!
The Sea Storm is moderately damaged!
The Sea Storm is crippled!
Maximum speed reduced!

You feel more experienced.

"Damn right I do," Ethan said, blowing out a sigh of relief.

Zoey came to his side and patted him on the shoulder. "You did well."

"Thanks to you," he said, turning to face her and toying with her hair.

Zoey shrugged. "Eh. Only following your lead."

Ethan stole a kiss, and she stole one back. As they parted and the *Victory* sailed away from the entangled ships, Ethan forced himself to part with her so he could take one last look at them with his spyglass.

The crews from both the *Sea Storm* and the *Fortune* continued to fight each other in the confusion, and Ethan suspected that by the time it was over, either ship would be lucky to still be afloat. A handful of cannon blasts from the *Sea Storm* at point-blank range only reinforced that idea.

Ethan put down the spyglass, convinced the ships were now out of the race. "Katryna!" he called out to her. "How much lead does the *Griffin* have on us?"

The swashbuckler leaned over the crow's nest, one hand shielding her eyes from the sun. "Half a league at most," she said. The ship rocked from an unexpected surge, causing her to fight for balance. "Something else, Captain," she called back as she pointed off to the east. "There's a storm brewing. Judging by its color, it's not one I want to be in."

Ethan's gut tightened, and he turned to Zoey for advice. "Something we should worry about?"

"Not yet," Zoey said. "But if it builds fast, it could cause problems."

Ethan nodded. "We'll keep an eye on it, then. Right now, though, let's go see how many holes we've taken on, and since no one is screaming, I'm going to assume no one is bleeding out."

"If they are, I'll be glad to assist with sending them on their way to the great beyond," Maii said, joining the two as they walked. "It's the least I could do."

Chapter XXII
Talks

With the sun set, the race well underway, and the other contestants well outside of any sort of engagement range, Ethan left the main deck and slipped into his cabin with Katryna in tow. He wasn't quite sure how he would bring up the discussion of turning Katryna with his better half, but he did know it was a conversation they needed to have sooner rather than later. So when she saw them enter, he did what any guy did critically fumbling his conversation roll would do. He started it off with one of the worst choices of words he possibly could.

"We need to talk," he said. "About us."

Zoey, who had shed her belt and her weapons at this point and was leaned back in her chair, feet propped on the table and bottle of rum in hand, turned her head and eyed them both with no small amount of suspicion. "This better not have anything to do with you hooking up with her. Or anyone else, for that matter."

Ethan retreated a half step, his hands coming up defensively. "What? No. Why would you think that?"

"Because you just rolled in here with another girl and gave me the 'We need to talk' line," she said, laughing and shaking her head. The vampire sighed and took a swig from her drink. "You really don't see how awful that is?"

Ethan shrugged. "Maybe? No? I don't know. I thought it was a fairly normal way to start a conversation." He turned to Katryna. "Was it really that bad?"

"No, it wasn't that bad," she said, grinning. "It was much worse."

Ethan's shoulders fell. "Sorry," he said. "Nerves from the race, I guess. It's nothing like that. I promise."

Zoey saluted him with her bottle and sighed with relief. "Good. So sit. Let's talk now that we got the heart attack out of the way."

Ethan motioned for Katryna to take one of the empty chairs, and then he dropped into the other, but he didn't say anything right away. Or even a few seconds later. It was only after Zoey gave him an expectant look and he drummed his hands on the table a few times that he decided being direct was best. "Katryna wants me to turn her," he said. A half beat later, he blurted out the rest. "And I want to."

Zoey froze, the bottle of rum brushing against her lips. After she finally put it down, she ran both sets of fingers through her hair and groaned. "I think I would've liked it better if you'd said you were cheating on me."

"You haven't even heard us out yet," Ethan said.

"I don't *have* to hear you out," she said, her tone growing sharp. "I know what's going to happen. I've seen it firsthand, okay? I've told both of you all of this already, and yet still you insist."

"But—"

"But nothing, Ethan," she said, slapping the table. "You promised me you wouldn't!"

"Hey! I haven't," he shot back. Immediately, he hated how he sounded and how fast this seemed to be spiraling out of control already, and so he managed to hold his tongue for a few seconds while Zoey steamed. And when he continued, he did so with a much more even tone. "I'm not turning her without your blessing, or approval, or whatever it is out here. I promise, but just hear her out this time. Please."

Zoey clasped her hands together and made a steeple out of her index fingers before resting her chin on them. She stayed like that, thoughts churning behind those dark eyes, and didn't share a single one. "Fine," she said before turning to face Katryna. "But if you don't have something new to say, you might as well leave now.

I don't want to relive how we spent the tail end of our time together from before."

"Look, I might have been…a little overzealous in asking before," Katryna admitted.

Zoey arched her eyebrows. "Might have?"

"I was. I was," Katryna said with a resigned sigh. "You know I'm terrible at apologies, so, I'm sorry. But this is more than all of that."

"How so?"

"The short, short version is, you two have to beat Azrael not once, but twice," she said. "First time for Ethan, and then again for yourself and the kids in the hospital. You might luck out now, but there's no way you'll surprise Azrael on a rematch."

"And what, you becoming one of us is going to tip the balance in our favor? Is that it?" Zoey guessed.

Katryna shook her head. "No. Well, it'll help. But the other part is Ethan becomes captain for *The Duchess*, and then we'll be unstoppable since not only will we have incredible powers, but a legendary ghost ship as well."

"Until we're caught, tortured for a century or two, and then outright killed when our screams become a bore to the vampire lords," Zoey said, folding her arms over her chest. "You left that part out along with the whole being slave to a ghost ship."

"I didn't forget," Katryna said. "We're going to hunt them down first."

Zoey burst out laughing. "We hunt them down? That's your grand plan?"

Katryna nodded. Ethan did, too, when Zoey looked to him. "The Duchess said she'd love to help, actually. Or is it *The Duchess* the one who talks? I'm still confused if the ghost is the ship or the ship is the ghost."

"It doesn't matter because either way, she'll say whatever she needs to get you to sign!" Zoey said, throwing her hands up.

"I know. I thought that at first, too."

"But?"

"But Katryna convinced me she's probably not evil and might just be misunderstood."

Zoey groaned and shook her head. "I'm not risking our lives, sanity, and souls on might." The vampire drew in a long, deep breath and exhaled slowly before looking at them both directly in the eyes. "I can't believe you two are running with this plan. It's barely been a day since we all agreed that Ethan signing that deed was the worst course of action we could take."

"I know, but I've had time to think about it more," Katryna said.

"And since then, the Duchess did speak to me again," Ethan added. "She wasn't as scary as she was before."

"And where's she now?" Zoey asked, looking around.

Ethan shrugged. "I don't know. She disappeared at the start of the race."

"Well, that's convenient," Zoey said with a snort.

"How's that?"

"Because now she doesn't have to answer any questions I might have you ask her," she replied. Zoey drummed her fingers on the table and let out an exasperated sigh. "Did it ever occur to the two of you that maybe—just maybe—that your sudden reversal on signing that deed has zero to do with having a good idea and everything to do with this ship manipulating you?"

"No, but that's not it," Ethan said, shaking his head.

Zoey shot him a deadpan look. "How do you know?"

"I just do," he said.

"Well, Mister I'm-going-to-channel-Aragorn, do you think those that picked up the one ring thought they were being manipulated?" she asked.

The cabin door flung open right as she finished her question, and Marcus came barging in. His eyes held a wild look to them, and his meaty hands gripped his staff so tightly that his arms bulged to such a degree, Ethan had no idea how the minotaur hadn't already pulverized the staff with grip strength alone.

"Did she agree?" he bellowed with unbridled enthusiasm. "I can't wait to get started!"

Zoey shot him an incredulous look. "No, I didn't agree! Why the hell would I agree?"

"Why? Why not?" he retorted. "How could you pass up communing with such a powerful spirit on a daily basis? Why wouldn't you leap at the chance to sail on the most legendary ghost ship to sail the eleven seas? On what realm of existence would you not infuse your soul with every ounce of power she'd grant you?"

"Oh, I don't know," Zoey said, overly exaggerating her shrug. "Maybe because you don't want to lose your sanity in the process? And that's not even getting into the whole sending innocent men and women to a watery grave."

Marcus shooed a hand at him. "Bah! You'd be mad not to! Think of the knowledge you'd gain! The abilities she'd grant! The places you could go!" The minotaur stopped his rant for a half second as he straightened, a new thought dawning on him. "Perhaps, Captain, in exchange for your service, she'd be agreeable to imbuing our skeletons with her power? Or granting a boon or two to your favorite necromancer? What ship, then, could ever stand up to us?"

"I don't know," Ethan replied. "Maybe."

"Ask her!"

"I can't. She's not here."

"Find her, then!"

Ethan shook his head. "I don't think it works that way. She appears when she wants to."

Marcus nodded thoughtfully and rubbed his chin. "I wonder if we need a sacrifice to summon her. Or maybe she wants a fresh body to possess? I'm sure we could use a prisoner from our next engagement."

"And on that note, we're done," Zoey said.

"Wonderful!" the minotaur said, ramming the bottom of the staff onto the floor. "I'm eager to see the Captain's transformation."

"No, I mean, over my dead body is the captain signing that deed, and you two," she said, circling her finger around Katryna and Marcus, "are leaving. This conversation is over."

An awkward moment settled in the room, but thankfully, when Ethan agreed, Katryna did as told, excusing herself and leading Marcus out.

"I won't turn her," Ethan said after he'd waited for a few beats once they'd left.

"But you still want to," Zoey said, sighing and then taking a drink from her bottle.

"I do," he admitted. "I think we could pull it off, and she's not wrong about needing more for Azrael after the race, either."

"I know. But you two honestly have no idea how strong these lords are," she said. "They've lived for thousands of years, faced down armies and empires. We wouldn't stand a chance. I don't care what *The Duchess* says she can do. I don't trust her, and I don't think we'll get to simply sail around the world in some sort of OP ship, doing as we please. We'll figure something else out for Azrael."

Ethan nodded slowly. He'd known this was a long shot, and truthfully, part of him wasn't as optimistic about the plan as Katryna was. So it was a relief in that regard that Zoey stayed the course. "I know we will," he said. "Thanks for listening, though."

Zoey smiled. "No, thank you for listening."

"I wonder what Marcus is going to do now you've popped his dream."

"*We* popped his dream," she corrected. "And honestly, I don't care."

"Does this count as our first fight?" Ethan asked. "As a couple, I mean."

Zoey shrugged. "Wasn't much of one. So, no?"

Ethan darted his eyes over to the bed. "I was kind of hoping it was."

"You were, were you?" she asked, grinning.

Ethan nodded.

"Think we need to make up?"

Ethan nodded again. "The thought had crossed my mind."

"Then yes," she replied, setting the bottle on the table and folding her hands in her lap. "It was the most terrible of fights we've ever had, and I'm quite appalled at your behavior, Master Ethan. I believe consolations are in order."

Chapter XXIII
Little Bargadine

Days came and went. The Duchess, or the ghost or whatever, never returned, which in a strange way both relieved and unnerved Ethan to no end. During that time, he and the crew kept the *Victory* moving swiftly across the waters without incident. Though they'd passed a couple more ships during that time, as well as several foundering wrecks of the defeated after not-so-cordial meetings, they still lagged far behind Azrael, who kept a sizeable lead on all.

Zoey, Jean, and Katryna spent most of the time keeping the crew on task while Marcus continued to hole himself away in the belly of the ship, researching and experimenting on the gods knew what. The minotaur said he was trying to come up with a way to create stronger, more resilient minions, but thus far, he hadn't found much success. At the very least, no one turned into a skeletal hamster, which Zoey pointed out was always nice.

Ethan, on the other hand, kept busy by putting his *Master Rigging* to use, constantly having the sails trimmed, lines adjusted, and courses shifted ever so slight, thereby tapping into the extra ten percent speed his skills promised.

Late morning on the sixth day, right after Ethan had reefed the sails again due to strong winds, Zoey walked up to him as he stood near the bowsprit. "Those clouds are building faster than I'd like," she said. "Any thoughts on what we're going to do about it?"

Ethan grunted as he folded his arms over his chest and tapped out some nervous energy with his foot. He'd been watching the storm continue to build behind them since the start of the race, and up until that moment, he'd talked himself into believing the thunderheads only *looked* like they were ten miles high and the immense wall the entire system formed only *seemed* menacing.

"I've taken in half the sails already," Ethan said. "I'm afraid if we play it any safer, Azrael will get too far ahead. He's setting the pace at this point."

"No, the storm is what's going to ultimately set the pace, not him," Zoey said. "It's not a question of if it will overtake us, but when. And for anyone who's caught in it in open water, that might be the last day they see alive. She's going to be a monster."

"Going to be?" Ethan asked with a nervous chuckle.

"She looks like a monster now. I'll give you that," she went on. "But mark my words. She's going to be more dreadful than a hangry kraken."

Ethan shuddered at the mental image. His encounter with a baby kraken was more than enough for him to never want to get within a thousand leagues of one again. "Point taken. I'm hoping, then, you've got a suggestion to our hurricane problem."

Zoey nodded and unfolded a cloth map she had tucked away. "I've been looking at our options. Coral Cay is the closest and safest, which is right here. We could be there in three hours, ride the whole thing out without trouble since the harbor's protected."

Ethan nodded but only needed a cursory glance to see the problem with that. "It throws us off course by, what, a quarter day once it's all said and done?"

"It does, and that's why we could look at trying to push for the Garagos Islands," the vampire replied, pointing to another spot. "They're about twenty leagues from here. Farther, but as you can see, we'd only lose two or three hours at the most."

"That assumes we outrun the storm long enough to make it there," Ethan said, finishing the picture on his own.

"I'd give us eighty-twenty odds that we do," she said. "Relatively safe bet."

Ethan tapped his fingers on the railing as he thought about what she'd said. Running for guaranteed safety at Coral Cay would keep them alive, no doubt, but it would likely have them lose the race as well. That left him with sailing for the Garagos Islands...or did it?

"What about making a run to Little Bargadine? We could shelter the *Victory* there and even send out a party to search for that wind in a bottle, right? I mean, if we're laying anchor anyway, we might as well use the time to be productive."

Zoey shrugged while an ill look fell upon her face. "In theory, yes, we could do that," she said. "But there's a lot of water between the Garagos Islands and Little Bargadine."

"I know, but do you think we can make it?"

"Maybe?" she said. "Not sure I'd give us even fifty-fifty on that. Probably closer to forty-sixty against."

Ethan grunted and went back to tapping the railing, but it only took him a few seconds to realize most, if not all, of his strategy had to be built around what the others were doing. With that in mind, he stuck his fingers into his mouth and whistled sharply for Jean.

As fast as a kite, the man peeked over the crow's nest. "Aye, Captain?"

"Can you see what the other ships are doing?" he asked.

Jean held up a hand and whipped out his spyglass. As he looked on, he narrated accordingly. "The *Royal Hawk* is still the next ship in line," he said. "A league and a half out. I think they're following the same bearing as the *Cygnet*."

"Which is headed where?"

"Maybe a point starboard," he answered. "It's hard to tell."

Zoey tapped the map. "They're making a run for the Garagos Islands. No doubt about it."

"Which means we can't afford to go to Coral Cay," Ethan said. "The only real question left then is: do we chance it all for a shot at getting ahead of everyone, or do we try to simply sail with the rest and essentially restart the race once the storm passes?"

"I wish I could say otherwise, but I'm not specced for this decision any more than you are," Zoey replied. "That makes it your call."

"I guess it does," he replied. He then flashed a quick grin. "Don't suppose we could make this a save point and somehow reload if it all goes to hell?"

Zoey laughed. "Hardcore, remember? No saves."

"Yeah, yeah. I know," he said. "But I can still dream." With that, Ethan turned his attention back to the crow's nest once more. "Jean! What of the *Griffin* or *The Popinjay*? Can you see where they are?"

Jean swept the horizon with his spyglass three times, in fact. When he finished, he reported back with a sullen face. "Afraid not, Captain. They're nowhere to be seen. I don't see the *Red Fish*, either."

Ethan grunted. "They're all going for the prize."

"They could still be sailing for the Garagos Islands, you know," Zoey replied.

Ethan shook his head. "They could be, but they aren't. Azrael won't squander this much of an advantage. Neither will Sedra or Sir Gideon. Trust me on that."

"How can you be so sure?"

"I played cards with them. They might have taken me for practically everything in the end, but that didn't stop me from knowing how they all think. And when you're about to claim the pot, the last thing you want to do is even the odds for everyone else."

"Okay," Zoey said, her face hardening with determination. "Let's get to work."

A streak of lightning lit up the aftward sky, followed by a deafening clap of thunder. A dark storm filled the southern horizon, one that looked as angry and vengeful as any elder god, and though Ethan had been trying to convince himself for the last hour that the sea wasn't growing rougher, and that the wind wasn't getting stronger, he couldn't delude himself anymore.

"Jean!" he called out, cupping his hands over his mouth and looking to the crow's nest. "See anything else yet?"

The man popped over the lip of the crow's nest, looking quite at home despite the gale at their backs and the constant roll and pitch of the *Victory*. "Aye, Captain!" he yelled, pointing. "I'm certain that's Little Bargadine at the horizon, and she's got ships at her shore now, too!"

"Whose?"

"Can't tell, Captain. But I count three of them."

Ethan cursed and folded his arms over his chest, only to have to shoot them out a moment later so he could grab a handrail when the boat rocked hard to port. "I wonder how long they've been there," Ethan said, looking to Zoey. "Maybe they haven't sent their landing parties."

The vampire, who'd been checking and rechecking the lines that secured the carronades, frowned. "I wouldn't bet on it," she said. "At the very least, we know they won't be leaving anytime soon. There's no way they'll outrun this storm, even if they weighed anchor right now. I don't care what skills they've picked."

Suddenly, the *Victory* lurched sideways before pitching upward. Zoey staggered, nearly losing her footing. Mister Potts, manning the helm, fiercely wrestled with the wheel to keep the ship on course, and he swore up and down every second he did.

"Holy hell," Zoey said, wrapping an arm around a line to keep her steady. "I'd call that a rogue wave, but I've got a feeling there are going to be a lot more like that coming at us shortly."

Ethan twisted his head over his shoulder. The apocalyptic clouds which had filled the horizon seemed ten times closer than they'd been not even five minutes ago. A massive curtain of rain fell from their bases, while the seas beneath continued to churn more and more violently than before.

"We're not going to have time to anchor and launch properly if this ship is going to make the cove on the other side of the island," Ethan said.

"You're absolutely right on that," Zoey said as her face soured. "We'll have to row in once we've found shelter. It'll be rough, but it beats having the storm smash us to pieces."

Ethan kept his gaze firmly latched on the island, jaw clenching, stomach tightening. He didn't like what she had to say one bit. From what he could remember, the layout of the island meant that if they played it safe, they'd lose at least another hour or two making their way around a small mountain to get to the fort compared to the landing at the southern shore and simply marching north. By then, no doubt someone would have that bottle, and this would be all for naught.

"We've got to go ashore now," he said, making up his mind. "We won't win otherwise."

"We won't be able to win if we break apart, either," Zoey rightly pointed out. "Look, I know sailing around isn't ideal, but maybe fortune will still favor us. Whoever gets to the fort first will have to deal with whatever traps they might have put on the chest."

"There are traps now, too?"

Zoey shrugged. "Maybe. Wouldn't be the first time the game makers have done that to spice things up."

"That figures," Ethan muttered. "What have they cooked up before?"

Zoey bit her lower lip as she gave the question a moment's thought. "Well, last year, it was a petrification blast that turned everyone into statues in a thirty-yard radius if they didn't make their saving throw, and at minus five to boot. Five years prior, a guardian ward had been etched on the pedestal that summoned a thousand giant, starving rats. I wasn't there, but from what I hear, four ships had their entire shore parties skeletonized in minutes."

Ethan shuddered. "I really didn't need that visual."

"Yeah, so while the early bird may get the worm, the second mouse gets the cheese."

Ethan nodded reluctantly, conceding her point. He turned her words over a few times in his head, and while he could see the practicality of playing this safe, he couldn't shake the feeling that if he did, he'd never cross the finish line first. Moreover, if anything, this world had taught him time and again he needed to be bold. Daring.

"I hear what you're saying," he finally said, "but we're not the second mouse at this point. We're the fourth, and unless there are three sets of mouse traps, we get nothing."

"Captain!" came a new call. "If the storm gets worse, our sails will tear apart! We've got to find cover!"

Ethan ran forward, stumbling as he did, until he could see Katryna at the bow. The swashbuckler had her hands full as she worked the lines along with a half dozen skeletons and a few of the crew.

"How much more can she take?" he asked.

"She sure as hell can't take that!" Katryna yelled, pointing to the approaching thunderstorm. "And we don't have much rigging to spare, either."

Ethan frowned, as he couldn't help but feel attacked over the last comment. He had, after all, lost money at the card table, money that could have, and should have, gone to loading the ship with more supplies. That, however, was in the past, he knew. Dwelling on it would change nothing, and he still needed to act.

"Jean!" he yelled. When the man looked back from the crow's nest a second time, he pointed at the island. "How hard are the waves hitting the shore?"

Jean held up a finger before aiming his spyglass. Given how much the sea tossed the ship, Ethan doubted he had even the slightest prayer of seeing a damn thing, but he hoped nevertheless. To his surprise, he yelled the answer he wanted. "They're pummeling the coast like a like a hammer on an anvil, captain!"

Ethan looked to Zoey and smiled. "Perfect."

"Perfect?"

"Yeah. Perfect," he repeated before giving a sheepish grin. "Well, perfect enough to fake like I know what I'm doing."

Ethan stuck two fingers in his mouth and whistled sharply. Everyone on deck spun to face him. He was only interested in grabbing the attention of two: Katryna and Jean.

"Katryna! I need you with me at the helm!" he yelled before turning his attention upward. "You as well, Mister Bayard!"

The woman nodded and barked some orders at a couple of others before relinquishing her position and running over. At the same time, Jean grabbed ahold of the lines and slid himself down to the deck. Together, they all ran for the quarterdeck, and midway, the *Victory* pitched upward as it caught a wave, nearly sending Ethan careening into a carronade.

"Mister Potts," Ethan said once they were all there. "How close can you skirt us next to the island without running aground?"

"Skirt?" he repeated. "Did I hear that correctly?"

"Yes, Mister Potts. You did."

The man sucked in a deep breath as an apprehensive look splashed across his face. "I could maybe get us a within couple hundred yards. Any closer and we risk the reefs, or worse, the rocks."

"Maybe?" Ethan said. "I was under the impression you knew what you were doing."

"Aye, sir. I do," he said, face hardening.

"Then I want you to get us within two hundred yards of shore, and once we're clear, make for the cove on the leeward side of the island. We'll meet you there after the storm clears."

The man gritted his teeth and forced a smile. "Aye, sir. I'll get you there."

"Mind filling us in what you've got in mind?" Katryna asked, tapping Ethan on the shoulder.

"We're going to surf a lifeboat into the island," he replied.

Katryna's eyes bulged with equal parts shock and excitement. "What? Are you crazy?"

"No, but I am super lucky," he said. "Besides, don't you want to live?"

"Do I ever," she beamed. "But I don't want to wind up pasted against the jetties, either."

"Don't worry. We won't be."

"And by we, who does that include?"

"You. Me. Jean, and Zoey, along with a few skeletons," Ethan said. He then shrugged at Zoey unapologetically. "You've just been volunteered for the away team."

"You put me in a red shirt, and I'm shooting you first."

"My dear, the only thing you can count on me doing is trying to get you out of your shirts," he replied. After she rolled her eyes playfully, Ethan clapped his hands together. "Now, then, this is what we're going to do: Mister Potts will get us as stupidly close to shore as he can. The four of us and some of our boney buddies will climb into a lifeboat and ride the surf in. I figure the waves ought to be plenty strong enough to carry us all the way there in one go."

"Captain, we're going to be lucky to be thrown overboard and land upright, let alone make it to shore," Jean said.

"I've got the luck part under control," Ethan said. "Trust me on this. Besides, we might run into Sir Gideon, and I thought you'd like to be there when we do."

Jean cracked his knuckles. "Oui. I would."

"What of the crew?" asked Zoey, throwing a glance toward them all over her shoulder. "Who are you going to put in charge?"

"Marcus will have command," Ethan said, already having thought of that point. He then called for the minotaur who came out from below deck, and once the monstrous crewmate had joined them all along with a curious Maii, Ethan filled them both in.

"I must say, Captain, I'm not fond of this rash plan of yours," he said as he crossed his arms over his chest. "But you have my word your ship will be in good hands with me."

"Glad to hear it."

"Unless, of course, you don't make it back," he said with a dark chuckle. "Then I suppose it'll be my ship."

"We'll be back. Count on it," Ethan said with finality, pointing a finger at the minotaur. "And for the record, it would become Zoey's ship, and Maii has my full permission to eat anyone and everyone who acts otherwise."

Maii flashed a wicked grin with razor-sharp teeth. "I'll keep them in line. Don't worry about that," he said before licking his chops and straightening. "Perhaps we make an example of someone while we have the time."

Ethan furrowed his brow. "No, Maii. We won't."

"But that one right there threatened you," he said calmly, eyes fixated on a nearby crewmember. "Or will, rather. I'm sure of it. I can smell the fear wafting from his skin."

"I said no."

Maii huffed and settled back down. "Fine. We'll play it by ear then."

The conversation ended at that point, and for the next however many minutes, as they sped toward the island, Ethan tried to visualize his plan coming to fruition over and over again. When he felt they were getting relatively near, he and his party sprang into action.

The group ran across the ship, Ethan proudly managing to keep himself from going overboard through the swells, while Zoey seemed to float across the deck seemingly without a care in the world, no doubt tapping into her well-developed vampiric attributes. When the four of them reached one of two secured lifeboats, they started to untie the lines as others of the crew helped keep the raft in place.

Once it was free, Ethan and his team took to the rails and hoisted themselves over. Ethan, leading the way, faltered halfway when he saw the raging waters beating against the ship's hull. His hesitation, however, lasted less than a second. He knew he couldn't balk if this was going to have any chance of success, and he certainly wouldn't be able to lead his crew anymore if they saw him cower. As such, he steeled his resolve, tightly gripped the rope ladder, and started down.

The moment his feet left the deck, the ship rolled starboard, flinging his legs into the air and over the raging sea. Immediately, Ethan tightened his grip and shot an arm through one of the ladder holes, wrapping that elbow and forearm in the line.

Reflex roll made!
You hang on to the ship!

Ethan groaned and rolled his eyes. "Thanks for the update," he muttered. "I'd forgotten how much I missed hearing you."

Narrator didn't reply, but Ethan tacked one last thing on. "Feel free to not update me on everything else that happens, too."

Zoey and Jean followed a few seconds later, with Katryna coming down last. The foremost two took positions on opposite sides of the ladder and worked their way down. When Katryna joined them all, she looked up from her spot and yelled to those back on deck. "Do you all have both sheets aft? Get that boat in the water!"

Ethan couldn't see what was going on at that point, but he could hear the shouts, the curses, and then what sounded like a tree breaking in half. A thousand nightmare scenarios raced through his mind over the next few seconds as to what the deck was like, pictures of snapped lines, shattered bones, and crushed sailors.

Before his worry got the best of him and guilt and fear took over, the lifeboat appeared at the edge of the railing. It hovered there for a couple of beats, and it looked like it might disappear when the ship listed portside. But then came a triumphant rallying cry of a dozen determined crew. The *Victory* rolled back the way it came, and the lifeboat slid over the edge.

Chapter XXIV
A Wet Landing

The boat nearly capsized when it hit the water. The bow popped back up a moment before it dug into the rise of a swell, which sent it flying toward the stern of the *Victory*. Despite the line attached, Ethan jumped, fearing they were about to lose the small craft completely.

How much luck did he need to make it? Ethan had no idea. But he dumped eight points—because eight, he decided, was a lucky number. As he sailed through the air, time slowed to a crawl. He could feel every drop of the salty spray against his face and hear every voice and gasp from the onlookers at the ship's rail.

He considered using one more point of luck, possibly two, to be sure. After all, saving any for later would be meaningless if he ended up swept away. Before he could commit to the extra points, his feet found the lifeboat, and he slammed into the center bench. Any hope at a graceful landing evaporated right after. His momentum carried him forward, and he barely managed to shield his face from the unyielding floorboards when they rushed up to meet him.

"Oh, damn, that hurts," he groaned, dazed and rolling to the side, due more to the boat's rocking than his own efforts.

The boat listed toward the *Victory* as he tried to find his feet and then back in the other direction right after. Each shift was marked by Zoey and Katryna's landings, respectively. Zoey managed to catch herself before spilling over the edge, but it was only a lightning-quick lunge by Ethan that ended up catching Katryna by the back of her belt, ensuring she didn't go for a swim.

"Thanks," she said, dropping into the seat at the bow.

"Watch yourselves!" Jean yelled. The man launched himself from his position on the ladder and managed to land square in the middle.

Six skeletons rained from above. Four made it into the boat, smacking loudly against its hull and collapsing in a heap. Two missed, and though they hit the water within arm's reach, they were swept away before anyone could grab them.

A wave took the little boat a split second later, raising it up a full six feet before spinning it into the side of the *Victory*. Everyone dropped as low as they could to keep from capsizing.

"Push off the ship!" Zoey yelled, grabbing and tossing oars to everyone. "We've got to get clear of her before she drags us under!"

Instantly, Ethan dug the tip of the oar into the *Victory*'s hull. There he waited for the half second it took for the others to follow suit, at which point he gave a fast count. "On three! One! Two! Three!"

The lifeboat rocked sideways and then rode the crest of another wave clear of the *Victory* as she turned portside, further breaking away from the group.

"Oh, thank God," Zoey said, sighing with relief.

"Told you guys I was lucky," Ethan said, driving his oar into the water and using it to bring the bow of the lifeboat in line with the coast.

"God, what a rush," Katryna said, sinking back in her seat, her face awash with exhilaration. "I could do that a thousand more times."

"You aren't going to be doing anything again if we don't keep at it," Jean chided. "We're still in dire straits."

As if on cue, the boat suddenly twisted starboard and lurched sideways. The four worked feverishly to correct its course and stay upright. They managed to do so, but the lifeboat then spun in another direction and nearly flipped again as it rose on the swell of a wave.

"Oh crap," Ethan said, clenching his oar even tighter than before. His muscles burned like fire, and somewhere in the rapidly unfolding chaos, he caught sight of the other ships in the area. The *Griffin, Redfish,* and *The Popinjay* all had anchors raised as they made for the western peninsula. He doubted any of them had the wind in a bottle yet, but he couldn't be sure. He could only pray this desperate beach landing wouldn't be made in vain.

"Ethan! Paddle hard to port!"

Zoey's cry snapped him back into the moment. Their lifeboat, riding fast on a wave that had to be eight or nine feet tall at this point, hurled them toward a long, naturally formed jetty.

Ethan's eyes bulged as mental images of the rocks tearing his body to pieces smashed forefront into his mind. He dug his oar into the water as hard and as fast as he could and repeated the one mantra that seemed appropriate. "Oh, damn! Oh, damn! Oh, damn!"

Even Katryna's usual zest for life in the midst of chaos faded, replaced by a dread Ethan never wanted to see ever again. "We're not going to make it," she said.

Zoey twisted in her seat and hit Ethan in the shoulder to grab his attention. "If you've got any luck left, now would be a great time to use it," she shouted over the roar of the storm.

In total agreement, Ethan committed it all. Where those points went, he had no idea. Hell, he didn't even know what skill was needed here. Was it a check on something like *rowing*? That was his first guess, and if that was the case, they were massively screwed. He didn't have any skill in that at all, and as he'd quickly learned when he first arrived, checks on untrained skills suffered massive penalties and critical failures the likes of which were nothing shy of spectacularly awful.

Or was he simply making some sort of saving throw? Did this game even have saving throws? Hell if he knew. Again, something that he'd probably have gleaned if he'd spent more time reading the manual. And if he got out of this alive, he resolved to do just that. Assuming it was a saving throw, what was it against? Save versus crush? Drowning? Death?

It didn't matter.

Narrator, the ever uncooperating fellow, didn't chime in with an explanation, either. At least, not until it all came crashing to an end. Literally. The small boat skipped off a set of unseen rocks before a large swell carried them up ten feet into the air and slammed them all into the jetty. The impact split the bow of the longboat, and though the midsection of the craft held together for a few seconds after that—a true testament to the craftsmanship— the violent torque produced by the waves tore the rest of the ship apart as it hammered it a second and third time against the rocks.

Rowing failed!
Ship suffers catastrophic damage!
Ship foundered!

Ethan, along with Zoey, Katryna, Jean, and their skeletal crewmates, flew out into the ocean as Narrator gave the recap. The frigid water ended up being far, far colder than Ethan had expected, and he was surprised at how fast it drained his strength. To make matters worse, Ethan couldn't see where the others ended up, but at the very least, he did have the presence of mind to tuck into a ball and cover his head, something that probably saved his life. The instant he struck the water, both forearms rammed unforgiving rock.

His skin split open, and lightning pain shot through his arms. His ears picked up the faint sound of bones cracking amidst the roar of pounding surf, and the coppery scent of blood filled his nose, even underwater with his breath held.

Rock hits!
You are moderately wounded!

Ethan gritted his teeth and fought the urge to scream. His body tumbled underwater, bouncing off rocks again and again. When he finally resurfaced, it was but for a split second in time. Still, at that moment, he managed to refill his lungs with much-needed air.

Under the surf he went again, tumbling along in the noisy, chaotic dark. His body lifted in the water, only to be slammed from above by a monumental force that he swore pulverized every bone in his body.

Still trapped underwater, his shoulder hit sand, and he rolled across the bottom. The waters suddenly receded, and Ethan found himself face down in coarse, wet sand. He gasped for air right as another wave struck him from behind. Cold, salty spray engulfed him, and as the wave receded, it tried to pull him back into the sea.

Ethan scrambled forward, gritting his teeth and squeezing his eyes shut when he put weight on his arms as he moved.

A set of hands took Ethan from under the shoulders and hoisted him up. "Come," Katryna said. "We've got to get moving before it's too late."

Ethan nodded as he found his footing right as another wave crashed into them. Thankfully, he remained upright. They hadn't made it to the central beaches as planned but rather had been swept much more east to where countless tide pools lay scattered about, and beyond them, towering cliffs they had no hope of climbing. The low grounds were a long way away, and he wasn't sure if they'd make it to them in time before the storm rolled in. Even if they did, Ethan realized they'd still be in grave danger.

Despite that, a greater concern washed over him. "Where's Zoey?"

"I don't know," Katryna said, tugging his arm. "I'm sure she and Jean made it."

"She might need our help," he said, rooting himself in place. His eyes scanned the beach to both sides, desperate to pierce the torrent of rain that fell. Wherever they looked, however, he couldn't see any sign of the vampire.

"Ethan!"

Another wave slammed into the two, one stronger than the previous. Ethan fell forward, striking his palms and elbows against rock. He pushed forward on instinct, splashing through water and fighting against the tow as the waters receded. Katryna scrambled next to him, her face hardened with determination, and within moments, they were running.

Their feet hit the first stretch of sand that belonged to open beach, and at that point, they redoubled their already intense pace. Ethan dared a glance over his shoulder at this point to check the open water. Not a ship could be seen, and the billowing clouds of the storm wall seemed right on top of them, driving the tide higher and higher with every passing heartbeat.

The two passed over a second set of tide pools, at which point there were barely a dozen feet between the rising waters and the sharp cliffs. Near-gale-force winds hammered the pair relentlessly, and the chill they brought sucked the heat right out of Ethan's body.

Another open stretch of beach came, bolstering Ethan's spirits, and they sped across them. But long before they cleared this final stretch to safety, Ethan's feet started to splash water with every stride. First, they sank into water not even an inch deep. That water turned to ankle-deep far quicker than Ethan would have liked.

Wind buffeted his face, and the roar of an approaching wave gave him enough warning so that when the chest-high monster hit, he managed to brace himself not to be taken down by it, and Katryna did the same.

Rain pummeled them from the sides, and between the deluge coming down and the fact that the clouds had blotted out the sun, not a single soul alive had a prayer in hell of seeing anything. Thankfully, Ethan was no longer alive, and the night vision he possessed was more than enough to compensate so that when they reached a narrow break in the cliffs, they didn't miss it. Or rather, he didn't miss it.

"Over here!" he shouted, grabbing the woman by the elbow and tugging her sideways.

"Thank God. I thought we'd never get off this beach."

They darted up a steep rocky incline. The rain made the ascent treacherous, as footing was slick. More than once, each of them went to the ground as their feet slipped, bruising knees, shins, and elbows.

After a few minutes of climbing, and at times clawing, they reached the top, lungs gasping for air that never seemed enough. Ethan flopped to his side before rolling onto his back. Goosebumps raised across his skin, and his body shivered.

Katryna appeared, her body kneeling next to his head, her face hanging over his. She shouted at him, but the storm drowned her words. His eyelids grew heavy, and all Ethan wanted to do was sleep.

Somewhere in his muddled consciousness, he knew he couldn't. But he could rest for a moment to catch his breath and warm up. With that in mind, he let his eyelids close and told himself it would be only for a moment.

Chapter XXV
Feeding

A slap stung Ethan's cheeks.

He jolted awake, eyes wide to find Katryna glaring at him with an open hand poised to strike again.

"Get up," she ordered. "Fall asleep on me again, and I'm leaving you."

Her words simmered in Ethan's muddled thoughts, and he had to spend a few seconds to get his bearing. Slowly, he pieced together his fragmented memory while the brutal storm raged overhead, pummeling his body with a chilling rain and vicious wind. He became acutely aware of the hard dirt and sharp rocks which dug at his back, which sparked images in his mind of them crashing into a jetty not long ago. Or was it a week ago? A year?

Ethan gritted his teeth and shook his head. No, that wasn't right. But when had they come? And why?

Ethan rubbed his temples, which given the numbness in his fingers, ended up being quite the task. A dull pain raced through his arm as he did, and his gaze fixated on the deep gashes he'd suffered on the inside of both arms. The skin had been severely torn, and the wounds in each forearm easily went to the bone as he could see deep into the tissue.

"Oh shit," he mumbled. "That can't be good."

Katryna slipped around him, stuck her hands under his shoulders, and hoisted him into a sitting position. "No, it's not," she said as she kept him steady. "It going to be worse though if we don't get to the fort soon. Now get moving already."

With a great deal of effort on his part and support on hers, Ethan stood on wobbly legs. "I can't feel anything," he said, teeth chattering.

Katryna gripped his sides and rubbed his upper arms as hard and as fast as she could. "Did that help?"

Ethan shook his head again. "No."

"You should be more resilient than this," she said. "Something's wrong."

"What's wrong is I can't feel a thing," he said. No sooner had the words fallen from his lips when a stab ripped through his gut. "Damn it to hell. I wish that were true now."

"What?"

"I feel like I haven't eaten in a week."

"I thought you had a meal," Katryna said as she threw his arm across her shoulders and started to pull him along.

"I skipped breakfast thanks to the storm," he said. "It's been a while."

"How much of a while?"

A splitting headache erupted across the back of his skull, and Ethan cringed as he tried to do the math. "Sixteen hours, maybe?"

"That shouldn't matter too much, unless—" Katryna stopped herself and shook her head. "Let me guess: *fast metabolism?*"

"Yeah."

"Great," she sighed. "That explains your near hypothermia. You've got nothing left to regulate your body temp."

Ethan cursed under his breath before shutting his eyes and taking in a deep breath, hoping it would help him steel his resolve. Instead, he took in the alluring scent of warm, fresh blood, and when he opened his eyes, they instantly fixated on Katryna's neck.

"Katryna?" he managed to eke out, gripping her hand tightly in his.

"Yeah?"

"I'm sorry."

With that, he spun into her and lunged, fangs bared in an attempt to open up her jugular. The swashbuckler moved gracefully with the clumsy attack, spinning around while catching him with an underhook with one arm and hip-tossing him to the ground. Much to Ethan's surprise, she helped him to his feet right after but kept him at a stiff arm's length.

"Please," Ethan said, somewhere between a plead and a growl. "All I need is a bite."

"I know," she said. "But not here. You have to wait till we find shelter."

"I'm not sure I can."

"I'm quite sure you must," she retorted.

Katryna spun him around, and with one hand on his shoulder and the other locked on his opposite wrist, she pushed him forward. Ethan shuffled his feet as best he could. They felt like sandbags had been tied to each one at the ankles, but that was all he could feel. From the thighs down, each leg was numb, which only further slowed him, as finding his footing with each step turned out to be only a couple of shades away from impossible.

Thoughts of hunger soon turned to thoughts of Zoey. By some strange twist, worrying about where she was, hoping and praying she'd made it out of the storm, eased the pain in his gut. That said, it put a new pain in his heart, one that grew worse and worse with every step.

The two pressed on, leaving the cliffs behind but unable to outrun the storm. The howling wind built more and more, assaulting his back and skin with a torrent of rain. Pieces of debris whipped through the air, leaving small bruises across his body for the most part, but at times tearing open exposed skin.

"There, I see something," Katryna said, increasing their pace. "Not much longer now. Promise."

"Thank God," Ethan muttered.

A couple of minutes later, Katryna led him to a single-story brick building that ended up being well shielded from the wind due to a dip in the terrain. As long as the trees remained cooperative and stayed upright, so they didn't crush the structure, Ethan felt they ought to be fine.

He shuffled through the arched entrance and collapsed, his body sprawling out on a moss-covered, stone floor. The room, barely twelve by twelve, not including a small side alcove, smelled like soot for some reason, and other than the two of them, held nothing of note inside. While a lit hearth, an extravagant couch, and a well-mannered butler with drinks and hors d'oeuvres would've been right up Ethan's alley at that point, the sheer fact that they were out of the biting rain was more than enough to raise his spirits.

Sadly, it didn't do much to raise his body temperature.

His teeth chattered away and continued to do so even when he managed to sit up and draw his knees to his chest.

"Your lips are purple," Katryna said, the tone in her voice sounding concerned. The woman knelt at his side, and she took his hand in hers and looked at his wrinkled fingers. "Also, your nailbeds."

"I think that should've hurt," Ethan replied.

"Why?"

He pointed to the inside of a forearm to where one of his gashes was. "Because of those."

"I can see. You're in bad shape," she said, sitting next to him. "But at least you won't get an infection—saltwater and all."

"That's the least of my concerns," he said as his stomach growled. Another pang shot through his side, and he clenched a fist and drove it into the ground.

"Hungry. I know."

Ethan nodded. He wrestled with the insatiable monster within, knowing he was only delaying the inevitable but feeling like he had to at all costs regardless. Enough of his humanity still remained that said it wasn't a particularly nice thing to snack on someone without permission.

"I won't let you suffer, don't worry," she said. "But there are two things you have to agree to first."

Ethan sucked in a breath through clenched teeth. "Anything."

"First, you stop when I say stop," she said. "And I realize that might be a little hard, so if I clock you, don't get mad."

"Okay. I'll try my best," he said. "What's the second?"

"After the race, you turn me."

"I already told you, Zoey—"

"—doesn't have to know," she said.

A beat passed between them, and as much as Ethan knew Zoey would likely be mad about it, he had to eat one way or another. And maybe he could get Zoey to come around to the idea. Or whatever.

It's not like this need wasn't being fulfilled under duress. And that's what he told himself when Katryna offered him her wrist.

In a flash, Ethan lunged forward, mouth salivating, and latched on to her wrist. His fangs hungrily sank into her skin, and the moment the first drop of blood passed his lips, his body relaxed, and he relished the taste—it was something like black cherries and hints of vanilla.

"What in the blessed Lady's name are you doing?"

Ethan opened his eyes with Katryna's wrist firmly clamped in his mouth to find Jean Bayard standing just inside the open doorway with three skeletons at his side, eyes wide with shock, hand gripping the hilt of his blade. Zoey pushed past him a moment later, panicked at first, but when her eyes met Ethan's, she froze in place, and tears of relief fell.

"Ethan, you—"

But that's all she got out. Ethan released his hold on Katryna and practically trampled her to the ground as he bolted to the vampire. He threw his arms around hers, and the momentum he had carried them both into the wall.

Jean threw himself into the mix, and the only reason he didn't stick a blade through Ethan's ribs was because Katryna joined the fray as well. Her hand found his, keeping his sword at bay, but she couldn't stop him from knocking Ethan to the side with his shoulder.

The four of them went down, Ethan striking his shoulder hard against the brick floor. The ensuing tussle lasted only a few seconds before Ethan and Zoey managed to back away while Jean came to his feet, cutlass at the ready, with Katryna standing between them all.

"What are you doing?" Jean yelled at Katryna. "The Captain's lost his mind!"

"Relax. He's fine now."

"Relax? He just tried to eat you!"

"I nibbled her," Ethan corrected as he stood and helped Zoey to her feet. "And she offered it willingly. No harm, no foul." When Zoey shot him a WTF-are-you-doing look, all he could do was shrug. "Would you rather he think we're cannibals?"

Jean inched back, the tip of his blade moving from Ethan to Zoey and back again a half dozen times. "We? What's this 'we' you speak of? What are you two? Demons? Blood mages?"

Katryna sighed heavily as she wrapped her wrist in a linen bandage. "They're vampires," she said. "Maybe not your typical king and queen of undead looking to enslave humanity, but vampires nevertheless."

"Vampires?" he repeated. "But how? I've seen them both in the sun with my own two eyes!"

"Ha!" Ethan said with a jump as he turned to Zoey. "I told you vampires are supposed to turn to ash in daylight!"

"I never said they never do," Zoey said. "I only said most don't around here, but that's not something we go out of our way to correct, either. It makes it much easier to move around if the world thinks it's always fatal."

"Vampires?" Jean repeated as if saying it in disbelief would make it not so. It didn't take him long to realize that wasn't going to happen. He shook his head, and lines of pained betrayal formed in his face as he turned to Katryna. "You knew?"

"Obviously."

"You let them mar your beautiful skin? Defile your soul? How could you?" He paused, gasped, and his jaw dropped as he faced Ethan and Zoey once again. "And the crew! You defiled them as well! Let their blood for your own sick pleasure."

Ethan tutted and folded his arms over his chest. "Says the man knowingly sailing with a necromancer and his undead minions."

"That is different," Jean shot back. "That is skill, craft. This...this is an abomination, and I will not stand for it."

Zoey took a step forward and narrowed her eyes. "Are we going to have a problem, Jean Baynard?"

"We? No," he said. "You? Most certainly. I will protect the lady and my crew with my life if need be."

Katryna groaned and rolled her eyes. "Stop," she said with an exasperating sigh. "I'm no lady."

"I shall not stop," Jean went on. "This is not something anyone should stand for."

Ethan squared himself up with the man, keeping his hands deliberately away from his weapons. He had a feeling he was about to need one hell of a *Leadership* roll, but sadly, he'd already used up his luck, and he wasn't sure if his meager investment in the skill would be enough. Still, he had to try. Maybe his unnaturally high *Charisma* would see him through. "Jean, there are a couple of things you ought to keep in mind before this goes any further, aside from the fact that I have no intentions of harming anyone under my command," he said. "First, we didn't hide who we are to protect ourselves."

Jean snorted. "Is that a fact?"

"It is," Zoey replied, smiling like the devil and giving a curt nod. "We did it to protect you."

Reality drained the color from Jean's face, and then it paled even more when he saw Katryna had no intentions of coming to his defense. To the man's credit, however, he found his backbone a couple of beats later. "And the second?"

"My plans won't change unless you intend to cause problems," Ethan said. "I'm going to get that bottle, get back to the ship, and win the race. And along the way, I'm going to help you get your revenge. So, the real question is: is that something you're still agreeable to, or do you just want to part ways now before we're at each other's throats?"

Chapter XXVI
Truce

"Well?" Ethan prompted. "What's it going to be, Jean? Do you want to sail with us, or shall we leave you to your own devices on this island?"

Despite all that had been said, done, and threatened, Jean still argued. "I don't like any of this."

"No one said you had to like it," Zoey said.

The man hesitated for a few more seconds before finally capitulating. "Fine," he said. "I'll not say a word, provided you do a couple of things for me."

"I don't think you're in any position to negotiate," Ethan said, feeling as if he needed to keep it clear who was in charge.

Jean ignored the remark and went on. "First, the two of you won't feast on me whatsoever," he said. "And second, the same goes for Katryna. As for the rest of the crew, well, I can't object to what I can't see."

Though Ethan was perturbed at the man's insistence, he also realized in the end, keeping him placated would ultimately be for the best. After all, they wouldn't be together for much longer as they neared the end of the race. "Then I guess we have an accord," Ethan said, shaking the man's hand. With the deal sealed, he relaxed and turned his attention to Zoey, embracing her once again.

"You have no idea how worried I was about you. I thought you were dead."

"I am dead," she replied, leaning into him.

"Yeah, well, more dead," he said. "What happened? We hit those rocks, and you disappeared."

"Turned to mist to avoid going under," Zoey replied. Her face soured right after as she went on. "Which ended up being a questionable move on my part. The wind grabbed me, and before I could get a handle on things, it whipped me away. I managed to reform somewhere down the beach, found Jean after that, and then we hiked up here through the storm, picking up our boney crew as we did."

Ethan whistled and arched his eyebrows. "Damn."

"Mm-hm," she said, using two fingers to wipe the bottom of Ethan's lower lip. "It's still pretty rough out there, but I think we can reach the fort, still, before it reaches its worst."

"Then I guess we better hurry," Ethan said. "Know which way to go?"

"Uh, yeah," she replied, grinning and sweeping an open hand off to her side. "It's somewhere over there."

"I figured that part out."

"Well, I didn't spec GPS, so that's the best you're going to get from me," she said.

Ethan laughed. "Right. Guess we better get moving."

After about ten or fifteen minutes of hiking, the group found a well-worn path that seemed to run from the beach to the fort, but it certainly wasn't found with ease. Every step of the way, the wind knocked the group around, and debris tore at their skin and bruised their bodies. Two thoughts constantly ran through Ethan's mind as they went. First, had he and Zoey not been vampires, blessed with unnatural abilities and luck, they both might not have made it half as far as they already had. Second, despite those unholy blessings, they might not make it through the storm alive anyway. How Jean and Katryna managed to stay alive, he had no idea, given the ferocity of the wind.

That last thought grew fivefold when a branch as long as Ethan was tall and as thick as his arm shot by his head and buried itself three feet into a nearby embankment. The only reason it didn't take his head with it as it flew by at Mach seven (or whatever the speed equivalent was in this world) was the fact that Zoey had made a diving tackle and now lay sprawled across him while he had his back pressed into the ground.

"Holy crap, that was close," Ethan said, his head craned up so he could gawk at what had nearly killed him.

"No kidding," she said. "Come on. Get up. I think the fort is nearby."

Katryna, standing a few feet away, shielded her eyes from the rain as a crack of lightning tore through the sky. "It's right up there," she said, pointing. "Few hundred yards at the most. I can see the tops of a wall."

Ethan grabbed the hand Zoey offered and hoisted himself up. "Good," he said. "Let's move."

On they went, and the path both narrowed and rose sharply along the way. With the rain pummeling them seemingly from all sides and gale-force winds racing through, every step felt more precarious than the last. As with the ascent off the beach, slips caused bruises and gashes, but thankfully, they reached the top of the climb in a few minutes.

The fort stood atop a hill and stretched a little over a hundred yards across on all sides. The path they'd come up put them at the southwest tower, fifty yards from the main gate. The stronghold's walls, made from a light, moss-covered limestone filled with shells, stretched some forty feet into the air. Along the tops ran broken battlements with watchtowers at the corners.

"God, I hope somehow we managed to get here first," Ethan said as they hurried for the entrance. "We could use the break."

"Maybe, but it would make for a much livelier adventure if we weren't," Katryna said.

Ethan shot her an incredulous look. "Running through a hurricane isn't enough?"

"I didn't say it wasn't enough," she replied, shaking her head. "I just said it could be even better, which it could."

"Yeah, well, I'm still going to hope that—" Ethan cut himself off as they slipped into the gatehouse and his eyes took in the scene before him. Sprawled across the floor were five bodies. Four lay facedown, clothes stained red, while a fifth had fallen in a corner, propped up with his back against the wall.

"And it got better," Katryna said, drawing her sword and pistol while her face lit up with excitement. She prodded the one in the corner with her weapon before kneeling close and feeling his arm. "Still has a little warmth to him," she said. "He's been dead maybe a half hour at the most. Hard to say, what with the wind and water and all."

"All these men are from two different crews, too," Jean tacked on. Though he'd been keeping his distance since Ethan's brief dining on Katryna, that was no longer the case. The man's concern now clearly focused on who might still be around as opposed to who he was with.

Ethan nodded. Half the men wore clothes with a black and white color scheme, while the others were olive and tan. He spent a few seconds looking at them all, or rather, looking for a specific individual among them. "None of these are the captains," he finally said. "Which means they're still here, I'd wager."

"Along with a third," said Zoey. When all eyes fell on her, she pointed to the wall left of the open gate. There, small chunks of stone had been carved out, and beneath holes, freshly fallen debris could be seen. "Missed shots that came from whoever was out there," she said, pointing toward the center of the courtyard where yet another body could be seen, facedown in the mud.

"Damn," Ethan said, drawing a deep breath and exhaling. "That means Azrael, Sedra, and Sir Gideon are all here, ready and willing to fight."

Katryna eased toward the courtyard for a better view. When she got it, she swore up a storm. "Stick me on a pike and leave me to dry," she said, shaking her head. "It is a slaughter out there."

Ethan trotted to her side, as did the others. Despite hearing her words, he wasn't ready for the sight before him. Nearly fifty men lay slain. "Holy snort," he said. "How many men did each of them bring?"

"More than we did, that's for sure," Zoey said after a long whistle. "We should've brought Marcus. He could've animated us an entire army."

"Guess that means we're going to need to be careful," Ethan replied.

Zoey nodded. "Agreed."

"Any chance Sir Gideon is among the dead?" Jean asked.

Ethan spent a few moments straining to see details through the storm. "I don't think so."

Jean grunted and frowned, toying with the hilt of his blade as he did. "I wonder how many men they all have left."

"As do I," Ethan said. "I'm starting to wonder if maybe we shouldn't be looking for a fight."

"One of them probably has the bottle by now," Katryna said. "I doubt they'll just hand it over."

Ethan nodded. "I'm sure they do. But we have something they don't."

Zoey tilted her head. "Which is?"

"You," he replied. "The greatest vampire rogue to have ever stalked the lands."

"Not sure if I'd call myself the greatest in the land," she said, playfully rolling her eyes. "But thanks."

"Well, on this island, anyway," Ethan said with a shrug.

Zoey lightly clapped her hands and rubbed them together. "Right. I'll scout. You follow a little bit behind. We'll start with investigating the chapel, since that's where it's supposed to be, and go from there."

Ethan bowed, making a broad sweep of the room with his hand. "Lead the way. And watch for traps. I don't want a thousand rats to feast on our bones and all."

"Don't worry. I'll be careful."

Off they went, Zoey taking the lead by a dozen yards and then two. Not even the faintest of sounds could be heard from her footsteps, and more than once, even when Ethan knew he was looking right at her, when she caught the shadows just right, she vanished before his eyes, only to reappear several yards away.

The first room they passed through was one of the guardrooms that flanked the gatehouse. In it stood a few old tables, barely upright, each one all but rotted away. From there, they passed through what had once been a set of sleeping quarters—broken bedframes for straw mattresses pushed against the walls.

A short hall later, they entered the southeastern corner of the fort. Old cannons stood on cracked carriages and platforms and pointed out small ports in the walls. Aside from the guns, like the previous two rooms, there wasn't much to this area, either.

On the trio went, quietly moving through the fort, heading for the chapel which had been built on the second floor on the northern side. At the northeastern corner, they ran up a small spiral staircase, halting for a moment to inspect four more bodies at the base.

"You been spending luck points I don't know about?" Zoey said in a moment of levity.

Ethan cocked his head. "Say again?"

Zoey pointed to the corpses. "Luck points ensuring they kill each other."

"No, but if that's a thing, I'm more than happy to spend all twenty-one to do so once they come back."

"Sadly, as far as I'm aware of, it's not."

Ethan nodded, and after a quick search of the bodies, which yielded nothing of interest, they moved on. The hall they were in ran only a few paces before turning sharply to the right. The area there seemed drier than below, and the stone floors didn't hold near as much mold along the edges. It was certainly nothing to stop them all in their tracks yet again, but what did, however, were the sounds of laughter.

"Azrael?" Ethan mouthed, brow furrowed in confusion.

"I think so," Katryna mouthed back, looking equally perplexed. She then nodded toward the doorway halfway down the hall where soft golden light spilled out into the hall. "Definitely coming from the chapel."

Zoey wrinkled her nose after a quick sniff of the air. "Oh, God. Wet minotaur."

Ethan became aware of the smell a split second later. It was like a moldy, musty footlocker filled with thoroughly soaked gym clothes that hadn't been tended to for months. "Great. Now I'm going to have to hold my breath for the next hour."

"Or four," Jean said.

"You three wait here," Zoey whispered, holding up a finger. "I'll take a look."

With that, the rogue slipped down the hall, gliding over the stone floor as quiet as a shadow with her cutlass held low. When she drew near the doorway, she flattened herself against the wall and cautiously eased forward. Zoey spent the next several moments waiting, listening, waiting some more, and then finally easing forward.

When she finally got an angle to see inside, she froze, not out of alarm, but rather...what *was* it? Ethan couldn't put his finger on the reaction, at least, not before she straightened, relaxed, and waved them over with a resigned look.

"Come on," she called out.

Ethan and the others exchanged confused looks, and after a shrug from each, they advanced. When they caught up with the vampire, Zoey stepped aside and gestured for Ethan to walk through first, which he did, weapon still at the ready, but not before he quietly ordered the skeletons to stay outside. Having a little extra insurance in the form of a surprise, he figured, wouldn't hurt.

Two steps into the chapel, Ethan halted. The room itself was a modest ten by twenty feet with a barrel ceiling and a small chancel. A single lit brazier stood in the middle of the room. Seated casually around it were the captains of the *Griffin, The Popinjay,* and the *Red Fish,* along with a few crew members from the ships, each man dressed in soaked clothes topped with blood and dirt and further accented with rip and tear. Despite their haggard appearance, they all wore smiles upon their faces.

Azrael's face lit up even more when his eyes found Ethan's. "Ah, there you have it, gentlemen. Master Ethan has indeed joined us before we left," he said. "I believe that's two crowns apiece you owe me."

Sedra, who sat closest to Ethan with his back turned, reacted first. The giant minotaur snorted as he twisted around. "I'm impressed," he said with a nod of respect. "Annoyed at myself that I misjudged you but impressed nevertheless."

Sir Gideon, on the other hand, simply shot a glare at Ethan over his shoulder before turning back around with a grunt. He fished in his coin purse, muttering, and slapped a pair of crowns in Azrael's open and outstretched hand.

"What's going on?" Ethan asked as he refused to believe what his eyes took in.

"We're weathering the storm in the merriment of good company, of course," Azrael said. He then motioned to an empty space nearby. "Come. Sit. Warm those bones of yours and enjoy a rest before we get back to the regatta."

The warmth of the brazier called to Ethan, but its temptations had nothing on the smell of warm blood hanging in the air. His stomach rumbled, and his mouth watered. Behind him, quietly, he could hear Zoey's stomach growling, too.

To combat the building *Hunger*, Ethan probed some more. "If all of you in here are rubbing elbows in good cheer, what happened out there?"

"Exactly what it looks like happened," Azrael said. "But as the storm grew worse and problematic, we negotiated a temporary truce between us all—a truce we're willing to extend to you, provided you act like the gentleman I know you are."

Ethan glanced over his shoulders. Zoey's grip on her cutlass tightened, and though Katryna kept her hands away from her weapons, he could see in her eyes she was ready to spring into action if need be.

"I suppose it's in the best interest of us all to stay cordial," Ethan said, facing Azrael once again and sheathing his sword.

Azrael clapped his hands together. "Wonderful! I knew you were a sensible man the moment I met you."

Ethan and his group took seats on the floor. While Katryna and Jean sat nearby, Zoey cuddled up to his side, rubbing her arms briskly as she did.

"Little cold," she said with a chuckle.

"You and me both," Ethan replied. He stretched his arms towards the brazier and enjoyed the warmth that returned to his fingers.

Jean paid the fire no heed and instead stared at Sir Gideon, hands twitching at his side, cords bulging in his neck. Though the man didn't move toward the Golden Templar, Ethan had no doubt that his self-restraint was but a stray word away from breaking.

The hatred sent by Jean wasn't lost on Sir Gideon either. The captain lolled his head casually to the side and returned a deadpanned look. "Something on your mind?"

"Do you remember me?" he asked.

Sir Gideon shook his head. "No. Should I even care?"

"Piram," Jean prompted. "You killed my brother. Left me for dead. All for a ring."

"Oh, him," Sir Gideon said with a smirk. "Perhaps if he'd been a more virtuous man, he'd still be alive."

Jean went for his pistol, but Katryna clamped onto his wrist. Despite the fact that she stayed his hand, his tongue still cut loose. "I'll have my ring and your life before this day is over."

"Once we leave, you're welcome to try," Sir Gideon said. "But as for the ring, I tossed it long ago."

"I'll—"

"Do nothing while we're in here. Truce and all," the Golden Templar said, cutting him off. "Lest you want all three of us to cut you down."

Tension reigned between the two, and after a few moments of silence, Ethan looked to Azrael and blew out a puff of air. "We're just going to sit here, then, hating each other, till the storm blows over?"

"No, Master Ethan, we're not," Death replied. He reached into a pouch that hung off his side and pulled out a small bottle of rum and offered it to him. "In the meantime, we're going to share drinks and company," he said. "After which, we'll race. We'll fight, and we'll see who dies and who does not."

Chapter XXVII
Bottles & Battles

Three hours later, Ethan, with a rumbling stomach, stood in the waterlogged courtyard with his crew at his side, a moderate wind constantly tossing his hair in front of his face.

The lot of them, skeletons included, along with everyone else from the chapel, formed a loose circle across the grounds, some twenty paces across. To his left, standing in front of the old well, were Sedra and his men, while Sir Gideon and his crew waited off to Ethan's right. Azrael, on the other hand, walked to the center of the gathering and placed a small wooden chest on the ground.

"And there you have it, gentlemen," he said, stepping away. Azrael straightened his long coat and clasped his hands in front of his hips before letting his gaze sweep over everyone. "Does anyone wish to speak before we start this grand melee?"

Ethan raised his hand, unsure if that was the proper etiquette but wanting to be sure he had a chance to ask his question.

"Master Ethan," Azrael said with a tip of the hat. "And what fine words of encouragement do you have for us?"

"Not words of encouragement, per se, but more of a question," he said.

"All the same, let's hear what's on your mind."

"Are we starting on ten or right after?" he asked. "I don't want anyone getting free shots on us because we misunderstood."

Azrael drew back the corner of his mouth with amusement but offered no chiding, despite the snorts and whispers that ran rampant amongst the others. "*On* the count of ten," he said, putting heavy emphasis on the first word, "anything goes. And, for the record, anyone can take the chest, or the bottle inside, at any time. The melee needn't resolve, first. Understood?"

"Understood," Ethan said with a nod.

Azrael clapped his hands together. "Wonderful, then—"

"I have something," Sedra interrupted. When Azrael acknowledged him, the minotaur snorted and pointed to the box on the ground. "Open it up. I want to see the prize is within."

Azrael shook his head with a disbelieving snort as he faced the monstrous captain. "Are you accusing me of cheating?" he asked.

Sedra's nostrils flared, and the muscles in both his arms tensed visibly. "I'm saying I want to see with my own eyes what's in the box before anything else happens," he said. "You're getting rather defensive over such a simple request."

Azrael laughed again, which did little to ease tensions, but when he held up a hand and casually made his way back to the center of the circle, Sedra and his crew seemed to relax. "I have nothing to hide, my most worthy competitor," Azrael said, taking a knee. "I'll not have anyone say our contest wasn't a fair and proper one."

Sedra let his hand drop to his side, coming off the butt of his pistol. "Good."

With a pair of clicks, Azrael flipped the two iron latches on the chest. He flipped the lid back, and the hinges offered a rusty squeak in the process. For a moment, Azrael kept kneeling as his mouth formed a tight line across his face, and he made a steeple with his fingers on which he rested his chin.

"It seems, gentlemen, some of us have taken to thievery," he said, slowly coming to his feet.

It took a moment for Ethan's brain to register what was going on, even when pistols and swords were drawn by all. But once he had, he saw that the chest was completely empty, and Sedra's rage was barely kept in check.

"I knew it!" the minotaur roared, leveling his pistol at Azrael's chest. "Hand it over."

"How dare you question my character," Azrael said, staring Sedra down without even much as making a twitch to draw his own weapons. "I am no so desperate or uncouth to resort to such trickery. In fact..." His words trailed, and he slowly turned his head toward Zoey, his eyes reflecting the tone of disgust in his voice as he went on. "There aren't thieves among us, but rather, there is but *one* thief among us."

In the blink of an eye, half the weapons from Sedra's and Sir Gideon's crew went to Zoey, and just as quickly, Jean and Katryna pointed theirs back.

"She didn't steal anything," Ethan said, stepping between Zoey and Azrael and raising his blade.

"Once a thief, always a thief, Master Ethan," Azrael said. "Her reputation is forever impugned, and while I'd hoped she may have reformed by now to prove me wrong, alas, she has not. Now step aside so we may deal with this matter and continue on, or I'll run you through myself."

Ethan narrowed his eyes and swallowed the lump forming in his throat. "No."

Zoey came out from behind him a moment later. "I didn't steal anything," she spat. She lowered her blade and did a slow spin so everyone could see. "Look at me! I've got nothing to hide and nowhere to hide it even if I did. My clothes are in tatters."

Sir Gideon, who stood off to the left, grunted. "Says the thief."

"Says the one who was nowhere near that box!" she shouted back. "You're the one who had the box the entire time," she said, pointing to Azrael. "And you, Sedra," she went on, shifting her finger, "were the one sitting closest to him! Why don't the two of you turn your jackets inside out and loosen those bags hanging from your hips?"

"As if that makes any sense, you stupid hedgewhore," Sedra said. "Why would I call attention to an empty box if I'd stolen the bottle already?"

"Because you're looking to slip out in the chaos you create," Katryna said as she took a few steps forward. "Hell, that's what I'd do."

"So, it was you!"

"The hell it was!"

A hundred more curses and accusations seemed to fly over the course of the next ten seconds, and all the while, pistols were aimed and re-aimed just as fast. All the while, Ethan stood his ground, his heart pounding in his chest, skin feeling unbearably hot.

And then without warning, the proverbial powder keg blew.

One of Sir Gideon's men shot first. Ethan was sure of that much. He caught the sight of smoke and flame burst from the flintlock pistol out of the corner of his eye, though he didn't see where the shot went. A split second later, everyone else fired their weapons.

Men dropped and staggered on all sides. One of Ethan's skeletons took three shots to the chest before its head exploded. Its body had yet to hit the ground when Sir Gideon outstretched his arms and spoke with a loud, commanding voice, *"Parva Sanctificem!"*

Golden rays of light burst from his hands, striking the remaining two skeletons dead center. Their bodies crumpled, their bones shattering into dust when they struck the ground.

Before Ethan could process anything else, he found himself locked into a duel with Azrael as the chaos of battle unfolded around them.

Fires of hate seemed to erupt from Death's eyes as if the politeness he'd once shown had been nothing but a mask, and his true, terrible self—the one every mortal feared—was on display for all to see. "If there's one thing I despise more than a cheat, Master Ethan, it is the man who knowingly sides with one," he spat, launching attack after attack.

Ethan scampered backward, parrying Azrael's blade in a panicked flurry. The clang of blade against blade filled the air. Another thrust. Another parry. A backhanded blow that Ethan barely ducked under to avoid losing his head.

All of these attacks and more taxed Ethan's skill to the breaking point over the next several seconds. Then, after another thrust by Azrael, Ethan managed to trap Death's blade along the hilt of his own and knock it aside. At that moment, Ethan, operating on pure instinct, drove forward, trying to take advantage of the gap in Azrael's defense and bring this duel to a swift end.

Ethan's lunge, however, skewered nothing but air. Azrael spun around the attack and stepped forward with the grace of a ballroom dancer, letting Ethan's blade slide harmlessly by. As he came around, he struck Ethan on the side of the head and sent him staggering backward.

Azrael hits!
You are lightly wounded!
You are dazed!

Ethan didn't know if Narrator had actually said that last bit or if he'd made it up on his own, but either way, he certainly felt it. The world around him blurred. Zoey screamed something, and he felt the tight clench of a hand on his elbow before it yanked him back so hard his shoulder nearly popped from its socket.

"Impressive," Azrael said, directing a flurry of attacks at the female vampire. He knocked her blade to the side and lunged after a few feints. In turn, she beat a fast retreat to recover her guard, but it wasn't enough. His blade cut across the top of her hilt in what should've been a good parry, but at the last second, he managed to raise his arm to dip the blade, letting it slice open the top of her shoulder.

Ethan yelled with an unmatched, unholy fury at the sight. His legs drove him forward with reckless speed, but before he could rejoin the fray, Azrael ended it all. With two strikes of his blade, strikes Zoey barely defeated, Death trapped her sword arm against his side and thrust the point of his main-gauche for a coup de grâce into her neck.

The tip of the dagger nicked her skin a moment before her eyes shot wide, and she disappeared into a fine mist, only to be blown away by the wind.

Ethan's charge continued, fear and anger surging him forward with a strength and fury that he never knew he had. He came at Azrael with a brutal overhead chop. Death spun on the balls of his feet and managed to deflect the blow, but it came so hard that the blow knocked both his rapier and dagger to the side.

Ethan pressed his attack, wanting—needing—to end this encounter as quickly as he could so he could find Zoey and make sure she was okay above all else. His rear leg sprang him forward, the tip of his cutlass leading the way, and he committed five points of *Luck* to see it through.

> *Five points of Luck used.*
> *Luck countered!*
> *You feel a little off!*

Azrael's expert footwork saw him out of danger, and his face brightened as Ethan's reckless attack failed to land. "Luck will only get you so far, Master Ethan," he taunted. The smile on his face grew, and he then added: "And it will get you nowhere with me."

"We'll see about that," Ethan countered.

Before the verbal exchange could go on, Ethan tried to seize the moment and attacked again. Azrael, however, easily deflected all four thrusts and cuts of Ethan's blade before issuing a counterattack of his own. His sword knocked Ethan's to the side faster than Ethan could comprehend, but at least Ethan had the presence of mind to leap backward and avoid being skewered.

To Ethan's surprise, Azrael didn't immediately follow. He simply adopted a more relaxed fighting stance and gave a brief salute. "You show much promise, Master Ethan, and I'd love to see how finely tuned we can train your swordsmanship," he said. "However, in the interest of time and the regatta, I believe this shall now be your final lesson."

Azrael lunged, sending a flurry of attacks that looked to cut, gut, and stab Ethan a dozen times from a dozen different angles. It was all Ethan could do not to let one land, to retreat as fast as he could without stumbling to the ground in the process. Azrael whipped his blade around the hilt of Ethan's, and then using it in conjunction with his main-gauche, he knocked Ethan's weapon out of his hand.

> *Azrael hits you!*
> *Azrael disarms you!*

Narrator had yet to finish those words before Ethan suddenly found himself staring Death in the face with not even four inches separating the two of them.

"Good day to you, Master Ethan," Azrael said. His eyes were both hard and filled with admiration, and his breath smelled of pipe tobacco. Then a wink came from those eyes, and his breath turned icy. "I shall think of you fondly as I cross the finish line."

Ethan straightened. His throat tightened, and his heart skipped a beat. He dared a glance down, wondering what it would be like when Azrael ran him through. Instead, Death drove a fist into his gut that sent him stumbling backward and then issued a swift front kick that would've pushed him another two or three feet easily if it hadn't been for the well they'd ended up at.

Ethan caught the lip of the well with the back of his knees, and momentum sent him tumbling down, bouncing off the rough stone walls and into the dark.

Katryna paused to regard the ragged group of men who stood between her and her goal: Sir Gideon. She'd driven toward him at the start of the battle with all the vengeance of a Fury, intent on helping Jean avenge his brothers and rid the land of such a vile being, but their advance had been plagued by a chaotic battlefield that constantly demanded their attention.

But now, all that changed. While Sir Gideon was locked in a skirmish with a few others, oblivious to Katryna and Jean's approach, all that stood between the two were three men, bloodied, tired, drowning in fear and fatigue.

She almost pitied them.

Almost.

But the fact that they terrorized the world under the guise of righteousness with Sir Gideon kept her from doing such a thing.

"Any last confessions you wish to make?" she asked, boldly approaching their line with Jean at her side. "I'm no priest, but if I were you, I'd hedge my bets regardless."

The man on the left retreated a few steps, and from behind his back, he whipped out a short-barreled flintlock pistol and pointed it at her. "Stay back!" he said, hands trembling. "You stay right there, or I'll shoot!"

Katryna raised an eyebrow. "Do you think that will matter?" she said, directing her question to Jean.

"Jamais," he replied, laughing. "But they probably think that it will."

"I guess we keep attacking then."

"Oui. I suppose we do."

"I mean it!" the sailor shouted, retreating a few steps more as his companions did the same. "I'll shoot!"

"Then shoot," Katryna said, not missing a beat.

The man's eyes glanced to the wake of carnage Katryna had left behind her. A half dozen bodies at least lay sprawled across the ground with surgical cuts across their necks. In that instant, Katryna drove forward, covering the ground that separated the two groups with blinding speed.

The man pulled the trigger before she reached him. The blast from his pistol sent the bullet driving square for Katryna's chest, but it never reached it. Her skill, *Deflect Shot* had already kicked in, and before the flint had even struck steel, she'd maneuvered her scimitar to make the intercept. The bullet skipped harmlessly off her scimitar, not even taking a nick out of its metal in the process.

Then she was upon them all. Her blade slipped between the ribs of the nearest man with such speed, he never had time to raise his defenses. The next had the wherewithal to issue a counterattack, but it came slow and wide, and even if Katryna hadn't positioned herself in such a way to beat a proper attack, she had all the time in the world to make the parry.

Which she did.

His weapon fell when she sliced open his inside forearm and finished him off with a stab through the gut. His body had yet to hit the ground when she was upon the last man, the one who'd shot at her. By the time she reached him, he had his cutlass up and was swinging wildly, trying to fend her off as his footsteps carried him back as fast as they could.

Katryna kept a measured pressure against him, not wanting to charge recklessly after him lest he find some measure of backbone and issue a lucky strike of his own. It would only take a moment, she knew, before an opening would present itself. Her prediction proved true. The man's left foot caught on a rock, and while it didn't cause him to topple whatsoever, it stole his concentration enough that by the time his eyes flicked back to Katryna, she'd already knocked his cutlass to the side, and his sword arm wrapped in her free one.

"Jean was right," she said, easily dispatching her foe. "It didn't matter."

Sailor killed!
You feel slightly more experienced.

Katryna paused as the body hit the ground. She hadn't paid Narrator attention in what felt like years. Hell, it might have been. The grind to the next level was taking a phenomenally long time, especially since most things out there granted her exactly zero points toward her goal due to the lopsided fights. Case in point, this one, and as such, she'd tuned him out long ago. But maybe these men weren't quite the cannon fodder she'd expected. Maybe she'd gained little bits of EXP here and there she hadn't noticed.

She ought to check her sheet when she had the chance, she decided. Maybe she'd be pleasantly surprised.

All of that fluttered through her head in a second at the most. She returned to the battle to see Jean launching himself at Sir Gideon, his sword coming down with a brutal overhead chop.

The Golden Templar parried the blade with his own, stepping to the side as he did so he could redirect the attack. Sir Gideon twisted his sword outward, further knocking Jean's weapon wide, and went on the attack. He hammered at the man with a pair of fast, low chops that sent Jean scrambling backward. Sir Gideon didn't press the attack. Instead, with a few feet now separating the two, he leveled his pistol—Ethan's pistol—at Jean and fired.

Jean tried to dive away, but he wasn't fast or lucky enough to do so. The bullet tore through his body, striking him high in the chest.

"No!" Katryna yelled as she desperately tried to reach her crewmate.

Even with all the speed she possessed, with all the talents and perks she'd picked up over the years, none of them mattered. As Jean stumbled, dropping his weapon and clutching his chest with both hands, Sir Gideon cut him down, first with a slash across his midsection and then a follow-up thrust to the heart.

Katryna's skin burned like a furnace. Her jaw set like a vice. Her legs launched her in the air, and she let loose a bellowing war cry that would've sent any wasteland barbarian running.

Sir Gideon spun around and dropped into a fighting base quick enough to defend her enraged attack. Her blade struck his, sending sparks flying in all directions and the clash of steel against steel ringing through the air.

"I'll kill you!" she said, hammering at his defenses time and again.

"Best not to make a promise you can't keep," he said, grinning as both footwork and blade work kept him safe.

The fight quickly turned into a series of complicated feints, cuts, and thrusts, taxing each to their limits. Sir Gideon, however, not only hit those limits first but went over them first as well.

Katryna knocked his cutlass down and issued a high thrust aimed for his neck. Sir Gideon, predictably, overcommitted to the parry, and while he managed to nimbly step back to keep his throat from being cut, he couldn't avoid the swashbuckler's blade when it dipped under his guard and carved a deep, three-inch-long gash in his wrist.

Sir Gideon hit!
Sir Gideon lightly wounded!

Katryna smiled at Narrator, and the sight of first blood drove her into a further frenzy like a hungry mako who'd gotten a taste of an upcoming meal. She redoubled the tempo of her strikes, each one coming at Sir Gideon from a different, yet no less deadly, angle. Another hit opened up the man's shoulder. Then a fine line across the top of his knee. A third put a gash in his thigh.

The color drained from Sir Gideon's face. His legs weakened from fatigue, and a moment later, he lost his footing and came crashing down, losing his sword in the process. "Wait," he said, outstretching his hand as he scooted away. "Please. I can pay."

"There's not enough gold out there for me to spare someone like you," she spat.

Katryna drew back her sword, and in that instant, the look on Sir Gideon's face changed from dread to elation. He snapped Ethan's pistol up to bear and pulled the trigger.

The magical shot punched through Katryna's blade, past all her defenses and talents, and struck her in the stomach. Her jaw dropped, and her legs gave out.

Chapter XXVIII
Turned

Ethan had never been a fan of wells. Ever since he'd seen his first one, he couldn't help but feel as if they were sinister contraptions whose sole purpose was to swallow wayward kids. Sure, it was an irrational fear, but one he'd never succeeded to fully shake himself from. And that damn movie with the girl who crawled out of them and killed everyone certainly didn't help things, either. When he'd gone and seen said movie when it first came out at the theaters, his fingers left gouges in the armrests, and his friends had to apologize profusely to the people behind them when creepy girl made her first appearance and Ethan sent his popcorn flying.

Thus, it was hardly a surprise that when Ethan hit the bottom, his first several seconds were spent in a mad flail, which was then followed by another half minute of him flattening his body against the mossy wall, all in an attempt to keep himself safe from whatever evil spirit called that place home.

Cries of fevered battle mixed with a few more pistol shots finally got Ethan to refocus, and thoughts of Zoey were strong enough to bolster his resolve and spring him into action. He had to get out of there, had to return to the fight. Had to make sure she was safe.

These were not new thoughts but ones he clung to and repeated as he began his slow ascent. The walls had plenty of finger and toe holds, but between the slick moss that grew on them, and the sharp, stabbing pain that attacked him through all of his limbs, progress was tenuous at best.

About a quarter of the way up, he wondered how many bones he'd cracked during the fall, if not outright broken. It didn't matter, he told himself. As long as they worked, he'd use them.

Halfway, his left arm gave out, and he slipped. Five points of *Luck* kept him from dropping more than a few inches. Once he felt stable enough to resume his ascent, he did, doing his best not to pull any weight with that arm but only use it to help keep him steady.

It took another five minutes of steady work to draw near the top; all the while, the sounds of battle faded away and eventually ceased altogether. His entire body burned like fire once his right arm reached up and grabbed the lip of the well.

Digging deep, Ethan pulled himself up and out of the well, body shaking, brow dripping with sweat. Staggering to his feet, he found himself alone in the courtyard. Or rather, he found he was the only one standing in the courtyard. Or moving, for that matter.

The dead lay scattered about by the dozens, crew from Azrael, Sedra, and Sir Gideon all in equal number. Jean Baynard, too, no longer could be counted among the living. He'd fallen with his back against a wall, shot in the chest, and struck several times. His head lolled to the side with a vacant stare in his eyes while his right arm clutched yet another wound to his gut.

"Oh no," Ethan muttered, feeling his mouth dry. His eyes scanned the rest of the battlefield, hoping and praying he wouldn't find Zoey having suffered a similar fate, but she was nowhere to be seen.

"Zoey?" he called out, willing himself forward. Every step he took felt shaky, and he paused long enough to check his character sheet and confirm what he'd suspected:

Severely wounded.

"Why the hell couldn't there have been a trampoline at the bottom," he said, stuffing his sheet back into his pocket. If he could feed, he could heal. Sadly, everyone still looked as dead as they'd been before, and Ethan wasn't sure how that worked, vampire-wise. More than one myth said vampires who fed off the dead died themselves, or at the very least, became severely ill. Given the fact that just the thought of nibbling a corpse made his stomach queasy, Ethan opted not to press his luck.

Besides, if he could find Zoey and they could make it back to their ship, he could always get a donation from his crew there.

"Ethan," called out a weak, feminine voice.

Ethan spun at the sound of his name. Across the courtyard, surrounded by six other bodies, he saw Katryna curled into a fetal position. Most of the color had left her face, and she held tight to her blood-soaked stomach.

"Hang on, Katryna," Ethan said, racing over to her. His hands instinctively went to the wound, but they retracted when he realized he didn't know what to do. "Damn, you're a mess. Should I try and bandage it more? Or do you think you can get to your feet? We can't stay here."

Katryna gritted her teeth and clenched her eyes as she shook her head. "Please, don't leave me like this," she whimpered.

"No one's leaving you like anything. Stop that right now," he said as he tore off part of a sleeve, folded it thrice over, and pressed it into her gut. The fibers instantly turned scarlet. "It'll do for now," he said, hoping he didn't need a decent *First Aid* skill to make this work because as of that very moment, he had none. Investing in it on his next level, he thought, might not be such a bad idea. But that was something he'd have to deal with later. He had to get her out of there.

Ethan snaked his arm under Katryna's shoulders and tried sitting her up. "Come on. We'll find Zoey together. She'll know what to do."

Katryna stayed upright for a moment, but the instant he let go, she fell to the side like dead weight. "I can't," she said. Water clouded her eyes, and there was a peculiar tremor in her voice. Not one born from pain, but terror.

"Come on, Miss Level Thirty-Four," Ethan said as he tried again. "A little gut shot isn't about to do you in, right?"

Katryna let out a wet cough and shook her head once more. She kept her bandage pressed against her abdomen with her right hand, and with her left, she fumbled inside her bodice for a few seconds before pulling out her character sheet. "No, Ethan, you don't understand," she said. "I literally can't go anywhere. Look."

Ethan took the piece of paper and quickly looked at where her health was written down. Two neat lines painted a dreadful picture:

Gravely Wounded
Permanent Injury: Paralyzed

"Paralyzed," Ethan repeated, falling back. His gaze drifted out to infinity, and his thoughts ran rampant with how disastrous his decision of coming here had become—how awful of a leader he was. "We can fix this, though, right?" he said. "We'll find you a healer or a cleric or whatever. They'll say a few prayers, light some candles, and you'll be walking again in no time."

"No, it's not that easy. You've got to turn me," she begged.

"Maybe Marcus can fix you."

"He can't fix me, Ethan!" she yelled. "Your stupid magical pistol ensured that no one can!"

Ethan fell back. "What? How?"

"It's enchanted against the living!" she went on, fully losing herself in grief and anger. "Its wounds are permanent. Always."

Ethan shook his head, his mind reeling. "No. No, that can't be right," he said. "I healed."

"When, Ethan? While you were still alive or after she turned you?"

Ethan felt his mouth dry and his eyes glaze. As much as he wished otherwise, she was right. "Oh, God. This is my fault. Isn't it?" he said weakly. "If I hadn't lost it playing cards..."

"You can still make it right," Katryna said. "Please, Ethan. I'm begging you. I can't be a cripple. Not here. Not again."

The swashbuckler's words snapped Ethan out of his shock. "What do you mean, 'again'?"

"I—" Katryna choked on her reply, and it was only when Ethan took her free hand in his and gave it a squeeze that she found the strength to get it out. "All I do back home—our real home—is lie in bed and waste away."

"Seriously?" Ethan reeled at his reply. The moment it left his lips, he knew how awful it sounded. Thankfully, Katryna didn't rip into him because of it.

"Seriously."

Silence then smothered the conversation for far longer than it should have, and Ethan said the only true thing he could think of. "I don't know what to say."

"You don't have to say anything."

"Did you get sick or something?" he asked.

"No. Someone mugged me in a parking garage after work," she said. "Kicked me down a flight of stairs. My neck broke when I hit the bottom," she explained. "Survived, obviously, but it left me—how do you say? Quad. All I can do is get fed like a baby. Wiped like a baby. Treated like a baby—only, I don't have a future to look forward to. At least babies get to grow up. All I can do is rot. So, don't you dare confine me to that fate here, and don't you dare let me die either. I won't go back to that hellish existence."

Ethan swallowed the newly formed lump in his throat. "I'm sorry. I didn't know."

"I don't want your pity," she said. "Just make it right. You owe me that."

Hairs rose across the back of Ethan's neck, and as he held Katryna's fearful gaze, he knew he was at a crossroads yet again.

He dug his fingers into his scalp, trying to decide what to do. On the one hand, it seemed that changing her was the only right course of action, but on the other, he couldn't shake the feeling that the hell that would eventually follow would still be somehow far, far worse for the woman. And that didn't even get into how badly he was about to break a sworn promise to Zoey. What would that mean for the future? He hadn't the slightest idea, but in the end, seeing her helpless broke his heart, and he chose compassion over fear—over integrity.

Zoey would understand later, he told himself. She'd have to.

"Okay," he said, taking a deep breath. "I'll do it."

"Thank you."

+1 Compassion gained.
You feel as if people will see you as less trustworthy and reliable.

Ethan sighed at Narrator's update and went to work. Though Zoey had never given him full instructions on turning anyone, he had a good recollection of what had taken place when Zoey had changed him from a hapless human to a newly minted vampire.

With that experience in mind, Ethan sank his fangs into his wrist. Blood spurt from the wound, ran down his forearm, and splattered on the ground. Right as he was about to offer it to Katryna, Zoey's cries cut through the air.

"Ethan! What are you doing?" she yelled as she raced toward him, face full of panic.

"I'm making her like us," he stammered. "*Saving* her. She's paralyzed. For good. All because of me."

"Look, I don't know what happened, but I know it's not your fault," Zoey said.

"No, it is," he said, looking away and shaking his head. "Just like Jean getting killed is my fault too."

"Ethan, you didn't kill him," Zoey said as she put her hand on his shoulder. "And you didn't do this to her, either. They did."

"My pistol did this," he shot back, his heart breaking with every word he spoke. "Mine. The one I looted from Lord Belmont, and the one Sir Gideon now has because I bet it in a stupid card game because I was too stupid to know any better."

Zoey knelt at his side. She framed his face with her hands and turned him toward her. "I get it. This world sucks a lot, sometimes, but don't do this," she said with a soft, even voice. "Please, believe me, you don't know the fury that awaits us all if you do. She's not playing for anyone. She'd be better off losing here and going home."

"No, she wouldn't," Ethan said as he squeezed Katryna's hand. "She'll rot away if that happens. And if we don't turn her, she'll rot away here, too."

Zoey's brow furrowed, and she reflexively pulled away. "What are you talking about?"

"He means I'm a quad back home," Katryna said. "You still remember what those are, right?"

"Yeah...yeah, I know what those are," Zoey softly replied. She then cursed and buried her face in her hands. When she finally let them drop, she folded her fingers together and rested her chin on top of them. "I'm sorry," she finally said. "I had no idea. Why didn't you say all of this before?"

"Because I don't want to be treated like a cripple," she said, her voice taking on a distinct edge. "All I want is to live."

"If you do this, they'll come for you," Zoey said, now sounding academic about it all. "I want you to understand that. I want you to really understand that some of the darkest, most dreadful beings in the world will come after you. Maybe not today, or tomorrow, or even next year. But they'll learn of what happened here, eventually, and when they do, you'll never be safe. Do you understand?"

Katryna nodded. "I understand. I am not buying a cat in a sack. I know what to expect."

"We still have *The Duchess*," Ethan pointed out. "Or will, at least. I'll sign the deed after the race, and we can go from there."

Zoey fell back on her haunches. Angst gripped her face, and water clouded her eyes. After a couple of slow, steady breaths, she asked him a simple question. "Do you remember what I said to you when you were dying?"

"That you didn't want to lose me?"

Zoey nodded. "I don't. And I can't. And I won't."

"You're not losing me," Ethan said. "I don't care who comes after us or what ghost thinks she can come between us. We're in this game together. Always, but we can't sacrifice everything and everyone else at our expense."

Zoey laughed. "There you go again, being the slightly naïve hero."

"You forgot the adorably sweet part," he said. "I'm that, too. Remember?"

"One of these days, it's going to get us killed," she said, clearing her eyes.

Ethan smiled. "But it is not this day."

"Okay, Aragorn," she said, laughing again. Zoey then exhaled slowly and nervously clapped her hands in front of her face several times. "Okay...okay, okay, okay," Zoey said, her eyes drifting toward the ground, "...okay."

The air grew silent and still, and Ethan waited for a beat to see if either would say anything else. When neither did, he pressed his still-bleeding wrist against Katryna's mouth. "Drink."

The woman latched on, holding his forearm tight with both hands. He felt her strength return more and more with each passing second and watched the hairs across her body stand on end. In turn, his own skin felt cold, and his head floated above the clouds.

"God, I feel amazing," Katryna said, pulling away from Ethan's wrist and wiping her mouth. "In fact—"

Katryna doubled over. Her face turned scarlet, and the cords in her neck bulged. Ethan grimaced, knowing full well the excruciating pain wracking her body as the unholy versus holy fought. He put his hand on her shoulder and tried to offer her some sort of comfort, but it didn't help. She screamed, arching her back and clawing at the ground. Dry heaving came next, followed by the spitting of dark, coagulated goo. When it was finished after what seemed to be an eternity, she lay there, panting.

The woman pressed her thumb into one of her new fangs and smiled. Her lips, however, turned downward, and her eyes widened a moment later. "I—I still can't move my legs," she said.

Ethan, swaying due to feeling extremely lightheaded, knitted his brow. "Say again?"

"I said still I can't move my legs!" she barked.

Thankfully, Zoey had a palatable answer. "You have to feed to regenerate," she said. "You should be fine after that." She then turned to Ethan and said the same. "You're going to need something soon, too. You look terrible."

Katryna bit her lower lip and nodded. Her eyes scanned the battlefield, and in the span of a few heartbeats, they lit up with determination. The newly made vampire threw herself forward and dragged herself across the ground with frightening speed.

"You can't feed on the dead!" Zoey yelled, giving chase.

Katryna didn't listen. She reached a fallen man before Zoey could catch her and yanked back his head while simultaneously taking a bite on his neck. The man cried out and tried to fend off his attacker with a few feeble strikes, but he was no match for Katryna.

"He was still alive?" Zoey asked, chuckling in disbelief. "Holy crap. I thought they were all dead."

"He's still alive," Ethan said. He repeated those words a couple more times so they penetrated the haze he was still in. Once they had, he staggered over to where Katryna was feeding and joined in, taking his prey by the wrist.

Sailor drained!
You heal some wounds!

Ethan relinquished his grip at Narrator's voice and relished the strength that had returned to him. His body still ached, and he still counted at least a dozen bruises with bruises across his limbs, not to mention felt a small knot on the back of his head, but at least he didn't feel completely broken anymore.

Katryna, too, had healed some. Though she still fed, she no longer was sprawled out on the ground next to the man but now had her legs tucked underneath her so she knelt as she drained what lifeforce was left.

A rumble in Ethan's stomach prompted him to take seconds. Two minutes later, refreshed and restored, he stood and offered Katryna a hand up.

"Come on," he said, pulling her up. "We've got a race to win."

"And a Golden Templar to send straight to hell," the woman said, beaming. "Should be easy enough now that Zoey has the bottle."

Zoey shook her head. "I don't have it."

Ethan arched his eyebrows as surprise splashed across his face. "What do you mean you don't have it?"

"I mean, I don't have it," Zoey said. "I never had it."

"But you're a thief."

"Yeah? And? That doesn't mean every time something goes missing, I had something to do with it."

Ethan groaned, and when she looked at him with annoyance, he held up his hands. "I'm sorry," he said. "Of all the times when you stealing something would've been really, really helpful, this would've been it."

"Believe me, I know," Zoey said.

"If you don't have it, then who does?" asked Katryna, furrowing her brow.

Zoey threw her hands up. "I honestly have no idea, but if we don't get back to our ship this instant, we'll never win. They've already got too much of a head start on us."

"Then we've no time to lose," Ethan said.
With that, the three raced out of the fort.

Chapter XXIX
Back to Sea

Ethan dashed through the forest, Zoey and Katryna following, trees and foliage zipping by in a blur. His legs drove him with powerful strides, and he followed the ever-increasing scent of saltwater and sounds of breaking waves on the shore.

More than one fallen tree along the way tried to slow him, but he took each with a hurdle without losing stride. For a while, he worried that the other captains had already reached their ships and now had an insurmountable lead, but after fifteen minutes or so, he heard the faint sounds of gunshots up ahead.

"Good," Zoey said between labored breaths. "Maybe they'll all kill each other."

"That'd be nice, but I don't think even I'm that lucky," Ethan said.

"All the more reason to run faster," Katryna tacked on.

Not long after, they cleared the tree line and found themselves on a wide, debris-filled beach. Three ships could be seen sailing away, while a fourth, the *Victory*, lay anchor a few hundred yards away. Thankfully, right after Ethan spied it, he also spotted a longboat beached fifty yards away.

"That's our crew! They're here already!" Ethan shouted as no one in their right mind could ever mistake who the raggedy group of skeletons by the boat belonged to.

The group redoubled their pace, practically flying across the sand. By the time they reached the craft, Mister Potts, who also happened to be in the group, was already knee-deep in surf, turning the boat around.

"Where's Jean?" he asked.

"He didn't make it," Ethan said. The words weighed heavily on his soul, and he was surprised at how hard they were to get out, how weak they sounded in his ears—how weak they made him felt.

Mister Potts frowned and nodded, pausing a moment before flashing a smile. "Then I guess we'd best win for his sake," he said. "Lest he haunts us the rest of our days."

"You're damn right we will," Ethan replied.

Ethan took a position next to the helmsman, with Zoey coming to his side. Everyone else found spots as well, and after a count of three, they spun the boat around and drove it into the surf. The lifeboat's bow punched through the waves cleanly, but the amount of force needed to do so was more than Ethan had expected.

After driving it far enough into the water, they each jumped into the longboat, Ethan being the last to throw himself in. A solid wave knocked him in the chest as he did, and it took a little extra help from two of the skeletons and a whole lot of flopping on his part to see himself in. At that point, he scrambled for a seat and an oar, and together, the crew rowed hard for the *Victory*. Thankfully, she seemed no worse for wear, and her colors still flew proudly.

"How far ahead are they?" Ethan asked as they started to row.

"They all raised anchors maybe twenty minutes ago," Mister Potts replied.

Ethan's eyes scanned the area and quickly found his opponent's ships near the horizon, and as much as seeing that sank his spirits, seeing his own ship, nearly a quarter mile away practically in the opposite direction, sank them even lower. "Why are we so far away?"

"Because Marcus didn't want us to take on any extra holes, Captain, and I was rather inclined to agree."

"Extra holes?"

"Aye, sir. From their cannons," he explained. "They've been trading shots at each other since the storm passed."

As if waiting to reinforce what he'd said, a series of booms carried through the air. Ethan leaned in his place on the bench to see billowing clouds rise from the portside of the *Griffin,* and Sir Gideon's ship, the *Red Fish,* no doubt took a heavy hit from the attack as it sailed by. What sort of damage Sir Gideon now tended to, Ethan couldn't tell, but he guessed it must have been severe, for the *Red Fish* not only didn't respond with a broadside of her own, but she turned away as hard as she'd go, running with the wind to escape the *Griffin's* firing arcs.

A few seconds later, *The Popinjay* sent out a volley of her own. Sedra had wisely kept her from the warring pair, but with that caution, he'd sacrificed a leading position as he sailed several hundred yards behind and off to the side. Whether or not his cannons hit anything on either the *Griffin* or the *Red Fish,* Ethan didn't know. He could only hope.

Minutes later, the ships exchanged another set of volleys. Ethan strained his eyes, trying to see what sort of damage they'd dealt each other, but he couldn't tell anything other than none had blown up in a spectacular fireball.

A minute later, their longboat bumped against the *Victory's* hull. The group hastily climbed the rope ladders, with Ethan being the last. As he hoisted himself up and over the railings, he saw some of the crew scrambling, trying to get the longboat aboard before it drifted away.

"Leave it behind," he ordered. "Weigh anchor! Full sails to the wind!"

The crew immediately abandoned the lifeboat and ran to their stations while Mister Potts went for the helm. Katryna started for the bow, intent on taking Jean's role at commanding the gun crews, but Ethan caught her arm. He had a much more important role in mind for her.

"How's the vision?" he asked. "Better, yes?"

Katryna laughed. "I could count the hairs on a fly's ass from twenty yards."

"Perfect, I need you up there," Ethan said, pointing to the crow's nest.

A growl escaped her lips, and her eyes narrowed. "The only reason I'm not flat out disobeying right now is because of what you did for me back on the island," she said. "But you've got another thing coming if you think I'm going to be happy sitting up there and watching while everyone else sinks the *Red Fish.*"

Ethan took her by the shoulders and squeezed. "I know. But I need the keenest eyes in the nest if we're to have a chance at winning. If the hooks go out, I definitely want you in the fray. But not a second before that."

"I'm going to hold you to that."

"Absolutely. Now go."

With a reluctant nod, Katryna raced up the ratlines. Less than two minutes later, the *Victory* was well underway, and a familiar, raspy voice drew Ethan's attention from behind.

"Sign..." Ethan jumped and spun to find the Duchess floating nearby, staring through him as she always did. In her hands, she held both the deed and a raven-black quill which she raised for him to take.

"How did you get that?" he asked, fighting the urge to take them regardless.

"It...is mine..." she said, her voice both powerful and chilling him to the core. "I always...have...it...just like...I...will have...you."

Ethan eyed both parchment and quill, unsure what to do. He was going to sign, he knew, but that didn't mean he couldn't try and tailor the deal to suit his needs more, first. "Okay, fine. I'll sign," he said, "but I have to finish the race before we do anything else."

The Duchess nodded slowly, keeping a wicked smile the entire time. "Very well...I...shall grant...three days...to...get...your affairs...in order."

Knots formed in Ethan's stomach and tightened even further as he took both the deed and quill from her hands. Its tip looked recently dipped in ink, and as he used it to sign his name at the bottom of the deed, it left scorch marks trailing across the page and sent wisps of smoke rising into the air.

The moment he finished, crossing the *t* in Ethan, the deed, quill, and Duchess vanished, and he was left standing there, dumbfounded for a few seconds until Zoey ran up to his side. "Finished gathering report," she said, oblivious to everything that had just taken place. "Our cabin's a mess. Some of our stores broke free down below, and the mainsail tore near a yardarm when they couldn't reef it in time, but it's been stitched already."

Ethan blinked and shook his head to snap himself back into the moment. He wondered if he should fill Zoey in on what had just happened but decided it could wait until later. They needed to concentrate on the task at hand. "That's not too bad," he said. "Let's see what the others are up to."

With that, he took out his spyglass and settled it on the *Red Fish*. The schooner, now out of range of the *Griffin*, had turned back on course, though it did so at a slow pace. Both the foresail and mainsail had a half dozen holes, and Ethan could see her crew scrambling and trying to fix rigging. He was also fairly certain he saw a hole near the waterline but had to admit due to the distance involved, he couldn't be sure.

He was going to watch them a bit longer, but Maii jumped up on the railing, claws holding him steady, and blocked his view.

"Jean Bayard is no longer, I assume," the ahuizotl said. "Or have you grown darker as of late and cast aside the weak?"

Ethan shot him a glare. "I would never. You know that."

"Only a question," Maii said, grinning. "After all, our dear Katryna has grown paler."

"Has she?"

"You and I both know she has," he mused. "Should we ask the crew what they think? Or maybe have her smile, first, and show off those pretty teeth of hers."

"Enough, Maii. I'm quite certain I've told you to stop causing mischief before," Ethan said.

"Who's to say what's mischief and what's mere curiosity?" Maii replied.

"I am."

"So you are," the ahuizotl conceded—or at least pretended to.

Deep down, Ethan didn't like the creature's tone and felt things were off, but that wasn't something he could focus on now. He had a race to win. He turned his direction to the crow's nest and called out to Katryna. "Katryna! Can you see Azrael or Sedra?"

"Aye," she answered. "But they're running fast over the waters. I'd say they'll be out of even my sight in a few hours at most."

"Damn," Ethan muttered. He'd wished otherwise, obviously, but knew focusing on that problem wouldn't do anything but frustrate him further. One thing at a time, he told himself. Before he could take first place, he had to take third.

"Katryna," he called again. "Any chance the *Red Fish* lost her guns?"

The woman held up a finger and looked through her spyglass. She spent a few seconds staring through it, leaning far out the nest, before lowering it and shaking her head. "I am afraid not," she said. "Looks like she still has plenty of teeth."

"Then we best treat her with respect," Ethan said.

Zoey came to his side, and after surveying the situation with her spyglass, she offered a suggestion. "Perhaps we should double load the carronades. If we do, there's a good chance we could cripple him with a single pass. The *Griffin* already gave her one hell of a beatdown."

"Don't forget to fetch the grapples," Maii added. When both Zoey and Ethan shot him a look, the ahuizotl grinned. "What? I'm hungry. I'm tired of salted meat."

"We're doing neither," Ethan said. "I don't want to risk an engagement, especially with Azrael and Sedra so far ahead. And like you said, the *Red Fish* is already hurting. I doubt she wants a fight."

"Maybe, but if Azrael is going to win anyway, the least we could do is get a fresh meal before it's all over," Maii huffed.

"No."

"I bet Katryna would like a fresh meal, too."

"No, Maii," Ethan said, brow dropping and tone sharpening. "Now knock it off."

Maii huffed. "This is why I like her much more than you. At least she'd want to avenge our fallen comrade."

"I haven't forgotten about Jean," Ethan said. "We can hunt down Sir Gideon after the race if need be."

Maii perked his ears, and he straightened as if he'd caught the scent of something delicious nearby. "Hunt down? Oh, I like the sound of that."

"Thought you would."

For the next hour and a half, Ethan carefully watched the *Red Fish*. They'd made a sizeable gain on her in the meantime and brought her to within a half mile. That, however, wasn't the only development. Up ahead, maybe twice that distance, the Isadora

Strait provided a tempting alternate, especially since Ethan was effectively in last place.

"I'm thinking we take it," Ethan said, gesturing toward the channel. "What do you think?"

Zoey sucked in a breath through clenched teeth. "I think we have to, but it's going to be messy."

"Only if *Red Fish* joins us," Ethan said. "And she looks like she doesn't want anything to do with it, judging by her course this last hour."

"Maybe, but I've got a feeling she's going to."

"Then we'll have to deal with her accordingly," Ethan replied. "Not sure how else we catch up to Azrael and Sedra." With that in mind, Ethan gave the order to his helmsman. "Mister Potts, a point and a half port, if you would," he called out. "We're taking the strait."

"Aye, Captain," he replied, turning the wheel.

"And load the carronades," Ethan called out, leaning over the rail. "Bar shot on all. I want her dead in the water if she wants to fight."

The gun deck became a flurry of activity as the *Victory* swung to port, sails snapping in response. The ship picked up the wind better than she had before, and Ethan felt her surge beneath his feet. Five minutes later, less than a quarter mile separated her from the mouth of the strait, and it was at that time Katryna whistled sharply from the crow's nest.

"Captain! The *Red Fish* is coming around!"

Ethan pivoted and dashed to his starboard railing to get a better look. It was just as Katryna warned. The *Red Fish,* six or seven hundred yards away, swung toward them. She straightened for a moment and unleased broadside. Most failed to connect, but one cannonball punched a neat hole in the mainsail.

"Two points starboard," Ethan said. "Let's close the distance and give her our reply."

The *Victory* cut back across the water, trying to get within range of the carronades before Sir Gideon had a chance to reload. *Red Fish* turned toward them, fired the chasers on her bow, and then turned to present her starboard guns. With three hundred yards now separating them, *Red Fish* unleashed another volley, this time, with much more severe results.

Three shots blew through the lower deck, while two others cut through some of *Victory*'s rigging. The sixth took out some lines to the main topsail, causing it to partially deflate and flap in the wind, while the last perfectly clipped the corner of the jib, ruining it as well.

Red Fish attacks!
Victory lightly damaged!
Maximum speed reduced!

Ethan cursed and cursed again when the *Red Fish* turned away from them to such a degree that if they tried to give chase, they'd sail into irons and be dead in the water. Realizing pursuit wasn't an option and that Sir Gideon would easily pick them apart, Ethan gave the only order he could think of. "Mister Potts, get us into that strait," he said as calmly as he could.

"Aye, Captain."

"Not that everyone doesn't already know it, but we won't be able to maneuver in there," Zoey said, taking his hand.

"I know, but neither will they," Ethan said, his eyes scanning the waterway. There, he took in the sight of at least three shipwrecks near the mouth of the strait alone, as well as a few treacherous rocks jutting out from the water nearby. Those warnings alone made it little wonder why navigating the strait had to be done in a slow, meticulous fashion, and even less wonder why Azrael and Sedra had opted to pass it by.

"I'm assuming you have a plan," she replied, sounding more hopeful than certain.

"Trust me. I do," Ethan replied before tacking on a grin and gesturing to his crew. "Or rather, trust them."

"Mind filling me in?"

"Absolutely, but first things first," he said before grabbing Katryna's attention. "Katryna, can you see what lurks below?"

The woman leaned out of the crow's nest and flashed a thumbs up. "Not as well as I'd like, but well enough to see us safe."

"Then from this point on, you're Mister Potts's eyes. I need you to keep him well aware of what's beneath the surface. Understood?"

"Understood."

With that, Ethan led Zoey below deck, taking a dozen skeletons with them in the process, all the while praying he'd somehow lead them to victory instead of utter defeat.

Chapter XXX
The Strait

Katryna saved them all.

Ethan had no doubts about that whatsoever. When he returned from down below, having packed a dozen skeletons with makeshift bombs, the *Victory* continued carving through the treacherous waters, missing both rock and shipwreck by mere yards as she went. The only reason they didn't strike any was all due to the fledgling vampire's heightened senses—a new trait Ethan had been counting on the moment they committed to the waterway.

As they went, the *Red Fish* kept her pursuit, following the route they took without err, firing the light cannons mounted in the bow every few minutes. In a perfect world, Sir Gideon would've misjudged something somewhere and run aground, but the captain wasn't cooperating with Ethan's plans. That said, Ethan hadn't been counting on that happening whatsoever.

"Captain!" Katryna yelled as she waved to get his attention. "Look, portside! Quick! We're clear for a quarter mile after this one."

Ethan bolted to the railing. When he reached, he saw a large formation of jagged rocks pass by, hidden under only a few feet of water. Up ahead, another rocky outcropping could be seen off the starboard side, ten yards away at the most.

"Perfect," Ethan said, gripping the rail. Not only had she threaded the *Victory* between the hazards perfectly, but she'd brought them to an ideal place for him to spring the trap.

For a half minute, Ethan watched the *Red Fish* close, now only a hundred yards away. Then, with a deep breath, Ethan went on the offensive.

"Mister Potts, bring us fully around, portside."

The man nodded and spun the wheel.

In response, the *Victory* rolled to the side as she changed course. Exactly as Ethan had hoped, the *Red Fish* turned into them, ready to match broadside for broadside. But before she could come around to answer Ethan's sudden charge, she turned sharply in the other direction to avoid running aground. In the end, however, the maneuver came too late. Her hull found the rocks beneath the waters and listed sideways.

To Ethan's dismay, the *Red Fish* neither came to rest nor foundered. She did, however, list, and less than a minute later, she presented her aft to the *Victory's* side—something Ethan took full advantage of.

"Fire!" he yelled.

Slow matches took to touch holes, and an instant later, the roar of portside carronades filled the air. Gouts of flame erupted from the *Victory's* hull, double loads hurling canister shot on top of solid, while thick clouds obscured it all. The short-barreled cannons rocked back in their carriages, straining their anchors as they slammed home, and the *Victory* trembled throughout her hull.

The Victory attacks!
The Red Fish is lightly damaged!
Maximum speed reduced!

"Cripes," Ethan said, shaking his head at the "lightly damaged" report. "What the hell does it take to sink you?"

"A lot more than a single volley," Maii replied. "But still, a good start."

Ethan nodded at the unexpected praise and brought his spyglass up to inspect the damage. With luck, he told himself, they were but a single nick away from sending the *Red Fish* from lightly damaged to moderately damaged.

What he saw made him think that very thought might be true. The *Red Fish* had its stern torn in a dozen places, gaping holes appearing in its hull. The mainsail, though taught and flying, suffered a large tear near the boom. Despite the damage, she continued to run with far more life than Ethan would've guessed or liked.

"Katryna, are we clear to show her our starboard guns?" he asked.

"Aye, Captain, but make it fast," she replied. "We're headed back to the rocks."

Ethan nodded and gave his command to Mister Potts, who in turn brought the *Victory* around another two points so that it had made a full circle.

The moment the signal came that the carronades were trained and ready, Ethan gave the order to fire. "Give 'em hell!"

The second volley flew from the *Victory's* side, another volley of double-shot blasting through the *Red Fish* with devastating results. Fires burned in two separate areas, yet despite this, it still wasn't enough. Through his spyglass, Ethan saw her crew fight valiantly to douse the flames and a deck gun break loose while Narrator gave report.

The Victory attacks!
The Red Fish is moderately damaged!
-1 cannons!

"Damn skippy, moderately damaged," Ethan said, grinning. Right as he'd finished those words, the *Red Fish* swung hard to port, no doubt intent on shaking them off her aft while also bringing her own guns to bear.

"Full point starboard, Mister Potts," Ethan said, wanting to turn into their enemy's maneuver and either buy some time while they reloaded, or better yet, stay completely out of the *Red Fish's* firing arcs by latching on to her stern.

The *Victory* listed with the turn, sails shuddering and taking more of the wind. Ethan tensed as the slow ballet unfolded. Though now tackling the wind nearly head-on, the *Red Fish* still managed to swing her guns around faster than Ethan had thought possible. That said, the *Victory* still had both speed and position on her side.

Even if Sir Gideon sent a volley toward him, surely they could weather it.

"Carronades ready and trained, Captain!" Zoey yelled.

"Fire at will!"

Again, thunder and flame erupted from the *Victory's* side. The blasts thumped heavily against Ethan's chest, and he could feel the tremble of the ship through his feet. A split second later, *Red Fish*, still turning close to the wind, fired a volley of her own.

Ethan's crew scored a handful of hits in the exchange. They tore huge chunks out of the mainsail and foresail and snapped the *Red Fish's* bow spirit, completely ruining both the jib and flying jib in the process.

The Victory attacks!
Red Fish ship moderately damaged!
Maximum speed reduced!

As much as Ethan would've liked, the *Victory* did not remain unscathed. Despite the three cannonballs that flew high and wild, most sending large plumes of water into the air as much as sixty or seventy yards away, nine struck the *Victory* in her midsection. One punched through the hammock netting, bounced off the deck, and shattered a pair of skeletal crew before clearing through the netting on the other side. Another split the rails not even five yards from Ethan before taking a small chunk from the foremast and blasting a hole through the opposite rails. The rest Ethan couldn't account for, and he could only pray no one was lost in the exchange.

Ethan took a deep breath and forced his anxieties out. Aside from being grateful not to have caught a twelve-pound cannonball with his face, he was thrilled not to have lost the foremast, as that would have been catastrophic.

"Keep us on her stern, Mister Potts," Ethan directed, refocusing all his attention to the battle.

The helmsman adjusted the wheel, and as the ship responded, Ethan threw a glance to his gun deck. Men brought powder from the magazine to the portside carronades while others ran sponges inside the recently fired guns to get them ready for the next volley. The group, including the skeletons who joined them, ran flawlessly, working as well as any crack naval crew. Despite all of that, Ethan worried they might not have the broadside ready in time.

Eighty yards from the *Red Fish*, the *Victory* continued to race across the waters, desperately trying to reach her prey's stern so she wouldn't have to weather a second volley. To Ethan's best judgment, it looked like they'd make it, especially given all the damage the *Red Fish* suffered. Of course, that didn't mean much. Ethan's judgment hadn't had a history of always being the best.

The crack of rifles drew his attention. From the tops of the *Red Fish,* sharpshooters began firing. Musket balls peppered the deck. One grazed Ethan's forearm, and he winced. Blood poured from the wound, quickly making a mess of his sleeve.

A gnawing hunger grew in his stomach and then tripled when he picked up on the scent of sweat and fear lingering in the air. Thoughts of the naval action gave way to longing to feed, and there was plenty of food to be had down below.

Ethan clenched his jaw, squeezed his eyes shut, and dug his nails into his palms to regain his composure. The hunger could wait. The hunger would wait. He could take his fill and then some once they'd grappled.

Thirty yards away, the *Victory* passed the *Red Fish's* stern. And while Ethan had originally thought her sluggishness had been due to a combination of fighting the wind and the ruining of the bow spirit, now that they were on top of her, he could see she was missing a third of her rudder, if not close to half, no doubt the result of ramming into the rocks earlier.

"Are we ready on the port?" Ethan yelled, twisting around to address his gun crews.

"Half a minute at the most, Captain," came the reply.

Ethan tensed, counted to ten in order to give them a little extra time, and then address Mister Potts. "Swing around and bring us to grapple," he said. "We end this now."

"Aye," he replied. "I'll have us stuck on her like scabs on a whore."

The *Victory* made one last cut back to starboard, swinging herself across *Red Fish's* stern one last time. The moment the carronades on the port side had their bearing, they fired. Blast after blast erupted in rapid succession. Thirty-two-pound shot obliterated large chunks of hull and railing and knocked several of

Red Fish's cannons off their carriages, while the packed grapeshot that led the way ravaged her crew.

"Cutting out party, standby!" Ethan yelled. "Send out the hooks!"

The gun crews abandoned their posts and took up their weapons. Lines with heavy iron grapples sailed through the air moments later, snagging the rails and tangling with the lines on the *Red Fish*. The two ships collided, scraping their hulls against one other, and sending the crews of both fighting for balance.

Somehow in the chaos, Ethan spied Sir Gideon slumped against a far-side cannon. Whether or not the man had been killed, was mortally wounded, or simply knocked cold, Ethan didn't know, but it didn't matter either. With the captain no longer a factor, Ethan knew their odds of winning had just increased threefold.

"Across!" he yelled, pointing his cutlass to their foes.

His men issued a terrific war cry in response, and Marcus's skeletons were the first to jump the rails. Each one bore a cutlass in one hand, a lit slow match in the other, and a chest stuffed packed with impromptu grenades. Though plenty of bodies littered the deck of the *Red Fish* thanks to *Victory's* last broadside, most of the crew remained, and they charged their attackers headlong.

In seconds, the first skeleton exploded. Fragments of bone and iron shrapnel ripped through a dozen crew, dropping half and staggering the rest. A heartbeat later, the second and third skeletons vanished in blasts of their own, taking more men with them as well. Panic erupted on the deck and grew more and more as the undead bombs went off.

From atop the quarterdeck, Marcus raised his staff high with one hand and used the other to hold open Lord Belmont's ritual book. Ancient words flowed from his mouth as he read, and dread filled the air. Bones scattered across the deck began to knit together, and the slain crew of the *Red Fish* twitched back to life. They staggered to their feet with groans and drew cutlass and club with jerky movements to the utter horror of the survivors.

"*Maiorem Sanctifica!*" Sir Gideon's voice thundered in the air, deep and resounding as if it came from the heavens themselves.

Brilliant light came from everywhere, forcing Ethan to shield his eyes and turn away. His skin burned and bubbled, and the smell of his own cooked flesh wafted into his nose as he staggered backward. The searing pain lasted only a few seconds. When he regained his composure, he saw that half his skeletal crew, along with those recently reanimated by Marcus, had been blasted apart, their charred remains scattered across the decks of both the *Red Fish* and the *Victory*. And though Sir Gideon stood with his mangled crew ready to fight, so did the rest of Ethan's, living and undead alike.

"Charge!" Ethan yelled, pointing his sword, launching himself into the fray. He made the jump to the *Red Fish* with ease, landing a good three feet into the enemy quarterdeck along with a few more of his crew.

He brought up his cutlass right as Zoey came to his side and took a quick survey of the situation. The main deck was awash in chaos, sailor fighting sailor, skeleton fighting man, and Katryna spinning a gleeful whirlwind of death in the middle of it all.

A blur of movement caught Ethan's eye, and he spun to find a trio of sailors running at Zoey and him with two more following right behind. The group spread out as they engaged the vampires, trying to land cuts and thrusts from a multitude of angles. To their dismay and Ethan's delight, once again, the vampire pair worked in complete concert with one another.

At first, Ethan and Zoey simply concentrated on fending off attacks, making well-timed parries and feints that defeated thrusts and cuts or sent men scrambling backward. Ethan spent a few points of luck in the process to stay safe, but within a dozen seconds, he felt their dance change. Then, without as much as a word or a nod to one another, the two vampires began setting up finishing strikes.

The first came when Zoey slapped aside one man's blade to such a degree it left him exposed. Ethan, coming around after a parry of his own, spun with his momentum and carved a deep gash in the man's forearm. The blow was far from lethal, but it was more than enough to get the man to drop his weapon, leaving him wide open for a thrust to the heart, which Zoey gladly took advantage of.

The next sailor fell in a similar fashion, though Ethan again had spent some luck to keep from being wounded. At that point, the morale for the remaining three dropped, and as they faltered, the third and fourth both lost their heads. The fifth died not long after, though he did put up a frantic fight and tried to regroup with the others. A slow slice across his thighs by Zoey sent him crumpling, and Ethan quickly finished him off with a thrust to the chest.

He'd scarcely pulled his blade free when the sharp cracks of musket fire filled the air. A nearby skeleton dropped, its head shattered, while Ethan's shoulder exploded in pain.

Most troubling of all, however, was the red stain spreading across Zoey's shirt.

Chapter XXXI
A New Wind

Zoey staggered sideways, and her hands clamped where her neck met her shoulder.

At that moment, every thought Ethan had vanished, save one.

"Oh, God, Zoey," he said, pulling her back so that the two were relatively clear of the fighting. "Are you okay?"

His hands fumbled with hers as he tried to pry them away so he could inspect the damage. They slipped over her skin time and again, thanks to a combination of the blood that covered him and his nerves getting the better of him. But after a few tense seconds, the vampire took a deep breath, relaxed, and pulled her hand away.

"I don't think it's deep," she said, exhaling.

"Are you sure?"

"Yeah."

Ethan was about to ask that same question again when his eyes darted up, and he caught sight of Sir Gideon taking aim at them once more.

Throwing six points of luck into his dodge, Ethan grabbed Zoey and heaved them to the side right as Sir Gideon took the shot. The bullet flew past Zoey's head and drilled into the deck nearby.

As the pair rolled to their feet, Ethan furrowed his brow and let slip a growl. "He's going to pay for shooting at you."

"And at you," Zoey added, matching his anger with her own.

Ethan nodded, and together, they leaped up the ropes that led to the marksmen's perch. Hand over hand they went, hearts pounding, fangs sharpening. Along the way, Marcus, from the deck of the *Victory*, fired shot after shot with four pistols he had stuffed in his belt. Not one landed, but they were all more than enough to keep Sir Gideon and his sharpshooters' heads down by the time Ethan and Zoey reached the nest and attacked.

The first man, and possibly the brightest, jumped over the side. Whether or not he made it to the water or broke himself on the deck, Ethan didn't know. His full attention landed squarely on the next, wide-eyed sharpshooter. This one tried to land a butt stroke on Ethan's head, but he easily ducked under the blow before snapping his neck.

Sir Gideon didn't last much longer. He tried to get one last shot off, but between the wounds he'd suffered slowing him down, and Zoey capitalizing on his distraction to *Sneak* behind him, he never managed to pull the trigger.

Zoey clocked him across the back of the head with the hilt of her blade. The Golden Templar stumbled forward, losing his grip on Ethan's pistol in the process. Before it could fall even a foot through the air, Zoey had him wrapped up from behind, one hand locking the man's arm against his back and her other hand clamped on his throat.

"I surrender!" he gasped.

Zoey narrowed her eyes. "You think that matters?"

"No, you don't—"

That was all Sir Gideon got out before Ethan grabbed the man's head, pushed it away, stretching his neck, and bit. Zoey followed suit, feasting from the other side. For a few seconds, Sir Gideon struggled vainly to get the two vampires off of him, but he was far too weak, and by the time they were finished satiating their hunger and healing their wounds, he was far too dead.

"He tasted like...chocolate fondue," Ethan said, wiping his mouth on his sleeve.

Zoey licked her lips. "Yeah. Kinda."

"Not sure how disturbing that makes me to think of people as tasty."

"Doesn't make you disturbing at all. You're not people anymore, remember?" she said, throwing him a wink.

Ethan drew in a quick breath and held it for a beat. "Right. Still forget that bit sometimes. So, what now?"

"We should probably get back to the fight," Zoey said as if it were some mundane event they were begrudgingly obligated to attend.

"Yeah," Ethan said. "I suppose we should."

Ethan knew their actions were odd. In the back of his head, his mind screamed that then was not the time or place for such wanderings, but his heart took control, wanted to relish this peaceful moment the two had where it was just the two of them—wanted to rejoice in the fact that they both lived, especially as the image of Zoey being shot was so fresh in his mind.

With a heavy sigh, Ethan forced himself to lean over the edge of the fighting top and see what was taking place below. To his surprise, he found that the battle was over, and the remaining crew of the *Red Fish* had surrendered, presumably to Katryna, who stood triumphantly over them all as they knelt.

Red Fish captured!
You feel a lot more experienced.
You feel like some skills could improve after some rest.

"Ooo, I leveled," Ethan said, brightening. "About time."

"Nice," she replied before draping her arms around his neck.

Annoyance then crossed his face. "Gah. I still have a set of question marks, though," he griped. "When am I going to find out about this last mystery trait?"

"No idea," she said, seemingly only half listening to his complaint. That thought was further accentuated when she gently took his chin and turned him away from his character sheet so she could look him directly in the eyes. "I missed you, you know."

Ethan cocked his head. "When?"

"When you got up here without me."

Ethan laughed, putting his hands around the small of her back and drawing her close. "That, what, whole half second?"

"It was a long half second."

Ethan kissed her softly and held it for a few beats. When they parted, he rested his forehead against hers and smiled. "You know, I can honestly say this isn't at all what I'd dreamed I'd be doing with the girl I'm stupid for."

Zoey's eyes lit up. "You're stupid for me?"

"I...well, yeah," Ethan stammered before giving a happy, resigned sigh. "I guess this isn't the most romantic place to make that admission, but you know, *Connected* and all."

Zoey turned to the side and shot him a playful look. "So, it's just the game talking?"

Ethan shook his head. "No, but I figured it was an easy out if I needed it."

"You don't need an out," she said. "Unless I do, too."

"No, you don't," Ethan replied. His heart soared so far he felt he could walk on the stars. He wasn't sure how long he stood there relishing the moment, but at some point, he realized things were still far from over. "We should join the others. Don't you think?"

"No," she replied.

"No?"

"No."

Ethan cocked his head and furrowed his brow. "Why not?"

"Because I think you need to kiss me again, first," she said. "You know, just to be sure this new confession of yours is real."

The two came together, losing themselves in the moment and each other until a shrill whistle ruined it all.

"Alright, you two. Seriously," Katryna yelled. "There are captives to deal with and a ship to repair, you know." She paused when Maii added something, which she then repeated. "And a race to win. We're assuming that's still on your agenda."

Ethan stole one more kiss from Zoey before pulling away with a heavy sigh. "It is," he said. Ethan spent a hot moment searching Sir Gideon's body before they left. From it, he took a small silver key that had been hanging from a chain around the man's neck, as well as the magical pistol Ethan had taken from Lord Belmont. After that, he followed Zoey down the ratlines, half sliding, half climbing his way down to the deck. When his boots struck loudly on the bottom, he surveyed everything and everyone around.

A grimace quickly followed. His ship and his crew had seen far better days.

"I need a damage and casualty report," he said.

"Marcus is working on the foremost," Katryna said, pointing to the minotaur who was inspecting every inch of the *Victory*, grunting and shaking his head all the while. "As for crew? Maybe a third of the skeletons are left. Ten men wounded, six of which won't be fit for duties."

"Any dead?"

Katryna nodded, lips pressed tight into a frown. "Four."

Ethan felt a catch in his throat. Jean's death was hard enough on him, but he'd told himself it was one he couldn't have avoided. *They* attacked them, and even though Ethan knew better otherwise, he'd tried his best to convince himself that no other lives would be in danger. But now, with four more killed, he couldn't pretend that was the case, and he couldn't help but wonder how many places he'd gone wrong. Hell, he could've at least learned something about each one who'd died. The guilt of treating them as fodder was a deep-enough pain in and of itself.

"Could've been worse," Zoey said softly.

"Yeah, it could always be worse," Ethan replied, hating the trite platitude. "We might have lost the battle and lost them all."

"No, I guess I should've said, it *should* have been worse," she corrected. "We lost what, almost fifty skeletons? Each one of those would've been someone alive had we a normal crew. Instead, we only lost four men—good men, don't get me wrong. But only four."

Ethan chewed on her words, and after a few moments, he nodded slowly. "True enough," he said before his eyes scanned his men. They all were tired and bloodied but looked at him expectantly, waiting for him to say something.

What could he say? What would he? Just a quick and simple, get back to work, and by the way, since we still have a race to finish, we might trade broadsides with Azrael or Sedra still, so I hope you have your last will and testament written?

Ethan opened his mouth to speak but stopped when he felt a tension build throughout his shoulders. Though he didn't have an official explanation from Zoey or Narrator, he knew deep down he was about to make one hell of a *Leadership* roll, so he'd better choose his words carefully. It was just too bad he didn't have enough time for an official "rest" so he could pick a talent that might help with this.

That said, these sailors were hardened, he knew. But that didn't mean they didn't need encouragement. And maybe he needed a little from himself, too.

"Men," Ethan said, taking on as much of a commanding posture and tone as he could. "It's been an honor and pleasure to sail with you all, and as we make preparations to get underway, I want each and every one of you to know that all of you have my undying gratitude, and not a single one of you will ever be forgotten, which is why it is my full intention that once we've won, I'll be erecting a monument to you all, with the names of all the *Victory*'s crew proudly on display for all to see, especially those who made their final voyage with us."

Nods of silent approval came from the ranks, but nothing else.

"But for that to happen, we need to cross that finish line," Ethan went on. "So, report to Marcus. Repair what's needed, and let's see this to the end."

The men scurried into action. As they did, Zoey prodded Ethan's side with an elbow. "Not bad."

"Thanks. I thought it would be longer, but I didn't know what else to say," he admitted.

"Sometimes brevity is best," she replied. She then pointed to the prisoners who were still kneeling by Katryna and Maii. "What do you want to do with them?"

Ethan's lips pressed together into a fine line as he crossed his arms over his chest and thought about his options, which seemed to number exactly two: kill them or let them go in a lifeboat. He didn't have a brig to take prisoners, and in the end, what would he do with them? Collect a ransom? From who? And what good would it do even if he did since his only goal was to win the race?

"Snacks?" Maii suggested.

"No, Maii," Ethan said, shaking his head. "They surrendered."

"And?"

"And you can't eat your prisoners," he said.

"We both know that's not true," the ahuizotl replied.

Ethan groaned and rolled his eyes. "You know what I mean. You *shouldn't* eat your prisoners."

"Again, I must beg to differ. Fresh is best, after all."

"Captain!" Marcus called out, interrupting. Once Ethan turned, the minotaur went on. "We've taken on a few new portholes, but nothing serious other than some snapped lines. Fifteen minutes at the most before we can set sail."

"How many skeletons can you mend?" Ethan called back.

Marcus grumbled a few seconds to himself as he counted all of the shattered and scorched bones scattered about. "A dozen, if we find favor with the Great Lord Charethes—may he always infuse my soul with his undying power. Even then, maybe not even half."

Ethan's eyes went wide. "Half? As in six or seven?"

"Sorry. I suppose I meant a third," Marcus said. "Sir Gideon's...regrettable purification spells did considerable damage."

A few curses escaped Ethan's lips before he reigned it in. Now was not the time to do anything but focus on what was, not on what he wished were. "She's not going to sail very well with such a minimal crew, is she?" Ethan asked, looking to his first mate.

"Sail? Yes," Zoey said. "Fight? Not so much."

Ethan nodded and drummed his fingers on his side. He wondered if they'd be fortunate enough to avoid both the *Griffin* and *The Popinjay*, but ultimately he felt relying on such a thing would be about the most reckless approach he could take.

"You all," he finally said, directing his words to the prisoners. "Do you want to set out on your own? There's only one longboat available."

The men exchanged nervous glances and some hushed words before one spoke. "If it's that or dancing the hempen jig, I think we'll be just fine cramming together."

"I ask because I could use more crew," Ethan said.

"You can't be serious," Katryna objected. "We all just cut each other to pieces."

"I am serious," Ethan said, "and as you so rightly pointed out, we just cut each other to pieces. The last thing any of us wants, I'm sure, is to fight one another again."

Rumblings came from the prisoners, and sensing he needed to speak more on the matter, Ethan filled them in on the rest of his thoughts. "Your captain is dead and whatever coin is in his strongbox is about to be mine," Ethan said. "On my honor, if you sail with us, fight with us if need be, I'll not only grant you your freedom after we've won, but I'll see to it you're paid a proper earning for fourteen days at sea, plus an additional crown each. If that's not good enough, I'll send you on your way right here, right now, in peace, but you won't have a farthing to your name."

Despite Ethan's words, the prisoners still wore looks of skepticism while some traded whispers of disbelief and suspicions of treachery. One man, stout with a handful of scars on his cheeks and just as many rings in his ears, spoke. "What of our wounded?" he asked. "Half of them can barely fit to hold their guts in."

"I'll see to it their injuries are cleaned and dressed, and they'll be fed and given space to rest. But before any of you even think about taking advantage of my generosity, let me be the first to say that our ever-hungry ahuizotl has my blessing to eat anyone who steps out of line."

"Or wanders near the line," Maii added.

Ethan glared at the monster. "Quiet. When I'm gone, you can terrorize to your heart's content. But not a moment sooner."

"As you wish," Maii replied with a slight bow.

Ethan tipped his head and turned back to the others. "Now then, what say you all?"

The prisoners conferred one last time, though it didn't last long. At the end of it, a large, burly man with olive skin and a split forehead took to his feet. "It is with great pleasure and considerable thanks that we accept your offer," he said, bowing deeply. "Where would you have our service, Captain?"

With the newest members of his crew being directed by Katryna and under the intense gaze of Maii, Ethan stepped into the Captain's quarters, cutlass leading the way. His muscles tensed when he crossed the threshold, half expecting some bullheaded, last remaining and loyal crew member to be hiding there and come out swinging. No one did.

A fine purple rug covered the polished oak floor, one that had seen better days for sure, but it was in far better shape than Ethan would've thought. Paneled windows, smashed due to recent battle, lined the back wall, and the remains of a desk and foot chest were up against the right side. Though the shot that had ultimately caused all that destruction had long since passed through, the exit hole, a good foot and a half wide, sat plain as day, letting in a small draft. Ethan did spend a hot second searching the bed on the left, but when it came up empty, he joined Zoey in rifling through the contents of said desk and chest.

"Find anything yet?" he asked, kicking away some debris that covered one of the broken drawers. "We don't have a lot of time."

Zoey looked up, one hand keeping the chest lid open. "No. Well, some coin, which is always great for boosting morale," she said. "But nothing of immediate use."

"I found a quill," Ethan said, plucking it from the debris. "Oh, and a mostly empty half bottle of ink."

"Half bottle? Like half-full?"

"No, I mean the other half is scattered over there," he said, pointing to a corner that was stained black.

"Oh, right."

The pair continued their search for a little bit longer until Zoey, having tossed all of the folded trousers and coats stored in the chest and coming up empty, stood, coin purse in hand. "I think this is it," she said. "I suggest we go topside so we can leave ASAP."

"I suppose a sack full of crowns is better than nothing," Ethan said with a shrug. He turned, intent on heading out, when an oddity in the desk caught his eye. Or rather, the center drawer, which had broken off its rails and was lying on the floor, caught his eye.

"Now that's weird."

Zoey turned and cocked her head. "What is?"

"This," he said, picking up the drawer. "It's not long enough for the desk."

"Looks long enough to me," she said, shrugging.

Ethan turned it over a few times, and when it didn't reveal any secrets, he knelt at the desk. It took him only a split second to see the metal box stuck underneath the desk, pushed to the back. Excited at finding a secret (and hoping that maybe there was an achievement for it he didn't know about), Ethan grabbed it with his hands. After a bit of coaxing, he managed to pop it off whatever mount it had been on.

"Tada," he said, holding it up proudly.

"Nice," Zoey said, looking and sounding genuinely impressed. "What do you suppose is in here?"

Zoey shrugged. "No idea. But why don't you let me take a look."

Ethan pulled away and playfully eyed her with suspicion. "Why?"

"Well, you can open it if you like," she said, stepping back and crossing her arms. "But if it's trapped, don't come crying to me when it blows up in your hand."

Ethan chuckled and handed it over. "Ah, good point. I happen to like my fingers."

"Eh," she said with a shrug. "They're alright."

"Alright? They're fantastic, thank you very much. Look how well they bend," Ethan said, wiggling them for extra effect. "Pretty sure you'd be sad if I didn't have them."

"Is that a fact?" she said with a teasing grin. "I bet I could get by."

"Get by? Sure. But they can do wonderful things for you, too, that you'd be sad about if that were no longer the case."

"Such as?"

"Such as freeing you from the chains of a lich, for one," Ethan said, enjoying the game.

"If memory serves, I freed myself by turning into mist."

"Yeah, well, that's only because I managed to mix the right reagents and blow up the gem—courtesy of my nimble fingers, thank you very much," he went on.

"Well, these nimble fingers are going keep yours safe," she said, turning her attention to the box. For the next several moments, Zoey turned it over in her hand, inspecting every inch before spending twice as much simply staring into the keyhole on one side. When she was done, she sighed heavily. "Well, it's definitely trapped," she said with a frown. "And the tumblers make me think it's going to be a complete pain to pick."

"We do have a key," Ethan said, holding up the small silver one he'd plucked from Sir Gideon's body. "Looks like it will fit."

Zoey took it but didn't give it a try. "We're missing something."

"Like what?" he asked. "We've got the key. We found where it was hidden. What else could there be?"

Zoey snorted. "More than you will ever know."

"Maybe Maii would know."

"Why would he? He's an ahuizotl, not a thief."

"I think you said that wrong."

Zoey raised an eyebrow. "Say again?"

"It should've been, 'Damn it, Ethan. He's an ahuizotl, not a thief!'" Though Ethan ended it all with a bright grin and expectation of laughter at the semi-obscure reference, all he got from his vampire lover was a stare and an uncomfortable silence. "Never mind," he said, huffing. "But we should still get him in here. He's the master of illusions, right? Surely he can spot them."

"Assuming there is one."

"You're going to feel silly when he marches in here and sees it right away," Ethan said, grinning. "Unless, of course, you're feeling threatened? I mean, you are a rogue, right? Can't have the pet ahuizotl taking your place."

Zoey narrowed her eyes. "I am not threatened."

"Then let's bring him in."

"Fine. Let's."

Zoey stood and marched out of the quarters, and barely a quarter minute later, she re-entered with Maii in tow. The ahuizotl looked perturbed, and the reason for his annoyance was obvious given the blood staining the fur around his mouth. Ethan could only hope that blood hadn't come from someone alive.

"This better be good," Maii said. "It's rude to interrupt a meal."

"I'll buy you a fattened calf when we win as compensation," Ethan said. "I need you to tell me where the magical trap is on this box."

"If he can even see one," Zoey tossed in.

Maii glanced at the box. "Two calves, and you've got yourself a deal."

Ethan nodded. "Two it is. Work your magic."

In the blink of an eye, the ahuizotl flicked his tail at the box. It glowed briefly, and the keyhole in the front disappeared while another popped into view in the back. "Not sure what the trap is, but that's the right keyhole," he said. "You're welcome."

Zoey's mouth hung open. "No...but..."

"I'm an ahuizotl, dear," he said with no small amount of smugness. "A simple illusion like that's not going to fool me."

With that, Maii turned around and strutted out the door. Once he was gone, Zoey frowned. "I knew there was an illusion."

Ethan grinned. "Mm-hm."

"I said we were missing something," she said as she stuck the key in and turned the lock.

"I know."

"Then why are you harping on this?"

"I'm not."

"I'm a good rogue, thank you very much," she said.

Ethan felt his brow wrinkle. "I never said you weren't?"

Zoey huffed but said nothing. She stuck the key into the lock, gave it a turn, and popped the lid to the box. Nestled in the velvet-lined interior sat a small crystal flask with a rubber cork stuck in the top and a red wax seal around the edge. Dark clouds swirled within while miniature streaks of lightning jumped from one to another.

"Holy crap," Ethan said, drawing near like a moth to a flame. "Tell me that's what I think it is."

"Wind in a bottle," Zoey said. She laughed and shook her head. "Should've known he was the one who stole it."

"How the hell did Sir Gideon get it?" Ethan asked.

Zoey shook her head. "No idea. Guess he had a few thief skills we didn't know about."

"I suppose that's not too surprising, given he was a Golden Templar, and from what I understand, they aren't exactly the most honorable type."

"Yeah."

"I wonder what else the guy could've done we didn't know about," Ethan said. "Hopefully not come back from the dead."

Zoey shook her head again. "That would be considered an abomination for them, so I'm going to go out on a limb and say, no, he's not coming back whatsoever."

"Good," Ethan said. His eyes drifted back to the bottle. "I can't believe we have this thing. Not only do we have it, but that also means Azrael and Sedra don't."

Zoey's face brightened. "This is big for us."

"I know."

"I mean, really, really big," she said.

"I *know*, Zoey," Ethan said, laughing. "God, this could be our ticket to an easy first place. Come on. Let's get out of here and put this to good use."

Chapter XXXII
The Final Run

Ethan stood at the helm of the *Victory* as Marcus inspected the bottle. Since he was the one with the most experience in this world when it came to magic, he was the one entrusted with opening the bottle. He'd taken on the task with confidence, but that had been ten minutes ago. And though the *Victory's* snapped lines had been fixed, and she gently glided through the strait's waters on a mild wind, the necromancer remained still, staring at the flask as if one wrong move might take out half the eastern seaboard.

"So," Ethan said, voice trailing, fingers nervously wrapping on his crossed arms. "You can still open it, right?"

"Yes," Marcus said.

"You balked," Ethan replied. When the minotaur glared, Ethan threw up his hands defensively. "I'm only mentioning it because we're on a time crunch, and as far as I can tell, that stopper is just as seated as it was ten minutes ago."

"I don't think any of you appreciate how potent a flask like this could be," he said, pointing a finger at it. "There have been some that have literally wiped out an entire seaboard with the tsunami they've generated."

Reflexively, Ethan sucked in a breath through clenched teeth. "You're serious?"

"Quite," he said. "So perhaps now you can grasp the fact that this is not the time to act rash. Savvy?"

"Savvy."

"We might still win without it," Zoey said. "We could play it safe."

Ethan shook his head without hesitation. "No," he replied. "We were already behind, and with that battle, we've lost even more time. We're going to use it." When he saw Marcus shoot him a glance out of the corner of his eyes, he tacked on one last thing. "I trust him. He'll make it work."

"I will," Marcus said, blowing out a huge puff of air through flared nostrils. "And I'll do it right now."

The minotaur extended a gigantic hand. In it, Zoey placed a long, hollow silver needle that she'd been holding for him from the start. Marcus eyed the bottle for a few more seconds, said a prayer so soft that Ethan could only understand its intent, and then carefully inserted the needle.

Ethan tensed as he did, and he heard Zoey suck in a breath and hold it. Ethan didn't know what to expect, but when all that came out was the faintest wisps of smoke, he couldn't help but feel let down.

"That was...anticlimactic," he said.

Marcus, still keeping his focus on the bottle, turned it slightly so it was more pointed to the aft sky than it had been before and held up a thick finger. "That's what happens when one is purposeful as opposed to rash," he said. He then gently tapped the side of the flask four times in a deliberate, slow rhythm. "Now, give it a moment, and you'll see."

It didn't take but half that. The breeze picked up, snapping the sails taut and sending a wave of excitement through the crew. Even Maii took an eager interest as he stood tall, forelegs on the railings and eyes fixated on the horizon as his ears perked.

The *Victory* began to accelerate, carving a small wake through the waters.

Ethan turned his attention to the crow's nest. "Eyes sharp, Katryna. We still need to clear the strait."

"I'm on it," she yelled back. "I'll have us through without a scrape."

The speed of the *Victory* continued to build, and within several minutes, she sliced across the ocean with a downwind run that surpassed all of Ethan's hopes and dreams.

"How fast does she run?" Ethan asked, directing his question portside to one of the men on the deck.

The man, skin a deep sunburnt olive from taking the sun more than it should, tossed a line overboard and began counting the knots as they slipped through his fingers. "Twenty knots and quickening!"

Thrilled, Ethan turned to Zoey. "Seems good."

"Very," she said with a nervous chuckle. "Now we see if the sails and lines hold."

"Think we should reef them?"

"Your call."

Ethan tensed and drew a breath through clenched teeth. He needed every ounce of speed he could get, but he also knew there was a point to where the winds would tear everything to shreds, and he really didn't need that to happen. Still, he had no idea how far behind Azrael he was, and with that thought, he shot her a grin. "Go big or go home, right?"

"Won't be the first time we've risked it all," she said, throwing him a grin back. "Can't say you keep a girl bored, that's for sure."

The ship lifted a moment later, rising on a giant wave. As the bow dipped, Ethan found his footing twisted in place. The sky grew dark behind the *Victory,* not even a half league away, and with the wind and waves it brought, so came worries that they'd be tossed into rocks or another ship before they could clear the strait.

"We'll make it," Zoey said.

Ethan nodded and forced himself to relax and stay confident. "Katryna," he called. "Can you see the end of the strait?"

The woman popped over the side of the crow's nest with unbridled enthusiasm. "Three leagues at the most!"

Ethan then directed his next question to Marcus, who was now at the very aft the ship, bottle still in hand. "How much more is in that flask?"

"Just ran out," the minotaur said, turning around and showing it off. "It's a strong storm for sure, but I'm not sure how long it will last."

The *Victory* caught another large wave, pitching the bow down and up once more, at which point he returned his attention to seeing the ship through to coastal waters. Minutes stretched seemingly into hours as wave after wave lifted her aft, and more than once, Ethan worried they'd plunge underwater, or the sails would tear.

His crew, however, seemed as determined as ever, keeping to their duties with a skill and resolve that left Ethan wanting nothing. And if they were giving it their all for his sake, he wasn't going to give them any less.

"We've got this, men," he said once he could see the end of the strait for himself. "I can taste the finish line from here."

"Never doubted the choice for a second," Zoey said, giving him another squeeze.

Ethan eased the grip he had on the railing as the storm abated about a minute before they broke free of the strait and hit the coastal waters. Portside, near the horizon, he could make out Fort Darvison, a small stone structure on the coast, which according to the maps, was the last point of interest before the finish line.

"We're almost there!" Ethan shouted, throwing a celebratory fist high into the air.

The words had scarcely left his mouth when Katryna gave a cry of warning. "Captain! *Griffin* and *The Popinjay* starboard side!"

Ethan spun, spyglass in hand. It took him only two breaths to find them both, each racing along the coast with full sails. "At least we've come out ahead," Ethan said, tucking the telescope away. "Swing us to port and follow the coast, if you'd be so kind, Mister Potts."

The helmsman spun the wheel, and the *Victory* turned, now running a near full two points from the wind. Their speed slowed, much to Ethan's dismay, and after ten more minutes of racing down the coast, what tension he'd been carrying in his shoulders doubled when he noticed both the *Griffin* and *The Popinjay* had made considerable gains.

Ethan rose on his toes and brought his spyglass up. He made several sweeps of the waters ahead, trying to find where the buoys were that marked the safe harbor zone—the final stretch of water where the use of cannons was forbidden. If they could get there before being blasted apart, he liked the odds of them winning. He tried not to think what would happen if they couldn't.

"Katryna, do you see the buoys for the safe harbor?" he called out after a couple more futile attempts to find them.

The newly minted vampire leaned over the crow's nest and shook her head, but after a second, she held up a finger and scanned the open waters not ahead but those far from the coast. "There!" she said, pointing. "That's them, I'm sure."

"There?" Ethan repeated, baffled. "That can't be right. They're supposed to be along the coast, a mile from the finish."

"That is them, Captain. I am certain," she called back after checking again. "Either that first storm we weathered or the wind we made must have blown them adrift."

Ethan shook his head and cursed. "Doesn't that figure," he muttered.

"They only mark the zone. They don't form it," Zoey said. "Everyone knows a mile from the finish, no fighting."

"Yeah, maybe, but will they honor that?" Ethan huffed.

"We'll see."

"Maybe we should lighten the load," Ethan said. "We could dump our carronades easily enough."

"We could, but we'd also be inviting a point-blank broadside that we couldn't answer."

"Crap," Ethan said, frowning.

"Captain! I can see the finish line on the horizon!"

Ethan's eyes lit up at Katryna's report, and he dashed forward, spyglass up once more, desperate to see what she was pointing at with his own eyes. Sure enough, a single lighthouse stood proud at the horizon, perched upon a large bluff. From that lighthouse, he knew, only a half mile of the race remained.

Ethan tried to run a few calculations in his head on whether or not they'd reach the finish before Azrael or Sedra overtook them. He hoped they would, but the wind direction clearly favored their ship design over his. With that in mind, he decided not to leave anything to chance.

"Stores overboard!" he yelled. "If it's not crew, shot, powder, or gun, I want it off this ship!" He paused for a moment and then quickly made an addendum. "And the chasers! Send them over.

There's no point in racing as if we're going to be in second place, ever. We win this right here. Right now."

The crew sprang into action, racing below deck and back up again as others sent the two nine-pound cannons on the bow overboard. The guns had scarcely hit the water when a dozen barrels of salted meat went over, followed by several sacks of flour. The skeletons who hauled the food had little difficulty bringing them up and even less remorse tossing them to the sea. Though what had been thrown wasn't nearly as much as what they'd started with, Ethan still guessed they'd dropped a few hundred pounds' worth, barrels included. It wasn't much, seeing how he only had to feed a minimal crew, but the amount of freshwater dumped overboard was considerable indeed.

The water stores came up in dozens of hogsheads and casks. Zoey, who'd been keeping tabs on the inventory since the beginning, answered the question he was about to ask. "A little over four hundred gallons," she said. "Maybe four-fifty."

"How heavy is that?"

"Four-fifty would be close to two tons," she said after a moment's thought. "Otherwise, a ton and a half."

"Good for us either way," Ethan said. The crew continued to toss the rest of the stores: lines, linens, tar, and even what few barrels of rum remained. As they worked, Ethan raised his spyglass once again. "They're still gaining," he said after a few moments. "But not as fast as before, I don't think."

"We don't need a lot," Zoey said. "Still, it might be a good idea to ready for battle."

"I know," he replied. He then cupped his hands around his mouth to give his next order. "Load the carronades! Double bar and chain both sides!"

Barely a minute had passed when the bow of Azrael's ship, the *Griffin*, erupted in smoke and flame. A pair of cannonballs sailed through the air, one overshooting the *Victory* by at least fifty yards, while the other punched a hole through her sails.

"Keep her running straight and true, Mister Potts," Ethan said. "All we need to do is cross that line."

Minutes passed, and all the while Ethan nervously rubbed his fingers together, and his crew finished preparing the carronades. He had no intention of turning, not with the finish line fast approaching, but as Zoey had said, they'd need to defend themselves if they were caught.

The *Griffin* fired again, and then a third time, scoring two more hits from the pair of salvos. Another ball ripped through the mainsail while the other came crashing down on the deck, shattering the chest of a skeleton before plowing through the legs of two more.

"A little over one mile!" Katryna yelled, pointing an excited finger toward the shore ahead.

Ethan tore his eyes away from his pursuers. Sure enough, the harbor and the buoys marking the finish line lay not far off the bow, seemingly within spitting distance.

"God, this is going to be close," Ethan said, biting down on a knuckle. He glanced behind him after a few more seconds. Azrael lagged by a little over a couple of hundred yards by his best guess.

Again Azrael's chasers fired, and again, Death scored a pair of hits on the *Victory*.

"He'll be going after our rigging next volley," Zoey said. "Probably a broadside."

"Been waiting for him to try, actually," Ethan said with a grin.

"You're not worried?" Zoey asked.

Ethan shook his head. "Not one bit. *Luck of the Devil* is ready. We'll dodge his broadside and be home free."

"Unless he doesn't shoot his wad all at once," Zoey said.

"What do you mean?"

"I mean, with as many guns as he's fielding, he can afford to space out the shots into smaller volleys, each ten seconds apart," she explained. "We'll only be able to dodge one group."

Ethan's heart dropped six inches in his chest, and he felt his mouth hang open as well. He hadn't thought such a simple tactic would essentially nullify the defense he'd been counting on.

"You think he'd do that?"

Zoey nodded. "I would."

"Crap," Ethan said. He tried to come up with something else he could do, but before he could, another cry filled the air.

"Captain! She's presenting!"

Ethan felt his heart jump into his throat and spun. Azrael's ship, lagging behind now by less than fifty yards, was turning starboard. Ethan only needed half of his spectacular eleven points of intelligence to see what was about to happen, and thankfully, he didn't waste a moment to react.

"Mister Potts! One point starboard!" he yelled. "Carronades fire at will!"

The *Victory* cut to the side as the helmsman maneuvered her, and a moment later, the gun crews brought down their slow matches, igniting the touchholes on each gun. Five of the carronades fired, sending a bar and chain ripping through *Azrael's* sails and lines. Before the remaining three could fire, however, *Azrael* answered with a full broadside.

The sheer amount of flame and smoke that erupted from the *Griffin* completely obscured the warship as two dozen eighteen- and thirty-two-pound cannons ripped into Ethan's ship. The heavy cannonballs punched through the *Victory's* side, sending splinters and shrapnel through hull and crew alike, while chain devastated her sails and rigging.

A half second later, the deck midship exploded, heaving his ship to the side, snapping what little lines remained, and toppling a mast.

Ethan, dazed, bloodied, and thoroughly stuck with wood splinters, picked himself off the deck. Smoke obscured everything in sight, and the smell of flames and burnt powder filled the air. The sight of total carnage before him drew out his insatiable thirst for blood. Fangs sharpened, and his eyes turned black. All he wanted to do at this point was feed.

"Abandon ship!" someone called.

The cry snapped Ethan back in control, at least for the moment. When he took to his feet, cringing from pain, he had enough wits to realize he had to take charge of the situation immediately before all was lost.

Wind swept across the deck, clearing the smoke enough for Ethan to see what was going on. *Victory* burned in a half dozen places, and her side had a hole the size of an elephant near the waterline. Seawater poured in, causing the ship to list, and no doubt she'd founder in less than a minute. Probably half that.

Griffin turned sharply, swinging her bow around to head for the finish line. Even with *Victory* destroyed, *Azrael* couldn't waste any time. *The Popinjay*, lighter and sleeker, cut through the water at full sail only a couple of hundred yards behind. And since Ethan had torn into *Griffin's* sails moments ago, *The Popinjay* was making considerable gains with each passing second.

Ethan stared at the third-place ship for a half second before realizing he had to do something to stay in the race.

"Belay that order!" he shouted.

"Ethan! We can't stay here!" Zoey shouted back, dragging herself out of a gaping hole in the deck. She, like many other of the crew, bled profusely, staining tattered clothes.

"We're not!" he shouted back. "All hands, boarding party! Grab our colors! That ship is ours!"

The men froze, but it only took them a second to understand. In an effort to shave off as much distance to the finish line as possible, the *Griffin* had cut back so hard that she sailed dangerously close to the *Victory*. If they could take control of the *Griffin* and hoist their flag, by the rules, the ship was theirs. And if it was theirs when she crossed the finish line, that changed everything.

The first grapple went out almost immediately, quickly followed by three more, then six after that. A few missed their mark, and a couple of others were promptly cut loose by Azrael's crew. But enough tangled with the *Griffin's* lines and caught hold of her rails that the two ships became intertwined.

"Everyone across!" Ethan yelled, charging forward with pistol and cutlass in hand. His feet pounded across the deck while his heart pounded in his chest.

The two ships pulled closer together, but the *Griffin* kept her rudder hard, making sure that they never fully came side by side.

Skeletons threw themselves over the railing, easily clearing the three feet that separated the two ships, while the men followed behind. Ethan, as he raced across the deck, even caught sight of Katryna, one hand tightly gripping the *Victory's* colors, make a flying leap from her crow's nest, catching herself on the *Griffin's* ratlines and making her way to the *Griffin's* fighting tops.

The moment his foot hit the top of the railing, he used every bit of strength he had to launch himself across. Air rushed by his face as he sailed between the ships. He landed with a thud a little forward of the quarterdeck. Immediately, he took aim at the nearest crewmember with his pistol, and the shot landed true. The man clutched his chest and fell to the deck, blood pooling all around him.

Critical hit!
Sailor killed!

Another sailor came rushing at him, cutlass held back for an overhead shop. Three of his companions followed suit, only a few steps behind. The one in the lead fell, catching a pistol shot in the gut, but not from Ethan.

"Charge!" Zoey yelled, racing by with her sword at the ready, trailing a wake of undead crew behind her.

Ethan surged with her and the others, and his group clashed with the *Griffin's* crew with violent results. Skeletal minion and man fell in equal number to blade and shot. While Ethan was glad the undead he fielded could hold their own, it was clear they didn't have the numbers to take the ship. Worse, the *Griffin* still sailed straight for the finish.

"Zoey!" Ethan said after ducking a chop and setting her up for the perfect counterattack. "We need that helm!"

"I don't think they're too keen on giving it to us," she said.

Ethan clenched his teeth as he was forced to retreat and acknowledge her point. Though the two of them continued to fight in perfect concert, they'd been effectively hemmed into one small portion of the deck.

A pair of explosions from within Azrael's ranks sent men stumbling. Marcus and Maii came crashing down onto the deck a few yards away, further adding to the chaos. The minotaur kept with the forward momentum and gored the nearest sailor with his horns, driving the poor soul into the others. The moment the man fell from Marcus's horns, the minotaur pointed his staff and unleashed jets of sickly green-and-yellow flame.

"Burn, the lot of you!" Marcus said, his voice booming. "Burn and serve me in undeath for the rest of time!"

Maii cackled in delight as the necromancer worked, fires consuming dozens of crew. As the chaos spread across the deck, the ahuizotl charged into the middle of it all. The sailors at first scattered but quickly swarmed the ahuizotl, stabbing him multiple times with cutlass and dirk. The lucky quickly realized the monster was never there at all, while those who were not so much screamed one last time before his jaws crushed their necks from behind.

Loud whistling noises filled the air, and then suddenly, a half dozen cannonballs from *The Popinjay* came crashing down, shattering skeleton and man alike and carving long trenches in the sea of combatants.

At that moment, Ethan pointed his sword to the helm. "Now's our chance! Let's go!"

Together with Zoey, he drove forward, using both pistol and cutlass to reach his goal. As he went, more skeletons and crew poured onto the ship to join the fight. He'd almost reached the stairs to the helm when a fiery pain erupted across the back of his shoulders, and he staggered sideways.

The sailor hits you!
You have been moderately wounded!

Ethan gritted his teeth and twisted to the side just in time to deflect the follow-up attack by one of Azrael's men. The two men's blades locked against each other, and as much as Ethan tried to free himself without getting stuck, stabbed, or sliced open in the process, he couldn't. His muscles strained against his opponents, but before he could work himself into a panic, Zoey took the man's hands at the wrists before issuing a lethal cut across his throat.

"Thanks," Ethan said with a brief sigh of relief.

"Bill is in the mail," she replied with a wink.

Their mini-celebration ended then and there. More of Azrael's crew began to swarm their position, and they beat a hasty path to and up the stairs. At the top, Ethan found another sailor waiting for them. The two exchanged a couple of quick attacks, which ended when Ethan slashed the man across the belly. When the sailor tried to hold his guts in, Ethan slipped behind him and sank his fangs into the poor soul's neck.

He hadn't intended to take a snack, but in that moment, his stomach growled, and *The Hunger* took over. Sweet, precious blood flowed into Ethan's mouth. His eyes rolled back into his head, savoring every drop and relishing the feel of wounds healing. Thankfully Zoey stayed close, fending off attacks with such fury, not a soul drew near.

"Ah, Captain Ethan and his lovely first mate," Azrael said, his voice piercing the chaos of the battle. "I must award you both full marks for effort. Truly, a valiant run if I ever saw one. Futile, but valiant nevertheless."

Ethan shoved his meal to the side as he turned to face his foe. Azrael stood at the top of the stairs leading to the poop deck, pipe firmly stuck in his mouth, cutlass and pistol both still stuffed in his belt, and not a care in the world shining in his eyes.

A split second later, Ethan felt Zoey press up against his back. Though they shared not a word between them, he knew that at least for the moment, none of Azrael's crew were trying to attack.

"This is your last chance to surrender," Ethan said, steeling himself for the duel of a lifetime. "We're taking your ship."

Azrael threw back his head and laughed. "Who is this we you speak of, Ethan?" he asked, gesturing at the ship as a whole.

Ethan glanced over his shoulder and ended up swallowing hard to rid himself of the lump in his throat. The *Victory* lagged, burning and listing and off the port side, and the lines she'd run to the *Griffin* cut. Worse, of the crew that had managed to cross, most of the skeletons had been cut down, and only a handful of men remained as well—counting Marcus with Maii near the bow, and Katryna, who'd fought her way up to a fighting top.

"That's, what, eleven of yours against my hundred and fifty?" Azrael said. "I must say, if you insist on sailing such treacherous waters, I shall find myself sorely disappointed in you. After all, what sort of captain condemns his own crew to such a grisly, inevitable fate over a mere dog?"

"She's not a mere dog. She's my dog," Ethan said with a growl. "And as long as we're talking disappointments, what sort of captain hides behind his crew for control of his ship?"

Azrael smirked. "Trying to wound my pride?" he asked before tipping his tricorne hat. "I'm insulted you think so little of me that it would work. Nevertheless, I accept your challenge—and Miss Zoey, I believe this means you and I have officially resumed our contest."

"I believe it does," she replied, coming shoulder to should with Ethan and narrowing her eyes. "Now call off your men."

The dread pirate laughed and tipped his tricorne hat to the two of them. "But of course," he said. He stuck two fingers in his mouth and blasted a whistle so loud and shrill, it put an end to the fighting on deck. "Listen here, you dirty scallywags," he boomed. "There'll not be a single blade raised or pistol shot while the three of us have a proper contest. If anyone here has the slightest inkling of going against that, you best be walking the plank right now because I'll be feeding you to Leviathan myself, one bone at a time!"

"Aye, Captain," cried one of his men. "But what of *The Popinjay*?"

"Reload the cannons and give her a broadside she won't forget," Azrael sneered.

"Sir? She's inside the safe harbor," someone called back. "We'll be disqualified."

"She fired first!" Azrael roared. "Now answer in kind!"

Death then sucked in a deep breath and calmly started down the stairs. "If I may offer one last bit of advice before we start, Captain. Try not to die too fast. It's bad for the crew's morale."

"You first," Ethan said, raising his magical pistol. The very instant he had a bead on Azrael's chest, he pulled the trigger.

The pistol kicked like a wild mule, sparks, flame, and a billowing cloud of smoke shooting out of the weapon. At the same instant, Azrael raised an open hand. The shot struck him square in the palm and didn't even break his skin. A split second later, the weapon flew out of Ethan's grasp and into Death's waiting hand.

"I think we can make this more exciting than that, don't you agree?" he said, casually tossing the weapon behind him. "Let's give the crew a show."

Ethan raised his cutlass. "Then what are you waiting for?"

"Absolutely nothing," he replied.

In a flash, Azrael closed the distance between himself and the two vampires with both rapier and main-gauche drawn. The moment he was within striking distance, he drove the point of his sword for Ethan's heart while at the same time using his dagger to fend off Zoey's counterattack with little difficulty.

Ethan twisted to the side, barely managing to catch the attack on the hilt of his blade and deflect it away. Instead of retreating, however, he launched himself forward, but also at an angle, so that Azrael now had to deal with the two of them from different sides.

It would've taken only a little footwork for Death to maneuver so that he could easily face both, but he didn't. In fact, he stepped forward so that Ethan and Zoey were on opposite sides. "For the record, a hundred years from now, I wouldn't dream of fighting you two like this," he said with a bright smile. "But as you two lovers are only starting to become one, I think this will prove more entertaining."

"You're going to feel stupid when we cut you down," Zoey said as her face hardened. She attacked a moment later, with Ethan following in unison. She went for a slice across Azrael's neck as Ethan opted for a feinting thrust to the gut where he changed the line of attack that ultimately drove for Death's chest.

Using main-gauche and rapier, Azrael defeated the attacks with ease, and the ones that followed, and the ones that followed those as well. All the while, he issued a few ripostes of his own that were half-hearted and only seemed to be nothing more than flourishes to the ballet he enjoyed.

After several more beats, the Angel of Death met Ethan's lunge with one of his own. He caught Ethan's blade on his handguard, and the two blades slid forward and locked against one another. Then, with a quick twist, he slipped behind Ethan so that he became a shield for Azrael against Zoey.

"Delightful, the both of you," he said, shoving Ethan hard so that he stumbled into his other half. "Might the two of you consider joining my crew? You'll find my employment quite lucrative."

Ethan and Zoey glanced at each other, both sharing the same unspoken thought. Together, they launched into a flurry of blows. Ethan relentlessly attacked Azrael's throat while Zoey kept going for Azrael's legs. Azrael maneuvered skillfully, all the while keeping his face bright and his tone light.

"Is that a no?" he asked.

"No, it's a hell no," Zoey said, redoubling her efforts. At first, even with the increased intensity, it didn't seem as if her bladework would ever be enough to pierce Azrael's defenses. But after the third attack, she managed to dip the point of her blade beneath Azrael's main-gauche and sent it slashing across the top of Death's knee.

Azrael's trousers split open, and bright red blood fountained from the wound. She'd have likely taken the limb in its entirety had Death been a little slower on his feet.

"The first point is yours," he said, his voice darkening. "From here on out, the rest shall be mine."

Death drove forward with blinding speed. He hacked and slashed from a dozen different lines of attack against both Ethan and Zoey, sending them both on their heels as they beat hasty retreats.

It took him only a few seconds to find a hole in their defenses and only a fraction of that to exploit it. Coming from up high, he trapped Zoey's blade with his rapier with one hand, and with the other, threw his main-gauche. The dagger spun twice in the air before its point found her stomach. As before, the weapon had barely pierced her skin when Zoey vanished into a mist, and before Ethan could even think about her reforming, Azrael snapped his fingers, and a blast of wind sent her overboard.

"So predictable," Azrael said, shaking his head. His eyes glanced over Ethan's shoulder before he shrugged. "However, it seems now that the race is almost over. Thus, it's time we wrapped this up."

Ethan didn't have a chance to reply before Azrael renewed his attacks against him. He managed to parry most, but for a few, it was only a hasty retreat that saved his life. He'd scarcely recovered when another blow came, this one even harder than all the previous seemingly combined. As blade clashed blade, the shockwave that rippled through Ethan's arm made it go numb, and he nearly dropped his sword in the process.

"Fast, Ethan, but not fast enough," Azrael said, stepping back and admiring his handiwork.

Ethan glanced downward and immediately wished he hadn't. His shirt was torn and his chest was split beneath the collar bone, and as the blood ran freely, he realized not only could he see a few ribs, but a couple had been cracked as well.

His legs gave out a moment later, and Ethan crashed to the deck.

Chapter XXXIII
Duel With Death

Ethan hurt.

A lot.

Apparently, being a vampire didn't exclude him from pain. Not that he hadn't experienced it before being a relatively new member of the guild of bloodsucking fiends, but this newest wound of his was so excruciating, it was all Ethan could do to push himself to his feet and not tip over the railing when he leaned against it for support.

"Never tasted silver before?" Azrael said. "I think from here on out, you'll have a new appreciation for it."

"I've had worse," Ethan said, gritting his teeth and forcing himself up. He had to fight. He had to win. He had to save his Anne and give Zoey a second chance at life.

The moment he'd straightened, Azrael attacked again. Ethan deflected a slice meant to gut him like a fish and ducked under another chop aimed at separating his head from his shoulders. Ethan countered, driving his blade straight for Death's heart.

Predictably, his blade was turned away, but Ethan didn't stay at arm's length. Instead, he kept driving forward, letting his pain fuel his anger, and his anger keeping him fast, strong, and deadly.

With their blades momentarily locked together, Ethan drove an elbow across Death's face. It landed with a satisfying crunch, which he would've been overjoyed at if Azrael hadn't come up with an even more devastating follow-up.

The Dark Angel drove his fist into Ethan's gut, the blow knocking the air out of him and causing him to double over. He then issued a quick snap kick that caught Ethan square in the face. As Ethan flew backward, he felt his wrist on his sword hand twist painfully, and he reflexively let his cutlass slip from his grasp.

Azrael disarms you!

"No shit, Captain Obvious," Ethan muttered. Thoughts of Narrator's intrusion flew from his mind when Azrael pressed the attack. Ethan jumped back and then dove into a sideways roll, barely dodging a finishing blow.

Thunderous booms erupted from the ship's port side a split second later, causing both combatants to steal a glance at what was going on. A full broadside from the *Griffin* slammed into *The Popinjay's* side, clearing half the deck, ripping lines and sail, and setting it ablaze at the forecastle.

Azrael backed a pace, giving himself enough room to quickly address his crew. "Make ready to fire again, but only if they want a fight," he ordered. "I'll not have anyone say we're not giving a fair sport."

"Aye, Capt'n," came the reply.

Death, who now happened to be next to Ethan's fallen weapon, glanced at it and then the finish line, which was now only a few hundred yards away. "Master Ethan," he said, lowing the tip of his sword a few degrees. "You could be a great asset to my crew. I'll even let you keep your dog as long as you sail with me. What do you say?"

Ethan's response came swift and without a second thought. "How about screw you."

"Manners, Master Ethan," Azrael said, shaking his head. "Manners. They'll get you everywhere in life."

"You want to talk manners? How about you give me my sword back?" Ethan replied. "Unless you think it's polite to kill an unarmed opponent."

Death laughed, and to Ethan's shock, he dipped his foot under Ethan's blade and kicked it over to him. "Whatever makes you feel better," he said as Ethan caught his sword in midair. "This isn't going to be a fairy tale ending, just so you know."

He was right. Ethan hated to admit it, but he was. He had yet to put a scratch on the man, and the finish line was, what, sixty seconds away at best?

"Forty-eight seconds, actually," Azrael said with a grin.

Ethan launched himself forward, hoping, praying, that *Luck of the Devil* would see him through. All he had to do was time it right on when to activate it.

Ethan swung wildly with zero respect for his own self-preservation. His blade cut through the air so fast it left a distinct hiss. Azrael parried, and then again and again, as Ethan kept up the ferocious assault.

With each blow, Ethan felt as if he were getting close to victory. With each ring of steel against steel, of feeling the shock of their swords clash together through his arm, he redoubled his attacks. He drove them from a dozen different lines of attack, forcing Azrael to backpedal more than once. Yet no matter how close he came to piercing Death's web of steel, Ethan couldn't land a single strike.

But he didn't let that stop him or even slow him down. Death had to lose, even if it was just this once. Hunger for victory seemed to tap into Ethan's hunger for blood, which only fueled his actions further, faster, and harder.

Their blades locked once again. Something hard slammed into Ethan's back an instant later. He cried out in pain but had the presence of mind to keep his guard up enough to keep from being skewered when Azrael kicked him in the chest and tried to finish him.

Death, however, didn't press the attack. At least, not as Ethan expected. The Dark Angel stepped back twice more and swept his free hand through the air like he was brushing aside a veil.

Ethan barely caught sight of the cannonball hurling through the air to duck in time. The iron sphere whistled by his head before careening into the water. Immediately, Azrael waved his hand twice more, and from the gun deck, another two shells shot through the air. Ethan managed to get out of the way of the first, but the second glanced off his ribs.

Pain exploded across his side as he could feel bones break. Azrael instantly took advantage of the situation and attacked. Ethan raised his cutlass and deflected the first blow, but not the second. The tip dug through his left shoulder, spilling his blood.

"You would need tricks," Ethan growled.

"I don't need them, Master Ethan, but I do enjoy them," Azrael said with a shrug. "But to prove my point, I'll have that hand of yours right now."

Azrael lunged forward, setting Ethan on his heels.

Ethan snapped his blade up to deflect an angled cut at his neck, but he overextended the parry. Death slid his blade down and under Ethan's guard and cut Ethan open at the forearm. The shock of being hit yet again was enough to keep Ethan from being able to act fast enough so that when Azrael spun twisted his sword through the air and brought it back sharply around, not only did it get by Ethan's meager defense, but it cleaved through Ethan's wrist with ease.

You have been critically wounded!

Ethan fell back, screaming and clutching his bloody stump. Water filled his eyes, blurring his vision, and his legs lost their strength. Time slowed to a crawl, which was exactly what he didn't want to have happen at that point, because not only was he acutely aware of Azrael moving forward to issue the coup de grâce, but he could also smell the fear of his own crew wondering what had happened to their captain, hear the cheers of the crowd watching the race's final moments onshore, and taste utter defeat in his mouth.

Despite the crushing weight of defeat on his soul, Ethan straightened, and life flickered in his eyes. He snapped his head to the side to make sure that it wasn't too late for his thoroughly insane idea to come to fruition. The *Griffin*, plowing through the water, had about fifty yards to reach the finish line. Better yet, Katryna still held her position, high on the mast, with the *Victory's* colors flying.

"You should've taken my offer," Azrael said, raising his sword.

"No. You should've taken mine," Ethan replied. Though he hadn't technically made one, he knew, it seemed like a snappy thing to say at the very least. And it did give Azrael a half-second pause which was all Ethan needed to start running.

Ethan shot across the deck of the ship, activating *Luck of the Devil,* legs driving him forward with every ounce of strength and speed they could. He weaved through the crew, dodging their attacks with automatic success while his eyes focused on the prize: the bowsprit of the *Griffin.* The wooden spar, sitting directly about the bronze figurehead, jutted forward at least thirty feet over the open water.

A strange sense of calm settled over Ethan as he ran. Maybe it was the blood loss or his mind cloaking him in the sweet embrace of denial as to what his ultimate fate would soon be, but Ethan liked to think it was the universe telling him to relax. He was unstoppable.

Guided by his talent, Ethan ducked his head and made a half twist to the left a split second before a pistol—from Azrael, he knew—fired. The bullet zipped by his ear and struck one of the crew manning the cannons in the back.

"Stop him!" Azrael roared.

But the crew didn't hear, thanks to a return volley of cannon fire by *The Popinjay.* The smaller ship's sixteen-pound guns weren't going to sink the *Griffin* with a single broadside, but they were more than enough for Ethan to capitalize on the chaos that they brought.

The cannonballs tore through the rails, sending fragments of wood and metal in all direction. One shot struck the ropes to a deck cannon, breaking the piece loose from its mooring. As the gun slid back, knocking aside crew, Ethan vaulted over it and was up the steps to the forecastle.

"Curse you all!" Azrael yelled. "I'll have every last one of you dance the hempen jig if he leaves this ship!"

Three men, the final three that stood between Ethan and his goal, apparently both heard the order and had the wits to respond. They turned from their station to meet him, weapons drawn. Ethan knew he hadn't a second to spare, let alone enough time to fight, even if he could. He'd have to rely on his speed to see him through.

Ethan made a mad dash to their right and then suddenly cut left when they followed his movements. With less than a couple of seconds left of unimpeded successes, Ethan darted by his opponents with ease.

His strides grew even longer, and he practically flew across the deck. Shots zipped through the air. Some missing by a foot or two, others tearing neat but otherwise harmless holes in his jacket. Right as this left foot struck the bowsprit, the Zen-like calm that had washed over him faded. In its place, panic gripped his heart with icy tendrils.

Luck of the Devil had run its course.

One last shot came from behind—a deafening boom that originated with Azrael. Ethan didn't have to be looking to know where it had come from. He could feel it in his very soul, and all he could do was brace for the hit and hope and pray whatever fortune he still had left would see him through.

The shot took Ethan through the side of the neck, sending his blood spraying out in front. His vision dimmed immediately, but he half ran, half staggered onward. Just a few yards to go.

At the very tip of the beam, thirty feet ahead of the main hull of the *Griffin,* Ethan watched as he passed over the finish line. A dozen more pistols fired, and he fell.

As the water rushed up to meet him, everything went black.

Chapter XXXIV
Fin

"Hey, sleepy. You finally waking up?"

The voice rang sweetly in Ethan's ears, drawing him out of his dark, near-comatose sanctuary. He forced his eyes open, barely at that. As the world came into focus, he found himself lying on his back in a large canopy bed. His right arm was bandaged at the wrist, making a white cap where his hand used to be, and something about his right butt cheek bothered him, too. Zoey sat Indian-style next to him, one hand stroking the top of his head, eyes awash with relief, while Maii stood at the other side of the bed looking impressed—as well as a little annoyed.

"No, you don't get to eat me. Sorry," Ethan croaked, his throat feeling like sandpaper.

"A nibble would've been nice," replied the ahuizotl.

Ethan sighed at the predictable reply and turned to his better half. "You have no idea how glad I am to see you."

Zoey leaned over and pressed her lips into his. She ran one set of fingers through his hair and around the back of his head as she repositioned herself, so she lay half on him and half on the bed. "I think I do," she whispered, drawing him into her gaze when they finally parted. Her eyes lit up, and she chuckled. "We're *bonded* now. Just so you know. Things will only get more interesting from here."

"Or annoying," Maii chimed in.

Ethan ignored Maii's comment and danced his fingertips down Zoey's spine and toyed with her hair. "Eh. I think we'll manage."

"I'm sure we will."

"Mind telling me what happened?" he asked. "My memory is a little fuzzy after I fell."

Zoey laughed, her face tightening in the process as if recalling a painful memory. "They fished you out of the water a little beyond the finish line, leaking blood like a sieve."

"Who did?"

"Azrael."

Ethan blinked, not expecting the answer whatsoever. "He did? Why?"

Zoey shrugged. "I don't know, but I'm not complaining, either. Not sure you would've survived if he hadn't. He was quick to bandage you up and pump you full of pots."

Ethan's gaze drifted as he turned this unexpected news over in his head a dozen times. He couldn't come up with anything other than Azrael was indeed a sportsman of the highest caliber. Despite that thought, he also couldn't help but think Death had something sinister in store for him as well. "How's the crew?" he asked, turning his attention to more immediate and pressing matters. "And the ship? And did we win?"

"Last I heard, Marcus and the crew went to get drunk," she said, shrugging. "The *Victory* sailed herself onto shore. She's little more than a wreck, but she's there, waiting for us. As for the race, I have no idea. Katryna went this morning to argue our case in front of the judges. It seems who actually won is hotly contested at the moment."

Ethan frowned and then cursed up a storm when a splitting headache erupted across his skull. At that point, he quickly became acutely aware of how agonizing it was to even breathe. Worse, his memory had a gaping hole to it. Deep down, he felt as if they should've won, and more importantly, he should know why, but sadly, try as he might, he could come up with nothing whatsoever.

Maybe Katryna had it worked out. He could only pray that was the case.

His stomach growled, and a stabbing pain ripped through his torso.

"Christ, I'm hungry," he muttered. "I need something to eat."

The door to the room flung open, interrupting it all, and Katryna raced inside.

"Hurry! Get up!" she barked. "They're going to rule if they don't hear from you!"

Ethan jerked upright. "On the race?"

"Yes, on the race!" she said. "What else would I be talking about? Now let's go!"

Ethan, hungry but not starving (thanks to Katryna supplying him with a bottle from an unnamed donor on the way), sat inside a decorative and packed courtroom. Zoey joined him at the table on the courtroom's right, while Azrael and his first mate occupied the table on the left. Ahead, on a raised platform, were the regatta's three judges, staring down at all of them from their benches with wrinkled eyes set under powdered wigs.

The judge who sat in the middle, the one who looked about as youthful and spry as a thousand-year-old mummy, toyed with a quill as he hummed to himself. Normally, Ethan wouldn't have paid him much attention, but the man had hit his gavel a couple of times moments ago and bid the room to quiet.

After a few more seconds and a thorough, hacking cough, the judge slowly turned his pale eyes to Azrael. "Do you care to make a closing statement?" he asked in a slow, raspy voice.

Azrael nodded and stood from his place. He wore a pristine navy-blue uniform, finely pressed with gold trimmings and shoulders, and a slew of gold medals hanging above his left breast. From his hip hung a ceremonial sword, and upon his feet were black leather boots polished so sharply, Ethan could use them to shave a hundred yards away. His attire, especially when compared to Ethan's sack-like trousers and white cotton shirt, was striking, to say the least.

"The court is gracious in hearing my case," Azrael said. "And while I will not insult the fine judges here today by repeating the details of what we've already spoken of at length, I will simply reiterate the crux of my argument, as well as what should ultimately guide your decision. Master Ethan, a resourceful and worthy opponent, was not in control of the *Griffin* at any point during the race, nor was he even on board as my ship crossed the finish line. As such, he cannot be deemed the victor."

The judge in the middle looked to the men on either side of him, and they huddled close for a few moments, whispering, nodding, and whispering some more. "Very good," he finally answered. He then rapped his gavel on the bench and added, "The record shall reflect the standing champion's case unless anyone has cause to deny its validity."

The pause in the courtroom was brief. The judge then turned to Ethan. "Does the challenger have anything he'd like to say on the matter now that he is awake?"

Ethan nodded and stood, wincing as he did. Despite the wounds that had already closed thanks to his unnatural healing, there were still plenty more to go.

"The *Victory* clearly was winning up until she was fired upon," Ethan said. "And when she was fired upon, she'd already crossed the line that separates open water from the safe harbor. Had my opponent not broken the rules, we would've crossed the finish line first."

"Objection, your honors," Azrael said, shooting up out of his chair. "We've gone over this before. The *Victory* never crossed the buoys marking the ceasefire zone."

"That's because those buoys were shifted by the storm!" Ethan fired back.

"We acted in good faith, your honors, thinking it was a legal engagement," Azrael went on, ignoring Ethan's retort. "It's hardly fair to us if such markers are not readily available to see, and we would contend Master Ethan's assertion that his ship was within the safety of the final run. All we have is his word to go by."

Ethan took to his feet as well. "I took an oath, and I gave my word," he said. "Does that mean nothing here?"

The judge on the right, the shorter, more wrinkled of the three, frowned as he played with a set of thin-rimmed glasses. "Under most circumstances, it does," he said. "However, something about you..." he said, now pointing a shaky finger at Ethan, "makes me think that perhaps your word is not as ironclad as we would like to believe."

"A fine observation, your honor," Azrael said, nodding. "If I may reiterate before this ends, no sizeable amount of crew from the *Victory* made it aboard. The *Griffin* was never in danger of being lost."

Ethan snatched a copy of the rules he had at the table and held it up for all to see. "That doesn't matter," he said. "The rules say, and I quote, 'While touching his ship with his colors flying, whichever captain crosses the finish line first shall be deemed the winner.' My colors were flying. The *Griffin,* at best for my opponent, was commanded by the two of us. I crossed the line first since I was at the bowsprit. Therefore, by the rules, I should be deemed the winner."

Azrael sighed as if he were embarrassed for Ethan's sake. "Even if that interpretation could be had, my esteemed opponent is clearly suffering from delusions," he said. "Master Ethan fell before the *Griffin* crossed the line. A captain who abandons ship cannot be crowned the victor."

"I did not fall before we crossed!" Ethan said, slamming his hands on the table. "On my word, I held on to the end!"

The center judge pounded his gavel like the god of smiths worked an anvil. "Enough, both of you!" he boomed. "This bickering stops now. Do you two understand?"

Ethan reluctantly lowered himself into the chair, and when he realized the entire courtroom was waiting for his answer as Azrael had already given one, Ethan nodded and gave a quiet reply. "Yes, your honor. I understand."

"Good. Now, do either of you have anything else you'd like to say that's both pertinent and new to the matter?" he asked.

Neither did, and the three judges sat back and conferred amongst themselves for a few tense minutes. All the while, they would occasionally glance at Ethan and Azrael but gave no other indication as to what they were talking about. Ethan tried listening in with his heightened vampiric senses but was dismayed when he quickly realized they weren't helping for whatever reason.

"We've come to a decision," said the lead judge, sending a flutter through Ethan's heart. "On the matter of whether or not the *Victory* was within the safe harbor or not, we find that the matter is not clear enough either way, and thus, the engagement stands as is."

Ethan cursed to himself and tried not to slouch. He also couldn't help but wonder if he shouldn't have taken help from the Duchess. That didn't matter, now, he knew, and all he could do was listen and pray as the judge went on.

"On the matter of whether or not the *Griffin* was sufficiently in the control of one captain or the other, the simple fact of the matter is that since Captain Ethan still had enough men on board to form a skeleton crew—pun not intended—and with colors flying, we deem that indeed the ship was contested at the time of her crossing the finish," he said. "Which leads us to the final matter: Was Captain Ethan aboard the ship or not when the *Griffin* reached the finish?"

The judge paused for a moment to take a small drink from a nearby glass of water. "In that regard, while we believe Captain Ethan is a skilled captain to have come this far in the race, we also believe his character is nowhere near impeccable enough to rule solely on his word. As such, with no clear evidence as to whether or not he was truly aboard the *Griffin* when it crossed, we have decided to declare this year's Grand Regatta a tie. All honors and accolades will be granted forthwith at the award ceremony tomorrow, and all prize monies shall be split evenly, excluding Master Ethan's bonus for successfully acquiring the wind in a bottle which shall go to him in full."

The judge slammed the gavel, and the courtroom exploded with cheers of excitement and shouts of enragement. Ethan flopped back in his seat, exhaling sharply and wondering what all of this meant for Anne. For Zoey. For himself, even.

He'd barely had time to ask that question when Zoey pounced on him, straddling his waist, grabbing his face, and kissing him hard.

When they finally parted, he leaned back and stared at her with a blank face. "But...but he won."

"We *both* won," she said. "He can claim victory, but not victory over *you*."

"Which means what? Rematch?"

"Yeah," she said. "But we can negotiate what sort of rematch later. Right now, the crew's going to want to celebrate, and I think we should indulge their request and maybe slip away for a bit."

"Oh, you do, do you?"

"Good for morale."

Ethan drew back a corner of his mouth. "Yours? Or theirs?"

"Well, if you have to ask..."

"Maybe I just like hearing you say it."

"I think I've got a little more you might like," she said, toying with his hair.

Ethan nodded with a stupid grin and hopped to his feet. He was about to make for the door with her when he saw his bandaged arm and frowned. "I still have stumpy, though," he said. "Any chance this will grow back?"

"Most definitely," Zoey said, walking a pair of fingers down his arm, starting at the shoulder. "In the meantime, however, we could always get you a hook, complete the pirate ensemble and whatnot."

"I'll think about it," Ethan said. He stuck an open elbow out to the side. "Shall we, then?"

Zoey nodded and slipped her arm around his. "On your lead, Captain."

The two left the courtroom, pushing through a sizeable crowd bent on getting answers as well as two reporters wanting more. When they finally broke free of them all and made their way onto the cobblestone street that ran from the courthouse back to the harbor, Azrael was there, waiting for them, leaning against a signpost.

"A commendable performance throughout the race, Master Ethan," he said with genuine praise and a tip of his hat. "I must say, I'm pleasantly surprised at how this all turned out."

Ethan stopped, unsure if he'd heard right. "You are?"

"Aye, I am," he said. "It's nice to know there are still those out there who can offer me a challenge. Keeps eternal life interesting."

"If you want to keep things interesting, how about we up the stakes on our next contest?"

Death chuckled as he reached into his jacket and pulled out his pipe and a bit of tobacco. "What did you have in mind?"

Ethan straightened and folded his arms over his chest. "Double the pot."

A slow, wicked smile spread across Azrael's face, and a fire that put a shiver through Ethan's spine twinkled in Death's eyes. "And how do you propose we do that?"

"I throw myself in for Zoey and her kids," Ethan said.

"Tempting, Master Ethan, tempting," Azrael replied as he packed the tobacco and lit the pipe. "But by my count, I'm betting three souls against your two, which hardly seems worth the risk given you're a proven opponent—especially now with *The Duchess* on your side."

Ethan froze as his breath caught in his lungs. "You know about that?"

Azrael grinned. "I knew it would happen before you even considered putting quill to deed."

Ethan's lips formed a tight line, and he considered his options. He had to get Azrael to agree, somehow. Sadly, only one way came to mind, and it wasn't a very good one. "I'll give you odds."

Azrael's grin became even larger and more sinister. "Will you now?"

"Ethan! Don't!" Zoey said, grabbing his arm. "We can figure something else out."

Ethan took Zoey by the hand and interlocked his fingers with hers, all the while never breaking eye contact with Azrael. "I'll give you odds. What say you?"

"I say that's a very intriguing offer."

Ethan reached out despite Zoey's further protest. "Do we have a wager, Master Azrael?"

Azrael chuckled and gave his hand a shake. "I believe we do, Master Ethan. We shall work out the details tomorrow, after the ceremony. And until then, I bid you farewell. Please do give *The Duchess* my kindest regards."

(End of Book II)

Acknowledgements

My heartfelt thanks to my fantastic editor Crystal for working on this new series with me, as well as the Mrs. for all her hard work and motivation for getting it done. The littles, too, for offering a lot of great creative input as we tossed around early ideas for the storyline.

Of course, another heartfelt thanks to all of my beta readers who read early drafts and helped smooth things out.

And *another* heartfelt thanks to all of my readers and fans of this book. Here's to hoping you enjoy the next as much (if not more) as the first.

And, and...I definitely need to thank Bob Kehl for both his talent as an artist and the license on yet another amazing cover.

About the Author

When not writing, Galen Surlak-Ramsey has been known to throw himself out of an airplane, teach others how to throw themselves out of an airplane, take pictures of the deep space, and wrangle his four children somewhere in Southwest Florida.

He's also rather fond of murder yoga and has a passion for choking out his friends. Thanks to his long legs, he tends to favor triangles but won't pass up a good cross-collar.

Drop by his website https://galensurlak.com/ to see what other books he has out, what's coming soon, and check out the newsletter. (Well, sign up for the newsletter and get access to awesome goodies, contests, exclusive content, etc.)

About the Publisher

Tiny Fox Press LLC
5020 Kingsley Road
North Port, FL 34287

www.tinyfoxpress.com